THE INMATES

To Joy Wilkins in Memoriam
March 25th, 1921

JOHN COWPER POWYS
THE INMATES

faber and faber

This edition first published in 2008
by Faber and Faber Ltd
3 Queen Square, London WC1N 3AU

Printed by Books on Demand GmbH, Norderstedt

All rights reserved
© The Estate of John Cowper Powys, 1952

The right of John Cowper Powys to be identified as author of this work
has been asserted in accordance with Section 77 of the
Copyright, Designs and Patents Act 1988

This book is sold subject to the condition that it shall not, by way of
trade or otherwise, be lent, resold, hired out or otherwise circulated
without the publisher's prior consent in any form of binding or cover other than
that in which it is published and without a similar condition including this
condition being imposed on the subsequent purchaser

A CIP record for this book is available from the British Library

ISBN 978–0–571–24215–3

Our authorised representative in the EU for product safety is
Easy Access System Europe, Mustamäe tee 50, 10621 Tallinn, Estonia
gpsr.requests@easproject.com

PREFATORY NOTE

I THINK that any book or picture or composition of any sort, once out into the world, so to say, produces a different effect on each person who seriously tries to follow it. I certainly do not think that the author of it has any monopoly in its interpretation. In fact, Thomas Hardy, from whom I learnt so much when I saw him in my early twenties, implied once to me that other minds, if sympathetic, of course, could get more out of a work than the author had the faintest idea existed in it. I daresay, too, there are quite lawful reactions totally different from any the author could have imagined.

What I've tried to do in this tale is to invent a group of really mad people who have the fantastic and grotesquely humorous extravagance that, after all, is an element in life. When Dickens gives himself up to enlarging on the monstrous and the macabre in his characters, you don't feel that they become less real. In a sense they become more real. Reality is not equivalent to dullness. It is not equivalent to solemnity. It is not even equivalent to Matthew Arnold's famous Greek word for describing what poetry should be, namely spoudaios, having the highest seriousness, or worthy of one's most serious attention. No! There is something in reality, and not least in the reality of insanity, that is caught on the wing when you are swinging your butterfly-net about in a mood of complete carelessness or even carrying it under some instinctive impulse in a rush of haste. Curiously enough, the Greek Lexicon of Liddell and Scott begins its interpretation of this very "spoudaios" with the words "in haste", suggestive of the eagerness with which we snatch at some particular aspect of reality that hits our fancy. What might indeed be called the "aboriginal levity" of the mother of the muses insists on the recognition of a vein of pure grotesquerie and simple gargoylishness

PREFATORY NOTE

in some of Nature's most natural creations, a vein in the world that made Heine refer on his mattress of death to the "Heavenly Aristophanes". There is, indeed, a vein of what might be called "devilish childishness", full of naive terrors and wild outbursts of ecstatic merriment in many of those among us who are suffering or have suffered from mental derangement; and this humour of the insane has not yet had the aesthetic homage due to it. In my own approach to it and in my imaginary characters in this fantastic book I have no doubt been influenced by my delight, itself almost amounting to a mania, in such figures as Rabelais' "Songe-Creux", who seems to have been a real clown-singer-dancer when the great Italian Renaissance—for this particular vein, sane or insane, has always been recognised in Italy—became popular in France. In Heine's *Florentine Nights* we get it, and of course it was present, as Rabelais himself recognised, in Villon; and nearer our own day we can trace it in Verlaine. In Poe, also, as I learnt from a hint from Thomas Hardy, there is not a little of it. Among the most moving characters in all literature, one, Don Quixote, is an actual madman and the other, Hamlet, pretends to be mad till he comes within an inch of being really so; while is it not inevitable that an old lecturer-actor like myself, struggling to describe the ghastly levities of insanity, should find that terrific scene in *King Lear*, where the professionally mad fool and the pretended mad Edgar are hustled by the really mad king into the hovel on the heath, exercising a peculiar influence over his fancy?

To obtain the particular effect required, that is to say some approximate reflection of those frivolous aspects of insanity which the gravity of religion and the inflexible "heavy weather" of both morality and science seek to suppress, I instinctively discovered as I went along that three things were essential if I were to get the required atmosphere: first a simplicity of narrative to compete with the macabre frivolity of the subject, secondly a shameless exploitation wherever possible of my own personal manias, and thirdly a savage avoidance of all the modern psychoanalytical catchwords, whether quasi-popular or pseudo-scientific, as leading us away from the heart of the

PREFATORY NOTE

matter, which is not the cause of the patient's mania but how it feels to himself or herself to suffer from it.

What in fact I am trying to do in this wild book is, if I may so put it, to defend the crazy ideas of mad people—in so far, of course, as they don't run to homicide and cruelty—as against the conventional ideas of sane people. I want to show that between all manner of quite different types of patients in a mental institution there is—when you come to these crazy ones' basic philosophies—sufficient mental agreement to constitute what I would like to have the courage to call the "Philosophy of the Demented". In other words, though these unfortunates differ greatly in their aberrations from one another, they really do possess, if we drain off or skim off those details of their manias which are obviously peculiar to the individual, certain dominant attitudes to life, to nature and to the cosmos, which, though contrary to all the accepted notions of the conventional minds who make up the world's judgment, have a deep abiding philosophic truth. But this "truth", this Philosophy of the Demented, is naturally under the ban of our authorities in Church and State. And being condemned at the top level it is very noticeable that it is anathema to the underlings, whose personal power and glory depend, of course, as they mount up, on the conventional ideas they have at last, after many rungs of the careerist-ladder, come to embody and represent. Incidentally, we may remark how very contrary to the way it was in the Renaissance in Italy, where money to support science and art was provided by reckless and unscrupulous despots, is our method of parliamentary and ministerial support of these things, a support that actually comes of course from the taxes paid by ourselves. Our popular ideas about philosophy and science and art—popular ideas that are now dramatically influenced by the extravagant lengths to which Jung's followers have carried the theory of the Unconscious, a theory that in a hundred years will probably be relinquished as a complete illusion—obviously cannot extend beyond our own intellectual limitations. Thus between the sophisticated experimental processes of our modern doctors'

PREFATORY NOTE

treatment of us when helpless in their hands and our own simple ideas criss-crossed by the catchwords of psychoanalysis, there is a vast gulf, a gulf that grows daily wider and wider. But when we look at modern art it is a different story. Strangely enough, some of the wildest, queerest, weirdest experiments of modern art, though totally obscure and even extremely repulsive to our conventional and popular taste, have a startling affinity with the ideas of the inmates of our asylums. The genius of great artists has always been in their unearthly and startling imaginations allied to madness. And this was true in the past as well as to-day. Thus I find no jarring note when I introduce Rembrandt's "Supper at Emmaus" into Glint. The unearthly fancies of the Philosophy of the Demented fall in naturally with a work of art like this, though they horrify the conventional ideas of ordinary people. In fact, our ordinary ideas have become a queer patchwork of uninspired conventionality criss-crossed by flashes of genius, a patchwork which the desperate truth in the blood of the Philosophy of the Demented naturally struggles to confound. I like to tell myself that one aspect of the Philosophy of the Demented is that daring cosmological theory about a real plurality of worlds; namely the theory of William James that we live in a multiverse rather than a universe. Everyone of my inmates is a symbol of some important aspect of its truth which seems to me especially alien to the schoolmaster-taught conventional mind with its passion for unity and oneness. For instance, the Zeit-Geist is an epitome of those lonely sensations when we feel ourselves to be isolated consciousnesses at some uncertain point in boundless space and time. It is at the emptiness round us all that this mad creature points his horribly wagging finger. The Commander, on the other hand, represents that recurrent struggle of the practical prophet to use the traditional values of our older Services for the purpose of making our political rulers at once wiser and more heroic than we are ourselves. Mr. Pantamount embodies that world-old secret of exultant and humorous self-escape which may have been the secret of the Mysteries of Eleusis and which may even revert to the sub-

PREFATORY NOTE

merged continents of "Mu" in the Pacific and "Atlantis" in the Atlantic. Echetus is the Homeric name in the Odyssey for that cruel king of some terrible coast whose title was the "Maimer of Men", just as the impervious head of Glint was a maimer of his laboratory dogs. The personage who appears at the end and disposes of the sadistic Gewlie is a Lama from Thibet visiting this country in his escape from the Communists. It is a symbolic rounding off of what might be called the self-escape-philosophy of Mr. Pantamount that the only memorial of their time as inmates of Glint left to remind John and Tenna of their old life as they begin their new is a liberated dog called Mr. Lordy.

CONTENTS

		PAGE
	PREFATORY NOTE	V
1.	"CERTIFIED"	13
2.	THE FIRST GLANCE	25
3.	THE FIRST ENCOUNTER	43
4.	FATHER TOBY	62
5.	THE NEXT DAY	82
6.	MR. FROGCASTLE	97
7.	THE TEA-PARTY	123
8.	THE COMMANDER	137
9.	HAMMER AND NAILS	153
10.	THE ZEIT-GEIST	166
11.	HITHER AND THITHER	179
12.	PANTAMOUNT	196
13.	THE POLISHED TABLE	216
14.	MIDSUMMER DAWN	243
15.	"ON ALL FOURS"	264
16.	THE ESCAPE	282

1

"CERTIFIED"

It was on one of the gravel paths of the institution that John Hush said goodbye to the young English statesman and his American betrothed, who at John's own request had not remained with him more than a few minutes after depositing him with the famous Doctor Echetus, the head of the place. He knew fatally well that it was a gravel path where he had said goodbye to them, because when they had driven away he felt that he preferred to stare at a small dandelion plant— flower, stalk, leaves and root—that had been weeded-up that morning and now lay withering in the sun upon that bed of immaculately raked-over little brownish stones rather than meet without a pause the scientific eyes of the well-known doctor. It was, all the same, more with his patron's future fate than with his own that John Hush's mind was occupied when the car drove off at last with the beautiful American and her handsome statesman and he found himself alone with Doctor Echetus.

"A brilliant man!" commented the Doctor admiringly. "May I enquire if you are related to him?"

"Oh no!" cried John hurriedly. "Oh dear no! No, I'm not related to him. He was very kind to my parents and I had an uncle in his service."

"A great gentleman of the old school," went on the Doctor. "You can see it in every movement he makes. You feel it before he utters a word. I think he told me your own parents were dead?"

"Yes," said John, "both of them."

"And that uncle, too, of whom you spoke?"

"Yes, that uncle too."

THE INMATES

"You've no relations at all?"

"None at all."

Doctor Echetus was silent, contemplating John with historic rather than scientific interest, as if he were the Last of the Mohicans.

Then he said, as if offering a hobby-horse to a Mohawk, "I expect you'd like to look round a bit before going in?"

"I would indeed, Doctor."

But John found his mind wandering away over and over again from what the ruler of Glint Hall was showing him. It kept wandering to the wonderful American lady, fabulously beautiful and incredibly rich, whom he himself with his own ears had heard fixing Midsummer Day as the day when she and his guardian should be married. And to-day was only the twenty-fifth of March; so it was a long way off!

But how well he knew—oh, how exactly and in what minute particulars!—all that it meant to this "great gentleman of the old school", to be married to this woman from the New World!

Wandering as his thoughts were, it did strike John Hush that the grounds of Glint Hall were as well kept as they were extensive and varied. The Doctor led him through lawns and shrubberies and orchards and gardens, all of them enclosed by a high and imposing wall, till they finally reached the great southern gates.

To the left of these gates there ran a small stream which had been allowed to flow under the wall; and John couldn't help noticing with a certain grim interest that there was a row of enormous and most threatening-looking spikes adhering to the base of the wall and descending into the weeds and mud at the bottom of the flowing water.

On the right of the gates, where the stream was crossed by an ornamental little stone bridge, was a grey-cement lodge built in one of the newest styles of artificial masonry, and to the door of this lodge the Doctor conducted the new inmate.

There was no need to knock or ring, for a tall and extremely angular woman whom John had perceived watching their

"CERTIFIED"

approach through her parlour window hurried to open the door.

"Good evening, Mrs. Squeeze," said the Doctor; and there was something in his tone and manner that drew to the two of them the full attention of the new arrival. Exactly what it was that startled him into taking so much notice of this bony but still handsome woman as she confronted his companion, John Hush would have been puzzled to say. One thing this arrest of his attention certainly did; it forced him to throw an analytical glance upon the master of Glint. Until this moment John Hush had experienced a singular reluctance to look at the man who now held him in thrall.

It is true he had had no very pressing need to look at him; in fact he had had no need at all. But now that the Doctor's personality was confronted by the personality of Betsy Squeeze something in the nature of a crucial dramatic crisis, not merely arresting but actually absorbing, took possession of the stage. Doctor Echetus was a substantially built man of middle height who possessed the sort of countenance that it would have seemed natural to find on the shoulders of an extremely competent manager of a country club. He had a well-trimmed pointed beard, rather small, vague, dreamy, unenthusiastic eyes, and, finally, a mouth that was so much the opposite of a sensual one, or a jealous one, or an emotional one of any kind, that it made you think of a professional cricketer or of the general supervisor of a well-kept public garden.

Betsy Squeeze, on the other hand, in spite of her tall bony frame and long bony face, had the most searching hazel eyes—yellow-grey they might have been called rather than green-grey—that John Hush had ever seen.

The "aura", as John's diplomatic guardian would have called it, of deprecatory discomfort which separated the polite Doctor Echetus from this impolite Mrs. Squeeze emanated, John was clever enough to see, from the man.

"The fellow's scared stiff of her," he told himself.

"How are you to-day, Mrs. Squeeze?" the doctor murmured.

THE INMATES

"How are *you*?" the woman returned with cheerful unction; and continued rapidly, "I was saying to Mrs. Cuddle only yesterday; 'It won't be long,' I was saying, 'before you and me, Mrs. Cuddle, will be using the term "His Lordship" when we mention the boss. If 'is 'ealth 'olds out,' I was saying, 'for only a gentleman of iron,' I was saying, and Mrs. Cuddle knows I never exsage, 'could bear the noise them dogs lift up when you be prodding their bowels with that fine teaser of yours what my Bill calls 'Little Prickly'. We'd 'ave any gent who weren't a man of iron like our Doc,' I was saying, 'setting up a 'owl, like a mad dog 'isself some fine spring night when the moon's in her ghost-bearing!

"'Weak women such as us,' I says to Tamia Cuddle, 'would have got the Jimimas after a month of them dogs; but Doc'll go on, you'll see, our Doc'll go on till he finds that dog-pearl he's after, the dog-pearl that'll bring us all long life and a lordship for him that found it!'"

"Well—well—well—well," murmured the master of Glint, looking first to the ground below the feet of Mrs. Squeeze and then to the roof above the head of Mrs. Squeeze.

"He'll be taking notice of me soon," thought John Hush, "if it's only to get away!"

But Doctor Echetus's eyes in their obscure distress seemed to have gone off on a quest of their own. Since Bill Squeeze was not under the mat or on the roof he might be at the back; and it was clearly through the house and out the other side that Doctor Echetus's blurred, obstinate, unenthusiastic, public-garden eyes had begun to search.

"Is Squeeze in?" he enquired.

"No, sir; no, Doctor Echetus. But I could soon fetch him. He's bound to be round and about. Fact to God, Doctor, we've had a bit of a tell-off, me and Bill, and when Bill got to 'ollerin' I told 'im the best 'ee could do was to take things easy, as you might say, in shed. Bill's most 'isself, you might say, in shed, same as I be in kitchen. As it 'appened, I *weren't* in kitchen this particular time; and that's why I saw you coming. I were in parlour reading the Sunday papers. You're the one, Doctor,

"CERTIFIED"

to know what 'tis with me and 'im—'im being funny and all of that, and me 'aving me 'eart. Not that Bill ain't a good man to me; and I don't say he's not a good servant to the Hall, for he is; but he's funny, and it's in consideration of that that the Hall gets a good servant cheap, as you'll be the first to allow, Doctor, though he was took over and me with him, before your time.

"But, as I tell him it's all right to get a job he can do well and please everybody, and a job nobody could get anybody else to do, and he doing it for a sum nobody else—I mean nobody who wasn't I don't know what—would consider for a moment, but it's quite a different thing to go on being funny when you're with the woman you married for better, for worse, and me being that woman, if you see what I mean, Doctor Echetus—*quite* a different thing it is! And when you consider, Doctor Echetus, how Bill's way of being funny is not only to go on talking about what passes through his mind —not that I'd trouble about that; for he thinks sillier thoughts than I've ever known a man to think, and I've known many— but about all he sees and hears up at Hall in his day's work; and when you consider what I do for him in house and all that and how days go by without my seeing my friend Mrs. Cuddle or hearing one word of what's going on up at Hall or whether you've took in anyone"—here Betsy shot a quick glance at John Hush—"who's been in the Sunday papers— not, I say, to talk to me of what he hears and sees up at Hall, but to talk to a wooden image he keeps in his pocket, when you consider all this, Doctor Echetus, is it any wonder ——"

But the Doctor had by this time gathered together all the conglomorate substance of his personality, all the praetorian cement of his position, all the sandbags of his prestige and all the tenon'd and mortised concrete of his discretion, and he now proceeded to make a firm but benignant motion with the little finger of his left hand.

"Well, Mrs. Squeeze," he announced quietly, "I don't think I'll trouble your husband to-night. We all gain, you know, by what he does with his axe in that shed of his. My

THE INMATES

fires as well as yours, Mrs. Squeeze, depend on that axe. I know well how these little peculiarities of our good Bill can be very trying sometimes. I find them so myself now and again. But we must be patient, we must be patient. But tell him, won't you, that I'd like to see him the first thing to-morrow. No, no, I won't stay now. Good evening, Mrs. Squeeze. This way, Mr. Hush!"

But as the absent-minded young man followed this new master of his fate, this lord of destiny whom he had just watched dodging, evading, propitiating and not without difficulty escaping a somewhat delapidated specimen of the classical Erinyes, he did his utmost to bring his attention to bear upon what was happening to himself. But there it was! Even as he dragged his steps after his guide and followed him through one kitchen-garden after another, along interminable gravel-paths under the ever-present prison-wall, till they reached the man's official residence with the monstrous annex, joined to it by a passage, where he kept his dogs, Hush still moved mechanically as if his guardian and the beautiful American had carried his soul away in the luggage-box of their smooth-running car.

It wasn't, indeed, till Doctor Echetus had led him around the whole circle of the place and they had followed for several hundred yards the barbed-wire fence that railed off an extensive plantation of young spruce-firs on Glint Hall's northern side, and shut away this forestry department from the stables and sheds and barns and the big cobblestone yard where the agricultural activities of the establishment were concentrated, that his attention was arrested by a sound that he knew perfectly well was the usual indignant cry of a blackbird angry at being disturbed in some remote part of the plantation where it was already hovering about its mate and her nest.

Since, however, Echetus had just led his new inmate past the main entrance to the research laboratory, where those experiments on living dogs were carried on that Betsy Squeeze regarded as a scientist's shortest cut to the peerage, the Doctor evidently mistook that blackbird's scream of anger for a dog's

"CERTIFIED"

howl of pain, and with the hurried exclamation: "Excuse me, Mr. Hush, I must see into this!" he disentangled a piece of wire from a small gate, pushed it open, and hurried down a grassy path between immature spruce-firs.

John replaced the wire as neatly as he could and followed at the Doctor's heels. He was still so absorbed in a mental pursuit of his guardian and the American girl that the colours of this path, especially a particular shade of trampled earth that resembled dried blood, though they had a vaguely troubling effect upon him, hardly roused his full awareness. Indeed, until this moment his whole consciousness had been so absorbed in the emotional strain of his separation from his friends and in the deep interior effort he was making to accept this separation in every one of its implications that his own consignment to Glint Hall had scarcely begun to impinge upon his mind; nor had the impressions so far made on him by the place begun as yet to take any definite shape.

His spirit was still trying to follow his youthful patron and his patron's betrothed, trying to imagine what the two of them were feeling as they arrived at their friend's abode, known locally as Halfway House; but there was something about this path quite apart from that bird's cry that was beginning now to bring him back to the immediate responses of his own nerves.

But while the bird's violent protests against disturbance died away in the distance, a much more intimate skin, so to speak, of his consciousness was now torn away as, at the heels of the Doctor, he suddenly found himself confronted by a horrible hole in the ground. It was clean in the centre of this blood-coloured path; and it was in a small clearing among some of the thickest-foliaged spruce-firs John had ever seen.

It was out of this hole that the Doctor had evidently fancied in his ignorance of birds' cries that the sound they'd heard proceeded. One of his assistants, the Doctor supposed, must have thrown a yet living dog to perish among the dead. For a dog's face did meet John's stare as he gazed down into that hole, and a dog's eyes answered his stare with a look of such unutterable loneliness under the infliction of pain that it revealed to him as a reality in the world what he had hitherto only ventured to approach in the imagination of exasperated nerves.

When the Doctor moved away and hurried back to the little gate in the fence, with himself following like a human dog, he began instinctively trying to cleanse his mind from the horrors suggested by that expression in the creature's eyes. And this he tried to do by plunging his own face into the foliage of those dusky-green spruce-firs; nor was the gesture an imaginary one, for he did quite deliberately let some of the lower branches of these sweet-smelling boughs flap against his mouth, brush against his forehead, and sting his half-shut eyelids.

Doctor Echetus seemed to recognise that this slight debouching to his dog-pit among the fir trees had disturbed the mental absorption of his new patient, for as they crossed the cobblestones of Glint Hall's extensive farmyard he took the opportunity to enlighten him a little about Betsy's husband.

"That fellow's an extraordinary case," he told him. "None of us have ever known a case like it before. It's a form of what I have come to describe in my case-book as *perverse doll-fetishism*; by which I mean the natural desire of young females for dolls perversely camouflaged in a mature male as a mystical idolatry of the inanimate. The relation between the human tendency to idol-worship inherited by us all, and the attraction of certain animals towards certain inanimate objects, is of greater importance than has yet been grasped. Where William Squeeze's case is a singular one is that he introduces into this perverse doll-mania a curious element of paranoiac superiority.

"What Squeeze does is indeed rather singular. He inflates the importance of his personality by conversing with this doll-image of his, which, if you please, he carved for himself out of wood; carved it roughly, you understand, in the shape of a classical head surmounting a six-inch pedestal.

"One of my former patients—he's dead now—was an authority on Greek philosophy, and in looking after him our

"CERTIFIED"

friend Squeeze picked up quite a few tags from the ideas of Heraclitus, whose name, for some cause deserving further study, must have arrested his attention. As no doubt you must have observed, that tiresome wife of his, with her vulgar and ridiculous ways, is the chief reason why his cure is so delayed; though I am not ashamed to admit that we shall all be rather sorry when he is cured, for his case is a fascinating one and full of importance for all students of insanity.

"You know, I felt pretty sure as we listened just now to that tiresome woman that Squeeze wasn't in his shed at all! If he had been I'm sure we should have heard his axe. My own belief is that you'll find him in the reading-room, the place of all places about which I have taken the most trouble! If you do see him there, my advice to you would be to say nothing of our visit to his lodge. Well! I see we've been seen from our other lodge, the one occupied by the best servant I possess here, the devoted Cuddle, whose good lady, unlike our friend Betsy, is more active with her hands than with her tongue I Yes, Cogent, yes indeed; I certainly think——"

Doctor Echetus was now addressing himself to a short but extremely broad-shouldered individual who, appearing to John as if he had forced his way through a dense undergrowth of spruce-firs from a hole that led straight to Hell, now filled a space where previously there had been nothing.

"I certainly think, Cogent, that you should see Doctor Splitting if he comes at the usual hour tomorrow. But I must be leaving you both now. I need my tea; and my tea, ha! ha! needs me! We'll soon be meeting again, Mr. Hush, soon be meeting again! I leave you in good hands. Cuddle will take you to the reading-room. Yes, Mr. Hush is our new inmate and he wants to rest in the reading-room until tea-time. Will you take him there, Cuddle?"

Remaining perfectly motionless for half a minute, just as if he had been watching the retreating backs of his own words, "until tea-time, Cuddle", flick the dust from their skirts and go mincing off across the yard, the master of Glint turned his back upon them and hurried away.

THE INMATES

Thus left to themselves the new inmate looked at the keeper, and the keeper looked at the new inmate; and an instantaneous electric-magnetic current of hostility, far subtler and deeper because on more equal terms than that between weasel and rabbit, passed from the nerve-centre of this official to the nerve-centre of this patient.

"Have you made any arrangements yet, Mr. Hush," were the first words that passed between these two antipodal human organisms, "with regard to your washing?"

"Why no! I can't say I have as yet. Isn't that sort of thing taken care of here? I mean, isn't there a—isn't there a laundry?" But even as he uttered these words there came over the newcomer a vision of himself setting out from those vast lodge-gates along a winding lane with his dirty clothes tied in a bundle and held up by a stick resting first on one shoulder and then on the other, and a parallel vision of himself returning later with quite a different bundle, smelling beautifully of soap, and wrapped around in a vast spotlessly white Mother-Hubbard's apron.

But the best of all the possible servants that Doctor Echetus could imagine interrupted these wandering thoughts.

"There's a laundry, of course, for public patients; but we find that when gentlefolk like yourself come here they usually want to make their own arrangements. I only spoke because I know how pleased Mrs. Cuddle would be to do for you, and not only to do for you, if you know what I mean—but to have the pleasure of meeting a young gentleman like yourself and—perhaps—you never can be sure—finding she can help you in other little ways. Many's the time I've heard my wife say:' It's wonderful, considering everything, what a woman can do for a well-spoken young gentleman who's really grateful for her help!' But I see Mrs. Cuddle is half-closing already. We are half-closing, you understand, at a quarter to five, and full-closing at a quarter past six. It's a custom of old standing, I believe. Maybe it's a good custom; maybe it's a bad one. They say, 'to obey is better than sacrifice, and to hearken than the fat of rams'. But it's not that

"CERTIFIED"

we've got to consider now. We've got to consider now whether you would like Mrs. Cuddle to do your washing. And towards your decision on this point I can contribute an important, some people might even call it a *decisive*, argument: Mrs. Cuddle would *like* to do your washing." And then without any pause: "I am telling our new young gentleman here, Tamia, that you'd be willing to attend to his mending and do his washing as long as he's with us. That's quite correct, isn't it?"

What John Hush felt at that moment was pure and simple astonishment, the cause of which was as simple as the feeling; for if there was one art in which Mr. Cogent Cuddle excelled it was the art that in modern fiction is known as "shepherding", and so skilfully had he practised this art on the new inmate that when the plump, active, girlish-complexioned, flaxen-haired woman, evidently a good deal younger than her husband, turned round from the half-closed gates, John felt a surprise that was by no means disagreeable.

It was a peculiarity of John's consciousness that it possessed the power of reducing its mental landscape to so small a size, or perhaps it would be better to say of reducing its field of vision to so small a size, that when one image occupied this inner space it became like a figure in a doorway entirely blocking the entrance, and making it necessary for any newly arriving thought or image to pass clean through the first if it, too, were to take its place in this exclusive enclosure. Thus it happened that just as a few minutes earlier the figures of his guardian and his guardian's girl had to endure the passing through them, in the entrance to his mental landscape, of a lot of scratching, scraping, brushing and stinging spruce-boughs and of a dog's face staring out of a horrible pit, so the kindly form of Mrs. Cogent Cuddle now had to glide into view through those boughs and across that hole in the ground. And it, moreover, turned out that this woman's face, once established in his field of vision, reminded him most strangely of his old nurse Maria, the only woman in his life, till he met his patron's American girl, whose personality he could enjoy without any physical, emotional, or nervous disturbance.

THE INMATES

"You heard me call Mrs. C. 'Tamia' just now," the man remarked a few minutes later, after he had indicated to John how to get to the reading-room through the back of Glint, "but you don't have no notion, do you, what 'Tamia' stands for?"

It was extraordinary how disturbing it was to John's newfound comfort in meeting someone so like his old nurse to have his ignorance of what Tamia "stood for" thus emphasised by Tamia's husband. "If I could only think of it! If I could only . . . If I could only . . ." And it came into his head how he had read in some book that the way to compel spirits to obey you was to know their names. And suddenly he *did* know! Clearly and for certain he knew. "Her name," he thought, "is Mesopotamia"; and instantaneously he decided that he would; conceal from Cogent Cuddle that he knew his wife's name, just as he would conceal from him that she reminded him of Maria Blackthorn, who had been his nurse from infancy to the age of five. "She's too good for him! She's too good for him! She's too good for him!" he thought. "No, Mr. Cuddle," he said, "I haven't the faintest idea! But I think 'Tamia' is a very suitable name. It's a pretty name, too. It sounds like Spenser's name for the Thames!" Oh, he was off now—doing what he delighted in doing—teasing, that is to say, a dedicated enemy! But as Cogent Cuddle, after giving him at the door of the reading-room a puzzled, suspicious, faintly bewildered, but also a shrewd and cunning look, the sort of look a cat might give a dog whom it left guarding its pet rat-hole, turned his back on the building to rejoin his lady in the north lodge, he caught a glimpse of himself in a mirror.

He was more than satisfied with the manner in which this mirror reflected him; and he paused for a second to indulge this satisfaction. The mask he beheld was mostly composed of brow, eyes and chin; for his human lips had so constantly been withdrawn into his mouth in the process of controlling some natural emotion that they looked as if—were the necessity for the mastery of all feeling by pure will kept up for

"CERTIFIED"

a few years longer—they might dissolve away entirely. Meanwhile his forehead was straight; his nose was straight; his chin was straight; and even his soul, putting aside its more intimate connection with these physical manifestations of his personality, might also, according to the strictest Euclidean definition of a "line", have been called straight. It was certainly basically, ultimately, and fundamentally so; though around and above this final "straightness", in which culminated Cogent Cuddle's residual and over-all purpose in life, there ran a twisted and complicated network of devious indirections, which made up the various crooked means by which this purpose was pursued.

Contrary to the human weakness of Bill Squeeze, whose temperamental anarchism could only be ruffled into action by the force that roused it and was alone capable of routing it, namely the tongue of Betsy his wife, Cogent Cuddle had succeeded in so completely depersonalising the ideal idol of world-communism that he never permitted himself even to think of it as anything but *It*. He himself had been converted in a public museum and it was only when *It* decided that the best way he could serve *It* was by converting to its service some famous champion of vivisection that he married Tamia, left his arrow-heads of flint, and came to Glint Hall, first to be cured of an imaginary aberration, and then to devote himself with implacable fidelity to the tremendous task, difficult but by no means impossible, of converting half the attendants at this asylum, and, if destiny so decided, the great Doctor Echetus himself.

2

THE FIRST GLANCE

"Escape for the certified!" thought John Hush as he entered the reading-room and looked round the books.

"'Isles of the Blest' for the inmates!"

The door by which he had entered faced a large window in

THE INMATES

the further side of this spacious room surrounded by bookshelves, a window through which the afternoon sunshine, floating between the still leafless branches and scarcely budding twigs of a tall tulip-tree, now fell with a palpable warmth full on his face. Towards this window he promptly directed his steps.

Very curious are the impressions that reach us when we enter any sort of a room for the first time. Not only are we confronted by the "aura" of the bodies and souls of those who habitually frequent it, but something quite different from any human atmosphere makes its impact upon us, namely the combined emanations from the pieces of furniture that have been longest in the room.

But John Hush, as he threaded his way between the chairs and tables with the intention of reaching the window, was now confronted by something beyond the room's human atmosphere, and beyond the impalpable emanations proceeding from such inanimate things in the room as had their own private histories.

He was confronted by a vibration of intense and concentrated curiosity, a vibration of surprise, of wonder, of a will to guard, to steer, to warn, to protect; but of this confrontation, and of the impalpable opposition it offered to his movement towards the window, he was entirely unaware. The personage who projected it, though Hush could have seen him, and indeed had actually been warned of his probable presence here by Echetus himself, was none other than Betsy's husband, the incorrigible Bill Squeeze, whose case, as the Doctor had explained to John, was so extremely interesting that it had become advisable to delay its cure. Bill Squeeze, as he now stared with this spell-binding intensity upon John's wavering progress towards the window, offered to such intelligences as might have been in a position to observe it a countenance that in all essentials was the direct opposite to that of Cogent Cuddle. For just as the husband of Tamia and keeper of the north gate of Glint was a perfect example of Spenser's mystic dogma that soul is form and doth the body

THE FIRST GLANCE

make; his countenance being entirely composed of the straight lines of predetermined conviction, Betsy's Bill had a visage literally composed of the rounded curves of arbitrary, whimsical and humorous caprices. His nose was as shapeless as a fungus on a willow-stump. His forehead projected over his nose like a wooden roller about to flatten out the dough of a pancake.

At the same time anyone watching him with as careful a scrutiny as he was bestowing on John Hush might have noticed in the fathomless curiosity of his eyes and in the incorrigible fantasies of his lowering forehead a resemblance to a well-known explorer contemplating an ensorcerised aboriginal of Central Africa.

The attention he was directing at John, however, struck its object without attracting that object's notice, while the interest of two other persons, by reason of their being directly between him and the window, could neither be by-passed unobserved nor glanced at and disregarded. Each of these two inmates, a man and a woman, must have experienced a certain unwillingness to stroll about the gardens of Glint Hall on this particular afternoon of the twenty-fifth of March in the present year. Their unwillingness, however, must have sprung from very different causes; for these two persons were almost as different from each other as were Cuddle and Squeeze.

John could easily imagine two reasons, all the same, for this man and this woman preferring to remain in this quiet place in spite of an afternoon of sunshine, reasons which it is quite conceivable *did* influence them both. The first of these may have quite naturally been, our friend told himself, a wish not to be accosted by, or even looked at, by any fellow-inmate; while the second may very well have been an insupportable distaste for, and an infinite weariness of, everything that this end-of-March sunshine could possibly reveal in the grounds of Glint Hall—a weariness of every flowerbed, of every shrubbery, of every rock-garden, of every lawn, of every fruit tree, of every iron post in every stretch of the iron railings that separated the gravel paths from the grassy pastures.

THE INMATES

Other reasons, no doubt, this man and this woman may have had for remaining in the reading-room on so sunny a twenty-fifth of March, but if they were wearied, as is quite possible, even of the very meadows of the institution, even of the sleek cattle that grazed in those meadows, it is also possible that such weariness extended even as far as the half a dozen wise old rooks who were generally to be seen lurching from side to side and jerking themselves forward across those pastures with the peculiar movements of winged creatures whom necessity has induced or compelled to walk instead of flying.

To reach the window our friend had to pass quite close to these ungregarious persons, and he forced himself to do so. The man was the first who was in his path; and he decided to pass him with a friendly nod as if he were a nameless tavern-acquaintance. The man was an extremely tall lean man with a very long neck on which rested, or rather from which hung, a head of such massive proportions that it looked as if it had belonged to some formidable broad-shouldered dwarf who had compelled this feeble-necked giant to exchange skulls with him.

What this dwarf-giant saw when John approached him was a gaunt, dark-haired, hollow-eyed, curly-headed individual who certainly looked—though as a matter of fact John had never acted in a play in his life—as if he had just stepped down from the stage of a provincial collegiate theatre where he had been rehearsing the part of the melancholy Jacques.

John was indeed on the point of greeting this dwarf-giant in a carelessly-natural and unselfconsciously-easy voice when he became aware that the fellow had fixed upon him a look of shocking penetration, a look that seemed to say: "I know exactly who you are. Your friends may have kept your case out of the Sunday papers, but I know it perfectly well and so does everybody else in here!"

Hurriedly switching off, therefore, the greeting he was on the verge of uttering, John hastened forward. Nor did he make any attempt to catch the eye of the other person in his path; for he told himself that if a male fellow-inmate could see through him

THE FIRST GLANCE

at the first glance, what might not a female one be able to do? He felt sure she was trembling with shameless curiosity, though as yet she had not lifted up, far less turned upon him, the lorgnette she was clasping so tightly on her black silk lap.

But it came to Hush as he glanced quickly at her that her purpose in carrying this thing was less in order to perceive obscure objects more clearly herself than to tap the knuckles of such unfortunates as might be unable to see what Providence had decided to reveal to her.

But he was at the window now, an excellently large window, and from it he could see, for it was on the first floor, the whole wide expanse of the gardens and meadows and walks and shrubberies on the southern side of the institution. There was hardly more than an air-gulf of ten yards between the window at which he now stood and the top branches of the nobly-grown tulip-tree.

Nor was this all; for extended on the grass beneath the tree and thus within the space of some twenty yards of the window-pane through which he was now excitedly staring, there lay a young woman the like of whom he had never seen in all the days of his life. And, now that he had caught sight of this girl under the tulip-tree, what had previously been the merest chance for Bill Squeeze became a certainty, the certainty that balanced on the lowest step but one of the reading-room step-ladder he would be able to watch the new inmate without being watched himself and able also to point him out to the personage he carried in his pocket.

"So that's the new bloke, is it?" he murmured as he contemplated with equanimity the nervously apprehensive actor-like individual with the decadent Roman nose, protruding upper lip and small deep-sunken grey eyes, who was standing like a mesmerised ghost at the reading-room window.

"He's watching Tenna Sheer. That's what *he's* doing! No, no, it's no use thinking you're invisible, young gent, for us do know all your little ways, don't us, Heraclitus?"

Bill was muttering all this in an audible voice; but the man and woman were so used to his mutterings that they took no

THE INMATES

notice of him; and John, after one hurried glance at him in which he realised who he was, gave himself up again to the girl under the tree. Bill now thrust his hand into the side pocket of his official jacket and brought cautiously and gently to the orifice of that spacious receptacle a small image of the weeping philosopher. This image he proceeded, with the most delicate and considerate nicety, to raise just high enough for its wide-open, staring, unblinking eyes to get a good glimpse of the man at the window. Then again he recommenced his mutterings. But John Hush, having once realised who he was, did not turn his head again to give him and his philosopher a second look.

"Up to his tricks, ain't he, Heraclitus? But he can't fool *us*, can he, old sport? For what you dunno, *I* know, and what I dunno, *you* know! Yes, *she's* there all right, ain't she, my wise one? Sitting under the tulip-tree she is, reading her book, and all the others afeered to go near her! What frights them so about that little girl, Heraclitus? That's what I want to know. She never talks back to none o' the lot; and when she does say anything, 'tis ever gentle and low, like Shakespeare says gals' voices should be! I don't say 'tis a warm-'earted voice, Heraclitus, old sport, and I don't say it's a neighbourly or a frolicsome voice. And yet, when you consider it, Heraclitus, you couldn't call it an icicle-proud voice. But whatever it is about that gal's voice, old tuppenny, it sure does give our poor little flock of natural lunies the tigly-wiglies. But what you can't tell me, Heraclitus"—and it was at this point that the husband of Betsy Squeeze decided that the moment had come for him to go home to tea—"is what it is that Mr. Hush finds so choosie-woosie, goosie-poosie, loosie-toosie, floosie-soosie about Missy Sheer. That's the mystery us has got to tackle, old sport, so don't jump the barriers or rush to conclusions.

"You may be a hell of a philosopher, Heraclitus, but I'm not going to have any bloody endings in this here tub of Diogenes, alias the old game-bag, alias Lizzie's temptation, alias the black hole of Glint. So be content with the peep into high life giv'd yer by Jupiter Squeeze. But home's the word, my hearty; so let's repeat the musical chairs—I mean prayers—we composed

THE FIRST GLANCE

the last time we sat on the steps of Parnassus. So good night, lords and ladies, and don't forget God and his prophet."

And with a glance at the back of the man at the window and an affectionate pat to his own left-hand pocket Bill went off. An onlooker would certainly have been induced to feel that the wavering channel of destiny and the fluttering trail of fate and the indecipherably scrawled map of chance, not to mention the sealed orders of necessity, were worthy of John's simplest and purest gratitude, if only for the fact that they had given him an extremely long-sighted pair of eyes.

A less clear vision would have missed half of the effect of the old-fashioned navy-blue dress, the plain black stockings, the filmy, straight, but rather rumpled and badly-combed hair of a subtle shade of brown that hovered between sepia and burnt-sienna, the nose that was slightly too aquiline for the pale oval face but went beautifully with the indescribably subtle curves of the girl's lips.

It was the general impression of all these, carried through the air from the grass to the window, just as if the flickering sunshine reaching out through the still leafless tulip-tree were a deviously designing artist, using that soft south-blowing air to create out of some unknown atmospheric element the perfect ideal, realised at last, of John Hush's life-long longing. He could see with a telepathic clarity all the appalling sensitiveness those rare curves implied.

So quickly would they be distorted that the very secret of their beauty lay in the strange prophetic quiver of agitation that stirred in them, like the wind in budding ash-tree leaves before there was any apparent troubling of the air. Tenna Sheer's chin struck him as so frail in its modelling that it seemed as devoid of the ordinary obstinacy of human self-assertion as a drooping currant moth; while her ears seemed to him like those of an exiled elf that has been blown on the wind from an island "where every sound gives delight and hurts not", to an island "where but to hear is to be full of sorrow and leaden-eyed despairs".

Frozen into a motionlessness that was like an icicle on the

THE INMATES

edge of Acheron, John Hush, as he stared through the shut window, felt that the prostrate form beneath that tulip-tree enshrined so absolutely the essence of all the maddening femininity he craved in his distraught idolatry, that all ordinary women, all ordinary beautiful women, struck him at this moment as belonging to a different sex altogether.

This enchanted creature struck him, in fact, as just as much more sensitive than ordinary women, as ordinary women were more sensitive than men. What in fact John Hush beheld with his long-sighted eyes was what old mediaeval learning called an "Elemental", and probably in this case would have been further defined as a creature of the air rather than of the earth or of the water or of the great zodiacal bodies of heavenly fire. For though it was certainly upon the earth that this ariel was now outstretched, Hush felt that no earth-magic could keep her there long.

Standing erect at that closed windowpane—for though the afternoon was exceptionally warm for the end of March it appeared to be taken for granted by the authorities that the inmates of a home like this would rather have their reading-room windows shut than open—John Hush thought, with the rational assurance of a man who has tried to regulate certain features of life according to his romantic wishes and has not always been aware of the ill-adjustment of these attempts to practical necessity, "I must go down to her at once."

Following this impulse, he moved towards the door, giving the dwarf-headed giant a wide berth, and glancing at the lady with the lorgnette as if she were less than the arm of the chair she sat in, in fact as if she were a certain nick in the woodwork of that arm that had been caused by an unskilled furniture-mover when it was first brought to Glint Hall. He tried as he went to visualise the girl under the tulip-tree as she would be when awake and sitting up or standing up; and he continued this process of mental visualisation down the main staircase, stepping aside to let little groups of inmates pass as they went up. Through the main entrance-hall he continued it and out of the front-door, where again he had to step aside to let

THE FIRST GLANCE

people enter; but by the time he reached the grass between the circle of gravel in front of the entrance and the tulip-tree, his mental vision was abruptly broken up by the sound of the bugle within the building and the sight of the girl herself crossing the grass towards him.

"*Damn!*" muttered John Hush with as much personally directed fury towards the jumble of large destinies and small accidents that had occasioned this mischance as if they had been embodied in the person of some preposterous rival. He opened his mouth as she passed him, but not a word could he utter; and if the mental vision of her by which he'd been obsessed had reduced the dwarf-headed giant to the nothingness of a blur and the lady with the lorgnette to the negligibility of a nitch, the way Tenna Sheer now hurried past him with her head bent low so as to see nobody and her fingers fumbling in the pages of that curst book blotted out the whole of the mental landscape that made such a vision possible.

"Swithold footed thrice the old!" was the blighted jingle that accompanied in John Hush's furious fancy the dying notes of that tea-time bugle, as he swung round to follow her across the gravel and into the hall and up the staircase. He suddenly felt a compulsion to tune his steps, and, indeed, to regulate every physical movement he made to some sort of rhyming tag.

"Follow her out," he murmured to himself as he went to the men's lavatory, "and follow her in; to *follow* a woman is no sin!" But later, when he discovered that the male inmates had their meals at one long table in the dining-hall and the female inmates at another long table in the same dining-room, his rhyming vein deserted him and his one desire was to find a seat from which he could see at least the back of Miss Sheer.

With a gasp of content he found one from which her face was visible. With this privilege in his possession, it was almost mechanically that he drank his first two cups of tea, though it did cross the threshold of his attention that both the attendants who carried round the tea and the attendants who followed with the milk and sugar spoke nicely if not respectfully to him and let him have as many lumps of sugar as he wanted.

THE INMATES

Chance had so arranged it that when John's head retained its normal position as he drank his tea he could just detect the shadowy curve of Miss Sheer's small white chin between or above or below the various opaque obstacles, organic and inorganic, which intervened; and not only so, but chance had also arranged that one of those mysterious shafts of light that so often break up the symmetry of a large apartment and do so in a manner for which a considerable experience of place and time alone can account, was now flickering, full of floating dust-motes that seemed to him like tiny magnetic whirlpools of occult affinity, between the arms and shoulders and sleeves and lifted cups surrounding that white chin, which in itself was worthy of any of those exquisite modellers of virginal-angelic chins in the studio of Leonardo, and a plate of brown bread-and-butter on John's own table into which that shaft of light sank and dissolved.

Towards this plate, upon which there remained only one last piece, John now stretched out his arm. But a youth at his side, and it had already struck him that there was only one grey head to be seen among the men seated round this long table, eagerly, almost passionately, forestalled him, snatching it up and swallowing it in a couple of ravenous spasms.

"Touch down!" chuckled this playful competitor, turning upon him a bland and serene smile. "All's fair in love and war! Besides, if your dad had seen as much as my dad's seen, and sailed the seas as long, and drunk rum with as many one-eyed admirals and as many fathom-deep pirates and as many lights-burning-bright-sir able seamen, north, south, east, west of Rotterdam, and east and west of Cape Horn, you'd have learnt, as I've learnt, the truth of that great saying of the king of the Cannibal Islands: 'For women and bread a man gives his head.'"

At this point Hush was aware of the turning towards them of a good many indignant countenances round that table, and aware, too, of the similarity of the expression written in marked language upon these faces. This was an expression not unlike what would have appeared on the faces of a group of boys on

THE FIRST GLANCE

their first night back at school had one of their number, breaking an unwritten law, begun bragging of his exploits in his native village.

John was likewise aware of a coming together, behind himself and the excited speaker, of at least four of the sturdy masculine attendants, two of whom were purveyors of tea and two distributors of milk and sugar. But John's mind, full of one matter only, and burning to make friends with his youthful neighbour purely with a view to gaining more light upon this one matter, completely disregarded these omens.

"And what," he innocently enquired, "has the wind at Cape Horn to do with your taking the last piece of brown bread?"

But in place of replying to this academic question, the son of the great seaman threw upon him a reproachful and upbraiding look and with anything but a genial "Excuse me", rose from the table and, with the assistance of the four attendants, stepped over the wooden form they were sitting on, and with haughty and silent submission allowed himself to be led out of the hall.

"You see, sir," murmured his neighbour on the other side, leaning closer to John than John found agreeable, since the fellow's clothes reeked of some peculiarly pungent disinfectant, "you see, he thinks his father was the Flying Dutchman!"

Evidently satisfied that the incident had passed without raising a disturbance, the attendants were now carrying round more tea and more milk and sugar; but John noticed that no other plate of brown bread-and-butter appeared to replace the one devoured so rapidly by the son of the Flying Dutchman.

But the white bread-and-butter was still there, and since the tea and the sugar seemed both inexhaustible, and he had eaten nothing since breakfast, our friend, though still hardly realising what he was doing, began to swallow slice after slice.

But all the while he was telling himself: "I'll sit here till she goes. I'll sit here till she goes; and then I'll go, and I'll speak to her outside!"

There had, indeed, been certain shiftings and readjustings and unsettlings that now enabled him, though the shaft of light had faded, to get a clearer view of that small oval face, aquiline

THE INMATES

nose, and perfect mouth and chin. She had seated herself, as it happened, next to the lady with the lorgnette, and now that several inmates from both tables had left the dining-hall it became clear that the lorgnette-carrier was concentrating on her fragile companion. The girl's head was bent over her plate, and as far as John could make out she was swallowing her white bread-and-butter as dreamily and absent-mindedly and with the same lack of any consciousness of the pleasure of taste as he was doing himself.

It was clear that though the lorgnette lady was addressing her with a continuous stream of low-voiced talk, her response was wordless. It was, indeed, confined to a few barely perceptible nods. At this point John Hush decided to be bold. A natural instinct, however, like that of a wild animal suddenly introduced into a concentration camp of circus animals, caused him to keep a wary eye on the attendants and to make no move till they were absorbed in a lively chat together near the door of the hall. Then without turning his head as he spoke, and, as far as appearance went, murmuring his words like a Ventriloquist, he appealed to the man who reeked of disinfectant.

"Are we," he enquired at large, "allowed to talk to each other at meal-time?"

As the man began replying to this question he did turn his head towards him just a little; but he noticed with relief that the stranger from whose person, unless they crowded up much closer on their common bench, he was divided, and glad to be divided, by a considerable gap, followed, no doubt quite deliberately similar tactics.

"Yes," the man replied, in a cautious and abstracted tone, addressing the backs of the women at the other table. "Yes, we're allowed to talk as much as we like as long as we avoid the facts of life."

"The facts of life?" echoed our friend vaguely; but his imagination had begun to call up several very curious memories that explained a good deal of what he now saw around him.

"I mean," the other went on, "real life, life that's the opposite of all the fables and fairy-tales and fancies and all

THE FIRST GLANCE

the silly escapes, in which the people who shut us up here love to indulge."

He was speaking so low now that John had some difficulty, with his head in its present position, in hearing him at all; and he knew by their voices, too, that the attendants, though still chatting cheerfully, were no longer in a group at the door.

"You mean," said John, "that we mustn't talk of anything that's important. But just tell me one thing, if you don't mind."

"You mustn't ask me," murmured the other, with scarcely a movement of his lips, "whether the stuff is stronger to-day or whether I still smell *It* through the stuff."

"Do you," whispered the cunning John, breathing his words as if the backs at the other table had been the wall of a fives court, "do you still smell *It*?"

"Hush!" returned the other. "Hush!"

"Hush is my name, you know," whispered John, "so it's easy to hush!"

"Pardon me," protested the disinfected one, "I'm afraid I don't follow."

"Hush is my name. My father was Thomas Hush and I am John Hush."

The utterance of this simple information gave John courage, and he turned his head far enough round to enable him to see that the speaker was a pitifully humble and a pitifully inconspicuous little man with sandy hair and large ears.

"May I use your name," enquired the little man, "when they don't put enough stuff on my clothes?"

Still dominated by his one sole purpose of learning more about Miss Sheer, John replied in his friendliest voice, "Of course! I'd be proud for you to use it! Do you find they take advantage of yours? Or have you turned against it? I won't ask you what it is."

The other leaned forward. "When I smell *It*," he whispered in an awestruck voice, "I become nothing but *It*; and the worst of it is, they have to put more on my clothes every day. Did you say you were interested in rock gardens?"

THE INMATES

This last sentence was spoken in a tone our friend had no difficulty in recognising. It was the tone of a boy who substitutes "Cato" for "catapult" when he becomes aware that the master is listening. But John experienced a thrill of crafty satisfaction. He had, it would appear, by means of all this selfish sympathy, made a friend already.

"What's that girl's name," he boldly enquired, though he knew perfectly well an attendant was already just behind them, "who is sitting next the woman who's got that eye-glass thing with a long handle?"

"That one? Oh, that's Tenna Sheer! She's been here a couple of years. She tried to kill her own dad, she did. That's what got her in here. It was only her dad being mayor of somewhere and swearing to be responsible for her that saved her from prison. And then a year ago she went for old Rumpibus with a door-scraper. He's got the scar still, and you can see it from here. He's descended from the great Doctor Rumpibus. He's the grey-haired one over there. He's a decent sort of gent and never holds it against her. I don't know him very well. He talks to everybody. He's not a bit scared of Miss Sheer. He gives her the time of day like everybody else. Jesus! If I had one grey hair I'd be fearful of being alone in a room with her! Tried to kill her own dad, she did, and he a great arch-builder and a' sir' in his own right. And only a year ago it was that she went for old Rumpibus. You know why he's in here, I expect, Mr. Hush? He's in here because he thinks he's God. It's because we say 'Our Father' that she went for him. It's wonderful, when you come really to think about it, mister, that there should be such a lot of people in the world who can't abide their own father and their own mother. That's what I always say. If love's wonderful, hate's wonderful, too, for there isn't a person who doesn't know that if love is heads, tails is hate. People aren't as thankful for being alive and for having mothers and fathers as anyone might think.

"In our gents' lavatory there *used* to be—they've whited it out now—a sort of music-hall song spelled out on the wall

THE FIRST GLANCE

above the third seat all about Tenna Sheer; and in this same song I'm telling you of, Sheer was made to rhyme with beer."

At this moment the disinfected one bent his back and changed his tone. "She is just like you, I expect, interested in rock gardens. No, you mustn't mind their not letting us talk seriously at meals. There is a purpose in it, no doubt, beyond playing the giddy goat with us. I can't see it myself. It seems just silly to me, but people are clever nowadays, and I don't know nothink myself. You've just come, mister, I expect? *Certified*, I suppose. Don't take it amiss that I say so, mister, will you? There's those here, you know, who aren't and never never can be. 'Tisn't lawful to certify in all conditions. But if you ain't had it done, the visiting specialist won't need to look you over. It's the certified alone they're interested in. To un-certify a certified—*that's* something worth talking about! It's about *that* the newspaper men come here; six at a time I've seen 'em come, Mister 'Ush. But, as I was saying," and the nameless one converted his animated three-quarter face into a severely inscrutable profile, "with the smaller kind of rock gardens, especially of this season, you never can be perfectly sure."

Hush was aware of one of the attendants slowly retreating towards the end of the table. "May I ask," his companion went on, "what they've got on you, chum?"

"Me?" Hush gave a self-conscious chuckle. "Me, do you say? What they've got on me? Well! I don't mind telling *you*, though I don't believe in talking about it to all and sundry. My trouble's an old one. I've had it since I was a schoolboy; and the war made it worse. Well! I don't mind telling you. But the truth is——"

He broke off. All the while the other had been speaking he had been repeating the syllables "Tenna Sheer" over and over again; trying to make them flow into that girl at the other table and diffuse themselves through her and become so intimately part of her that every wisp of her hair and every feature of her face, and every pleat and hem and fold and crease and curve and hollow and wrinkle of every garment she wore, and every beat of her pulses and every stir and every stillness of every part of her body under her clothes, together with the whole atmosphere and aura of her personality, should in some occult manner be contained in the actual sound of those three syllables of her name!

His feeling became so intense as he sat there listening to this gallant but inconspicuous victim of a maniacal sense of smell that he imagined himself holding Tenna Sheer on his knee; and, with every caress he gave her, calling upon the fitful precipitation of airy mist that composed her name to identify itself more fully with the being of which it was the vibratory symbol.

"You were telling me," recommenced the disinfected one, "about the particular trouble that caused you yourself to be thrown among us? I'm afraid I turned your attention from the subject."

If John Hush hadn't just seen an inch or two more of Miss Sheer's forehead from where he sat he would have been sharply arrested by his neighbour's choice of the word "trouble".

It had occurred to him to wonder at least twice in the motor car as he sat beside the fair American how the inmates of an asylum were accustomed in ordinary conversation with one another to refer to their personal aberrations; and one of the occasions when he had been thinking of this was when the lady was speaking of the recent purchase by some American friends of hers of the old mansion called Halfway House whose lights they both assured him must certainly be visible as soon as darkness fell from any window at Glint Hall that faced the hills to the west.

"What *is* there about your name," enquired John Hush, "that makes you want to use mine instead?"

"My name?" echoed the other. "Did you say my name?"

"That's what I said," sighed John, with a peculiar and almost petulant irritation. "What devilment is this," he went on, "that two honest men like you and me can't exchange the simplest remark about the mystery of names without having to produce the name of the person who baptised us, of the god

THE FIRST GLANCE

whose worshipper we became by being baptised, and of the king whose subject we became by being born!"

He now found without any too palpable twisting or peering that he could see quite a lot of Miss Sheer's face as she listened to the lady with the lorgnette. He even went so far as to pretend to himself that he could catch the identical expression of her face under that lady's concentration.

"Do you want really to know my name?" repeated the little man. And when John nodded abstractedly, wondering whether it would have to be in that leather-smelling reading-room that he must struggle to snatch his first exchange of words with the object of his obsession before they had to separate for the night, there suddenly took place an event which, of all the events that could conceivably happen at that moment, was the one that John Hush least expected.

He was compelled to remove his eyes from Tenna Sheer. The truth was that the insignificant little sandy-haired creature who was addressing him became suddenly endowed—at least as far as John was concerned—with an authentic power of hypnotism. It was as if he had suddenly been compelled to follow, in full daylight and in the centre of a dramatic moment that required all his attention, and not only to follow but to understand all the ghastly events of the life-tragedy of somebody else, of somebody who was not, and had no wish to be, connected in any way with John Hush. This had never happened to John before.

Living in his own insanity, if insanity it were, other people's identities—always with the exception of his guardian—had until this moment been like the sound of rain on the window, or wind in the trees, or waves on the beach. But now as he listened to this disinfected nonentity he found himself compelled to share the tragedy of a person whose weight of character was like that of a fly among a herd of bison.

The small creature told him in a rapid whisper that his name was Lordy—Osbert Lordy, he told him—and that from boyhood he'd been so used to having exclamations of "O Lordy!" addressed to him that he'd come to hate his name. His father

THE INMATES

had died before he ever saw him, and his mother had married again, and not only married but married a man fifty years older than herself.

It was this stepfather who had become the horror of his life. It was in fact because of the moral superiority of Tenna's father over his stepfather that Mr. Lordy felt critical of this young woman's conduct. She—so Hush was now compelled to learn—might have a selfish father. She didn't have to wait on a decomposing corpse who was no relation to her at all!

"In the end," Mr. Lordy said, "I completely lost my temper. He had been looking forward to his hundredth birthday. I hadn't touched him—to wash him, you understand—for years. He had begun to stink. The neighbours complained. As I say, I lost control of myself. It was on his hundredth birthday, and he said he could dance for the joy of being alive. 'And dance you *shall*, Daddy Lug!' I cried out. And I *did* make him dance. I held on to him and danced him up and down. He was a big man, but I felt as strong as a gorilla. You *do*, you know, when it comes over you like that! Well! *I danced him to death*; and that began it all. Daddy Lug was dead—dead and buried! But *It* got out of his grave and came to make *me* dance. *It* wasn't *him* any more, mister. No-no. And it wasn't *quite* as bad as him. It was his stink. I expect you didn't know, mister, that old men stink like corpses? You didn't? No, I thought not!

"And that's why I have to be kept from cracking up with stronger and stronger disinfectants. It's a pity. I don't know what they'd do if I began smelling' *It*' in my sleep. Perhaps you've never heard this, but it's the truth. Jesus Christ goes down unto the hell of sleep where all living things are given a tiny-weenie blotto, or crazy-dazy holiday from God's waking creation; and Jesus Christ strolls about down there as easy and careless as a sailor at the fair, and spits as the rest of us do, and dawdles round, so that his blessed spittle's as common down there as cuckoo-spit on the longest day, and that's why none of us poor devils, except now and again in a nightmare, meet *you know what* when we're asleep! Our priest here doesn't

THE FIRST GLANCE

live round here, you know. I *think* he comes from Horsesmouth. Anyway, he comes every Wednesday, and his name's Wun—Allen Wun—that's what his name is; and Wednesday's the day he comes. I know *that* because I don't need as much disinfectant on the day he comes. I don't say I don't need *any*, mister. Even the father from Horsesmouth can't be a total disinfectant for one like me.

"But he goes a long way; and if a poor devil could live at Horsesmouth and see the father Mondays, Tuesdays, Wednesdays, Thursdays and Fridays there's no telling what mightn't happen. All this bloody life might get as blotto as the hell of sleep itself. Anyway, I've found *this* out, that as Eno's Salts are good against bunged-up guts, so Christ's spittle's good against corpses in the hell of sleep. I haven't liked to ask the father why it's not used regular—Christ's spittle, I mean—in our *waking* life. Mind you, I'm not underesteeming its use in the hell of sleep; but if ever I dared ask Father Allen Wun such a question I'd ask him point-blank why the Lord don't stroll about in our *waking hell* now and again. Maybe he's got a stepfather in our waking hell who won't let him spit.

"If I *did* ask——"

But John Hush interrupted him. "I'm terribly sorry, Mr. Lordy, but I *must* go now. Will you be having tea here tomorrow about this same time?"

But all he could catch of the little man's reply as he stepped over their bench and hurried off towards the door was the word "disinfectant", and even that reached him with a faint sound as if it came from far away.

3

THE FIRST ENCOUNTER

He was feverishly making a little round pellet with his thumb and first two fingers from some crumbs left on the table near the brown-bread-and-butter plate as he came out of the dining-hall; but the moment he had shut the door behind him and

THE INMATES

realised that he was alone with the girl he shook this pellet to the floor, rubbed his greasy fingers against the edge of his jacket, and walked rapidly past her, down the corridor, just as if he were hurrying to the main staircase.

The moment he had passed her, however, he made a desperate and convulsive motion of his will, swung clean round, and confronted her.

"Miss Sheer!" he gasped. He could feel in his own nerves the shock that made her draw back. It was just as if he had flicked that little pellet of brown bread straight into her face.

"Oh!" she cried.

"Please, *please*, Miss Sheer," he implored in a low scarcely audible voice. "I don't want to be rude, and I won't keep you a moment. I only wanted to tell you that I think I know—something—about the book you're reading—that would interest you a lot, if you'd only listen to me just one moment.

"I'm fond of reading alone, too, just as you are, but there's something I know about that book that would be—that would make—that would surprise—that would, in fact, thrill you quite a lot! Please, Miss Sheer, believe me! I have discovered something—I'd like to tell you something—about that book—that—that explains a great deal."

She shrank back and cowered away from him like a wind-blown leaf that shrivels at its corners and seems to hesitate, as it gives little taps to the hard road, whether to resign itself to the cart-track or aim for the ditch. Then to his intense astonishment she stood quite still. Finally she gave him the swiftest and at the same time the most understanding look he had ever had from anyone in his whole life.

It was as if the crumpled leaf had turned into a bird—not an ordinary bird, but a bird made of some sort of living air that was more penetrating than thought itself. And this thought-bird seemed to flutter through the very pores of his skin and to dart up and down and round and round inside him, soothing with its gentle air-feathers the nervous tension of his whole being.

His cunning in walking past her and then turning so as to bar

THE FIRST ENCOUNTER

her retreat down the passage had evidently justified itself completely, though he was far too absorbed in the personality of Tenna Sheer to have any heart to glory just then in the success of his manoeuvre. But his strategy had had the effect of catching her between himself and the large window with which this second-floor passage terminated.

Behind him now was the reading-room from which he had first seen her. Behind him also was the popular smoking-room with its tables for games and cards. The only important room that wasn't behind him just then was the dining-hall from which they had just emerged.

For various practical and psychological reasons the massively built window at the end of the corridor which now formed a grandiose frame for Miss Sheer's small but beautifully shaped head was, among all the windows of Glint Hall, the one out of which the fewest number of inmates were in the habit of looking.

By this time the book she had been reading, which was a small thin dark-blue volume of Henry James's *Daisy Miller*, had been slipped into her handbag, a receptacle which had already struck our young man as having a tendency to remain imperfectly closed. But he now forgot both book and bag in contemplating the effect of her head against this easterly view.

The window behind her revealed an undulating expanse of arable land, broken here and there by hedges and trees. But this expanse terminated in a clear-cut unploughed grassy ridge, in the centre of which rose some kind of ancient fortification surmounted by a couple of gigantic Scotch firs. The whole ridge at this moment was in the process of being atmospherically affected by what was happening to the opposite horizon as the sun went down. In that western sky, where his guardian's lady had told him could be seen the lights of the American-purchased mansion called Halfway House, there must indeed have been visible at that particular time an unusual sunset.

John Hush's service in Various Balkan capitals in the combined role of private secretary, poor relation, and outspoken valet, hadn't encouraged him to make any but rather feeble and

THE INMATES

sporadic efforts to correct his city-bred ignorance of Nature. He may therefore have been in complete error when he interpreted the atmospheric condition just then of that eastern ridge with its prehistoric camp and its pair of majestic Scotch firs as due to the sinking of an especially blood-red sun over the rim of the opposite horizon and consequently over the chimneys of that Halfway House that now was sheltering his friends.

But the actual cause of the enchanted look of this eastern ridge mattered nothing to John Hush at that moment. The important thing was its ensorcerising effect as a background for Tenna Sheer's delicately shaped skull and soft brown hair. From the twilight that had begun to fall upon that prehistoric ridge there certainly emanated a heathen influence, and to the imaginative but not very scholarly mind of John Hush the small head that now appeared between that horizon and himself might have been the head of Ariadne or Andromeda or Atalanta or Arethusa or any other immortal nymph.

As he stared at the brown hair and white face before him, and beyond that head and face at all that was revealed through the great window terminating the second floor of Glint Hall, he began to feel so happy that he couldn't utter a sound. That he'd got her to look at him, that he'd got her not to run away from him, that he'd got her to give him her sympathetic attention, was so wonderful to him that for the moment he was unable to think of anything else. He just stared at her in speechless enchantment and she noticed that his under-lip was trembling as if he were going to cry. He was clearly helpless and wholly at her mercy. Nothing like this had ever happened to her before. Here was a real person, a person as mysterious as all other persons but completely different from all others in the fact that he belonged to her. She could be nice or horrid to him. She could make him happy or make him unhappy. But beyond all this, he was an endlessly winding path that she could follow at ease and leisure, not caring in the least where it led but free to trim the branches and dig round the tree-roots and look at the newts in the forest pools.

She was an old inmate. He was a new inmate. But they

THE FIRST ENCOUNTER

fitted into each other as naturally as the shadow of a tree fits into the ups and downs of a stretch of grass. Whether men knew such things as quickly as women she couldn't tell; but one thing she knew for certain: he wasn't a spluttering, banging, stretching, creaking, stamping, shouting, boasting, laying-down-the-law sort of man! He wasn't *any* sort of man! He was an inanimate. He was more like a doll than like a person. If he couldn't know what she was feeling, he knew she liked him to be there and knew he liked her to be there.

"And I don't *have* to talk to him now I've got him," she thought, "if I don't want to! I can think my own thoughts just as I always do, and sometimes not tell him! At any minute I can say to him: 'What are you thinking?' Or I can say: 'What does that noise remind you of?' Or I can say: 'What does that taste make you think of?' Or, 'What did you feel when you first knew you were certified? 'Of course, I *needn't ever* ask him things like that. And, of course, I'll never know for an absolute certainty how much he's hiding when he answers! He wouldn't be an inanimate doll if there weren't a mystery in him I can never, never get to the bottom of!"

To any onlooker the queer thing about this meeting between John Hush and Antenna Sheer would certainly have been the length of the time they just stared at each other between their ejaculatory questions and their slow, pondering answers! Miss Sheer was really only half listening to him when he fell into a rambling discourse as to the manner in which he would run Glint Hall if he were its chief. "I could think anything," she was now saying to herself, "with him there. I could do anything, dust anything, clean anything, pick up anything, put down anything, sew anything, weed anything, pick up leaves, trim bushes, draw pictures, make patterns! His being there doesn't bother me at all!" And by "there" she didn't mean "in sight". Now she'd got him, she could talk to him whereever he was, or wherever she was!

And she could never get to the end of him. Yes! that was the thing! He was her doll, but she would never know all he had in his mind, or might suddenly have in his mind, though it

THE INMATES

wasn't there before; and she needn't know it! No, she needn't!

What they thought need never be quite the same. She couldn't bear it if it were quite the same! But he must feel a lot that she felt. He must feel that things were pressing in upon her and jeering at her, and saying to her: "Yes, you see how brown I am! How yellow I am! How grey I am! You see how dusty I am, and the same as always! Yes, I am those same hairs in your comb, those same fish-bones on your plate, those same door-handles one after another in your house; I am that same dust and that same duster!" "No! they can't ever again say those things to me! Simply and solely because I've got a thinking man-doll for my own! And I needn't bother any more whether people hate me or don't like me, or whether I'm ugly and plain, or stupid and silly! Nothing of these matters any more! I've got a walking, moving, thinking animate-inanimate of my own, one that can say to itself: 'Has she gone for long? Will she be back soon? What will she have to tell me when she comes home?'"

All this while beneath their hurried spasmodic words and queer intense silences their souls were calmly, quietly, and with infinite relief, simply enjoying themselves. But at last he told himself that he must begin to talk to her or she'd take him for an imbecile.

"What do you think of Glint Hall?" he asked.

She waved her hand. "I can't bear its name."

"Yes. It's a short name, isn't it."

"Too short. I like long names."

"What kind of names?"'

"Oh, I don't know; a name like Rhyd-y-Groes-ar-Havren."

"That sounds Welsh to me."

"It is Welsh. A girl in the laundry told me it was her home. I made her write it down because I liked it."

"Did you work in a laundry?"

"Only for a week, to escape keeping house. But I wasn't strong enough. I couldn't do it. I had to go back."

"Did you try anything else?"

THE FIRST ENCOUNTER

"Lord, yes! I was always trying things! But the nice places wouldn't keep me. I wasn't clever enough or strong enough; and in the places where it wasn't nice I couldn't stick it out."

It was at this moment that the big clock in the artfully constructed belfry of Glint Hall struck half-past six. "The bell for everyone to be indoors will ring in a second," murmured John Hush anxiously. "And, anyway, there'll be such a crowd in the garden now. Hadn't we better find a good corner in the reading-room where we can go on talking?"

Miss Sheer glanced nervously round and at once made her accustomed hurried and timid step backwards; and then, looking straight into his eyes, gave a long-drawn, infinitely contented sigh, and with her head tilted just a little to one side allowed her face to relax into the ghost of a smile.

"Wouldn't the smoking-room be better?" She uttered these words, not in the sort of whisper that is conventionally described as "lighter than air," but in a low sound that exactly resembled the fretting of one feathery reed against another on the edge of a small pond. "They'd take less notice of us," she added, "and there are heaps of games there; so we could pretend to be playing."

He clapped his hands in pure delight. "And cigarettes," he suggested, "that we could pretend to be smoking!"

"Don't you smoke?" she enquired.

"No," he confessed, feeling rather ashamed, "no; I can't honestly say I do. But I'll love to see you do it, one after another!"

"Have you never smoked?"

"Oh yes! And it's queer how I came to give it up. But we mustn't waste time talking about that now. Let's go in there quick. Better not be seen hanging about in the passage like kids at school."

He gave her sleeve a jerk, and his agitation was such that without releasing his hold on this small segment of cloth, though he wasn't dull to the fact as he clung to it with his finger and thumb that it was warm inside and cold outside, he

THE INMATES

hurried her down the corridor to the door of the smoking-room, which they found open. It had only been left a few inches open by the last person to enter, but the sound of men's voices and women's laughter issuing from the room broke upon them as they paused on the threshold with the disturbing impact of a sudden puff of unexpected steam from a stationary locomotive. The whole thing was indeed far easier than John Hush had imagined it could possibly be.

He led her nervously and shyly into the further end of the darkest corner, threading his way like a water-diviner, while she glided after him like a shadow. Between table and table and chair and chair they made their way; and when they did at last discover an empty place it was to find they could settle down there in complete isolation without exciting anything beyond a sympathetic smile.

What he had found with his invisible divining-rod was nothing less than a tiny walnut-wood table adorned with inlaid squares, squares appropriate to romantic chessmen but at the present moment invaded and successfully occupied by business-like draughtsmen, who though of fungoid rather than of anthropoid shape seemed to John Hush to click their heels with secret joy and respectfully salute their new pair of opposing generals, as who should say: "*Now* we'll be having an easy time!"

And it certainly is true that the new generals and their respective men were in a secure position. They were in a recess behind two rather noisy groups of card-players who were far too occupied with their own skill and their own chances and their own flirtations to feel more than a remote flutter of faint interest over Miss Sheer and her new friend.

As to what they were supposed to do with these sturdy little toadstool-fighters, her white ones defying his black ones, neither of them had the remotest idea. Sir Warden Sheer had had as little time for parlour-games as he had had for tavern-games, and since he believed more strongly in daughters looking after those to whom they owe all than in successful builders humouring the fancies of spoilt young women, Tenna's leisure

THE FIRST ENCOUNTER

moments had a tendency to be spent rather in reiterated ponderings about her mother's death than in learning to understand the meaning of "checkmate".

Mrs. Warden Sheer—for this occurred before the house-builder had been knighted for his contributions to progress—had been drowned in the over-turning of a solitary canoe, and her daughter's balance of mind, like the balance of that canoe, only in a more gradual decline, had been tilted still further on the sinister side by that event.

"Did *your* father have *you* certified and put in here?" Tenna now enquired across the patient draughtsmen.

"God, no!" he chuckled. "I wish I had a father, if only as someone to damn and curse! No, I'm what you call an orphan. I've got no relations at all. There is a person—as a matter of fact he's a well-known political figure—who calls himself my guardian. It's he who chose my school for me when my parents died, who got me into his own office abroad when the war broke out, and in whose service—I mean as whose secretary, for he treats me like a younger brother—I stayed abroad till the end of the war. It's been since the war, since we've both been back in this country, that our troubles—mine and his too—have mounted up. I'm not blaming him, Miss Tenna. No, you mustn't think I am. Don't look so angry with him! It wasn't his fault any more than it was mine. He had to put me away. He had to put me in here! I'd have disgraced him completely, ruined him, in a sense, if he hadn't put me here. In plain words, Miss Tenna, if so I may call you, I deliberately begged him to have me certified.

"Of course, really, I'm no more insane than you are; I daresay no more than a lot of us are in here. In fact, now that I've met you, and now that you've been so nice, I wouldn't be surprised if I don't get quite cured of my mania, or crazy-wickedness, or nervous complaint, or whatever you like to call it. Yes! I really mean it, Tenna Sheer. You don't know what you've done to me."

She bent down sideways and squeezed the life out of her latest cigarette by pressing it against the wooden edge of an

THE INMATES

empty waste-paper basket that was so large and solemn and grandly recriminatory that it made John think of a certain second chamber in a Balkan republic.

Then she said with a frown: "But, Mr. Hush, you must have met hundreds of girls far cleverer, far prettier, far smarter, far more lady-like, than me——"

Her frown deepened and she made a vague gesture with her hand as if constructing a little viaduct through the smoke of the dead cigarette along which her soul could cross over the heads of the lazily listening draughtsmen.

"Say 'John'," he broke in. "Don't mister me!"

But she went on without heeding the interruption. "And far better able to interest anyone like you—and not only that, but far nicer than I am; for the truth is—"Here she began the gesture of pointing a finger at her own ribs, but thinking better of it she bowed her forehead low down over both her hands. Then she pressed her slender palms and widely-divided fingers against her cheeks, rubbing the skin as if such friction removed some teasing and irrelevant train of thought. "For the truth is," she went on, taking her hands from her face and sitting up straight, "you've no idea how far from nice I am inside!"

She sank back after this confession and looked steadily at him as if challenging him to go on being the friend of a creature so monstrous.

"She's got an absolutely elfish face," he thought. "It's not human. It's I don't know what! It's a leaf on the water-face, a root in the hedge-face, a frost-picture on the window-pane face, a feather on the wind-face, a foam on the wave-face, a 'Virgin of the Rocks' face! I've seen something like it somewhere; but I can't think where!"

Antenna Sheer was indeed watching him at this moment with an expression completely different from any expression he'd ever seen on a human face. It gave him the feeling that at any moment she might vanish altogether out of his sight.

"How terrible," he thought, "if I were really and truly insane and she were only a fancy of my madness?"

THE FIRST ENCOUNTER

He couldn't help noticing that as a smoker of cigarettes she had the peculiarity of making more smoke, thicker clouds of smoke, than any smoker he'd ever known!

As they whispered together across these orderly ranks of opposing draughtsmen, their thoughts seemed to swim in and out of their quaintly contrasted skulls like fish between a couple of under-water rock caves.

In his skull the question was now swimming about as to how she managed to create such a cloud of undulating smoke. Was it, he wondered, because she swallowed less and inhaled less than other smokers, and drew at the same time much more desperately at her cigarette?

And what an extraordinary number of cigarettes she possessed! And she appeared to be keeping them all quite loose at the bottom of this handbag, into which *Daisy Miller* had retreated. And the handbag itself, as he surveyed it shyly, respectfully, surreptitiously, and with a queer sense that it was a sort of indecency to notice it at all, how unlike all other handbags he had ever seen it was! It made him think of certain sacred objects used in extremely ancient ritualistic observances, objects of which the symbolic significance had long ago been lost; but objects which retain, so he told himself, like the ghostly notes of Roland's horn in the forest of Fonterabia, some inner quintessence of the actual matter, in *that* case the "matter" of sound, in *this* case the "matter" of fabric or gold or silver or bronze or ivory or semi-precious stone with which the "object of mystery" had been—during long centuries of time—ceremoniously charged.

"Is your father—I mean your guardian," was the next question she asked, "a married man?"

He looked at her in astonishment. "Why do you ask that?"

"You needn't tell me," she replied, "if you don't want to."

He thrust his arm clean across the draughtsmen and touched, not her hand, for he felt she wasn't a person to be lightly touched, but, as an Israelitish ox or mule might have done, that ark of mystery, her handbag.

"Of course I want to! I want to tell you everything.

THE INMATES

There's not one single least little thing I wouldn't like you to know. That's not why I asked you why you asked me. It's only that it makes you such a witch! No wonder you like Welsh words! For, do you know, it's just because he isn't married, and wants so awfully to be married, that we agreed I really had to be shut up!"

Antenna Sheer's face became at that moment what some of the old writers in the shelves of that reading-room from whose window he had first seen her would have called a palimpsest. Her perplexed and slightly suspicious frown didn't vanish, but it was overtaken and, as you might say, overlapped by a flickering smile. Beneath this smile it was still just discernable, like the scaly back of a small crab seen through disturbed water.

"Go on," she said; and it was clearly all she could say.

"As I told you," John went on, "since he's been back from abroad he's become much more important. They need him, you know; I mean this present government needs him, needs him terribly. In fact there's nobody else who can play with the other side as he can, and make them hop and skip with their own weapons! You will say, I expect—("Mercy!" thought Tenna," *I* have nothing to say! ") you will say that a man as clever as he is ought to settle down and write books and not fool about with politics; but the thing is he's not good at writing books, and he *has* a perfect gift for politics, and if he married this lady they'd have the best drawing-room in London and she swears she'll marry him on Midsummer Day if by that time he's got a constituency."

It was Tenna's turn to lay a rapid hold on her bag. She extracted a cigarette and began to breathe forth, like the elfin daughter of a dragon, clouds of white smoke. She even had a temporary coughing fit. But how could her companion possibly know that the word "constituency", though its connection with the building-trade might be obscure, brought Sir Warden into her mind; and along with Sir Warden there came as so often happened the whole problem of her mother's upset canoe.

THE FIRST ENCOUNTER

"Do you like her? Is she nice to you?" she enquired, rather painfully.

John Hush pondered. It was all very well to want to tell Tenna Sheer everything; but how could he get it into that angelic little forehead rising before him through its cloud of smoke as if it had come straight into Glint Hall from those rock-caves that "kept the fallen day" of such dangerously "deep seas" about them, the worldly fact that once having embarked on the fatal ship of politics, the influence, the insight, the discretion, the social power of some wise and tactful and, for such was the truth, wealthy woman, were absolutely essential to a prosperous career?

But the girl with feminine intuition had touched the danger-point. "I told him," confessed John Hush, "that he'd better keep me out of it altogether—not mention me, you know, or anything! Why should he? He's only my guardian; and anybody can be a guardian to anybody. I might easily be a black man from a cotton-patch in Alabama. He didn't like what I said. He's a real one, I tell you, but I kept at him. I told him that when he was in Parliament and had what they call 'a stake in the country', and had children of his own, and had 'saved civilisation', he could get me out of here, have me de-certified, or whatever they call it. And I kept reminding him what luck we'd had" (Miss Sheer thought she'd never seen anybody's eyes shine so bright or any face become so transparent as John's became now) "in keeping me out of the papers; and what he'd feel like if at tea somewhere they'd seen—you know? —a picture of me in the—the act of—oh, but of course I haven't told you yet——"

Tenna gave a shiver, dropped her cigarette on the walnut table, pressed the joints of all her ten fingers, including the thumbs, against her navel, gazed nervously round to make sure no one was listening, watched with relief while the uniformed attendant, who had recently appeared on the scene, turned his back to them in the course of his march up and down the apartment, and at last murmured hoarsely: "I'd rather not hear about it if you don't mind."

THE INMATES

"But you *must* hear, Tenna! I want you to hear! It's important to me you should hear!"

Tenna was aware of a dark wave of familiar misery mounting up on her horizon. This was the sort of thing she dreaded: a man bent on telling her about his sexual peculiarities! It made her feel all that she really and truly was, all that Sir Warden took for granted she was, and all that Sir Warden—and to this she could have sworn upon her mother's drowned body—secretly gloated over her being!

But the light had gone out of John's face and his eyes were slowly becoming glazed. Wearily and mechanically he was stretching out his arm over the draughtsmen, not to draw virtue from her handbag but simply to pick up her smouldering cigarette; and, just as he had recently watched her do, he now began to extinguish it by rubbing the crumpled blob of white paper flecked with brown fibre up and down that inch-wide rim of the recriminatory waste-paper basket.

Antenna suddenly felt as if the man opposite her were himself that blob of matter he was squeezing into a little ball and as if the fingers pressing the blob against the rim of that calmly-yawning Avernus were not his fingers but hers.

She suddenly felt that at all costs she must save that little brownish object from rolling down into that horror-pit of lost and discarded sentences—sentences of torn-up letters, sentences of torn-up newspapers, sentences of torn-up books, sentences like hibernating butterflies drowsing in dusty rafters, sentences like dead flies on the window-sills of unopened windows, sentences that wanted to be set free, to be blown through the air, or over the water, or into the fire—anything but to be carried off with the garbage in the cavernous dust-cart to the smouldering rubbish-heaps of Glint Hall!

As she looked at his glazed eyes and squeezing fingers, and at that whitish-brown blob on the point of being flicked into hell, she suddenly felt such a rush of protectiveness towards John Hush that she could not remain inactive a second longer.

Biting her under-lip, in a reckless abandonment to her impulse, she flashed down with the swoop of a shrike, snatched

THE FIRST ENCOUNTER

the round blob from those squeezing fingers that seemed to be her own, and opening her handbag quick as thought dropped this paper-ball of damnation among the virginal cigarettes that strewed the sweet-scented leather-tapestried bower of *Daisy Miller*.

"No, no, Mr. Hush," she whispered in an impassioned and excited tone, "I didn't mean at all what you think! Oh, not at all! I can't wait to hear exactly what you felt and did; what indeed you *had* to do since you felt as you did, and just how you came to do it."

The change in John Hush resembled the emergence from his shroud of the resuscitated Lazarus.

He licked his fingers and began vigorously rubbing at the mark left on the walnut table by the recently burning cigarette. But he didn't wait to finish this ablution of the battlefield of the draughtsmen. He broke into a fountain-jet of rapid murmurs, the words issuing pell-mell, in a disordered flight of narration.

"It was a mania for girls," he explained, using expressive words as he went on, and yet words so refined and delicate and fastidious that they couldn't have offended the ears of the chastest of women.

"Everything about them," he declared, "since I was a boy, has thrilled me so that I could hardly bear it! The way they're made, the way they move, the way they speak, the way they dress, the way they do their hair, the way they look, the things they do, the things they say, have grown to be more and more exciting to me; so exciting that I couldn't stand it without throwing my arms round them and hugging them! The moment they stopped being children—for female-children had no interest for me at all—I didn't give a damn whether they were pretty or not, whether they were tall or short, plump or thin, dark or fair! Just the fact of their being girls was all I bothered about, all I cared for!

"Well! you can guess how far this obsession of mine led me. I used to go down to the beaches and sands of all the seaside resorts available from London and stare like a crazy

THE INMATES

hypnotised vampire at some particular girl whom I discovered I could watch without attracting hostile attention.

"I had acquired the habit when I was abroad of searching public places for the sort of figures to which I was specially attracted; for as time went on I wasn't equally attracted to every aspect of them in the indiscriminate manner I had been at first. And even among the particular things about them which I made, as they say, into a fetish, I began to discriminate.

"And then, beginning about this time last year, a mysterious change appeared in my mania. It was curious. I can't explain it; and these doctors who ask us all these questions have never explained it—at least not so that I can understand or can associate—you know what I mean—what I *feel* with the words they use! But I reached the point when the only thing that gave me the real ecstacy I've always had from something or other about girls was to carry a pair of scissors about with me and cut off a tiny little lock of hair when I saw the kind I wanted, the kind I had this queer mania for. Isn't that an odd thing? But its oddity isn't the point! The point is, or *was*, Tenna, my Tenna, for I shan't call you Sheer ever again because there's something frightening to me about the name Sheer; and though I don't know any of your people, nor have ever seen anything about them in the papers, there must be something, mustn't there, to make me feel like I do?—but the point is that a girl's curl is like the curve of a wave, or the tail of a bubble under ice, or the crest of a wisp of foam or the smooth arch at the top of a waterfall!

"And girls with curls never get caught. They always turn and laugh at the great helpless hunters who are hunting them! They are like foam on waves, ripples on lakes, currents on rivers, feathers on precipices, thistledown on winds, leaves on waterfalls. Girls with curls always escape! That was the whole idea in carrying a pair of scissors wherever you went. You only had to creep up behind one of them and—*snip-snap*—it was done!"

John Hush gave utterance to a quaint little murmured chuckle, light and low, husky and yet airy, like a wrinkled

THE FIRST ENCOUNTER

piece of bracken crossing a dry flat stone as it worked its way along a path of spruce-needles under a roof of dark-green spruce-boughs. "*Snip-snap!*" he repeated, "and it was all done!"

Antenna Sheer had kept her eyes earnestly fixed on his face all this while. When he stopped speaking she lifted her hands to her head and ran her fingers gravely and scrupulously through her own hair, as if to ascertain, once for all and beyond all question, whether it was straight or curly.

"Oh, I'm quite different now," he whispered eagerly. "Since I've met you I'm quite different! When I had that crazy mania for curls it was because I wanted Undines and nothing but Undines! I changed completely this afternoon when I saw you under the tulip-tree. I've never seen anyone in the least like you, Tenna. And you've made me into a different person.

"I've come to my final conclusion about girls, Tenna. And shall I tell you what it is?"

Deep in her heart—while with her elbows on the table and her frail long-pointed shell-brittle chin, propped on her two clenched hands, gravely supporting her small skull, from whose metaphysical frontal-lobe she had pushed back the hair—Tenna thought:

"Yes, he's mine. He's my doll. He's the one I've waited for all my life. I never thought I'd find him. I thought I'd die and he'd die without one ever knowing the other. But *there he is*, sitting opposite me in this smoky, noisy place, with that keeper walking up and down, pretending not to be thinking of anything, while he gives a suspicious peep into everybody's face, trying to read their secretest thoughts.

"But let him peep and peep into *my* face He'll never read mine! Nobody, nobody, nobody, nobody will ever know what my thoughts are! There he sits! There sits my actual doll! And does God think, and do the doctors think, and does that devil who calls himself my father think, that I shan't know what to do with him now I've got him? Oh, you'll all of you soon see whether I do or don't! But there's no hurry about it. We're both here for good. We're both certified.

THE INMATES

"We're both under control. Under control? Don't you be afraid, my precious doll, what they can do to us! They can't do anything to us as long as we're *both* certified, both under control! It's the ordinary outside world that's liable to hurt us!

"Oh, take care, my only doll, oh, take care! Isn't it beyond all hope that we should be as safe as we are? That's to say until *he* comes at midsummer to make sure there's no chance of my running away!

"And it's at midsummer you said your guardian hopes to get married. Well, there's plenty of time to think everything out before then. And I'm the one to do it! So slow's the word, Antenna, my girl. There are days and days and days; and if I want the nights to think in as well, there are the nights too!

"What a good thing days are so long and nights are as long as days! I never did justice before to the length of days! Now I love to think of them stretching out, one after another and full of such a lot of hard things and soft things and of blue things and green things and of things that go in and of things that stick out. And I love to think of the nights all black and white and full of things that don't matter and things that don't count, and you just following things, and things just following you, and *him*, the great devil, never there at all, and they stretching out and out; and no hurry about anything!"

Miss Sheer's private thoughts had by this time been accompanied, though not interrupted or disturbed by yet further revelations from John Hush, who had reached the point of explaining to her that the beautiful brilliant lady his guardian hoped to marry on Midsummer Day was an American born and bred, when the tallest of the attendants announced with benignant authority, a *little* as if it had been a council-of-war and he the chief-of-staff to a commander-in-the-field, and a *little* too as if it had been a London pub and he an imposing but kindly landlord, that it was time for bed.

John and Tenna rose to their feet like a couple of animals who have been disturbed, not so much by a dog, as by some harmless pedestrian; and hurrying between the tables and the

THE FIRST ENCOUNTER

groups of players so as to get out into the passage and to be alone as quickly as possible, they discussed in an hurried colloquy as to when and where they could meet on the following day.

John Hush was by no means pleased to learn that an able-bodied young man and an able-bodied young woman, such as they confessedly were, would not be free to enjoy each other's society till after the midday meal. "I'll have to help in the house," she explained to him, "and you'll have to do something in the stables or in the garden. This special Bedlam is half an expensive school and half a luxurious hospital. It's not like a workhouse—at least I don't think so; nor like a prison. I can't imagine prisoners being allowed to go about together as we've been doing, can you?"

As she spoke to him thus hurriedly in that dimly-lighted passage, Tenna Sheer presented to the enclosed world of John's awareness as indeed she would have done to the unenclosed world of his guardian's awareness, a contented and satisfied countenance. Had the head of Glint Hall, to whose experiments on dogs the scientific journals had been of late more than responsive, seen her face at that moment he would have been at no loss at all to explain this profound change for the better in a patient obsessed by a patricidal mania.

But his explanation would have had little to do with what actually went on in the conscious soul of this evasive young woman. That she regarded John as a doll she had had all her life without knowing it, or rather as a doll she had lost in the desert and that now had come back to her of its own accord, wouldn't have drawn the ghost of a smile from the famous doctor; while that John Hush regarded her as a miraculous combination of the elementals of air and water, that is to say of an Ariel and Undine, though confided to him by John Hush himself, would have aroused not the faintest comprehension in the water-right pigeon-holes of his mind. That to follow the actual feelings of his patients' afflicted nerves *as they felt them themselves* should be one of the first steps to any real cure was the last thing the famous doctor could imagine or conceive. Indeed, it could be said of him

THE INMATES

that he owed his high position to his gift for making himself not only immune but absolutely impervious to what might be called the imponderables of his cases, whether canine or human. He possessed, indeed, the two supreme qualifications for success in this world: an undeviating one-track mind and the power of putting first things first.

But though the expression upon the face of Miss Sheer as she gave her hand to John and bade him goodbye "till two o'clock tomorrow under the tulip-tree" would have conveyed little to Doctor Echetus, it conveyed a great deal to John Hush as he followed the girl with his eyes till she vanished at the top of that staircase to the left, on the wall of which were written, in unmistakably clear letters, the words "Ladies Only"; and only then, and not till then, did he begin ascending the staircase to the right, on the wall of which were written, in equally clear letters, the words "Men Only".

4

FATHER TOBY

IT HAD already been conveyed to the new inmate, though through whose mediumship he had now entirely forgotten, that supper at Glint Hall only consisted of milk and biscuits, or, for those who preferred it, of a bowl of hot bread-and-milk, and that this modest repast was served in the dining-room, when, as at this moment, the reading-room and the smoking-room were closed for the night.

But John had been led to understand that only a small number of patients partook even of this light supper; most of them preferring to retire to their solitary bedrooms where they all discovered awaiting them on their toilet-table quite a substantial stick of chocolate. This had been a bequest to the institution by a certain great and wise chocolate manufacturer who had found in the course of his long and charitable life that in prisons and mad-houses, and other places where people

FATHER TOBY

pine, the only sticks held in greater veneration than sticks of dynamite are sticks of chocolate.

But even beyond finding chocolate in their bedrooms, the inestimable privilege at Glint Hall, and one held sacred by all inmates both male and female, was the rare and heavenly privilege of having bedrooms to themselves.

And it was with this thrice-blessed custom that the chaplain of the institution, Father Toby Tickle, was associated. It was not Father Toby himself, however, who was mainly responsible for this supreme solace. It was his extremely ugly and extremely good-natured wife, Mrs. Ursula Tickle, a personage known to the whole establishment both indoors and out-of-doors as "Ursie Mum". Mrs. Tickle had acquired this nickname in a very natural fashion, and she was constantly justifying its use. There apparently existed for her only one unpardonable human fault, and this fault was fastidiousness.

"Didn't your mummy teach you no better than that?" she would say when in the presence of this weakness. "Did Snow-White come into the world," she would say, "between powder-puff and soap-dish?"

"Mr. Pick-and-Choose," she would say, "never got to Heaven." And it was the same when instead of scolding, she was praising some unfastidious inmate. "If I were your mum," she would say, "I'd be proud of anybody working with slops till you're as muddy as sin, and messing with filth till you stink like a sewer!"

John Hush was still standing in a sort of daze on the third step of the staircase marked "Men Only", letting the loitering and arguing stream of men pass him by with casual and friendly "good nights" when Ursie Mum, accompanied by her husband, appeared as his side. The pair were pursuing their blameless way to their bedchamber, an apartment that could only be reached by ascending the same staircase that led to John's.

Observing the dazed condition of this newcomer, Mrs. Tickle indicated to Father Toby that it might be a good thing if he escorted the young man to his room; and, even as she

THE INMATES

made the suggestion, proceeded, as you might say, to put on steam herself so that in her own peculiar movement, which was as if she possessed at the centre of her being a mechanical engine that gave her complete control over the whole of her unwieldy frame, she projected herself forward so rapidly that she was already half-way up the staircase before John had time to respond to anything but the presence of her husband, which made itself felt as if it were an old-fashioned battleship rather than a person—a ship of the line, we might say, heaving-up beside him rather than approaching him, and throwing out, in place of grappling-irons or the voice of a speaking-trumpet, a peculiar shipyard fragrance that suggested a newly-painted lion-and-unicorn at its prow, as well as an ancient mainmast steadying its deck, from whose historic pennon, representing our island of sea-dogs, more sacred emblems had evaporated in the free-blowing airs.

Father Toby was indeed a striking figure, and John Hush stared at him in astonishment. He was quite as tall if not taller than John himself, and his weather-beaten leathery face, though it might have struck some who saw it as having a resemblance to the Emperor Hadrian, was in reality a physiognomic composite made up of the expressions of old-fashioned squires, poachers, keepers, farmers, hedgers, ditchers, cattlemen, shepherds, fishermen, timbermen, pictured in passing by field and forest, grassland and cornland, downland and moorland, fenland and marshland, from Carlisle to Colchester and from Shrewsbury to Penzance, a typically insular face, stamped with the diurnal endurance of the most changeable weather on this planet, gathered up from all the counties of Britain, caught anywhere and found everywhere, confused together for the confounding of enemies and the comforting of friends, moulded into a mood of incorrigible resistance to everything alien, a weather-created mask of obstinate defiance to every veering of the weather that created it!

"Hullo, young gentleman!" cried Father Toby. "Didn't I see you arrive this afternoon with those Americans who've bought Halfway House?"

FATHER TOBY

John felt in such a dazed condition after his talk with Tenna that he would have willingly confessed to arriving at Glint Hall that afternoon in the company of the Emperor of Constantinople. He emerged at once from his confused lethargy and indulged in an outburst of violent politeness.

"Yes, sir," he responded eagerly, "yes, sir, yes, Father! I hadn't the pleasure of a proper talk with you just then; but I look forward to one later, Father. I'm afraid more people want to know you better, Father, than you'll ever know."

Whatever the Father knew, or didn't know, upon this particular point, few could have possibly surmised—certainly not his present interlocutor—that he had already guessed correctly as to the cause of this same gentleman's unnatural excitement.

"I was very glad to see ——" went on Father Tickle. "No, no! We mustn't stay talking here. I'll come upstairs with you. We live in the same wing. My wife's just gone ahead. By the way, I'd like to give you the general hang of things here if I might—if it wouldn't annoy you—so that you'd feel more at home—'at home *from* home', and all that—when you wake up to-morrow."

"I'd like it very much," murmured John Hush, not having the faintest notion what this weather-beaten cleric was talking about or with what "general hang of things" he was to be made acquainted.

But he hadn't to wait long. When they reached the floor above and had passed the open door of the Tickle apartment where Ursie Mum, upright in the middle of the room and free from her conventional outer garment, had already assumed the voluminous house-wrapper with which the females of the establishment had come to associate her endearing hideousness.

Father Tickle always told her that her ugliness was a thing of magic; and that what she really was was one of those "Messengers of the Grail" who one day—so he would say—would "drop the mask".

At this moment all that Ursie Mum did was to wave them away with an exaggerated gesture of outraged modesty; and on they went down the passage.

THE INMATES

It was only when they had passed John's own small room, the door of which was also open, and its unappealing though neat appearance revealed to all it might concern, that the nature of his guide's intention became clearer.

It was a very long passage and there were many other doors on both sides, from a few of which came voices, but from most of them only those various less significant sounds, hard to particularise, made by human beings of the male sex as they prepare for bed.

At length the passage terminated in a small, squat, covered-in tower, barely lifted a storey's height above the rest of the wing, but raised high enough to contain a square chamber empty of everything but flowerpots, some intact, but most of them broken, and the intact ones containing not very promising and extremely chilly-looking cuttings and seedlings. This squat tower-room, John soon realised, overlooked the whole massive structure of Glint Hall. It possessed four windows each of which opened on one of the four quarters of the horizon.

There was no moon that night; and the starlight was obscured in certain directions by floating grey clouds, blown listlessly and sadly upon a chilly wind; but there was enough light in the sky to give John Hush a rough if somewhat blurred idea of what the handsome chaplain of Glint Hall meant by his queer expression "the general hang of things".

The first thing Father Toby did was to light a small wax-candle that stood securely fixed on its own dried wax on a rough wooden bench among scattered potsherds. The second thing he did was to light a short clay pipe and begin puffing out clouds of sweet smoke. This latter was in itself a sufficiently simple act, but it was one that Father Toby performed in so challenging a manner that it made John feel like a degenerate uncle in the presence of a manly schoolboy.

Emitting one defiant puff after another between his set teeth as if he were a moral locomotive, Father Toby guided John to the particular window of this tower-room that looked south. Here he could see directly beneath them the tulip-tree under which he had had his first sight of Tenna. Looking further

FATHER TOBY

afield he realised now that the whole landscape round and about Glint Hall was dominated by the river. The importance of this river was a surprise to him. He had grasped, with an odd satisfaction, the nearness of that ancient heathen camp with its two Scotch firs that lay east. He had been thinking all the evening, save when too stirred by Tenna's presence to think of anything else, about the massive stone manor called Halfway House that lay west; and where his guardian and the American girl were now with their American friends.

But of the river he had taken no thought. Now, as he surveyed the whole southward-stretching landscape, he noticed how, although the lawns and flower-borders and shrubberies and the railed-off green meadows and vegetable-gardens of Glint were enclosed by the institution's towering prison-wall, the height of the wall itself seemed considerably reduced from this observation-point.

Thus reduced, however, it served rather to accentuate than diminish the peculiar appeal of the unusual river. John realised, indeed, that the natural protagonist of the whole scene in this particular place was neither Glint Hall nor Halfway House, nor even the pre-historic camp with its monumental pines, but was simply and solely the winding river.

And, moreover, there was, he suspected, some mysterious link, perhaps in the very act of being created, between this monstrously walled-up citadel and the river that so nearly surrounded it.

As they stood side by side before this southern horizon John realised that more than smoke was issuing from the formidable game-keeper jaws of the tall chaplain. "Of course, it's not a deep river and it's not a fast river. But what makes a river the kind that satisfies a person has to do with the nature of the water."

As John listened to these murmurs he got the feeling that he was being conducted through the intricacies of a scene more seductive than anything in real nature: a scene like an ideal print in some old romantic masterpiece; a Holbein illustration, for instance, of More's *Utopia*.

THE INMATES

"Our river," Father Toby went on, "often makes me think of a place I once visited in South America. Those reedy ditches and pollarded willows have the sort of look—though of course the particular trees and the particular reeds are quite different—the sort of look..."

But as John watched the man's face in that criss-cross mingling of light and darkness, he received the impression that this river-worshipping chaplain of Glint had no more idea of what ordinary human beings go through in their diurnal endurances and nocturnal nightmares, whether the vegetation runs to bulrushes or to bamboos, than has the south wind that moans round their patience or the north wind that rouses them to revolt. "Toby of Glint," so he rhymed it to himself, "has a heart of flint, though he smokes a pipe of clay; and Ursie Mum would have taken to rum if she hadn't had her way."

But the new inmate of Glint Hall was not allowed to spend his time shifting from foot to foot in that tower-room composing rhymes about the authorities. He might have been a visitor to some four-square lighthouse on some historic ocean rock, judging by the polite persistence with which he was now conducted to the eastern window.

Here he was encouraged to observe, though from a loftier position, all that he had already seen that evening with Tenna's head in front of it. The curves of the old camp would have scarcely been distinguishable at all under the cloud-dimmed stars if there hadn't been that couple of Scotch firs whose monumental old age divided the ridge into three sections—the one to the right of the two trees, the one between the two trees, and the one to the left of the two trees.

It indeed began to occur to John Hush that there was something like theological unction in the precision with which his self-appointed guide was mapping out the eloudy horizons of Glint Hall; and the impression was increased rather than diminished when he noticed the perceptible rapidity with which the view from the northern aspect of their tower was slurred over.

This view embraced what he had already seen of the abode

FATHER TOBY

of Mesopotamia Cuddle, the woman destined to do his washing, and who had already made him think of his childhood's nurse, and it comprised the cobble stone yard surrounded by stables and barns and pigsties on which his bedroom-window looked.

It also included a wide sweep of the hideous prison-wall, broken, as he had already discovered, by the same type of model lodge and terrific lodge-gates as had confronted him, beyond the gardens and the meadows, on the southern side of the grounds.

"Why is the fellow," he thought, "so unwilling to give me any time to take in what he calls 'the hang of things' from this outlook?"

John Hush was not an unmitigated fool. Possibly by reason of his birth in Derbyshire, one of the most central of our counties, he carried about with him a conjunction of geographical and astrological birth-seeds that endowed him with a peculiar kind of cunning.

This was a cunning that certain particular animals and a certain class of human neurotics alone possess. It is a cunning hard to define, and not at all easy to catch at work; and on the occasions when the herd, or the pack, or, in more conventional language, public opinion does discover its base of operations, it hunts it down in a savage rush of fury.

It was this special kind of cunning in him that led John at this moment to delay the slurring over of the northern outlook from the tower of Glint and to compel Father Toby to pause in his circumnavigation of the four horizons.

Whether it was by pure chance, or, as seems more likely, by the passing of some sort of hostile vibration between them, John obtained this delay by a reference to the unusual appearance of the river from their high observation-point. "It looks like a huge white serpent," he murmured, "like that world-snake in Norse mythology. You'd think it was working its way closer and closer to us with the aim of eventually making a leap and squeezing us to death!"

As if in reply to these sinister words of his visitor, Toby Tickle pressed the switch of an electric bulb in the wall of the

THE INMATES

tower-room. By the light of this bulb John could see that his guide's expression had changed. He now looked grave and slightly worried. John could have sworn that across those weather-beaten features that had become so representative of life on British soil under changing British sides there even passed a flicker of something like fear.

"What a pathetic crew we educated people are!" thought the new inmate. "There isn't one of us who hasn't got some bruised spot in the landscape of his soul, where morbidly sensitive moss or perilous grass or electricity-charged lichen grows and where the mere approach of an alien presence sends a shiver through our whole being."

But the chaplain was protesting vigorously now: "Oh, you mustn't, my dear lad, you really and truly mustn't speak of our Glint river like that! Serpents—snakes—dragons—squeezings to death? Oh no, no, no! I cannot allow such expressions to drop into the air from this observation-post of mine! I must confess to you at once, my dear boy, that that river down there, about which you talk so lightly, is my whole life in this place: well, of course I can't *quite* say that, for obviously my work here is the reason I am here at all. But I can say—and you'll forgive me, won't you, for taking you into my confidence? —I can say that the river is my whole life when I'm not at my job! I go down there practically every day and all the year round. It's the fish, of course, chiefly. But it's everything else, too! Though the fish are the only creatures I *kill*. Cold-blooded, you understand, Mr. Hush. I mean the fish, of course, not myself! I'm extra hot-blooded, as everybody who knows me would say. But I don't shoot. And I've never hunted. Fishing's my one and only! And it's mostly coarse fish, too; perch and roach, you know. Though I often catch quite good-sized dace with a fly. I've really become quite a specialist over the flies that dace will take. I'll show you when you're free from this little temporary trouble.

"I'll take you on what I call my round. It's the nature of the land that makes the river curve so. Oh, I assure you, Mr. Hush, there's no serpentine malice in it! Purely the lie of the land.

FATHER TOBY

But it's unique, you know. Nothing like it in all the British Isles! Why, it curves clear round the whole place except for one little quarter of a mile!

"I sometimes think it's these curves that make me love the river as much as I do; and, of course, the fish I catch in it. In God's truth I sometimes hardly could say whether I love the fish for the river or the river for the fish! Cold-blooded they are—the fish I mean—and the worms, too, of course! That's why they don't feel, though they wriggle and flop. Cold-blooded—that's what worms and fishes are.

"And yet it's curious how when the juice comes out of them—out of either worms or fish—it doesn't *feel* cold. And, do you know, Mr. Hush, I've asked some of the cleverest scientists in the kingdom why it is that the river curves round this place, and do you think any of them gave me a sensible answer? Not a one! I mean not an answer that a simple chap like me, whose only sophistication is to put worms on a hook and catch great greedy old perch through their tough gills, can understand.

"My rival cleric here, the Roman priest from Horsesmouth, pulls my leg about this river. He makes out she was once a heathen goddess—yes, a real heathen goddess! It's funny, isn't it? I expect our good Doctor thinks I've become in-fected—*affected*, shall we say—by my concentration on the work here. But that's absurd, of course! I've always been eccentric in these things!

"The truth is I've got my own idea as to what the Church should be; and this idea includes quite a lot of things that would shock some people. We're all Christians nowadays. Christ, by' being lifted up', as he himself predicted 'has drawn all men unto him'; but the reason why Communism has grown so strong is that it has stolen half the thunder of Christ.

"And who is the chief enemy of the Roman Church? Communism? Well, Communism you will say, has stolen the other half of this divine arsenal. But notice this, my dear boy—notice this!"

THE INMATES

"Don't worry, master," thought John, "I'm noticing quite a lot of things!"

One of the things he was noticing had no direct connection, though doubtless many indirect ones, with the ecclesiastical ideal now being communicated to him by this hot-blooded killer of the cold-blooded. It had to do with the way in which this formidable clergyman with his barge-pole physiognomy was lighting his clay pipe. He lit it like a pilot, he lit it like a boatswain, he lit it like a gamekeeper, he lit it like a yachtsman, he lit it like the oldest member of the oldest white-man's club in Central Africa.

And with every pressure of his broad thumb he seemed to be saying: "To hell with your aesthetes and ritualists! What is needed to-day to keep up the old historic church to which we have dedicated our lives is more of our national character. What the world needs isn't pious United-Nations martyrs. The world needs adventurous Americans, scientific Germans, inventive Italians, practical Frenchmen, independent Australians, and strong, tough, sporting English!"

John Hush couldn't help allowing his mind at this point to recall a discourse of his guardian's at a club in Belgrade on the varieties of religion in the Church of England. "You can catalogue them," his guardian had declared on that occasion, "by the way they eat and drink and smoke. For example, if you want to understand the beautiful simplicity of the Evangelical party in our Church, you ought to see them at a Sunday-school treat eating strawberries and cream. The High Church, on the contrary, imitates the Papists and goes in for bouts of poetic alchoholism. But it's the Broad Church who are the most representative of us. They're the sporting parsons, and with them a weakness for the wriggling of worms on hooks and the flapping of dying fish on grass naturally coincides with the grimness of strong teeth biting the stems of sturdy pipes."

"God doesn't want," this river-lover continued, for by this time he seemed to have accepted John's diplomatic politeness as the first stage of a convertite's interest, "God doesn't want an emasculated world of planetary puppets. He wants a world

FATHER TOBY

of richly contradictory and finely complicated individuals to whom every country has given its quota of special peculiarities!"

John Hush stared in wonder at the only official guide supplied to him in this home by his national government. Toby Tickle's countenance automatically assumed as it met his gaze the expression it must have worn afternoon after afternoon in sun and rain and mist and drizzle and sleet and snow and through many a dull day of composite neutrality along the banks of his obsessing river.

During the passing of quite a number of moments of reciprocal personal scrutiny, the Reverend Tickle tried more definitely than was usual with him to sum up the character of this young man whose nervous and sulkily philosophical appearance suggested nothing so much as a would-be actor dedicated with any luck to be allowed to play Hamlet.

John's mind, on the other hand, had never been less restricted by what we have been taught to regard as the fatally procrastinating tendency in Ophelia's lover. His thoughts were of the kind at that moment that no possible action, however swift and successful, could embody. The bronze head in front of him became a microcosm of the whole round earth, while the four horizons visible from this tower-room, one of which alone—that is to say the eastern one—was entirely free of the ubiquitous river, became four infinite recessions of uninterrupted space.

The peculiar thing was that the imaginative urge in John's mind, an urge that was electrified by a considerable amount of emotion, was so pathetically devoid of all logical and mathematical and even metaphysical machinery that once having seized upon the notion of four corridors of space receding endlessly northward and southward and westward and eastward, always with Glint as their common point of departure, he felt absurdly puzzled as to how to fill up the four gaps between, these four corridors so that the natural rondure of the earth's complete horizon should remain unbroken.

He decided that towards the circumference of this vast

THE INMATES

ultimate spatial rondure there must be for ever emanating from their centre at Glint, and for ever arriving at their destined point on this far-off tremendous circumference, just as many streams of magnetic energy as are required "to go", as children say, "round".

And thus, according to his pictorial but extremely unscientific cosmology, John Hush visualised his four great spatial highroads as a four-fold objectively parcelled-out stratification of this perpetually streaming radiation. Consequently, as he went on staring at the bronze physiognomy of his country's fish-hooking representative of the absolute in Doctor Echetus's home of rest, he found he was able to follow the spatial corridor behind the chaplain's head, which happened to be the one to the east and the only one free of the river, as clearly as it was possible for him, without indulging in any particular acrobatics, to visualise through the back of his own head the one to the west, the Halfway House one, which he himself just then liked as little as the chaplain liked the riverless one.

Never in his life had John's thoughts whirled through his head as fast as they did at this moment; and the thought that dominated all the rest was strictly rather a nervous sensation than a thought, namely the present physical position of the curious entity he felt to be his conscious soul at an actual point in space from which four infinities radiated. It suddenly struck him as positively comical that such a wavering, fluctuating, and morbidly shrinking creature, as was the living thing in which dwelt the consciousness of John Hush, should possess a zodiacal position in space at all; but that it should also find itself confronted at this dizzy planetary centre, where four such pendulous space-roads met, by such a sturdy home-bird as this fisher in perch-pools, seemed to be carrying comedy into burlesque.

But his thoughts were now scattered as completely as if they'd been a swarm of midges dispersed by a cast of the chaplain's fly. Father Toby took his pipe out of his mouth, strode to the potsherd table, and snatching up half of a flower-pot

FATHER TOBY

pressed it down upon the flickering wax-candle and held it there until that troubled flame, spluttering and hissing, was transformed into a thickly oozing, rapidly dissolving cloud of reeking fumes.

This drastic action, like most actions of such a kind, not only broke up the pregnant moment that had enveloped these two human forms as a long drawn-out operatic syllable envelopes a pair of lovers, but completely changed the atmosphere of the whole situation. With the firm and quiet authority of an experienced moral leader, Father Toby now conducted the new inmate to the western window of the tower-room. It became clear that of all the four horizons visible from his watch-tower the chaplain felt that the one best adapted to the troubled soul of his new recruit was this one to the west.

He pointed out to the newcomer how upon the upward slope of the hills dominating this view, which was indeed exactly what John had been told before he ever caught sight of the place, could be seen the flickering lights of Halfway House.

It certainly gave John a queer feeling, full of conflicting currents of emotion, when he was thus encouraged to admire the lights of Halfway House.

"Nothing like knowing the ropes," said Father Tickle. And he repeated the words with yet greater emphasis as they descended the half-dozen steps into the passage. "When you know the ropes," he concluded, "you're ready for anything."

At the door of John's room he stopped again. "It's curious to think," he remarked in a contemplative tone, and as if the idea had just come into his head for the first time, "that today's the twenty-fifth of March. Do you know, Mr. Hush, I believe I've really twigged at last what the Church had in mind in putting the Annunciation into this week."

"Have you, Father?" murmured John respectfully, while in his heart he thought, "Why is it that High Church clergymen always make you feel uncomfortable? This fellow's what's called a decent chap. He wants to put me at my ease. He wants to heal my trouble. He wants to make me happy

THE INMATES

in this place. Why in the name of God, then, must he use the word 'twig' in talking of Mary and the angel?

"It's our class system that does it. The public schools don't aim at making Christians. They aim at making self-controlled, brave, polite, modest, chivalrous pagans. They teach us to be courageous, honest, patient and enduring. To be stoics, in fact. And then we expect our clerics to be as unselfconsciously Christian as Irish or French or Italians who have lived in religion, like minnows in a stream, from childhood, and to whom the poetry of Christianity is as natural as eating or drinking, and its restrictions as natural, though sometimes as annoying, as relieving ourselves."

While these thoughts passed through John's head, Father Tickle, who had the quick psychological perception of a man who has wrestled all his mature years with a tendency to paederasty, decided that it would have to be through that extremely difficult young woman called Antenna Sheer, and only through her, that any successful approach to this polite young man could be made.

"Yes, but," the chaplain went on, "it's too nice a point —too human a point you might almost say!—to be discussed as late as this! Oh, by the way, you saw where the men's lavatory is? You saw the door, didn't you? We passed it at the top of the stairs. To tell the truth, we've got quite a nice well-kept lavatory in our wing. I confess it's a little too near my wife's apartment—but she doesn't mind. She's a remarkable woman. You will meet her in due course. She's in the women's domain all day, and we're pretty quiet up here during the night.

"But you and my wife will get on like a house on fire when you do meet. . . . Oh yes, you can open your window still further if you like, Mr. Hush. Or you can keep it entirely shut. It's just as you like. Those bars? Yes, I know; they *are* rather like a nursery-window, aren't they? You see, it wouldn't quite do, would it, to have people roaming the countryside all night? Here's your electric switch. May I turn it on? Well! Sleep well, Mr. Hush."

Very carefully and meticulously, the moment the Father

FATHER TOBY

was gone, did John explore every aspect of his small room. There was a neat little chest-of-drawers with a couple of deep square drawers at the top into which had been carefully put not only his collars and handkerchiefs but also his socks; and in the same drawer as these latter and placed there with equal care he found the books he had brought with him.

And he responded with quite a little glow of satisfaction as he noted that these books of his—which had been selected with some nicety and consisted of Hesiod in the Loeb Classics, a French volume of Selections from Paul Verlaine, Walt Whitman's *Leaves of Grass*, Longfellow's *Poetical Works, The Mabinogion* in Lady Charlotte Guest's translation, Milton, and Edgar Allen Poe—hadn't been shoved together or stuck in at random but had been carefully isolated from one another and laid to rest apart, as if the person who unpacked them desired to treat them with some special kind of respect.

"I wonder who arranged these?" he thought. And then—and, as it happened, quite correctly—he attributed this to Mesopotamia Cuddle. There was no wallpaper on the walls, but they had been newly whitewashed, and though this whiteness would have thrown into effective relief any crudely coloured picture, the only picture actually hanging there—and it was a very little one—was a reproduction of Rembrandt's "Supper at Emmaus". This picture, in any case, depended for its effect on something other than colour.

It struck John, indeed, when he approached close enough to it to get the almost disturbing effect of the light thrown by the electric bulb as it encountered that other light diffused by the small central figure under that massive arch, that there was something in the expression of this resurrected deity that reminded him of the look he had caught in the dead eyes of one of those dogs in that horrible pit among the spruce-trees. It was as if that small figure were totally unconscious of the divine light that was filtering and leaking from him and drifting away to the ends of the earth.

"But though *he* doesn't know it," thought John, "it *is* there—man's hope against hope—under that cavernous arch

THE INMATES

which hides all the oppressions that are done out of sight of the sun. But while that very homely Son of Man breaks the bread of—damn it all! "—thus did John interrupt John—" if I'm not in the picture myself! On my soul, I believe I'm that boy there who's changing the plates for them!

"But what does that fleshless fish-head on the plate he's changing think of it all? That boy certainly looks as if he felt friendly to these queer guests; but he also looks as if he wouldn't be sorry for this supper to be over!

"As to that little god-man with the light leaking out of him, he looks as if he were too sodden—no, not exactly sodden, too saturated with suffering to understand that he has redeemed the world. He certainly looks far too humble to believe he's the Second Person of any Trinity, and too shocked and puzzled by what they've just been telling him to have any heart left to enjoy her resurrection!"

John Hush began walking up and down between his chest-of-drawers and his bed. "Oh, dearie I! Oh, dearie I!" he kept muttering. Then he thought: "But I've got Tenna. That poor fleshless fish-head on the dish hasn't got her! That young dish-washer hasn't got her! That pipe-smoking cleric with a wriggling worm on his hook and a dying fish in his basket hasn't got her!"

He crossed the room, and going to the window opened it as far as it would open. Then he began to shake the bars with his clenched hands. One after another he shook them, making an ugly face each time he did so. Then he shoved his hands deep into his pockets and leaned forward, pressing his stomach against the window-sill and his forehead against those upper panes that refused to move, just as the obstinate stone of Sisyphus, bewitched in the same sort of purgatory, refused to *cease* moving.

He tried to forget his anxieties by taking in every pool of liquid dung and every heap of befouled and bedraggled straw. The cobblestone yard out there was certainly a large one; and the number of stables and barns and sheds was beyond what anyone would have expected in a place like this. From

FATHER TOBY

the yard his gaze moved to the dimly lit upper room of the northern lodge. Was the woman who resembled his old nurse already in that upper room? Yes! yes! he could see "vast formless things moving the scenery to and fro" up there.

"What a mystery it is," he thought, "that it should be in our power to look or not to look at what strikes us as unbearably horrible or as intolerably alluring! But I fancy," so John's thoughts ran on, "I'll grow so practised in these mental tricks before I get out of this incredible place that, weak fool as I am, with about as much will-power as a pond-newt, I'll steer my own mind and regulate my own feelings quite as successfully as that pathetic perch-catcher."

But he left the window now and extinguished the electric light. Irritably he tried to throw off, with coat, waistcoat, shirt, collar, tie, braces, trousers, drawers and socks, as if they had been scales growing upon the skin of his very soul, his odd vague misgivings not only about Father Tickle's hurry to by-pass the northern view, which was the view from this window, but about those shadows he had seen through the yellow blinds of the Cuddles' upper floor.

Safe in bed, he stretched himself out at full length and remained for some minutes on his back wondering whether to yield to his cowardly desire to turn away from the window or whether to lie boldly on his side facing it. It was a fear that cowardice might hurt him more than courage rather than any courage that made him decide to face it, and it was facing the window that he finally closed his eyes and set himself to think of Antenna Sheer.

But though he faced the terrifying window, and though he closed his eyes and used all the visionary energy he possessed to summon up the precise appearance of Miss Sheer's small head and clear-cut features against the peculiar rich blackness encrusted with zigzags of dazzlement that had been substituted for ordinary sight by his tightly shut eyelids, what he felt impelled to do, as he lay thus with his knees bent and his fingers clutching his lean thighs, was to envisage not merely the lineaments of the daughter of Sir Warden Sheer or of the

THE INMATES

rising young statesman he called his guardian, but of that dramatic mask of destiny which was his own life.

He pondered on his passionate devotion for the man who was spiritually so much more than a father to him, and on the curious fact that, though his feeling for this person was completely devoid of every sort of homosexual vibration, it was extremely intense and desperately jealous. He also pondered on the odd fact that, jealous as he was, he found no difficulty in making friends with his guardian's betrothed, or even in feeling a certain affection for her, though—and this rather bewildered him—he experienced not the faintest attraction towards her.

Gradually these thoughts about Tenna and about his guardian lost their personal intensity, and it was not long before the faces of both his girl and his friend were absorbed into those dizzy encrustations of dazzling light that kept appearing and disappearing against the inky blackness.

And it was then that the palpable body of his life itself rose up, not as a memory of anything, nor as a hope for anything, but simply as a huge, shapeless mass of pain-bearing and pleasure-bearing substance, pressing upon his consciousness, yielding to his consciousness, wounding and caressing his consciousness, like the shores of a vast continent opposed to an inflowing sea-tide. The "I am I" behind this consciousness that flowed round his experience was certainly an entity of an extremely evasive kind; but the consciousness itself was a sequence of very definite impressions, moving and tossing up and down, many of them very delicious and many of them horrible.

"It is a battle," he told himself. "It has always been a battle between me and the whole pressure of my experience as to whether I can enjoy life or not. Yes, it's a battle between me and life. 'The wrestling of this world asketh a fall', and, when I'm dead, either the world will say: 'That crazy little weak silly creature of a John Hush got me down', or I shall have to say, 'Well! You beat me, you damned world, and that's the truth. I tried to enjoy being alive, but I simply couldn't; and I'm glad it's over! Life, World, Existence, whatever you prefer to call yourself, *you've won*, and John Hush is beaten!'"

FATHER TOBY

He clutched at his thigh still more tightly and bent his body still more firmly into the shape of a buried skeleton in a cist or of an unborn embryo in a womb. And as he did so he sought to envisage in one amorphous "lump", as it were, the varied reactions he was feeling to all that surrounded him at this moment. "I *will* enjoy my life!" he kept repeating, as he obstinately wrestled with this enormous swaying and heaving mass of mingled impressions. "I *will* enjoy my life!"

What he felt at that moment was that it was really possible for him to force himself to enjoy this battle with life even if he couldn't enjoy the particular experiences with which life was challenging him at the moment.

Although he actually continued in that bent position, clasping sometimes his ankle, what he felt in his imagination was that he was moving about quite freely over the surface of the earth. "I've got to hold my soul in readiness," he thought, "for struggle after struggle. But no struggle, however intense, need prevent my enjoying it, and if I enjoy life—I mean enjoy the *struggle* to enjoy life—nothing else need come into it. That's the whole thing: to reduce the battle to its simplest elements. But how *can* it be thus reduced?"

And John answered his own question as his lean fingers tightened his grip upon his lean thigh. "It can only be thus reduced by concentrating my mind on my mind's own power of enjoyment as if this power were a magnetic stream of invisible energy drawn from unfathomable reservoirs in myself and turned upon outward things like a moving searchlight, a searchlight that is transforming by its magical force"—and certainly no buried skeleton and no unborn embryo could have worn a look of more self-satisfied relief than John's face assumed when to himself he used the word "transforming"—"of painful as well as of pleasant things; and forcing them all, pell-mell and *en masse*, into the enjoyment circle!"

Having thought of the word "transforming", John suddenly, and without knowing it, came near the ocean-brink of sleep, and his thoughts reverted to Tenna.

THE INMATES

"I've got her," he thought, "and that's the great thing. If I decide to enjoy my life under any condition, under that condition I can *make* myself enjoy it! It's all in my power. But what *wasn't* in my power, what was a matter of fate or of providence or pure chance, was my meeting Tenna at all! . . .

> 'Childe Rowland to the dark tower came
> His word was still Fie, foh and fum,
> I smell the blood of a British man.'"

5

THE NEXT DAY

JOHN HUSH slept until three minutes after four on the morning of the twenty-sixth. Then he awoke with a groan and a gasping cry; but, for all his struggles to recall what had troubled him, he was unable to remember.

"I believe I've had a nightmare!" he told himself, as he lay staring into the darkness with his fingers trembling and his forehead sweating, while his whole soul jerked itself back in spasms of relief to a shaken but normal consciousness. "It's some weakness in my heart, of course," he thought, and he repeated several times over: "But the heart's nothing; the heart's nothing." And while he repeated these reassuring words he did his best not to think of a monstrous, heavily moving luggage-train that had got mixed up in some way with an appalling mass of darkness pressing in upon him from every side. "I mustn't think of it," he told himself. "I mustn't think of it."

And although this "mustn't think" was quite as definitely concerned with the intolerable weight of darkness around him as was his "nothing" with the pounding of his heart over the luggage-train, it was attended by much more serious apprehensions. And this was proved by the fact that each time he told himself he "mustn't think" of the darkness, his

THE NEXT DAY

whole power of mind hovered on the edge of a panic-stricken sensation that made him draw back in terror from the black darkness round him and mentally try to push it away with both his hands.

An old, old trouble with him it was, this spasm of night-terror. It had to do with an imaginary difficulty in breathing; difficulty that sometimes took possession of him with such horrible tenacity that, although the whole thing was entirely mental, he would feel on the point of rushing wildly out of the house, while he shouted with a terrifying cry: "Air! Air! Air! Air!"

On this occasion—though it did not seem to increase his nervous tension—he was thoroughly conscious that it was impossible for him to rush out of *this* house or even to break his neck by throwing himself out of a window. But he had recourse to an old device of his, that had often proved successful, as indeed it did now. He set himself *to breathe consciously*. He did this by drawing his breath through his mouth and disregarding his nostrils completely. He became, indeed, an animal that possessed no other aperture for imbibing air except a mouth; and by the trick of making each particular motion of inhaling and exhaling a separate undertaking, and of carrying through this undertaking in triumphant defiance of the darkness, he reached a condition wherein by continuing his monotone of vocal dichotomy, "in-out, out-in, out-in, in-out", obstinately repeated, he began to feel that his own secret, private, unique consciousness was a match and more than a match for this ink-black cuttlefish of not-being, this huge epitome of ultimate negation, this mother of nothingness, this absolute of nonentity, this unspeakable hole in the bosom of Abraham, this grandfather of chaos, this paradigm of the final abyss that had taken into its fearful head to swallow him up!

"The great thing," he thought, "is to have faith in your own power. If you have faith that you can get on happily without God, you *can* get on happily without God! If you have faith that by some trick or other, or just by waiting till

THE INMATES

your chance comes, you can marry your love, or kill your enemy, or live till you've outlived your friends, you can do all those things. faith is everything! It's infinitely more precious than hope or love!"

All theology, like other exquisite things, is allied to madness; and had the soul of Tenna Sheer been watching over her new friend's pillow, under the compulsion of driving away devils, she might have witnessed, for at night in Glint Hall there were strange symposia of telepathic dreaming, a curious dialogue between the spirit of Father Toby and the spirit of Father Wun, in the course of which the schismatic priest, defending himself against the orthodox priest, protested that had this aggressive mystery of Faith really possessed a magic denied both to hope and love, the only way of making certain of this superiority would simply be to wait till the horror of darkness were actually at our throat and then boldly and desperately try out this power in the soul to hypnotise the soul; and see what happened!

But even if in this conjectured vigil of Miss Sheer it happened that the magic of faith did work the miracle and thus prove itself more god-like than hope or love, there would remain much more for it to do. The actual nature of the faith-power thus exerted would have to be experienced—and this also would be, if not an act of, certainly a labour of faith —so fully, that there would inevitably come to pass an intensification of the link between the consciousness enjoying the struggle and the struggle enjoyed.

But whether if was the mental concentration implied in forcing himself to be conscious of each breath he drew, or whether it was his faith in the hypnotic power of his own soul over his body, John Hush did fall asleep and managed to remain asleep till he was roused by a violent beating of a gong in the passage outside his door. The state of his mind when he awoke astonished him. Instead of any feeling of horror at being where he was, he was instantaneously aware of a childish thrill of simple interest and excitement. He felt as he might have done when instead of being twenty-two he was

THE NEXT DAY

eight, and instead of hiding *Leaves of Grass* in his collar-drawer he hid his catapult.

He awoke, indeed, with a vague sensation of extraordinary happiness. He felt as he had once felt at the seaside when his childhood's nurse, with whom even after he had gone to school he still spent his holidays, had let him make friends with a little girl who was a relative of hers, on a well-known beach in East Anglia. That particular fortnight on the east coast had indeed been the period of the most perfect happiness he had known in his whole life. It had even surpassed those thrills when he first snipped off those entrancing curls with his scissors.

Nor did the whole morning of that twenty-sixth of March, long though it was, play him any trick or grow sandy or gravelly under him, as he trod his appointed round and did everything he was directed to do in the stables, in the cow-sheds, in the woodsheds, and in that big cobblestone yard.

At breakfast only about half the men and only about a third of the women were present in the dining-room at the official hour, and Tenna was not among them. So it was with a lively excitement at one o'clock, though he was both hungry and tired, that he stared at a segment of her oval little face at dinner while he talked with more sympathy than he had dared to hope he could muster up to poor little corpse-haunted, badly dis-infected Mr. Lordy.

He learnt from this latter that Father Allen Wun, the Catholic priest, had had an unexpected invitation to lunch at the American-owned mansion that afternoon and might pos-sibly drop in for a cup of tea at Glint Hall with his handful of believers in the older faith.

"If the Father does do this," Mr. Lordy explained, "I'll get him to sit here with us and we can hear all the news about that house. They say some very grand people from London are stopping there this week. Anyway, it'll be great to hear what the place is like."

"It will indeed," Hush heartily concurred. And he won-dered whether his guardian and the lady had decided to spend

THE INMATES

a couple of nights there before returning to London. Mr. Lordy was authentically sympathetic.

"What kind of night did you have, Mr. Hush? To some people their first night here is the worst they go through, and I only pray that wasn't your experience."

John hesitated for a second; and then he thought: "But, after all, what's the point of being reserved and superior with a decent chap like this?"

But Mr. Lordy had gone on quickly; and it was obvious that the little man felt happier than yesterday. The truth was, John told himself, that everybody was so hungry, and the Irish stew was so good, and even the vegetables on the side, such as mashed potatoes and cabbage, not to mention turnip, were so well cooked that there was little fear, if they spoke low, of attracting the attention either of their fellow-inmates or of the attendants.

"If I can persuade the Father," Mr. Lordy went on, "to have tea with us here, there'd only be a few other gentlemen—and I'm sure you wouldn't mind crowding up a little so as to fit them in—and it would be such a perfect chance for our telling him something of what really goes on behind the humbug these people talk.

"The Catholic Church *has* its faults, Mr. Hush. Please don't think I'm bigoted; but with *it*—I mean with *us*—religion does really come first. And it is genuine religion. In fact it's *so* genuine that those who hate religion call it superstition. But superstition or not, Mr. Hush, with us it comes first; and isn't that what all the great world leaders are always telling us to do—in the papers I mean—put first things first?"

John fixed the little man with all the power he could throw into his look and "words."I'll be eternally grateful to you, Mr. Lordy, if you do get the Father to have tea with us tonight. I heard of 'Halfway House' before I ever knew there was such a place as Glint Hall; and I long to hear about it from someone who's been inside. It's one of the great historic houses of these islands. They taught me all that's true about

THE NEXT DAY

it at school; and they taught me all that isn't true about it at college. And now from Father Wun Allen——"

"Father Allen Wun, if you don't mind," corrected his neighbour, "for it's the Father himself who makes jokes about his name, for he's full of fun, the Father is, and All-in-One, if you catch his meaning, in a manner of speaking is what he means——"

John nodded more energetically than irritably; for he was as desperately grateful to this murderer of a life-loving step-Either as he was disturbed by the disinfectant that drove off that old gentleman's ghost.

"And from Father All-in-One," he thought, "I'll *really* get what this Anglican chaplain, Tickle, who showed me round last night, called 'the hang of the place'—but shall I?"

They finished their Irish stew, in spite of Mr. Lordy's having a second helping, in silence after this; but as soon as the pudding appeared, which consisted of hot apple-dumplings, to which could be added all the creamy milk and brown sugar anyone could possibly want, Mr. Lordy, who had clearly, from the frown on his expressive face, been thinking things out, began again with intense seriousness.

Fortunately for John's reputation for courtesy, Tenna Sheer, out of some obscure feminine impulse, or even, perhaps, intention, had been trying for the whole length of that hungry meal to avoid meeting John's eyes, and even to avoid if possible— at least so it seemed to him—his catching sight of her at all. Thus as he tipped up his plate with his left hand—a childish trick of which his nurse could never cure him, and in which his guardian from one Balkan capital to another had shamelessly encouraged him—and scooped up with his spoon—his guardian was only waiting, he once told him, to see him lift the plate itself to his mouth—the last drop of milky juice and melted sugar, destiny—for this really was *not* chance—enabled him to give his full attention to his excited neighbour.

"There's something I'd like to ask you, mister," began Mr. Lordy gravely, "on this twenty-sixth day of March, now that the Announcement of the Immaculate Miracle is already a day old; and you not being a Catholic, but being what you might

THE INMATES

call an outsider, makes it easy to ask you, whereas in a matter like this, a heaven-and-hell matter if you follow my meaning, another Catholic might misunderstand what was up, and seek to acquire merit with the blessed saints by blabbing to the nearest Father or even to the Lord Bishop, if the Father was scared of going outside his orders and borders in such high matters.

"Well, it's concerning what I heard Doctor Echetus say to that sly devil Cuddle when they were talking in the fir-plantation, and me all the time aloft in one of the tallest firs like the little short man in the Holy Gospel. Cuddle was asking whether he knew the kind of devil that fellow Gewlie actually was, and the Doctor was saying what did he think he was if he didn't know Gewlie to be the worse case of a sod—only he called it 'sard' but it rhymed with 'lard'—he'd ever handled; and Cuddle was going on about the games Gewlie were up to all the time, when Doctor asked him straight out, flipperty-flap, straight from the tap, didn't he know that these sorts of crack-ups were always hiring themselves out to places like this?

"And so what I'm asking you, mister, you being a free-thinking man and one who don't believe in Church or Judgment, is just simply this: whether I ought in fairness to our fellow-inmates to give the Father a straight tip about friend Gewlie, who, to tell you the honest truth, is a practising Catholic and will be sure to be round here at tea-time, sucking up to the Father and putting the idea into his head that any stories he may hear about him are ridiculous nonsense."

"You mean . . ." began John hesitatingly. He was anxiously waiting the faintest move Miss Sheer might make to leave the hall. He felt as if he had already exhausted all the springs of unselfishness in his soul by just listening sympathetically to Mr. Lordy and treating him with the attention of a fellow conspirator. To be responsible for the man's actions or to give him advice as to this stand of his between the appalling Gewlie and the formidable All-in-One were imperatives of social behaviour that just then seemed to be retreating to outside the circumference of his conscience. "You mean," he repeated,

THE NEXT DAY

"that we might decoy the great Catholic Church herself, in the person of this good Father, into exposing Doctor Echetus's tolerance of an active sadist among us when his English chaplain, Father Tickle, either doesn't realise what's going on or is powerless to do anything to stop it? But has there ever been" —he interrupted himself to make a movement of rising, but sat down again, for his training as half-valet and half-secretary to a diplomat in the Balkans had taught him that to leave any building with a girl and to descend any staircase with the same girl and then to drift casually into any garden together would be less noticeable than to hurry from a hall alone, and to await the girl under a tulip-tree—"has there ever been a case, Mr. Lordy, when the word of an inmate of an asylum, or the words of a lot of inmates of an asylum, were accepted as evidence against a warder, still more of a warder supported by a doctor? Has there ever been such a case, my friend, and can we imagine—— But forgive me—I have an appointment—we'll meet at tea— and I'll be interested"—he was on one foot now with the other suspended above their bench—"to see the Father—and friend Gewlie, too, if he comes. So long, Mr. Lordy!"

Not a word of greeting did the lovers exchange, in fact not a word of any kind, till they had rounded the laurel hedge at the first curve of the nearest gravel path. Then Antenna said, speaking rapidly and low, and gazing gravely into his face as she swung her big-brimmed brown hat by a string of loose elastic inside it, "I stayed awake a long time wondering whether you'd be able to sleep. I slept *my* first night like a dead rabbit hunted to death, for *he* had come here with me; but my second night they had to give me a drug, I screamed such curses at him. But after that, when I knew he was back at home and was all those hours away and there was no chance of his coming back—for he never leaves his business unless he's forced to—I settled down quite happily. In fact, except for certain times when I hated him so much that just for him to be alive spoilt everything, I was happier than I'd ever been since she killed herself to escape him and left me alone with him. Think of her doing that—leaving the child she'd brought into the world

THE INMATES

alone with him! Oh, this place has been a heaven to me just simply because I've escaped from him! Before yesterday I had only one happiness—to be where he wasn't! And only one misery—that Midsummer Day would *have* to come, when he'd be here again—only for an hour or so—for he'll hardly sit down he'll be so keen to get back to his houses—but just to *see* him—but I mustn't think about it! You're here now; and everything's different. But *did* yon sleep all right? I don't seem able to stop talking when I'm with you! But *did* you?"

John Hush nodded. "I certainly did," he said, "but I confess I had a nightmare later on. I don't know how much later on, for I went to sleep again. But you know how it is when you wake up with a nightmare and it's still pitch-dark. But I went to sleep again and stayed asleep till the morning."

"I won't ask you what the nightmare was," said Antenna.

He stood still, and she stood still by his side. He looked at her closely.

"Better not, perhaps," he said. "Though I *could* try to tell you. I *could* try to tell you anything, Tenna."

She looked away from him; but standing as they were, she couldn't altogether hide her face from him, and he was shocked by the nerve-strain that was upon it, that was in fact drawn tight and quivering over it, like a new skin over a palpitating sore. "I don't believe," he burst out, "it *is* fair for me to go on telling you things when you don't tell me anything of the same sort!"

He saw her bite her under-lip. He saw her lower her head and stare at the ground. He saw the sun throw the shadow of her skirt and the shadow of his trousers upon the well-weeded gravel path and the shadow of their heads upon the smoothly clipped laurel hedge. Then he saw her lift up her head and fix her resolute eyes full upon him.

"What you and I, my friend, had better do," she told him in a calm low voice, "is to get to know each other as quickly as we can! But, on the other hand, if we tell each other too agitating things at the start—it's a queer thing, my dear, but then we *are* a queer pair—I have an odd sort of feeling that it'll get in the way of our knowing each other, rather than help us.

THE NEXT DAY

I'm bad at expressing myself. I'm not clever like you, John, and I'm not educated like you.

"But I can *feel* things like this; and you being what you are to me, I know I've got plenty of time. And, after all, John, there's a lot in us both—more than a lot—that all the agitations in the world can't change or turn into anything but what's—

well, I needn't go on, need I, for you know all this?—what's important to you and me is just our own ordinary selves, not all these terrible things we've been through!"

She had got as far as the sentence, "what's more important to you and me" before she realised that he had ceased to listen; the sudden manner in which this revelation arrested her increased the shock of it. But the relief that went through her like wine through a sieve when she realised the extremely practical, masculine, and even military reason why his mind had wandered from her words, was so great that she seized his sleeve between her finger and thumb and pinched it violently.

"Stay just as you are," he whispered stiffly, "and don't look as if I were telling you anything that I *oughtn't* to be telling you! As a matter of fact, I've come to the conclusion that, if we ever decide to escape from here, this is the place where we could do it. Only, we'd have to go slowly and get ready slowly! Take a good look at it, my dear." He lowered his voice. "But we mustn't be caught standing here and staring like a couple of frogs at a water-snake! I'll explain later; but if we went in with that water and came out with that water we couldn't be more than a couple of minutes at the whole job. But we'll have to get those real spikes out and we'll have to slip some artificial ones in, and we'll have to deepen the bed of the stream a bit to make sure there'll be room for us to get through that great hole and come out on the other side. But come along now, for Christ's sake!

"Yes, I know that's the south lodge over there where that fellow lives who was watching me in the reading-room yesterday when I first saw you. But come along! Don't look at it! And don't say anything aloud here about the water, or the spikes, or the hole under the wall."

THE INMATES

Antenna hurriedly quickened her steps, and as she passed the south lodge she swept its windows with her eyes; and there, sure enough, just within the porch, serenely mending her husband's woollen drawers, but keeping her eyes fixed in a patient dreamy reverie upon the gravel path, sat Betsy.

"'Ow are you to-day, Mr. 'Arsh?" she cried at once, in her clear ringing voice.

To John's nervous companion this voice became at once a living creature, a creature something between a flying-fish and a water-rat; and since Tenna's eyes were reluctant to glance at those spikes in the stream, it was precisely there that she now was conscious of the oily and polished spine of that embodied voice that was now being scraped by those same spikes as it followed the stream beneath the wall.

But then, in a still louder tone, Betsy went on: "We must all join together, mustn't we, Miss Sheer, in making a nice young gentleman like Mr. 'Arsh feel a 'ome-from-'ome feeling amongst us 'ere!"

"He's going to show me the cattle in the field that he was looking after this morning. He's made friends with your husband already."

These words were uttered by Miss Sheer in the voice that all the Glint attendants had come to know well, and Betsy cursed her savagely in her heart.

It was not concealed from John that there was danger in the air, and he raised his voice accordingly. "I tell her," he cried, "that it's going to be 'round and round the mulberry bush', the sort of walk I'm going to take her!"

With this he drew Tenna away, giving Betsy no chance to utter another word; but when they were beyond her voice and yet were still well under her eye, he allowed a discreet space to appear between himself and Tenna, a space almost as wide as a whole yard, and as if well satisfied with this outward and visible sign of propriety, they quickened their mutual pace, he swinging a last-season's dead artichoke stalk, of which he had possessed himself, he couldn't have told how, as they approached the south lodge, and she "arranging", by plucking

THE NEXT DAY

at them with the fingers of her right hand, five or six short-stemmed clover blooms and a couple of wisps of ground-ivy that she had snatched up as they walked and now held captive in her left hand. Thus following the gravel path that ran along the edge of the meadow, they vanished from the resentful eyes of Betsy.

"Snobbish little bitch!" thought that lady ferociously. "I'd give her the gallows with a look of my eye, I would! Try and kill the poor old dad what begat her, would she, the proud little hat-pin? If I were Master Doctor I'd soon uncertify *you*, you little toss-head, and give your case a good re-trial, too, and when the judge was talking about attempted murder and telling you you was in luck not to be hanging by the neck till you was dead, do you think I'd have looked away and been sorry for you?

"Not on your life, Missy Too Proud-to-speak! Not on your little life! I'd be glad you'd got what you ought to have, getting let off like you've been, and being cooked for and waited on like you are, by them that's known how to restrain theyselves!"

But another thought followed hard on this one. "Yes, restrain theyselves, I tell you, when they might right and proper have killed their old men over and over, so aggravacious are all men and so much have us poor women got to suffer from them!"

As soon as they were out of sight of Betsy the new inmate drew close to Tenna Sheer. "I don't think that good lady is very partial to us!" he remarked.

But the girl didn't reply. Nor did she lift up her head or look at him till they'd come to the end of the railings separating them from the grazing cattle.

"What's the matter, Antenna?" John asked her, standing still and trying to look into her face.

"Oh, nothing particular!" she murmured, fidgeting with the flowers in her hand and still avoiding his eyes.

"There *is* something," he went on, "I feel certain there is. Please, please, Antenna, tell me what it is?"

THE INMATES

But how could she tell him that the light, frivolous, indifferent tone with which he had referred to Betsy as "that good lady" had been a curious shock to her. She knew from what he had already revealed of his past that this upper-class tone wasn't, so to say, native to him—wasn't, that is, the tone he had heard in childhood. It was an acquired tone, imbibed like a special atmosphere, through his senses, though not through the pores of his skin, while with his guardian in those Balkan embassies.

As a matter of fact, Antenna's mother had belonged to identically the same class as John's own relatives in the crowded body of our wave-tossed social ship; while in spite of his financial success and his knighthood, Antenna's father belonged to the same class as Betsy herself, whose parents had for years peddled geraniums in south London.

If John hadn't lived on such intimate terms with his guardian he would have been more careful about his tone on an occasion like this. For he would have been more class-conscious. He would, in fact, have resembled his own parents and Antenna's mother; all of whom had been what used to be called decayed gentlefolk. The atmosphere of these embassies, on the contrary, was anything but old-fashioned; and if it was decayed it was teeming with parasite life. It was on the crest of time. It positively tripped and tumbled into the future. Thus it was with an air artificially acquired from a closeted clique of devil-may-care cadets of historic houses who were more at home with ex-royalties and ex-conspirators than with retired florists, that John had cleared his mind of Betsy.

"Well! I won't tease you, child, if you don't want to tell me!" he announced gravely. "But come on! I want to follow this damned wall all the way round to the other lodge, so that we'll know exactly where our cage ends!"

He gave a gentle tug at the sleeve of her grey jacket, while with his left foot he kicked out of her way a dead branch that had a thick knob at the end of it.

"Don't do that!" she cried in a voice that he hadn't heard from her before.

THE NEXT DAY

He swung round at once. "Sorry, Tenna!" he muttered. Then, after gazing at her bent head with a puzzled frown as she raised the branch to examine it: "Is it something you've seen before?" he asked. "Does it remind you of anything?"

She made no answer. All she did was to drag the thing off the grass and thrust it with deliberate care under a new-leafed elder-bush.

"That wasn't where it belonged!" he grumbled. "What's the idea?"

Again she made no answer. And this time he grew troubled. Was she really vexed with him for something? What the devil *was* there about that piece of dead wood with tiny little fungi on its underside?

"Please, my dear!" he pleaded. This was the first time since her mother's death that anyone had called her "my dear". That Welsh girl in the laundry had called her "ducky", but that was different; and here, at Glint, Ursie Mum's endearments by one of those cruel laws of nature that tend to flatten out familiar things, seemed hardly to count at all.

But hearing this man of hers, who was now her wooden doll for all eternity, utter these two syllables, an almost intolerable happiness seized her. The spasm of rapture that shook her was like a Maenadic cry, and for a moment her two arms shot up into the air as if they had become bird's wings and were going to fly off by their own volition, leaving her human body staring after them.

Her head was thrown back; the expression on her face could only be called a contortion of ecstasy, but as soon as her arms sank down and she had clasped her hands behind her head, there rose from her lips a sign of such supreme contentment that it seemed to expand into a vast vaporous cup, capable of containing the whole dim, windless, warmly-chilly, misty green atmosphere round them, lifting up the sap of a million stalks and a million grasses and a million buds towards a sky that was so old and sad and weak that it looked as if it might melt into grey, tasteless, colourless water and drip and drop and drain away over all the horizons of the world from pure weariness of

THE INMATES

having seen so much beneath it and so having to see so much more beneath it before the end.

And John Hush thought: "She's not human! God knows what she is, or what she's got in her mind! What was she up to, pushing that dead thing under that elder-bush? Can young elder-bushes put new life into old rotten black stumps? Or did she *see a face* in that knob? Did she think it was doing something to that elder-bush? Or was the elder-bush jeering at it with its new leaves?"

But he felt, as he stood there before that thrown-back head, as if Nature were offering him, for once and for once only, a glimpse into one of her strangest, most terrifying, and yet most healing secrets, but a glimpse which, by some weird necessity of life's peculiar ways, when once it has been offered, when once it has been received, irrespective of whether it has been understood or not, can never return again.

Antenna's eyes had been wide open as she stood like that, and they had been facing him; but it struck him as though she were neither seeing him nor thinking of him. She seemed in fact to be seeing and feeling something that baffled her own mind and yet at the same time completely absorbed it. Was she feeling happy or unhappy as she stood like that staring out of this world into something else? It was impossible to tell.

Hush watched her as an astronomer might watch a star, a hunter might watch a deer, a fisherman might watch a trout, a prophet might watch a bird of unknown augury, a monk the parted lips of a miraculous virgin, and a laborious creative god the frantic antics of irresponsible and chaotic chance.

Suddenly her arms sank down, her head hung, and feebly, weakly, and absent-mindedly she pushed the stalks of the flowers she'd been carrying into her belt.

"Well," she sighed, as if waking up in a hospital bed on the sudden apparition of a privileged relative, "I feel as if I'd just come back from sailing round the world! Do you ever feel like that, John—falling asleep while you're on your feet? But, come on, my friend, I do want to go the whole circle together on our first day in this place."

6

MR. FROGCASTLE

It almost seems as if certain particular human thoughts associated with certain special human feelings often remain hovering in the air, or slowly dissolving into the air, above certain particular tracts of ground. This does not imply that everybody who passes or crosses such a spot is affected by these bodiless "revenants" or invisible creations of intense feelings that have come and gone; but when destiny brings people to these places who are dedicated by their special sensibilities to respond to these derelict emanations curious and startling results can come of such encounters.

The place which John and Tenna were now on the point of leaving could hardly be said to possess any very remarkable characteristics. It was a chance-given spot on the fringe of a crowded and flourishing plantation of young spruce-firs with a sprinkling of other trees.

With their backs to this spot, what they faced was the gravel path by which they had come and the green meadow, with a few healthy-looking cattle grazing in it, which was terminated by their impregnable prison-wall.

What exactly it had been that caused the unloved, and many would add the unlovable, Miss Sheer to be seized with such an ecstasy because a neurotic young man answering to the name of John, with the look of an old-fashioned Shakespearean actor, had called her "my dear", must, of course, remain conjectural, but an element of not altogether negligible value in interpreting it might be found in the fact that the head-gardener of Glint, who lived outside the walls and whose name was Frogcastle, had paused this very morning, as he passed this spot after listening to a quarrel between Betsy and Bill, to thank the gods that he had remained a widower.

As the two now moved away, with the gardener's unuttered cry of gratitude to fate clapping its wings like a bird caught in

THE INMATES

the girl's hair, it was she this time who put her hand on his arm; but he noticed that before they went on she gave a nervous glance at the end of the dead branch which could be clearly seen protruding from beneath the fresh leaves of the elder-bush that grew so low that they touched the grass.

She walked fast after that; and he noticed that she was absorbed in some difficult train of thought, for she kept silent, and the lines in her forehead kept deepening and twitching.

"Do you mind if I ask you something, Tenna?"

"Of course not! What do you take me for, John Hush?"

She turned to him without slackening her speed, and he was struck by the grave intensity of her look. "She believes I'm going to reveal to her some extraordinary secret of superhuman endurance," he told himself, "whereas what I really must get from her is a practical idea of the points of the compass in this infernal hole!"

"Do you know if that south gate we've just passed—that gate between the stream where we looked at those spikes and the lodge where we saw that chattering female—is really south? What I mean is this. Suppose *there weren't any wall at all*, should we now be able to see Halfway House where I fancy my guardian intended to stay the night?"

"Halfway House?" she repeated vaguely. "Oh, I suppose so. Yes, of course! At least I think so. They've often shown it to me—I know that—from the window of the linen-room on the top floor. I suppose the west's over there!" And she made a careless gesture with her free hand—the hand that wasn't clutching his coat-sleeve with all its five fingers—a gesture that swept the horizon from south-west to north-west.

John made two resolutions: firstly to avoid rather than cultivate the habit of referring to his guardian; secondly to make careful and exact investigations of his own, quite independently of Tenna, as to these ticklish compass-points in regard to Glint Hall and its surroundings.

"Yes," he replied, in answer to that extremely comprehensive wave of the thin arm in the grey jacket, "yes, that must be just about where it is."

MR. FROGCASTLE

"Is that the creature you were going to show me?" enquired the girl, pointing to a large deep-uddered grey cow standing by itself under the shadow of the enclosing wall and beneath a couple of small silver poplars.

"No," he replied, "I don't think so. No, I'm sure it isn't! The one I took a fancy to was grey—certainly it was very grey—purely grey, not light grey, nor dark grey, but just grey. There! There are some more of them near that haystack. Perhaps the one I wanted to show you is with that lot. It had longer horns than the one over there—yes, much longer horns! And I think it was greyer, too, than the one over there—yes, longer horns, and greyer still—you've never seen a cow so grey!"

Hush was silent; and, as far as Antenna could tell, his mind was completely absorbed in estimating the comparative greyness of Glint Hall's grey cows.

Her own mind was following very curious patterns of thought, patterns whose effect upon her companion, had he been able to apprehend them, would have startled her as much as *her* thoughts would have startled him.

"Longer horns," the girl was thinking, "and greyer cows!" And instead of the actual cattle before her she saw in her mind wide-stretching meadows extending under a sky even more mistily sun-pearled and even more vaporous with golden interstices than the one now above them; and, feeding in these meadows, beyond all the rivers she knew, beyond the reedy water-courses and the deep weirs, beyond the salt tide that carried down her mother's canoe, she saw grey cows that moved among the tall shadows of leafless poplars and white horns that kept piercing yet whiter mists!

But as she walked on by his side and he kept rejecting one particular grey cow and then returning to it, and kept rejecting one pair of white horns and then returning to them, his curious absorption in this unimportant game began to get on her nerves. Why must he be like this? Why couldn't her newly-discovered lover, who had so much about him that was like a helpless, puzzled, bewildered inanimate, walk about these

THE INMATES

gardens without comparing white horns with white horns and without worrying and fussing whether he was showing her the precise creature whose shed he'd cleaned that morning.

So intensely irritated with the absurd fuss he was making about his precious cows did she become at last that she flung one thought at least against such a jagged block of blue-black ice in the sluice of her consciousness that it broke into sharp-edged bits of ice. And then as she clung to the railings, while he hesitated and stared across the grass, she felt as if her mind were being pricked by the horns of cows wherever it turned; not only so, but her imagination began playing tricks with this tedious talk until it made him say the most silly, crazy, and grotesque things.

And at last her mind actually began twisting his words and mixing up his words and using his words as leaping-off places for sheer madcap fantasies. For John, by reason of having all that morning looked forward so much to telling her about these cows and to showing her their peculiarities, was agreeably lingering over the lengthy business of resolving into proper order their various shades of greyness and their various lengths of horns without, as happens so often when men talk to women, noting her reaction to his words.

Tenna's imagination, indeed, began playing with these ubiquitous horns till they seemed to tear themselves and their owners' heads and rush about in an independent pack. They seemed to be joined by the horns of the moon, by the horns of the deer in Windsor Park, by the horns of every tricorn and unicorn in the forest in Broceliande.

And then she suddenly wanted to stop them in their mad rush. For she saw where they were heading, these horns without a head! They were heading for the brick-yards, gravel-pits, saw-mills, and cement-works, of the Firm of Sheer and Shot, house-builders and estate-agents.

But when the actual horns he was pointing out to her began leaving their owner's heads she felt compelled to turn her own head away from him lest he should see she wasn't *properly* listening. She felt as if her mind were doing something that was

MR. FROGCASTLE

wicked and wrong; so before she had the power to stop herself she began crying out: "I see the one you mean clearly! I see her! I see her! I see her! I see her! And oh, how grey she is!" But she dared not look him in the face as she uttered these false and treacherous cries; for though in her mind the rush of horns had been swallowed up in Sir Warden's brickyard, there was left behind one old grey cow, like a creature of painted wood, and this old cow was sitting up on its hind legs in the manner of a performing dog, while the grave John, himself looking like a wooden figure from an old-fashioned Noah's ark, was milking her into a child's seaside bucket! And all this while the real John Hush was saying to himself: "She's here! She's here! She's here! And I'm telling her just what I swore I would tell her! Yes, she's the one I can tell all my thoughts to, and everything I do! Nobody else in the world would care to hear what I've been doing in the north yard all those long hours!"

And then he spoke aloud, swinging round happily towards her and away from the cows.

"Come on!" he cried, pulling her forward by the sleeve of her coat. "And what about it being your turn to show *me* something!"

"Sure! I'll show you something!" she murmured cheerfully; and indeed it was really such a relief to her to wipe those comic Noah's ark creatures off the slate of her mind that she could actually smile at him as they moved forward.

"Oh, there's Mr. Frogcastle," she whispered presently. "I'm so glad. I'd like you to meet him. He's not an inmate. He comes from the village. He's an expert gardener. And do you know, John"—Hush noticed she spoke with more eagerness and animation than she had shown all this afternoon—"he's been the one and only person since you and I met yesterday who's taken the faintest interest in me, or gone out of his way to discover anything about me, all these two years!"

Hush followed her with willing alacrity, and they advanced quickly along the gravel path under their prison wall. He

THE INMATES

didn't feel in the least jealous of the man they were approaching. He felt nothing but pure unmixed gratitude; and he contemplated Mr. Frogcastle with alert equanimity and friendly interest.

The gardening expert was halfway up a short ladder fastening little bits of soft woollen cloth round thin sprays of old indented peach-branches and tender young nectarine-twigs; but as soon as he heard them approaching he began hurriedly to descend. They met at the foot of his ladder and the girl introduced the two men.

Seldom had John Hush seen a person more entirely satisfying to his taste in human beings; and if the other wasn't equally reassured, he answered John's greeting with a friendly handshake. Mr. Frogcastle wore a flimsy, very new cloth cap at the back of his skull. The whole of his head was covered by a thick crop of close-cut grizzled hair that so much resembled a wild beast's skin that John's first thought as he surveyed him was that the neat cap was his natural skin and the rough hair some savage creature's fur. Frogcastle had hollow, rather pallid cheeks, a wide friendly mouth, an extremely low broad forehead, and very pale greenish-grey eyes.

These eyes supplied the whole clue to the gardener's character. They were so wide apart that they appeared to focus in a completely different way from ordinary human eyes. Instead of concentrating upon any particular point in what they surveyed, they seemed to take in the whole length, breadth, height and depth of the object. The object wasn't isolated from its surroundings but absorbed and included in all its peculiar relations to its position in the world, so that a considerable segment of the object's environment, together with a fair stretch of the causes and antecedents that had made the object what it was, were embraced in one glance by the unnaturally wide scope of Daniel Frogcastle's vision.

If this had the effect of diminishing the intensity of the gardener's gaze, it also had the effect of giving it a weight, a balance, a dispassionate consideration that seemed to challenge the cosmos to catch such a gaze off-guard. It was largely for

MR. FROGCASTLE

this very reason that Miss Sheer felt so comfortable and relaxed when she talked with Danny Frog. She felt as if he treated her like a shrub rather than a girl.

In fact she forgot she *was* a girl when she talked to him. She felt that, while she couldn't bear either Father Toby or Father Allen to come near her, still less Doctor Echetus, she wouldn't have minded having her hair cut by Mr. Frogcastle.

"I've just had a scene with that fellow Gewlie, Miss," said the gardener presently, after answering some questions that John put to him about wall-fruit, "You remember telling me about his meddling with Mr. Tackle and Miss Tutty and frightening them by following them about and saying things to them? Well, what do you think? I caught him at it yesterday; and when he grew insulting and even accused me of being jealous over poor Miss Tutty, do you know what happened, miss? Something very rare with me!"

Tenna glanced quickly at John, and then she burst out with a little laugh. "You didn't *hit* him?"

"That's exactly what I did! I knocked him down!"

It was John who intervened at this point. "But I've got to meet this awful chap at tea today! I'm glad you've dealt with him already, Mr. Frogcastle, or I might be forgetting I'm an inmate and not a visitor! It's through my good neighbour in the dining-room, Mr. Lordy, that I got the invitation. He's a Catholic, and so apparently is this awful Gewlie. Well, I'll be well primed with the facts; and if I don't give this same reverend Father a few hints about his dear son, my name's not John Hush."

"Will *you* be at this tea-party, miss?" enquired the gardener; and it struck John that he spoke rather anxiously, but it was hard to tell, since the wide gaze of his eyes was such that it turned a person's attention away from any expression there might be upon his face to follow the faintest hint of his meaning from his voice, which always tended to resemble the voice of an oracle speaking out of the air.

"Well," the girl murmured with the fleetingest shadow of a smile, "I'll be in the same room, anyway. And you may

THE INMATES

depend on it, Mr. Frogcastle, I'll take in all I can of what's going on."

There was something in the wide stare of the gardener's eyes when she had said this that created a curious silence round all three of them. This silence continued even after Danny-Frog had bidden them goodbye and had reascended his ladder. It even accompanied them till they were well out of the far-flung shadow of that high southern wall.

"Can we get back without passing that tiresome woman again?" enquired John Hush.

Antenna hesitated. "Of course," she said to herself, "there *is* that twisting path I found last year through this damned wood, but it led ——" And Antenna shivered at the memory of what she had found. "No, John," she said, "not to-day. Another day—perhaps—but not on our first day. But old Betsy will have gone in by this time. She'll be in her kitchen. I know she will! And, anyway, we'll walk quickly past the lodge. She'll not bother us, John. I swear to you she won't."

"But we'll get back too soon if we walk so fast," he protested.

"Well"—and she looked at the wood on their right and the meadow-railings on their left—"we might——"

But their discussion was interrupted by a party of their fellow-inmates—about half a dozen of them—who came laughing and shouting and giggling past them, slapping and pummelling one another. Some of this noisy band shouted at them; others laughed at them; others waved to them with genial friendliness. There were a few of them, however, who actually hunched their bodies into knots and tightened their garments round them as if in desperate fear of contagion.

When they had gone and the pair had turned to each other with the same unspoken wonder as to what Mr. Frogcastle would do when these people reached him, whether, for instance, he would remain on his ladder with his back to them or swing round to greet them, they became aware that two more Glint Hall inmates were advancing towards them, evidently as unwilling as they were themselves to get entangled in any group.

MR. FROGCASTLE

But unlike themselves this pair was not walking side by side, for the rear one was clearly pursuing the foremost one, who was striding forward with her head in the air and an expression of haughty disgust on her face.

Nor was this all: for at a little distance behind this couple there strolled one of Glint Hall's tallest attendants, a man with a countenance that reminded John Hush of the profile of George Washington on a five-cent postage-stamp. This man was indeed as clearly bent on doing to a nicety what he regarded as his duty as was the first president; for his immovable face seemed to say: "Let the grass and the railings and the grey cows and the birds and the bushes, as well as that noisy set of people who have just crowded past, understand once for all who I am and what I am: I am here and I am *not* here. When anything goes wrong, behold! I am there. When all goes well I am as though I were nowhere." Getting rid very quickly of the erroneous idea which at the first moment crossed his mind, that this tall attendant was none other than the egregious Gewlie, John was able to give his entire attention to the woman who was now approaching them. And he now knew her as the person he had come to think of as "the lady with the lorgnette".

He recognised her luckless follower, too. He turned out to be that first inmate he had encountered after he had been deposited in the reading-room by Mr. Cogent Cuddle. He was the man who might so well have been a foundling from a circus, of which his father was the giant and his mother the dwarf.

And it was upon this freak of nature that the lady with the lorgnette, swinging suddenly round on both her polished heels, now turned the full ferocity of her terrifying fashionscope. She turned it upon her bewildered follower as if it had been the shining muzzle of a machine-gun, and its effect on the giant-dwarf was instantaneous. Being the sport of Nature that he was, he was peculiarly sensitive to the heat of the sun, and this was especially so—though nobody in Glint Hall except Ursie Mum would believe it—in the month of March. He had

THE INMATES

therefore placed upon his head, when he followed the lorgnette-bearer into the garden without time to get his hat, an enormous blue handkerchief, bought at a fair in the County of Essex, of whose border he made a fresh knot, snatching it from his head and replacing upon his head every time the lady paused in her march.

There must have been latent in this poor *manqué* some abortive germ of an inspired diarist after the fashion of Pepys, and these knots in his headgear were his method of recording the momentous pausing places of his idol. His appearance, however, was not improved thereby as every new knot reduced the blue handkerchief in size. Never had a lorgnette revealed such a grotesque apparition.

But the giant-dwarf was as unable to cease celebrating the lady's pauses by tying knots as the lady was unable to prevent her expression from saying: "How dare this peripatetic abortion cross my horizon?"

But it was the lorgnette that won. The infatuated freak suddenly flung up his great hands to his head, dragged the handkerchief down over his eyes, staggered as if he'd had a sunstroke, and retreated in shuffling panic towards the south lodge, whither, John noticed, it had also become the apparent whim of the Washington-like attendant casually to direct his loitering way.

As soon as they were alone again between the railings and the thick plantation of small firs, they both stopped.

"Tenna!" John whispered, as if Mr. Frogcastle, with his eyes wider apart than ever, were looking down on them from his ladder against the wall. "Tenna! What are you ——?"

But Tenna's eyes, as John now saw, and every nerve in? Tenna's body that could be reached through her eyes, were absorbed in the slowly approaching figure of the woman with the lorgnette. This singular creature, whose whole body and soul appeared to be drawn inwards out of the surrounding air towards the proud protrusion of her under-lip, displayed herself to Tenna as a perambulating symbol of all those forms. of British snobbishness, whether of blood or of taste or of

MR. FROGCASTLE

moral judgment, that her father—long before he had become Sir Warden Sheer, long before he had become the head of his firm, long before he had married Doctor Cataract's only daughter and begotten Tenna—had worshipped as the true Shekinah or Cloud of Divine Glory into which money, and money alone and yet more money, could enable a self-made man to thrust his reverential head.

What never ceased to fascinate Ursie Mum Tickle in her work among the inmates of Glint Hall—a work that was more than saintly, that was in fact goddess-like, for if saints redeem, goddesses recreate—was the fact that, though nobody else among the authorities in Glint Hall seemed to notice it, there were no two inmates in the whole place even faintly resembling each other in the nature of their mental afflictions.

Now in Britain, as we all know only too well, there are degrees of ladyhood. Some are born ladies; some achieve ladyness; and there are—though this may be hard to believe—those who have it thrust upon them! Miss Arabella Bolster belonged to a fourth category—those who worship the Middle Ages.

And it was this interior, spiritual pride in Miss Bolster that Sir Warden Sheer, that thick-skinned master-builder, dimly and dumbly felt with uncomprehending awe.

Unluckily for Miss Bolster's mental balance she actually did have in her veins a drop of blood inherited from Boule d'Enterre. This noble gentleman, who was himself a Crusader, is known to have claimed descent, when his right to the family's coat-of-arms was challenged by Ralph Boylestarre, from Baron Boltstraigne of Bolt who was killed at the Battle of Hastings.

Miss Bolster's half-brother, when a handsome boy of fifteen, had fled from her devoted care and escaped to the Continent, where after many ambiguous adventures—for *his* hobby or mania had nothing to do with the Middle Ages—he was finally befriended by a benevolent Turk. It was under this Turk's protection that, rendered prematurely old by the life he had led, he settled down as a sort of door-keeper at a villa on the shore of the Sea of Marmora.

THE INMATES

From this neo-Gothic retreat he despatched once a year to the only other descendant of Boule d'Enterre a picture-postcard upon which was written an affectionate but stiffly conventional greeting, "couched", as Miss Bolster told Father Toby, "in language of Oriental restraint".

The number of these cards—that were pictorially always exactly the same and in their pious brevity might have been composed by Boule d'Enterre himself—now amounted to thirty-three; but as Miss Bolster re-read them more than thirty-three times every year their romantic value for a victim of the medieval frenzy was beyond the science of numbers.

And there arose in Arabella's "noble mind o'erthrown" the desperate illusion that a certain blotch or blur or disfigurement that was in reality a flaw in the printing, and which always appeared, as the picture remained the same, in the same place, in the Turk's garden, was a ruined wall of Gothic rather than of Turkish masonry. To this heap of stones, or rather to this defect in the print, the authentic though very thin and wavering line by which Arabella "deduced her lineage" from Boule d'Enterre had now been destined to lead.

The blur was a wall. The wall was a Crusader's castle. And the castle had been built by Boule d'Enterre. And to say that this discovery endeared these unchanging tokens from the boy she had brought up to Miss Bolster's heart would be to underrate their effect upon her. If they buoyed up her heart they intensified her pride to the breaking point.

Thus, with her lorgnette elevated as if it were at least a broken handle—"gules in bend between two cross-crosslets sable"—of a Crusader's sword, she advanced upon our two friends like the avantgarde of Charlemagne, not of course really seeing them at all and, indeed, seeing nothing at all but the infatuated offscouring of the old-fashioned circus known when she was a child as the "Tom Thumb Circuit", alias "The Roystering Laxatives".

Tenna's mind was diabolically clear about her danger. Her feelings were writhing like insect-dogs under their vivisector's terrible microscope, but she held them down. It

MR. FROGCASTLE

would have been an ecstasy to her to snatch the lorgnette from the advancing woman and hit her—*thud, thud, thud*, only *that* wouldn't have been the sound—full in that contemptuous face. She ceased to be Tenna Sheer, exercising self-control: she became the wild clutch with which she seized John's arm; she became the frantic fling-away of her whole body; she became the desperate pull with which she dragged him after her among the thickly planted spruce-firs. She was forced to let him go in a minute or two because the branches so hurt her face, but *that* was all right, for now she knew he'd follow her!

Nor did she force her way in a straight line through those firs. One mad terror strove with another in her nerves; for she hadn't forgotten what she had once come upon in this plantation—that very pit for dead dogs that had shaken John to such a point. At last, completely exhausted, she lurched forward for a few paces bent double and then crumpled up and lay motionless, her chin against her knees.

John Hush knelt down on the ground at her side. The ground was damp, though fallen spruce-needles made it much less so than it would have been in any other portion of the earth encompassed by the great wall of Glint.

"She'll be gone in a second, Tenna, my Tenna!" John whispered in her ear—though there was really no need to whisper—"and they'll all be gone in ten minutes!" He looked at his watch. "Yes, sweetheart, in ten minutes the first bell for tea will ring. So we'll have a quiet walk back!"

Tenna was hit to the heart by his calling her "sweetheart". Flashing like forked lightning, her mind zigzagged back to the days of her girlhood when she used to play a game with all the twigs and sticks she could pick up under the poplar trees in Corncrake Crescent. She would pretend these sticks were people. She would turn one of them into her father; and that stick was always destined for some horribly ignominious end. And one of them would be her lover. She had never had a lover and never expected to have one; but she was an inexhaustible reader of love-stories.

And though all that the proud, thin twig with a little grey

THE INMATES

lichen on it that she chose for herself would allow to her heroic warrior, covered with moss, was to He with its head — that is to say with its club-like end, whereon the wind that tore it from its branch had left a knobby oblong excrescence — resting upon her foot, which was the point of the Tenna-twig from which the bark had been peeled she was reminded of these solitary games when John Hush threw himself down by her side, and a queer thrill ran through her that was compounded of a variety of tremendous and exciting shivers.

There was real alarm in what she felt, for though he had confessed to her as if she were sexless the peculiar nature of his obsession for young women, she couldn't help being a young woman, and although it was impossible not to feel herself different from those others, different in herself and totally different in her relation to him, she felt that in these things the shrewdest intuition that any girl had might easily fail to predict what could happen.

But as if he read her thoughts and had resolved to show her that from the sex-mania that affected him she had nothing to fear, all he did was to clutch tight with the finger and thumb of his right hand the fringe of her coat; and pinching this fragment of cloth with such intense violence that thumb and first finger soon began to grow numb, he turned over upon his face, so that the feeling of the ground beneath him gave him an obscure sense that in clutching the hem of Persephone's garment he was, like the impious Jasion, enjoying the Great Mother herself.

But that inch or two of cloth, just because it *was* unyielding cloth and not responding or relucting flesh, reduced his maniacal vice to a quite controllable measure; and though he was, you might say, after his own crazy cerebral fashion making love to her, it was all so remote from ordinary love-making that it wasn't calculated to draw from her any faintest trace of the automatic response that the ordinary sex-excitement of the male is wont to arouse in the nervous system of the female; and he himself was able to do what he never could have done six months ago in the crazy obsession of his

MR. FROGCASTLE

ringlet-snatching, that is to say he was able to enjoy Tenna's nearness to him and his worship of her in widespread sensuous connection with the immediate surface of the earth.

It had always been an integral element in his erotic temperament to embrace figuratively and imaginatively, but with every sense he possessed, the particular expanse or segment of the earth's body which happened to be the geographical background of the human contact he was enjoying.

And at this moment, therefore, with his whole nature absorbed in the cerebral ravishing of Tenna's evasive spirit, he derived a complicated satisfaction from reminding himself of all he had discovered in the last twenty-four hours as to the elemental foundation upon which his new temple of Eros was rising. The temple itself might be inchoate, cloudy, shadowy, wavering in outline; but its base, at any rate, was solid and four-square.

Bending over his girl's form, as she lay on her side on the ground facing him, it gave him a peculiar satisfaction to remember every geographical detail of this river-circled plateau on which they were stranded at Glint. His mind pieced together for itself a sort of spiritual helicopter upon which he proceeded to fly north, south, east and west!

He flew in a straight line, for instance, though all the while he was anchored by her side, to that pit of horror on the northern fringe of this fir plantation. He even flew across that appalling spot to the vast farm-buildings and cobblestone yard where this morning he had worked. He visualised the way in which the lodge, where the woman lived who reminded him of his old nurse, confronted the yard beneath his bedroom-window and guarded the hideous iron gates beyond which the road stretched away through a patch or two of fir-plantation like the one in which he was now lying by Tenna's side until it reached an expanse of willows and rushes and a bridge across the river. Then he thought of the two enormous Scotch firs on the crest of the ancient British camp to the east of Glint Hall. That prehistoric fortress seemed to possess the power of holding back the river and hindering its approach.

THE INMATES

And again, completing his exploration of the four-square foundation of his tower of Eros, for where they lay now was on its south side, he visualised to the west the park-like upward slope, where, beyond a more stately bridge than any of the others, rose the singular mansion owned by his guardian's American friends.

Returned from these aerial journeys to the four sides of the imaginary square, upon which, disregarding both the wall and and the river, he was resolved to build his temple to the son of Aphrodite, it occurred to him to wonder what connection there could possibly be between his depraved mania for girls, that until yesterday had made it impossible for him to fall in love, and the curious magnetic attraction he had for such things as ruinous bridges, obliterated mile-stones, fallen breakwaters, forgotten boundary-posts, broken park-pailings, moss-grown weir-dams, derelict boat-keels, stranded barges, crumbling walls, indecypherable signposts, obsolete mill-wheels, deserted wharves, earth-sunk grave-stones.

In some weird way all these things seemed a natural, an inevitable background to his feeling for Tenna, who was now *all girls in one*. Yes, a natural background; and yet he now began to feel as if this four-square elemental foundation, upon which, along with Tenna, who so strangely resembled them, all these half-ruinous things, that had been lying there for a thousand years, could be lifted up, Tenna and himself with them, not by any violent eruption or any startling miracle, but easily, naturally, smoothly, quietly, as if they were figures carved in stone and soon to be poised between heaven and earth, as oblivious of the walls of Glint as they were of the waters of the river—that river with Father Tickle catching its perch, that river that would have encircled them clear round, if it had not been for some unknown deity in the old hill-camp who kept thrusting its waters away!

What was Tenna thinking about now as she lay facing him with her eyes so tight shut and her breathing so steady and even? Well, you could love one of these strange creatures to the limit and yet have no idea of what went on in that delicate

MR. FROGCASTLE

brittle skull or beneath those maiden breasts. Absolutely no idea! No idea whether she was angry or indifferent; no idea whether she was full of rebellious devilry or full of infinite resignation!

"I don't even know," he thought, "whether at this second she's fast asleep, or watching me, as in the stories they always say they watch you, through their lovely eyelashes! Sometimes I could even wish"—he made a face as this thought danced like a goblin through his head—"that I were a stone at the bottom of the brook that goes under those iron spikes and under the wall! I'd be a stone then that couldn't slip or sink or roll or slide among litter and rubbish! I'd be safe then in a niche, a ledge, a crack—and I'd be safe from the spikes and I'd be safe at the bottom!"

She was lying all curled up, with her high white forehead, which suddenly made him think of an old print his guardian possessed of Bernard De Fontenelle, author of *The Plurality of Worlds*, almost touching one of her knees, knees covered by extremely old-fashioned black stockings, things that were almost unattainable that spring, as John, an expert upon girls' attire, knew very well. He himself, now seated on his haunches with his hands clasped round his shins, was gazing down at her, endeavouring to conjure up a plurality of universes to help him exorcise the thought of nail-scissors.

The recoil of his mind from this temptation had the same effect upon him that pushing with a punt-pole against a verdurous bank might have had if he'd been in a boat on Father Toby's river. It started him thinking of barges and barge-poles and encircling rivers and exhausted females prostrate upon pine-needles: examples certainly rather than symbols of the plurality of life's dimensions. And he said to himself: "I believe the chief cause of madness is our absurd admiration for *personality*. Everybody longs to have a striking personality, a personality full of humours and whims and fancies and prejudices and eccentricities and grotesqueries.

"Everybody would like to hear it said of them: He or she has got such a great personality! That's what does all the

THE INMATES

harm! A great personality? A great ass! This whole damned place is simply chock-full of great personalities, the whole lot of us simply wallowing in our bloody personalities! I'd like to collect together the whole crowd of the inmates of Glint in that reading-room up there and give them a discourse that would astonish Father Toby, but with which I believe old Ursie Mum would entirely agree! I'd tell them that the whole business of being cured and getting out of here consists in ridding ourselves of our blasted personality!

"I'd tell them we should reduce our lives to two dimensions, and cut out this damned personality once for all: Be in your bodies, I'd tell them—be in your bodies to the limit, and then when your bodies don't satisfy you, be *in the spirit*! You ask, my dears, I'd say to them, what I mean by being in the spirit? Well, I'd say to them: *That's* just what I'm telling you now!

"You've heard all this chat, I'd say to them, about evolution producing civilisation? Well! What did Jean-Jacques Rousseau tell us, eh? To pick up a few home-truths from the trusty savage, and let evolution tread water for a time! In other words, instead of letting this blind conceited idiotic evolution-impulse do what it likes with us, why not play at being gods ourselves and do a little wholesome self-creating on our own? Yes! And begin, too, I would say to them, with the nature of our own being! What drives us mad? I'd say to them. And I'd answer: The over-complicated nature of our own identity!

"Of course that's the exact truth; for it's the real truth that always has to be dug up from the pit, like Aristophanes *Eirene*, when you're going to improve things. These are grand days for manufacturing what they call Robots.

"Well! Why not substitute *creation* for manufacture; and play at being gods ourselves? Why not, I'd say to them, start creating a different kind of human being than the one that can only be scared by hell-fire into behaving properly? That crazy fellow Kirilov in *The Possessed* says that the human race has to he *physically changed*.

MR. FROGCASTLE

"Well! Let's be the ones to change it. That's what I'll tell them! And I'll add: Where in the name of Holy Jesus could be found a better place for changing it than Doctor Echetus's home for lost dogs? But how to do it? Ah! There's the rub that makes calamity of so long life!

"But listen, my dears, I'd say to them. Here we are, all together, in this nice comfortable reading-room, with the biggest tulip-tree in the United Kingdom outside the window. Isn't it natural to us all, though not always easy, I admit, but isn't it natural to us all, to change our nature by getting rid of certain fancies, caprices, whimsies, mischiefs, furies, manias?

"We've all heard of *conversion*, haven't we? We all know what the Salvation Army can do for the souls it saves? But that, you'll say, means faith in God! Of course it does! But let me tell you this, my dear. The thing that works these miracles isn't God, but the *faith* which these people have in God. It's faith, I tell you, that does it. Jesus is perfectly right there, and so is Paul. What works the miracle is faith. And whose faith, I'd like to know? Ours, of course!

"And faith in what, you'd like to know? *Faith in our power to change ourselves!* All right, I'd go on, so far all is granted. The change is to be made, this terrific, this terrible, this startling change, this change that's as extreme as a physical change, this change that the Salvationists call 'a change of heart'. But the change I'm telling you about is more than a change of heart. It's a change of *dimension*. It's a *metaphysical* change.

"In our human mental world it's like splitting the atom! In plain words, I'd tell them, in language you can all understand, my dear fellow-inmates, what we've got to do is to reduce the embodiments of our identity *from three to two!*

"And just here, my darlings, so I'll say to them, lies the miracle. What took theology—starting with Plato, long before Jesus was born or Paul had preached in Athens and converted half the household of Caesar—what took, I'll say, about two thousand years for theology to do we must do, like spiritual atom-splitters, in a few months, in fact, I would add, before midsummer!

THE INMATES

"And what we must do, I would go on, coming now to the essential point, is to liquidate completely from our individual human nature this preposterous and troublesome something in each man and each woman, namely that grandiose projection of ourselves that we are in the habit of describing as our personality.

"It is *this* part of us, so I would tell them in my speech in the reading-room, which is at the bottom of all the worst troubles and quarrels and misunderstandings in life.

"Of course it's with our bodily senses that we enjoy things and suffer things and it is over the appetites of the body that in our most animal moods we fight with each other both individually and as a pack. But wasn't it from the frustrated desires of their flesh and blood as individual men or animals that Alexander and Caesar and Hannibal and Tamburlaine and Ghengis Khan and Frederick the Great and Bismarck and Hitler brought such devastation to so many?

"I'll tell you, fellow-inmates; I'll tell you in one single word. These famous men weren't more lecherous or treacherous, more cruel or hard-hearted, than the rest of us. They were probably less so! They were certainly more hard-working and in most cases more magnanimous. How, then, is it that their names have become so satanic that the smoke of them mounts up to heaven? What brings down this doom upon them that they should be accounted worse among men than plagues or famines? In one single word, fellow-inmates, in one single word: *personality!*

"These murderers of thousands, these manufacturers of widows and orphans, these burners of roof-trees, these blackeners of hearth-stones, these sackers of cities, these scorchers of the earth, don't do what they do because of their bodies. They don't do what they do because of their appetites and sensations. Far less do they do what they do because of the spirit that exalts all men and makes the souls of all men equal! They do what they do because of this accursed *third dimension* of our nature, this thrice-accursed devil or a thing we call Personality!

MR. FROGCASTLE

"This, brother-inmates, this, sister-inmates, is the 'abomination of desolation' set up in the holy place—that is to say, between the sacred animal-earthly *body* and the sacred human-planetary *spirit*; in other words, brother-and-sister inmates, between the dust that returneth to the earth from which it rises and the spirit that returneth to the air from which it descends.

"There are many worlds and many universes, fellow-inmates, but we, human beings, are constructed of only two dimensions—matter and mind, body and spirit. All the horrors and evils in life come from the accurst Platonists or Gnostics or Prae-Christian mystics, whoever they may have been, who confused the whole issue by inventing, out of some subtle confusion in the mysterious relation between our conscious self and our bodily self, this proud, insolent, ambitious, indecent, arrogant, and entirely illusory concept of personality.

"Don't you see, brother-inmates and sister-inmates ——" Here John realised that in his ambassadorial pride in subtle distinctions he had begun murmuring aloud this "counter-blast", as the old covenanter would have styled it, to history's great men, and that Tenna had opened one eye and had fixed it steadily upon him. The reading-room and its imaginary audience vanished completely then, as John's two eyes encountered this dazed and puzzled stare.

But like a man who has long been practising a particular jump and has thrown himself so absolutely into this practice that all other mental energies must remain numb and void till the contest is over, John Hush didn't stop murmuring this imaginary speech. Nor was he content with his position by Tenna's side. Rising on his knees, he swayed above her for a moment, his two eyes fixed upon the eye she had opened, an eye which, just because it was only one, didn't seem to be fully aware of the nature of the situation, and then he sank forward across her, plunging the palms of his hands and the undersides of his wrists into the spruce-needles on the further side of her. In this position, Tenna's body being so thin and her dress being so flimsy, there was nothing of her he could

THE INMATES

really see, although to his fancy the sepia-coloured fir-needles, a few miniature funguses, a spray of yellowish moss, and a patch of grey lichen became a firmament of staring puzzled brown eyes.

As for Tenna, she lay like a dead sycamore leaf that all the winter had been blown from spruce-fir branch to spruce-fir branch, hating the rich incense-heavy Christmas smell of their massive green foliage and longing to sink down amid funguses and damp moss and those fine thin patches of grass-blades that seem to rise out of larch-needles, like the spears of fairy warriors sown by the tender gums of lizards and slow-worms and secretive toads.

She was fully awake now, but hesitated to open her other eye lest this man of hers should start doing in this perfect hiding-place whatever it is men do to women. Those were the exact words she made use of in her curled-up blind soliloquy, and the unspoken words were followed by a fretful, petulant, troubled protest against the whole nature of normal life which apparently refused to make it clear to one like her, *who had nothing to go upon*, except the vaguest virginal fancies, what at such a moment it were best for a girl to do. She had never felt quite so confused and bewildered as she did at this moment.

Hitherto there had only been one Tenna in her heart, head, her neck, her stomach, her bowels, her legs, her arms. Now to her consternation there seemed more than one "queen of the castle". There seemed indeed several Tennas within her, and these different Tennas wanted different things.

None of them, however—and this was the most troublesome part of it—had a clear idea of what it did want. There had been a Tenna—could it have been only yesterday morning?—whose secretest and deepest ideal was to have a mate who was barely human, who was in fact the extreme opposite in human polarity from the hard-working, hard-climbing, male-conscious, class-conscious, race-conscious, brick-yard owner, who had been made a "Sir" for his services to society, and for whom, not only because he'd begotten her, and not only because her mother drowned herself, but simply and solely

MR. FROGCASTLE

because he was *himself*, because his eyes were *his* eyes, his nose *his* nose, his ears *his* ears, his hands *his* hands, his smell *his* smell, the hairs on his head, on his hands, on his chest, and everywhere else where there could be hairs, *his* hairs; for whom she had a loathing as if he were "the worm" Jesus talks of "that dieth not"—yes, there had been a Tenna whose ideal mate, in order that he might be the extremest possible opposite to Sir Warden Sheer, resembled an inanimate doll, of human size and human appearance, of course, and certainly not in the least effeminate, but so much her very own that he could be trusted never to touch her when or where she didn't want to be touched, and who could be trusted when she wanted to be quiet never to ramble on in a tiresome, pedantic, stupid, tedious, obscure way about white cows or spikes under bridges or Halfway Houses belonging to rich Americans!

But last night, after they separated, and once in the night when she woke and stayed awake, she had found that her heart, her senses, her nerves, her whole body, had come to be, in a manner that caused her several queer shivers and tremors, not entirely satisfied with a companion so completely inanimate.

And yet there was still a Tenna struggling for the mastery against the one that made her open her left eye. This Tenna, though her body was so feminine and so soft, was the fierce man-hater who, a couple of years ago, had got herself into Glint for trying to kill her father. Had it been Mr. Frogcastle rather than Mr. Gewlie who had been the one to be spying upon the inmates of Glint that cloudy end of a warm-breathing day, it is hard not to believe he would have paused in a humorous reverie as he spied on those two human forms, one bent like a new moon on the ground and the other bent like an arched bridge across her body and both ensorcerised in a queer unnatural silence. The convulsive tremors that had passed through them separately before their bodies assumed this queer almost zodiacal position would have been unknown to him; but it would have struck him that some serious tension vibrated in the atmosphere about them, a tension that sug-

THE INMATES

gested the approach of an unusual nervous crisis or at least that such a crisis was on the wind.

But no such crisis, whether projected by the terrible urge of Eros or by the terrible necromancy of Nemesis, occurred at that time; nor, indeed, was there anybody spying on them. But, all the same, a startling change in the situation did occur, of which the cause, though it had nothing to do with human emotion, was a simple and natural one. It was, in fact, a series of long-drawn exquisite notes from an unseen blackbird; and under the impact of this recklessly shrill yet liquidly raindrop sound, the tense, opaque, heavily covered, humanly compact bodies of those two inmates of Glint were magnetised into a vibrant alertness.

John's body instantaneously stiffened and straightened. He drew his fingers out of the thick mass of pine-needles and knelt upright by Tenna's side, listening. She remained prostrate, but turning round she now lay on her back, and drawing up her knees clasped them tight with her clenched hands. Extended like this, he kneeling with his hands clasped behind him and she on her back with her hands clasped about her knees, they both listened to this invisible bird which had flown across the Glint meadows on an exploring expedition, but at this moment was tempted to take a holiday from the nesting-season's labours and to make a little music for the pure pleasure of making it.

The two listeners to this divine burst of aesthetic selfishness were queerly affected by what they heard. As there is an irresistible and fatal regularity in Nature's pulsings and throbbings and spasms of erotic sound, so there are also in the recurrent motions of the ebb and flow of the life-stream certain unexpected, unaccounted-for in-rushings of completely incalculable forces. These forces, although they are forces "that Nature makes", disturb and interrupt the normal rhythm of things; and when in their startling unexpectedness, like "bolts", as we say, "out of the blue", these extra-normal invaders from far outside the ordinary system of life's ebb and flow rush upon us, it is as if we felt a sudden cosmic crack in

MR. FROGCASTLE

the thick rondure of our universe, through which the-devil-knows-what invasion takes possession of us.

To these highly-strung lovers of two days' acquaintance it was as if there came rushing on the notes of this unseen bird an airborne shaft of unnatural revelation, in fact a revelation assuring them of the irrational fact that the madness that had lodged them in this weird walled-in place was not in its essential nature an evil thing at all, but, on the contrary, a sort of miraculously winged ichor or elixir which as it came fluttering down from some completely different dimension had overflown its mark and had hit the wrong nerve in each of them, so that she was not inspired to start a revolt against the cruelty of old custom but only to try to kill complacent old men; while he was not inspired to perform some miracle of valour for a maiden but only to cut off the curls of provocative maids.

"Oh, my one of all," he thought, "it doesn't matter whether I touch you or don't touch you as long as we are together, as long as you are alive and by my side!"

And she thought: "I don't care whether he makes love to me or not. From the heart of my skull to the heart of his skull there's some kind of air-bridge and over that bridge our thoughts keep passing, not speaking a single word, but—what's that?"

She sprang to her feet, and so did he, for quite close to them they heard gaspings and pantings and a desperate scrambling. Before they could decide what to do, a pair of inmates, a man and a woman, people just known to her, but quite unknown to him, rushed wildly past, evidently in a pitiful panic, while behind them came a uniformed attendant.

John Hush knew at once that in all the days of his life he had never seen any human face more appalling in its possibilities than the face of the person who was following these frightened inmates.

Tenna, of course, knew well who it was, but she had no time to explain anything to her companion. With a movement as swift as the blackbird, who with an angry scream broke off its impassioned celebration of solitude and noisily flapped away,

THE INMATES

she flung herself between pursuer and pursued. Her instinct had risen to the occasion.

"Oh, how lucky it's you, Mr. Gewlie!" she cried. "Mr. Hush here—Mr. Hush, this is my good friend Mr. Gewlie—Mr. Hush was telling me he hoped to meet Father Wun at tea to-day. I believe they have friends in common at Halfway House. Will you help us to get back to the path, Mr. Gewlie? Mr. Hush and I have begun to feel nervous in this wood. And we feel we have been trespassing, too! Please be so good as to take us out of the wood, Mr. Gewlie!"

The man removed his hat with his right hand, wiped his forehead with the palm of his left hand, and stared at Tenna hesitating. John also stared at her in absolute astonishment.

"What a thing a girl is!" he thought.

And then he, too, addressed himself to the man, carefully and deliberately, using his most pronounced Embassy voice.

But still the man hesitated, glancing in the direction whither the panic-stricken pair had fled.

Then Tenna "took", as Homer would say, whether of a mortal or an immortal, "other counsel". She, too, glanced in the direction followed by that panic-stricken pair.

"I hope," she said, speaking slowly and clearly, "those excited people who have just passed us won't come out from the wood exactly where Mr. Frogcastle is nailing up fruit trees—because I'm sure he won't at all like to be disturbed." She had done the trick!

Into the countenance of the attendant, Gewlie, came an expression of a terror even greater than that which she had seen on the faces of the two fugitives.

"Follow close behind me!" he gasped from his distorted lips, and, swinging clear round, led the way back towards the south lodge.

7

THE TEA-PARTY

JOHN'S admiration for Tenna was as boundless as ever when, in the watchful but extremely respectful company of Mr. Gewlie he entered the dining-hall and made his way to his usual place. Yes, there was Mr. Lordy, keyed up to an intense excitement of expectation; but no sign as yet of Father Wun.

As for the man Gewlie, it was clear that the departure of Tenna had restored his equanimity. He assumed the role of introducing John Hush to the expectant group of Catholics. "And here," he announced, "is our nice, good, new gentleman, most comforting to us all, I'm sure—aren't I right, Mr. Lordy?—so healthy and strapping and upstanding—aren't they the words Miss Bolster herself would use? Except 'strapping', perhaps! Do you know I once asked Miss Bolster if she liked the word 'strapping' as applied to a handsome spirited young man, and do you know what she said?"

It was at this point that Mr. Lordy paid John one of the greatest compliments he had ever received in his life. John hadn't been in Balkan embassies for nothing; and well enough did he know that the humbler, shyer, more timid and less self-assertive a person is, the greater is the honour of such a person's confidence.

And now Mr. Lordy lifted him, with a gesture like a delicate accolade, into the innermost circle of his friends! This he did with a flicker of his left eyelid across the breast-bone of the the man Gewlie. It wasn't that he gave John a wink. That would be to put it grossly. It was rather as if he took the eyelid-flicker with which a wink would naturally begin, caught it with impalpable fingers and released it, like an invisible thought-moth, in the kitchen-garden of John's brain.

Meanwhile the man Gewlie went on. "She said 'yes'! Yes, Miss Bolster said 'yes'! She willingly admitted that the

THE INMATES

word 'strapping' gave her a nice feeling and was one of her favourite words. She told me it made her think of football!"

By this time John and Mr. Lordy had already devoured between them almost half the whole plate of brown-bread-and-butter; and it was clear that Gewlie, who, though in uniform, was obviously playing the part of an invited guest, was too nervous to do more than nibble at this feast.

John could catch only an occasional glimpse of Antenna from where he sat, for she had taken a place at the furthest end of the women's table. She had found Miss Bolster's society too reminiscent of that particular social ideal that always hovered before Sir Warden's "inward eye" and which, though beyond the reach of bricks and mortar, had been one of the main inspirations of his undeviating, undistracted, and, you might almost say, devoted struggle to become rich.

As for the man Gewlie, he also kept giving troubled glances at the unfilled gap on the further side of Mr. Lordy which had been clearly reserved for the Father; for beyond this gap there were about half a dozen inmates who were murmuring among themselves in a manner that had for an onlooker, even for an onlooker who had so recently been "certified", a curiously unpleasant effect. Hush would have been hard put to it to define this particular unpleasantness. It wasn't an indecent effect. On the contrary, it was nervously proper. But in some peculiarly ghastly way it struck Hush as if all those half-dozen people, though so strictly correct in their gestures and in their sentiments, had no modest covering of ordinary *skin* between their clothes and their bowels, lungs, bladder, gall, kidneys, liver, and several other familiar human organs!

Was this due, he wondered, to their carrying the ancient psychoanalytical habit of confession much further than it could possibly be carried in Catholic countries where everybody was a Catholic or an atheist; or was the Catholic Faith itself such a protection against the religious element in all insanity that there was something almost indecent about a mad Catholic?

Some inmates who had come in while John was occupied with Gewlie and Mr. Lordy now entirely concealed Tenna

THE TEA-PARTY

from him. This was a serious matter, for the agitating conclusion of their afternoon walk had prevented them from arranging together where they would meet after this meal; and John would have liked to have signalled to her by some sign she would have recognised at once—for instance by treating bits of bread-and-butter as if they'd been draughtsmen—to suggest that they should meet in that same corner of the smoking-room.

He felt sure Antenna was only hidden by those new-comers. She couldn't, surely, have slipped out of the hall altogether without his having noticed it? But all the same he felt extremely nervous. He must arrange with her a minutely circumstantial plan of campaign for an occasion of this sort!

He made a feeble attempt now to enter into the Gewlie-Lordy dialogue by forcing himself to turn upon them both a certain engaging and beguiling smile, a smile full of the aristocratic roguery of diplomatic confidence-tricks, to show he had heard what he hadn't heard, caught what he hadn't caught, divined what he hadn't divined, and understood what nobody but God could possibly have understood, but the only result of this almost feminine manoeuvre was to involve him still further in the ghastly and tragic chatter, like the twittering of a flock of purgatorial long-tailed tits, at once weirdly jocular and reverentially apprehensive, of these half-dozen Roman Catholic inmates.

They even struck John, though he was anything but an Homeric student, as if they were gathering to meet Father Wun as the Homeric ghosts under the earth gathered to greet Odysseus—pathetic shadows of their own past, longing to do, to say, to feel, in fact to play, the living part which they no longer had the substantiality to fulfil.

He couldn't follow what these men were saying. Indeed, they spoke very low. But it almost looked as if they were conversing with the empty space on the bench which would soon be filled by Father Wun, for they kept throwing quick glances at that unfilled gap and then looking hurriedly and reverentially away, until Hush began to feel that he would experience only a faint

THE INMATES

surprise if some shadowy manifestation of at least the lower portion of Father Wun's material envelope had been revealed to them for a second, even though it had been withdrawn in a flash.

But what was this? All the inmates who were having their tea in that hall, not merely the men at John's table but the women at Tenna's, had ceased to talk and were gazing awestruck at a group of people who had just entered. It caused John a sharp pang that he couldn't be absolutely sure, since only a few inches of a girl's shoulder and about an inch of her sleeve were all he could see of his friend at this agitating moment, that these adjuncts did belong to her, or that she was there at all.

He had reached that crucial point in a love-affair when a lover feels that all those extra-dramatic occasions which normally he would appreciate with his whole nature could only reach half of his attention if the object of his attraction were not there to share them.

But even with half of his nature, waveringly combined with those two inches of feminine attire, John Hush did note with no small interest the impressive group that had now entered. One was Doctor Echetus himself; and rarely had any of the inmates there present been more conscious of the greatness of their lord and master. He was an impressive-looking individual; and the impression he made was certainly one of great authority. Authority, perhaps, would be a better word for the head of Glint than any other. The impression he made at first glance couldn't in any sense be called an impression of distinction.

To the man's essential quality of self-centred assurance had been added, as I have already presumed to hint, a curious air of integral officialdom like that possessed by the established overseers of parks, public gardens, and even of royal castles; and Doctor Echetus certainly looked at this moment, as his calm gaze moved from visitors to patients and from patients to visitors, as if he were an embodiment of all the most formidable insignia of authority from the Black Forest to the Gobi Desert, and from all the imperial ante-chambers from China to Peru.

But it was the Doctor's companions that drew John's interest most vividly just then and made him snatch almost

THE TEA-PARTY

angrily and with the eye of a shrike at that morsel of sleeve and that reverted shoulder-tip to make them share what he felt. For one of the visitors was a lady. This lady John felt sure must be the new owner of Halfway House and the identical person under whose roof his guardian and his guardian's betrothed had spent last night.

It seemed to him that her gaze, though she was a short plump personage who looked decidedly short-sighted, took every chance it could of scanning the faces of the inmates at the men's table; but he hurriedly told himself that even if this were true it might easily be that his friends had respected his pride and had scrupulously refrained from referring to him at all, and that this kindly creature who bore, he now decided, a striking resemblance to a picture he had once seen of the youthful Queen Victoria when under the escort of Lord Melbourne, was simply behaving as she always behaved.

There was nothing about Doctor Echetus in the least like Lord Melbourne, and as for Father Wun, he was the mortal antipodes of any conceivable British statesman, but it was quite clear to our well-trained diplomatic friend that this short plump uncomely American lady possessed that imponderable feminine quality of regal magnetism which enabled Victoria to out-queen it even over the Empress Eugénie. She was now advancing to the bottom of the table, where Hush was painfully and desperately trying to snatch a glimpse of more than his friend's sleeve.

As the American advanced, she asked one question of Father Wun and another question of Doctor Echetus in such a manner as to transform both these gentlemen into organic ornaments upon the prow of that exquisitely-steered ship which was herself under reduced sails.

John was so absorbed in his guardian's hostess that he only gave a cursory and fleeting glance at Father Wun, and it wasn't till both Echetus and the lady had disappeared that his attention returned to his own table.

Oh, how fearful he was lest Tenna shouldn't have been there at all, and not only so, but should have gone without their

THE INMATES

having made any definite arrangement as where they would spend their evening!

But he had to deal with the immediate situation now, for he was being introduced to the Father by Mr. Lordy, and he was particularly anxious to notice the effect of the priest's presence upon the egregious Gewlie.

No sooner, however, was he alert to what was happening round him than he saw Tenna. Yes! There she was! And, oh, how thankful he felt! Two or three women had suddenly moved away from that end of the table, and there was Tenna clearly exposed to his view—yes! and actually smiling at him, and watching what was happening at his Catholic tea-party as closely as he had been watching the entrance and departure of the queenly American!

"No doubt," he told himself, "she will wait now till I make a move, and then we'll be together in the passage near that end window as we were yesterday."

Father Wun greeted him in the friendliest manner, but he clearly had so many of his own faith on his hands that he couldn't remain in conversation with him for more than a minute or two. But the Father did reveal the important fact that his guardian *had* spoken about him. What had he said about him? Not very much; so at least he gathered from the priest's brief words. And John was glad that it hadn't been very much!

But now the whole situation was moment by moment becoming much more dramatic, and John could see across the two tables that Tenna was missing nothing of what was going on.

Mr. Lordy, who had begun to treat the pot of freshly-made tea brought by an attendant as if it had been made by himself to be served by himself at a party presided over by himself, now proceeded, without the slightest preliminary warning or challenge, to plunge into his appalling charges against Gewlie, who, perfectly unmoved, and with a patient, protesting, wistfully indulgent expression on his face, appeared to be assuring the Father that there was no reason why they should permit this agreeable meeting of fellow-religionists who knew one another

THE TEA-PARTY

so well to be seriously disturbed by the unfortunate manias of a person as unimportant as this voluble epitome of all that is negligible.

While Mr. Lordy plunged on and on into further and further details of Gewlie's sadistic behaviour, John had time to study at close range the whole figure and countenance of Father Wun. No one had told him that there was any oriental blood in the priest, but "Wun" certainly sounded like a Chinese name, and soon all sorts of obscure odds and ends of information about the ancient Chinese classics of Confucius and Mencius if not of Laotze and Kwang-tze came drifting into John's head in vague association with Jesuit missionaries.

And yet somehow he couldn't imagine the authorities appointing a priest with Chinese blood to a parish in so populous and important a town as the one which was now the centre of the Father's activities, though for himself John saw no reason against it.

But whether or not he had any Chinese blood, Father Wun's face was as impenetrably polite as if he'd been a direct descendant of Confucius. It gave no sign of annoyance or of impatience. It betrayed no anxious concern about Mr. Lordy's plunging into such dangerous matters.

John thought he detected at one point a movement of the priest's expressionless eyes—not of his head—in the direction of a couple of attendants who were discussing some private matter of their own, but who now and then directed a faintly amused glance at the group of Catholic inmates gathered round their spiritual guide; but even of this glance he wasn't certain.

John's own chief preoccupation, as this scene appeared to be intensifying to a point where an explosion of some sort was unavoidable, was to keep his eye on Tenna, and if possible exchange with her some sort of wordless commentary on what was happening, while he missed nothing of what actually *was* happening. Unfortunately upon one of these occurrences he couldn't comment with Tenna simply because, by reason of the distance between them, she couldn't possibly see it. This was the curious way in which from having been slightly paler than

THE INMATES

usual, the egregious Gewlie—for there was a sort of comical abominableness about the man that possessed a lurid attraction, and John didn't conceal from himself that he derived peculiar satisfaction from mumbling the phrase "the egregious Gewlie" —now displayed at various places in the skin of his face certain dark-red spots.

"It isn't, Father, believe me, it isn't"—Lordy was now explaining—"that I've any malice or hatred or any personal grudge against Mr. Gewlie! What I *have* seen, I *have* seen, and what I dread seeing, I dread seeing, and the truth is, Father— yes, you may smile your sneering smile, you cruel wretch, but you can't stop my telling the Father everything!—the truth is there are certain unfortunate people in this place this smiling devil won't leave alone. He has the whole place, as all the attendants have, to wander about in just as he likes. He has a pass-key to all the rooms. Don't you see, Father, how horribly wicked this whole system is, and how dreadful for this demon's victims? Mind you, Father, I'm only telling you what everybody in this place knows to be true, only they're too afraid— and naturally enough they're too afraid—to tell any outside person what's going on here all the time. Yes, you can smile and tap your head." At this point John was able to exchange a completely understanding look with Tenna; for it was evident that the last thing the egregious Gewlie felt like doing at that moment was tapping his head. He was, in fact, rather absurdly straining his neck, so as to be able to keep an eye on the nearest group of his fellow-attendants, where, though they were still talking among themselves, there was one man who by some tacit agreement never took his gaze away from the encircled figures of Lordy and Father Wun. "But the truth—" Mr. Lordy now burst out, "the truth is that instead of this place being a place of healing for the wretched people singled out by this man for his devilish tricks, it has become a place where people on the edge of being cured are driven back, harried back, hunted back into raving fever!"

Mr. Lordy's voice had a definite touch of hysteria by this time, and his fellow-religionists began to huddle closer and

THE TEA-PARTY

closer to Father Wun, like a woolly flock suddenly aware that in their midst is a creature not entirely sheepish; an insignificant beast, but a beast with at least a drop of the blood of a yak or ibex.

And the eyes of John Hush and Tenna Sheer, meeting across the two empty tables, told each other how the faintest quiver of hysteria in *any* voice attracts human attention to the exclusion of everything else.

The attendant, who was, so to say, in the crow's-nest of that near group gave a quick glance at his companions and they all moved forward. Parallel with this forward movement of his fellow-keepers, the red spots in the countenance of the egregious Gewlie faded away, and he resumed his original smile, so volubly saying: "Isn't it touching how insanity creates such monstrous accusations in simple minds?"

But the hysterical quiver in Mr. Lordy's tone rose higher yet, and as it rose the man himself became more and more negligible, till, as that high-pitched cry ceased to be composed of coherent words and became like the discordant quavers and semiquavers of a bar of broken music, there did not seem, at least to the eyes and ears of John and Tenna, to be any Mr. Lordy at all, but only a thin quivering gnat-like vibration in the air that kept repeating, "Let me alone! Let me alone! Let me alone! Let me alone!" and then, on a yet wilder and more defiant note, like a whirring of invisible grouse-wings over a rain-soaked moor, "Go away! Go away! Go away! Go away! Let me be! Let me be! Let me be! Let me be!"

The moment was a very painful one to John, and not less so, he could clearly detect, to Tenna, for they both could see that in another minute the attendants would surround this vibration from the void and hustle and rustle it back into the darkness, as if an abortion had presumed to criticise creation and had to be hugged to death on the downy bosoms of celestial midwives!

But—and for the first time to-night—the weary, inscrutable countenance of Father Allen Wun moved like a mountainous sheepfold to protect his frightened flock of huddled sheep.

THE INMATES

"Mr. Lordy and Mr. Gewlie," he remarked calmly, "have anticipated by a few minutes the talk I have begged them to have with me after tea in Mr. Lordy's room upstairs. You will excuse us, the rest of you, I know? If I hadn't to catch the eight o'clock bus I would have joined you all in the smoking-room presently, but as it is, I'm afraid I must bid you good night. Both Mr. Lordy and Mr. Gewlie belong to our Saint Patrick's Dramatic Club and their different approach to all these difficult mental problems has begun to extend, I'm afraid, to regions where, quite naturally and properly, we laymen—I speak as a novice in the presence of so many expert ministers of the great healing profession—must confess to being out of our depth. But it is as a priest of the Church that I must insist, if you'll permit me, to have a little talk with my two sons here—with you, Mr. Lordy, and with you, Mr. Gewlie—so if you don't mind, gentlemen . . ." and Father Wun turned his eyes in his buttressed, bastioned and bulwarked face without moving his skull by the faintest flicker of an inch. He turned then towards the stealthily advancing but obviously hesitating attendants on one side of him and the fidgety, furtive, feverish group of frightened fellow-Catholics on the other.

It was, as John saw, and as he realised when he caught the expression on her face that Tenna had seen, a crucial moment. The attendants, in spite of the Father's rock-bastioned skull, were still advancing, With the evident intention of laying their hands upon Mr. Lordy and removing him, by the exertion of irresistible though patient force, bodily from the dining-hall, and of conveying him to the particular wing of the establishment where unruly inmates were encouraged to develop second thoughts.

It was clear to John that in these two or three beats of the dragging pulse of time a Very great deal was happening, and happening, it seemed to him, to the advantage of Gewlie and to the disadvantage of Mr. Lordy. Gewlie's face had triumphantly petrified itself into his superior smile and there was a movement of his lips as if he were articulating the words, "I will see you later, Father. Yes, a little later, when I have attended to the removal of this ridiculous individual."

THE TEA-PARTY

Gewlie's eyes were in fact now alight with a sinister magnetic power that seemed to be actually drawing the attendants towards Mr. Lordy. John found himself so absorbed in his recognition of what was going on that for the moment his mental contact with Tenna was broken, and he missed the fact that the girl had moved forward and was now standing alone, half-way between the women's table and the spot where Father Wun was holding the enemy at bay.

John's fear that Mr. Lordy was on the point of losing this terrible tense struggle was now accentuated by the fact that Father Wun himself suddenly moved. This movement arrested John's full attention. It struck him in a curious way. It was as if something much more than an Oriental-looking personage in a dusky cloth suit and a round collar were changing a physical position.

The priest moved so close to Mr. Lordy that the lower portion of a notably ecclesiastical, tightly buttoned, gastronomical abdomen touched one of the disinfectant-reeking side-pockets of that feverish nonentity.

John himself had actually begun to shiver with sympathetic apprehension. This physical change in Father Wun's position troubled him greatly. He felt convinced that it wouldn't have occurred if the priest hadn't been pretty sure that the attendants would carry off Mr. Lordy, and that he, priest of Omnipotence as he was, would be forced to catch his bus without having achieved anything in the service of his God, or of his Church, or of his conscience.

John's one hope, though he would hardly have dared to confess such a crazy thing even to Tenna, was that the contact of that almost episcopal abdomen with Mr. Lordy's coat-pocket might somehow, in the mysteries of magnetic transference, whirl the man out of danger.

It was at that extremely crucial second that the voice of Tenna Sheer, sounding like the wind through a husky, threshed-out hollow straw almost at John's elbow, became audible. There had been a cessation of talk among the Catholics when the priest made that paternal move to Mr. Lordy's

THE INMATES

side; and it was therefore in a silence that gave to her words a startling emphasis that everyone heard her say: "I think I saw Mr. Frogcastle just now crossing the grass. He must be going to see Doctor Echetus."

It was like the explosion of an occult bomb. Thrusting himself between the two attendants who were nearest to Mr. Lordy, the panic-stricken Gewlie dragged them off towards the only window in the hall.

As for Tenna, she hurried back to the women's part of the room, where, completely indifferent to Father Wun's momentous tea-party, a group of female inmates was listening with not a few nudges and giggles and chuckles and spasms of delight—for it was evident that the springtime aura of this twenty-sixth day of March was as active inside as it was outside Glint Hall—to a scene between a big plump bouncing girl, whose real name was Lavinia Tatters, but who from a very early age had been christened Tottie Creambo, and the elderly gentleman whom, as Mr. Lordy had pointed out to John at their first encounter, because for some reason he'd reminded her of her father, Tenna had on her first appearance at Glint Hall blindly attacked.

But fortunately for everybody except Gewlie, Tenna had turned her back on the women's table before the appearance of old Rumpibus and Tottie. It was, therefore, with a free mind that she could join the alliance, not unknown in history, between orthodoxy and insanity and assist them, for the time being at any rate, to defeat the Devil.

John himself had switched his gaze from the girl to Gewlie, in time to mark before the man dragged the attendants away the look of ghastly panic on his face. Gewlie's features had indeed contorted themselves into a horrible mask of terror.

"What does he suppose," John foolishly asked himself, "that a pruner of peaches and a planter of raspberry canes can possibly do to a medically approved attendant at a scientifically conducted lunatic-asylum?"

But as Gewlie's victims forgot, or they wouldn't have been where they were, and as Father Allen Wun seems to have

THE TEA-PARTY

forgotten or he wouldn't have been where *he* was, the inflictors of physical pain in this world are, as a rule, save under special conditions, less deft in their poignant art than their brethren the inflictors of mental pain.

That the opposite of active sadism is passive masochism is undoubtedly sound logic, but the appallingly intimate link between a distorted imagination and the horror-nerve which the power that creates our particular dimension of the multiverse has inserted in the human-animal nature, as the vivisectors in their research laboratories know well, is by no means confined to sex-perversity.

The expression of horrible terror that convulsed the features of the man Gewlie at that moment lodged itself in John's secret gallery of memorable images, and became a *memento crudelitatis* and a lasting warning against projecting the faintest sadistic vibration into the ebbing and flowing ocean of floating subhuman thoughts that surrounds us all.

The red blotches on Gewlie's face increased as rapidly as the skin between them became deathly white. It was as if all the blood in his body, rushing inwards to quench the mad thirst of the terror-monster in his soul, had lost its way, and while drops of it had got caught in various skin-holes, other projections of it were drumming at his eyes, pounding at his ears, gurgling in his chest, and, like condensed steam in an engine gone wrong, were not only causing the nerves in his face to give mechanical twitches but had even gone so far as to force certain muscles in his throat to utter inarticulate terror-sounds that were not only beyond anything human but even beyond anything animal.

It was as if the unfortunate man's paroxysm of terror had reached such a point that it had broken down some biological barrier between animal sensibility and the sensitiveness of such inorganic planetary substances in the stellar galaxy as can be imagined shrinking at the threat of some atomic explosion that could throw them back into the void of non-existence! The unhappy wretch had returned from the window, leaving the other attendants to watch the scene from a distance; for it

THE INMATES

was clear that Mr. Lordy was now quite calm and that Father Wun had the situation well under control.

Gewlie was in fact now standing in baffled, frustrated, defeated helplessness, like a convicted criminal, who, having exhausted every vista of assault, was watching the closing of every corridor of escape. And yet nothing about the man's figure or about the expression of his face suggested any change in his essential nature. His defeat had nothing to do with what we call conversion. It was merely a reduction to temporary helplessness.

"Well, my friends," Father Wun began, looking steadily at Mr. Lordy, who with his mouth dribbling and his eyes dilated, was staring at his dumbfounded enemy much as a spell-bound rabbit might stare at blood-sucking weasel, half of whose head has suddenly been blown off. "Well, my friends, will you let me say good night now, good night to all of you here? My sons, Lordy and Gewlie, are going to talk matters over with me upstairs. Come, my sons, we will soon find out what's wrong with Glint from the viewpoint of the blessed saints. 'Tis *they*, after all, isn't it, who are the true astronomers and the true discoverers who know where to look for the real zodiacal signs in our human darkness? Come, Gewlie! Come, Lordy!"

And incontinently, taking advantage of the abnormal and almost embarrassing quiescence into which everybody had fallen, including the attendants, who now acted like well-drilled troopers who had been disbanded, Father Wun led his submissive captives away. Past the other table he led them, past the group who had collected round Tottie Creambo and old Mr. Rumpibus, past the loiterers drifting towards the reading-room and the smoking-room, until he reached the foot of the stairs leading to the men's quarters.

It was as soon as Tenna turned her back on Gewlie and Lordy that she perceived old Rumpibus and Tottie. At the sight of them she forgot John altogether and walked straight towards them. John followed her somewhat anxiously, and the Catholics from the tea-party followed John.

Meanwhile the discomfited attendants, talking in a less

confident and less casual tone than was usual among themselves, came slowly behind.

"These gentry," thought John, as he became aware of their presence bringing up the rear and caught their murmurings, "will be giving short shrift to any *other* signs of revolt among us! Father Wun, is he? Well! With the help of Tenna, for to-night at least Father Wun has won!"

8

THE COMMANDER

"YOU DID it," whispered John to Tenna as soon as they stood together. "I thought that devil had beaten us! And he sure would have if it hadn't been for you. You're a wonder, you really are! Do you think the Father will put a spoke into his wheel?"

Tenna made no reply, and when he bent down to get a look at her face he was surprised and distressed to see an expression upon it he had never seen there before. It was an intent look and yet an abstracted look.

It was an awe-inspiring look and yet it was a wild and reckless look. It was the look of an agitated revolutionary torn between two very different if not opposite methods of revolt. In fact, Tenna's face had become an arena where a gladiatorial struggle was going on.

John followed her gaze. It was fixed upon the dignified and venerable old gentleman whose first name he had already discovered to be Zedekiah, commonly shortened to Zed, and whose surname was Rumpibus.

And suddenly John remembered Mr. Lordy's words about Tenna's crazy assault upon this old man soon after her arrival here two years ago. Yes, Tenna's eyes *were* fixed on Mr. Rumpibus now, and her whole body, as he could feel when he took hold of her arm above the elbow with his right hand, was quivering.

THE INMATES

But that she was struggling valiantly against her obsession was clear, for he could see the twitchings in her forehead, and he could see she had drawn her lower lip tightly into her mouth. This time he began to pray that the grumbling attendants behind him would intervene and pack Tottie off to the reading-room and old Rumpibus to the smoking-room—at any rate, separate them. Wasn't that sort of thing exactly what these cursed attendants were for?

Missy Creambo was obviously teasing her old gentleman with every accusation, tantalisation, provocation, instigation, manipulation, implication, improvisation, monopoligation, desquamation and titillation that came, it could hardly be said into her head, but into whatever nerve-centre connected with the head is dedicated to the exciting and provoking of what are popularly known as "the senses".

Although John had come to suspect from what he had already heard about him that the "Dean" of Glint Hall was an expert at drawing to his person every vibration of persecution, every brand of mockery, every gesture of provocation that occurred in his neighbourhood, it had never crossed his mind that this insanely masochistic old gentleman could have any effect on Tenna or revive that weird storm of perilous feeling that had swept through her when she first saw him two years ago.

"I must get her away," he thought. "I must take her to our corner in the smoking-room."

"Shall we—" he demanded of his companion in a tone sufficiently loud to be heard by those who were near and sufficiently conventional not to arouse the attention of those who were further away, "shall we have another game of draughts, if our place of last night hasn't been stolen by anybody?"

As he spoke he offered her his arm with as much natural ease as if they had been in a dancing-hall rather than in an institution, but she snatched at the wrist he offered and began whispering to him in a low, concentrated, agitated voice. What she was saying as the spluttered syllables and broken sentences, each one of them growing more disturbing and more startling, as it

THE COMMANDER

followed its predecessor, was a dramatic denunciation of Mr. Rumpibus.

"He leads her on," Tenna murmured. "Can't you see what he's doing? He's driving her crazy. He's forcing her to go further and further! He's drawing her on to make her strike him; and when once she does that, it'll be all up with her. She won't be able to restrain herself! She'll pick up something from somewhere, don't you see, that will really hurt him before them all! Oh, it maddens me to see him do it! He oughtn't to be allowed to do it!"

Tenna's silence when her whispers ceased was more agitating to John Hush than her words, for her clutch at his wrist tightened and the pressure of her pulse upon his pulse united them in a dim, blood-dark, cowering riot of throbbing dread that gave him the feeling that they were both wrapped in the same bundle of hunted guilt, a bundle that only wanted to roll, of its own volition, out of the room into the corridor, and out of the corridor down the staircase, and through the door into the garden, and out of the garden under those spikes under the bridge!

It was for John the most unpleasant moment he had had since his arrival in the place. And his discomfort was increased by the way the attendants were now obstinately pressing upon them from behind, longing—he could actually feel the vibration of this longing—to reassert themselves over the inmates after their defeat by Father Wun.

And John had also begun to be troubled by something much more serious: namely by the fact that he had begun to look at Tenna in a way he had prayed to avoid. This was due partly to the vibratory aura of Mr. Rumpibus and partly to a telepathic wave of suspicious viciousness from the attendants behind him, who were obviously jostling both Tenna and himself towards the reading-room in the manner of silent but sharp-toothed sheep-dogs who can hardly wait for some of their flock to behave badly so that a modicum of barking if not of biting might be in order.

Until this unfortunate minute his feeling for Tenna had

THE INMATES

been entirely ideal and romantic. He worshipped the startling originality of her mind; and as for her strange, aloof, evasive face, it reminded him of the angel in the Virgin of the Rocks with the long-extended finger pointing towards the divine child.

But now at this confused and disturbed moment he couldn't resist staring at one particular wisp of her hair disarranged in her present agitation and twisted into the special kind of tangle, that, for some fabulous cause which none of the doctors who had dealt with his case could discover, his demon made him so desperate to clip, cut, carry off, and keep, till, perhaps—oh, madness!—he burnt it with a match.

Yes, this was the first time since they had met that his curious perversity had brought *her* into the circle of its casting-net. John Hush was not one to miss the appalling seriousness of this shock to his feeling for Tenna. The danger hit him a blow in his most vulnerable place.

"This will never do!" he groaned, and in the strength of his trouble he uttered these words aloud.

"Never do, never do, young man," echoed one of the attendants with a patronising chuckle just behind his back. "No, it'll never do, will it?" the man jeered on. "Never, never do, will it?"

When they had all been projected into the corridor, and John was beginning to feel just as if the two of them really were in serious truth the congealed and aggregated bundle he had imagined them, they were accosted, or rather Tenna was accosted, by the only inmate of Glint Hall who actually behaved as if he *were* out of his mind; that is to say, who behaved in the manner in which most visitors to lunatic-asylums find the inmates behaving—not as ninnies, freaks, antics, and mountebanks, nor as howling, ranting, gesticulating, gibbering, posturing, dribbling, chattering maniacs, nor acting like so many perambulating images of absolute silence or moving masks of irrevocably sealed damnation, but very much as ordinary people.

This was the ex-naval officer, Commander Serius-Ocius, who, after his famous infatuation for Weeny Wimple, the

THE COMMANDER

beautiful Tahitian dancer, had retired to the Canary Islands. It must have been his unfortunate return to London from this pleasant retreat that disturbed the balance of his mind. For, once in London, Commander Serius-Ocius got into the habit of behaving in such a manner outside the entrance to Parliament that his conduct compelled the Cabinet to introduce a Private Bill, the passing of which enabled the Home-Secretary, in the interests of the state, to place the gallant gentleman in some appropriate home.

"Are you two people going," enquired the Commander of our friends, bowing before them, as the poet says, most politely, "to the reading-room or to the smoking-room?"

At this point-blank and perfectly direct challenge John Hush would certainly have extemporised some absolutely fantastic excuse, if he hadn't just then had the double shock of discovering that not only his new girl-friend but his new-made self—yes, the unfamiliar new self which had been born of his resolve to make the way smooth for his guardian's union with the beautiful American—were both liable, quite apart from their private affinity, to relapse into their original and totally different aberrations.

So disturbed, indeed, were both our friends by the scene that was going on between Mistress Creambo and old Rumpibus that they were forced to gaze blankly at each other for a second or two in order to realise what these places were to which Commander Serius-Ocius was referring when he talked of reading-rooms and smoking-rooms. Then, speaking simultaneously, and far too impulsively to bother about what words they used, they assured him they were going to the smoking-room.

"Not to play cards, I hope?" remarked the officer from the Canary Islands.

"Oh no!" cried Tenna. "Mr. Hush and I aren't at all sociable. If we did anything, we'd play draughts."

"Will you let me share your draughts for half an hour?" enquired the Commander.

Again they were compelled to look at each other; and their looks carried the bewildered blankness that a boy and a girl

THE INMATES
might have displayed if in the midst of sailing toy boats on the Serpentine they had been suddenly accosted by a foreigner in a turban, who wanted to know the way to the Tower.

"We can find—we can show—we can share," responded Tenna, with what was at once a curiously eager and a completely absent-minded voice.

"By all means," John assured him. "We'll take you straight to where we were sitting last night. It's a quiet corner, and there'll be no need to play draughts or indeed play anything else if you don't want to. There'll be no need to do anything at all! It really is a quiet corner, isn't it, Tenna?"

But the girl, with her fingers still clutching his wrist and, if it is permissible to say so, teleporting him forward by a sort of streamlined vibration of invisible will, was far too absorbed in watching Tottie Creambo and Mr. Rumpibus moving towards the reading-room, from which already came the sound of piano-playing, to take any part in this propitiation of the Commander from the Canaries. Miss Creambo's yellow hair had never been twisted more loosely round her small head, nor had the old black-silk dress that clung to her voluptuous torso and rounded limbs ever given its wearer a more languorous droop or a more enticing allure.

John found it difficult not to imagine himself entering the lists against old Rumpibus, for there could be no disputing Tottie's lecherous desirability. And though he couldn't bring himself to share Tenna's solicitude for Miss Creambo, as opposed to the subtle provocations of Mr. Rumpibus, he was intensely fascinated by that gentleman's exquisitely ascetic features and by the indescribable deftness with which he manipulated his clean-shaven spiritual profile, causing it to cut its way like the prow of a wave-clipping vessel through all those siren enticements, even while he dizzied himself and dazzled himself and dallied and dangled and danced in the aura of that heavy yellow hair and those luxurious caress-inviting curves.

But the Commander from the Canaries, now that he'd grappled with them, was not to be lightly thrown off; and it only needed a second or two of uneasy tension before the

THE COMMANDER

disappearance of Miss Tottie's yellow hair and silk-swathed limbs, followed by the incisive and almost papal profile of Mr. Rumpibus—just in time, John couldn't help thinking, to avoid being beheaded by the reading-room door—threw the two friends completely into his power.

And the Commander lost no time in boarding the vessel he had captured. There was no great stir, nor any particular flurry of speculation as the three of them entered the smoking-room and made their way between the tables to last night's corner. Yes, the waste-paper receptacle was still there, and the draught-board with its opposing black and white bodyguards was still there; and it was easy for John Hush, who for all the Commander's quarterdeck presence of mind was much more socially alert, to borrow, with hurried apologies, an empty armchair, a chair much more suited to a philosophical symposium than to a round game; and ensconced in this throne "out of time", as Father Toby might have called it, or "out of space", as Father Wun might have corrected him, Serius-Ocius of the Canaries dropped anchor.

John Hush and Tenna Sheer sat as still as mice listening to the murmur of his hypnotising voice and struggling with all their concentrated attention to follow his startling ideas. They kept their eyes fixed upon him, never once, as most lovers would have felt compelled to do, exchanging a glance of sympathetic bewilderment, and never once, not by as much as one timid question, interrupting the flow of his words.

The Commander was no mean exponent of original ideas when once he was fairly launched. He was a clean-shaved man of about fifty, with closely cut grey hair; unusually small ears, growing as near to his skull as seemed possible if they were to fulfil the purpose of ears; a large, leathery, weather-beaten face; a mouth that was permanently open with a painfully striving look that suggested hard-drawn laboriously-taken breaths and an intelligence concentrated, at the cost of a well-concealed strain and at the risk of the snapping of some secret muscle or dynamic valve or metallic spring, on the single and sole purpose of keeping the ship afloat.

THE INMATES

Since every inmate of Glint Hall had strong ideas about every other inmate's most intimate case-history, it was a commonplace of gossip that Commander Serius-Ocius had officially been directed to take a prolonged holiday under Doctor Echetus by reason of a peculiar habit he had fallen into of waylaying Members of Parliament of both parties on their way to Westminster and informing them of the absolute necessity of being more philosophical in their attitude to public affairs if the ship of state was to weather the present storm.

Little did the incorruptible officer know that this wisdom of the ancients to which he desired to recall the rulers of our lives to-day had never been more realistically justified than in the immediate effect of his personality to-night on these two agitated friends.

John Hush, as he listened to him, was telling himself that his own particular mania, a purely erotic one, was no illusion, no hallucination, no fixed idea of an erroneous kind. The curls of girls *were* alluring. Only fanatical miscreants and ferocious misogynists could deny it. His trouble was therefore purely a matter of degree. To *look* at a girl's hands or knees or mouth or neck or bosom or ankles or eyebrows or hair with delirious and dissolving ecstasy could not be called insane. It was legitimate fetish-worship and had multitudinous roots in Nature; indeed, as used by Nature in a myriad ways for the propagation of life.

But was insanity used by Nature? Well, maybe it was! John sucked in his lower lip in a grimace that with him took the place of that mysterious mental gesture that people call "smiling to themselves". But at any rate for to-night, with Tenna herself so upset by *her* lack of degree, or proportion, or whatever it was, in *her* particular mania, it was hardly a moment to dally with the limits of Nature's indulgence.

In a fierce effort to forget what deliciousness it would be to snip off that maddening brown tress which at the moment wasn't only "disarrayed", as the poet Spenser would call it, but was damp with tie perspiration of agitation as well as of the heat of the room, John Hush now set himself to stare at

THE COMMANDER

the Commander's mouth, which revealed what his eyes and nose and chin and the whole shape of his skull did their utmost to conceal, namely the desperateness of the man's obsessed concentration.

At several of the card-playing tables in their neighbourhood people looked at each other between the moves of their game with a vague faint quizzical amusement, as much as to say: "Poor wretches! That's what comes of being kind to the father of all bores!"

What the card-players couldn't see, and what the Members of Parliament he waylaid couldn't see, was that this competent and experienced naval officer, whose eyes and nose and chin and forehead were to the highest degree professional, conventional and class-conditioned, revealed not only by the words that issued from his mouth but by the form and imprint, by the psychological tension and stress-moulded expression of the mouth out of which they proceeded, a power of spirit that was positively apostolic. They couldn't see that in the course of every single day and in the course of every single night, whether he were awake or asleep, for it was a peculiarity of Commander Serius-Ocius to practise his philosophy in his dreams, the spirit of this man gave orders from the quarterdeck of Nature to the rudder of the human ship, directing its course and navigating it through windless calms as well as through water-spouts and typhoons.

"I've been waiting for you two," was what he was now telling our friends. "Yes, waiting for you; for I knew by the law of averages that, if I stayed in this place for as long as they let me stay, the chances were that I should find the undivided persona humana. As somebody says in the Symposium of Plato, men and women were once one person, a person who must have moved through life in a circular manner . . . in fact like a wheel . . . and I have learnt from this inspired hint that an 'undivided persona' . . . such as is formed by the conjunction of certain unusually harmonious lovers like yourselves . . . is bound to understand me . . . for when this person . . . I mean the 'undivided persona' . . . who advances into truth like a

THE INMATES

wheel . . . hears my message . . . yes, when this circular person, this undivided person, this 'persona humana', as you might say, 'in the round ', this real two-in-one who is much more divine, as Pythagoras taught, than any Trinity, being wholly free from the diabolical taint of odd numbers and wholly embodied in the divine potency of even numbers . . . when this two-in-one catches, that is to say when *you two*, my dear friends, who are now listening to me, catch the drift of my message, you will understand why the truth has been delivered to me once for all by great creative Nature and why it is that she compels me to tell the rulers of land and sea how to rule and the creatures of land and sea how to be ruled."

He paused at this point and looked in turn at his two hearers. He looked at Tenna first and was at once aware of a wave of tenderness towards him, but at the same time was conscious of an intangible spiritual something, a sort of shimmering opalescent resistant object that was about the size of an ordinary dish-cover and which she seemed to have the power, while she shot at him eager, hurried, sympathetic, and even appealing glances, of projecting from her bosom, like a Highland target or Homeric buckler, as if to make sure no unfair advantage was being taken of her yielding mood.

Oh, how well did Commander Serius-Ocius know the various sensations of pride, some exciting, some soothing, some *Just there*, to be put up with, as he would put up with the advertisements in an absorbing magazine—that he experienced now! But his pride soon had a fall. With his left hand resting on the rim of the waste-paper receptacle, and his skull pressing against the side of the raggedly-covered wooden back of his faded armchair, his exultation made his receptivity so intense that his conversion of our lovers actually began to be seriously interrupted by the sub-human consciousness of this same ancient chair whose last-century mischief and antiquated malevolence began obscurely teasing this polite occupier of a piece of furniture formerly used by chair-ridden great-aunts with large tabby cats on their laps.

The Commander now surveyed the young couple before him

THE COMMANDER

with the neatly arranged draught-board pressing against her silky black sash and against his silver watch-chain, and it struck him how easily at a signal from some Doctor Echetus in the world of the inanimate that draught-board might obediently cut them both asunder and reduce them to a half-woman and a half-man!

Ah, and how well did he know the sensation he now experienced as he watched those young heads in front of him and saw behind them all those card-players so absorbed in their games that they were like a fleet of little skiffs in a great mist, diminishing, dilating, advancing, receding, outlining themselves with menacing clarity, and then again vanishing like phantoms!

And then the Commander looked from the young woman to the young man, and as he did so a whole set of disturbing memories assailed him. His own grey sleeve about the wrist of the hand that dallied with the rubbish-box exchanged itself for a much darker one with gleaming official stripes, and he felt as if he ought to be uttering brief, clear, practical, technical words of command; anything but strange intimations of mystical wisdom!

But now instead of those old mechanically jerked-out laconic syllables such as, "yes sir! no sir! three feet to starboard, sir!" what he heard from the young man opposite him were the diplomatic words: "I don't want to tire you with questions, Commander, but if you could put into a plain and simple sentence the chief points of your new philosophy it would be of the greatest interest to us both. Miss Sheer has been very good to me since I arrived yesterday afternoon and I hope you too, sir, will help me with your advice. It isn't easy, is it, sir, to get reconciled to the routine of a place like this? But Miss Sheer tells me the worst feelings come *after* a patient has just got through the first settling down. There's a revulsion, she says, that comes then, that is worse than any of the first shocks, because there's an unpleasant sense of the thing going on—if you can follow me, sir?—for a rather long time—going on, in fact, if you will let me put it crudely, *for ever*."

THE INMATES

From its expression of simple concern Commander Serius-Ocius's face became a living mask of heroic compassion. Both the young people opposite him were regarding him with the look of a pair of precocious children who in the midst of an elaborate game have got themselves, for all their cleverness, into such appalling trouble that they can't get out of it without the help of a competent as well as a kind policeman.

"Well, well, well, well!" he repeated sympathetically. "It's clear that you two are born—yes; I can't refrain from saying so—born to be recipients of my doctrine. And it's very simple. That's the beauty of it, my dear children; it's so very simple. All you've got to use is your mind. And, mark you, it needn't be a clever mind. It needn't even be a sane mind. That's what people are too stupid to understand. It can be a crazy mind or a silly mind. It can even be an idiotic mind."

At this moment John Hush made a scarcely perceptible movement with his head so as to get one of his eyes, his left eye as a matter of fact, into focus with one of Tenna's.

"The mistake," the Commander went on, "that everybody makes, is to assume you have to be wise and clever and intellectual to get at the truth about life. My philosophy teaches the opposite of all that nonsense! You've got to clear your mind at the start of all other ideas. In fact you've got to clear your mind of *all* ideas! You've got to use your mind: that's what I teach. But not for the purpose of thinking. You've got to use your mind to stop yourself from thinking! What do you suppose our minds were made for? For the low, corrupting, insidious, perverse, drug-like vice of thinking? The gods forbid! The mind is far too rare a thing, too delicate a thing, too subtle a thing, too complicated a thing, too noble and sacred a thing, to be used for thinking! That would be like using a magic wand for a walking-stick or a porridge-spoon to move a manure-heap.

"The mind's everything. But you don't want to wash your feet in everything! The mind's air, water, earth, fire. It's life; it's death; it's the world; it's the end of world. A

THE COMMANDER

mad mind is simply a mad world. A weak mind is simply a weak world. There's nothing else, I tell you, my children, except reservoirs upon reservoirs of surplus matter.

"And don't forget this, my friends, you *are* your minds! When people talk about the soul surviving the body they're only reminding themselves of the importance of their minds! Our minds *are* our souls. Whether any of them succeeds in surviving death is a question none has ever answered or can ever answer. Our minds are surrounded by what used to be called 'matter' and now is called by a lot of other names.

"But calling it other names doesn't change its nature. Only one thing changes the nature of matter, and that is the diving into it of mind. It is by plunging your minds, my dear children, into what you touch, hear, see, smell and taste, that you endow poor, patient, humble, passive, enduring matter, which by itself is nothing, with all its magic attributes. They are all in you, for you are a multitude. Every self is a multitude and every self is a mind, and the plunging of every mind into matter creates a new world.

"That is why it is ridiculous to say that there is only one world. There are as many worlds as there are minds to plunge into matter, and these are beyond counting.

"And don't you see what a revolution this makes in our whole system of life? What do we all want? Only one thing, children, only one thing! To enjoy ourselves! But do we want to enjoy ourselves in the same way? Of course not. For no two of us are alike. Well then, what are the things that hinder us from enjoying ourselves? Who doesn't know the damned list? Pain first of all; then cold and hunger; then fear; then illness and discomfort; then disappointment, frustration, humiliation; then sex, sex in too big, or too little, or too eccentric doses; then some mental disturbance, such as those that get us here; and finally—and this is far the worst of the lot, save raving frenzy or extreme pain—what we call boredom, *ennui*, feeling dead-sick of everything!

"Now let me ask you a plain question, my children. Is there any way, even for a very short period of time, by which

THE INMATES

we can shake off these obstacles to enjoying ourselves? And, if there is, *what* is it? Well, children, I would answer this question at once. There is such a way. And I'll tell you what it is in one word. *Forgetting!*

"Great creative Nature has given us the power of forgetting everything except extreme pain. As we know well enough from our life in this place, madness doesn't necessarily follow a person into his sleep. Nobody sleeps sounder than a certified lunatic.

"*Before* you're certified you suffer from two quite special horrors. The first of these might be called the fear of insanity in general. The second can only be called by some very queer name known to the person who feels it and known to nobody else. In fact this horror I will call our personal and particular mania.

"*After* you're certified—at least this I understand to be the usual experience—you lose the dread of madness in general but in place of this you begin to experience an increased terror of what I might call your' old particular'. And now I come to a very peculiar phenomenon, and it is this. Though your horror of your 'old particular' is increased, when it is actually *upon you* you can endure it much more easily when you're 'certified' than you could before. And there is a curious reason for this. There emanates a certain aura from the pressure around us here of so many souls exerting their divine power of forgetting!

"There isn't an inmate among us here—no, *nor* an attendant"—and Commander Serius-Ocius gave a little jerk of his close-cropped gentlemanly skull in a direction that might be described as backward and upward—"who is not concentrating on forgetting. Nor is it concealed from any inmate of any asylum in this country that the attendants grow very quickly more dangerously demented than their patients. Thus, taking patients and attendants together—and of course it wouldn't do to exclude from these creators of such blessed clouds of oblivion the illustrious head of our institution—thus there is created here an aura of what might be called retrogressive nihilism, or the power of *uncreating the created*, the power, you might say, of unliving life, unsolidifying matter,

THE COMMANDER

unactualising reality, and of reducing the *is* to the level of the *is not*.

"Further than this, in the sublime art of' retrogressive nihilism', it would be difficult to go, unless we reduced the historic *was* to what never under any condition could possibly have been. But now I will tell you, my dear friends, what we've got to do with our minds instead of letting them give way to this worse than bestial vice, this *human* vice of thinking. I tell you we have perverted the true direction of Nature's spontaneous movement.

"Some devil has done it, some proud morbid degenerate depraved-perverted devil who has hated the large free motions of the stars in their courses, and of the constellations, and of the galaxies, and of the nebulae, and of the revolving planets! What we must do, my dear friends, is to break away for ever from this vicious, stinking, polluted, maniacal habit of using the mind to think!"

At this point the intense emotion surging up behind the Commander's own mind brought it about that his tone ceased to resemble either the tone of a quarterdeck voice, or the tone of a lights-burning-bright-sir voice, and became the kind of fatally well-known tone that in a second drew the two tall attendants towards the utterer of it.

"Pardon me, sir!" whispered John hurriedly, bending forward over the elbow of the Commander's armchair. "Pardon me, sir! I believe those officials are going to meddle with us!"

The naval man screwed up his eyes as if to look through a telescope. Then, turning his neatly-shaped head a little to one side, he closed one eye and surveyed the tall attendants through the other, as if he were measuring them from the mouth of a turret-gun in preparation for giving them a broad side fore and aft.

Relaxing after this, as if he really had disposed of them, he continued his disclosure in a quieter voice. "You will say," he went on, "that there's nothing for the mind to do if it stops thinking. I reply there is *everything* for it to do!"

As John listened, with his eye on the attendants and on some of the tables, too, where people had paused in their game, he

THE INMATES

began to wonder whether the leading statesmen of our island, as they were arrested by this ancient mariner on the threshold of Parliament, actually heard a single word of what he said ere they looked round wildly for a policeman.

"Sane people are really rather stupid," John said to himself, "to take no interest at all in our ideas. If Hamlet pretended madness and Don Quixote survived madness and Ajax died mad, madness can't be a negligible thing."

But Serius-Ocius had begun again. "A mind virgin to all thought," he said, "can become a diving-suit for the soul to enjoy itself in! I am not asserting that the mind is independent of the body. I'm only saying that it can take from our body, and from the bodily senses, and from time and space, all it needs to form a diving-suit, which, though remaining attached to the body by a sort of umbilical cord, has the power of plunging into any substance it likes outside itself.

"And now I arrive at my central point. What we all live for is happiness. And what is happiness? Happiness is a series of pleasures, of pleasures that in the long run satisfy us completely. Without a number of single pleasures, delicious in themselves, it's impossible to have any satisfying sequence of pleasures.

"And of what do single pleasures consist? They consist of *simple* pleasures; and here we reach what people call the heart of the matter. All matter is a mass of material outside ourselves. All pleasure is the sensation we experience when we plunge into something outside ourselves. Mind is the self within us and matter is the self without us.

"This plunge of the *self* into the *not-self* is what we call pleasure; and the more we enjoy this plunge, and the more often we make it, the more pleasure we get from life. Therefore we must struggle to disregard and forget all the impressions that hinder this plunge and we must force ourselves at every possible moment, and along with whatever else we may be doing, to keep a portion of our mind free not only to make the plunge but to immerse itself in the element into which it plunges."

THE COMMANDER

Commander Serius-Ocius's voice had again risen to a disturbing pitch and again certain of the groups of card-players had stopped their play to listen. The two attendants had now become three attendants and were clearly only waiting to pounce till it was unavoidably evident that the ex-naval man had gone far enough to justify his being placed in the punishment wing of the institute.

And suddenly the Commander, grown aware that there was opposition to him in the room and a hostile silence, leapt to his feet.

"It is my duty," he cried in a thundering voice, "to announce to everyone here the beginning of a new world! The new world will not be given us by religion, nor will it be discovered for us by science, but it will be created by ourselves as if we were gods! We shall create it out of the reservoir of ever-fresh material which lies at the back of space and time. I have only been able to discover this because of my training in the Navy, and it is as a discovery of the Navy that I announce——"

But to John's and Tenna's consternation the attendants had laid hold of him now and were taking him by the arm as he stood confronting the whole room as if he was quelling a mutiny at sea. With his compact close-cropped skull, his straight figure, his square shoulders, his hands in the side-pockets of his grey well-fitting jacket, he looked as if he were the Admiral of all the West defending the Straits of Gibraltar from an armada of Mongols.

9

HAMMER AND NAILS

THE TWO attendants who had seized the Commander by his arms were not his only menace. There was a third person there, who was already beginning to unfold with scientific nicety what Tenna from her experience of the place knew well

THE INMATES

as a special kind of strait-waistcoat recently invented by Doctor Echetus and which had the peculiarity of being able to be compressed into so small a space that it could be carried about in the pocket of any attendant who understood how to slip it neatly and quickly over a patient's unruly torso and rebellious arms.

But suddenly the attention of each of the three keepers as well as of their powerful antagonist, was diverted by an excited inrush of a new crowd of inmates who bursting into the room began calling out: "Where is Commander S.O.? We want Commander S.O.! The Father says Commander S.O. is mentioned in the paper this morning! The Father says the paper says Commander S.O.——"

Undeterred by the presence of the three attendants, the newcomers, whom Hush recognised at once as the group of Catholics he had met at tea, were soon hurrying and scrambling into our friend's corner. They were all excited and they were all in high spirits.

"Had they," John asked himself, "been crowding round the door of Mr. Lordy's bedroom in the hope of seeing in the flesh some palpable exorcism of Satan? And had their enthusiasm for righteousness taken the form of hero-worship for the Navy?"

Suddenly John Hush saw Mr. Lordy among them. But it was a Mr. Lordy in a transformed mood. The cloud of predestined insignificance which habitually emanated, like a subhuman aura from the man's eyes, nose, mouth, forehead, cheeks, chin, head, neck, shoulders, hips, legs and feet, had, so to say, changed its colour. It was still there, this emanation of something as typically and normally insignificant as the smell of a fox is foxy or the smell of a fish is fishy; but it was no longer blurred by the smoke of self-contempt.

It was as unobtrusive as ever, but it was satisfied to be itself. Its radiation, like a wavering flickering of light following the dragging footsteps of some unknown tramp-saint, caused its possessor no embarrassment.

He felt no pride in it. But if he ever were conscious of it,

HAMMER AND NAILS

it gave him a faintly agreeable sensation, like a small acid-drop in the mouth.

"This must be," thought John Hush, "the magic of the Church of Rome. How on earth can that Father have worked it? Did they all see him putting the fear of God into Gewlie? No, that wasn't the way the Church of Rome did things! Father Wun must have won again by some subtle appeal to some secret virtue in this horrible man known to nobody else; and this momentary release from his obsession must have created such a vacuum in the soul of the egregious Gewlie that the living waters of natural feeling must have rushed to that spot from every quarter of the compass and brimmed up so over-poweringly in the soul of everybody there that they had to find an outlet in some traditional popular channel, which of course the accident of the Commander being mentioned in the paper had beautifully supplied."

But that gentleman's voice was being raised again to its more than quarter-deck resonance and John Hush noticed that one of the attendants, the one with the Doctor's patent strait-waistcoat, had vanished from the scene; doubtless to fetch reinforcements for the forces of order.

In desperation he turned to Tenna, who was standing by herself with a strained and troubled frown and with her eyes on the door of the room. She clearly was listening intently; and John's imagination began conjuring up a sea-fight wherein the rest of them were all engaged on deck while she alone at the stem of the vessel was scanning the horizon in the expectation of the spouting of a whale.

Alas! John knew only too well who his friend's whale was! It was a human person. It was that old gentleman who not only derived satisfaction from being teased, tormented, and tantalised by Tottie Creambo, but would have derived a similar satisfaction from being beaten up by Tenna for permitting such liberties to be taken with him by Tottie!

"For God's sake, tell me how to quiet him!" John now kept whispering in Tenna's ears. "Listen to me, Tenna! For God's sake listen to me! We must quiet him before any more

THE INMATES

of them come! They'll keep him shut up for months if we let him go on, and you know how he'll feel if they do that!"

At last she heard him. With a deep sigh that seemed to shake her whole body, her tension relaxed, and very slowly, as if on the countenance of a patient recovering by degrees from an anaesthetic, a whimsical smile flitted across her face. What puzzled John as completely as it delighted him was that she didn't seem to need any further elucidation of that moment's crisis or of what had to be done. She seemed to awake from her own private grief straight into the Commander's private grief, and to understand them both equally well. She was like a sea-bird who has dived after a fish, and who now, safely returned to the surface, flies through the air with as much knowledge of what that more rarified element requires of it as it displayed beneath the water when it caught the fish.

And what she did now was as astonishing to John as was the calm and collected assurance with which she did it. She went straight to Mr. Lordy and had a hurried word with him; a word which John, who was watching her with as much anxiety as he was feeling for the Commander, felt impelled to overhear.

"Can you remember, Mr. Lordy," she asked him in a clear whisper, "what it was you told *him*?"—and she gave her head a little jerk in the direction of the Commander, who was now standing, though the men were not actually touching him, with an attendant on each side.

"I mean," she continued, "that night he was so excited on the staircase and what you said calmed him down so completely."

Seldom had John Hush felt more respect for a living creature than he felt for Mr. Lordy at that second. The intense guilelessness of the puzzled and baffled gaze the man turned upon Tenna would have made anyone, he decided, trust him with their wife, their child, their country, and their country's gods!

"What did I say to him? Oh, Miss Tenna, please believe me when I tell you I had nothing I *could* say to him. But wait

HAMMER AND NAILS

—wait! Doesn't it say in the Bible or in Shakespeare, 'Nothing can come of nothing?' Oh, but I *do* remember now! I told him about Lieutenant Lordy, a member of our family in the what-do-you-call-it century when there was a hole in the ship and the water was rushing in and our relative said to him—I mean to the captain, or admiral, or whatever he was then—I mean to Lord Nelson—'If you please, sir,' our relative said, 'we'll be in Davy Jones' locker by this time to-morrow!' And all Lord Nelson answered—and our relative remembered his very words, because when he was paid off and back home, as you might say, he was took by what in those what-do-you-call-them days they called 'horse's fever' and he repeated Lord Nelson's very words to the Reverend who was anointing him, and that's how he came to be called 'Lord Nelson's Pint' because you'd only to treat him to a pint and the admiral's very words were yours——"

By this time not only John Hush but everybody within hearing, including Commander Serius-Ocius himself and each of the two attendants, was listening intently; nor did it take John very many minutes to become aware that the attendants had begun to edge away as rapidly and imperceptibly as they could, and had even begun to present the appearance of having no longer any particular interest in that corner of the room.

It was at that critical moment that John perceived that the man with Doctor Echetus's latest invention in his pocket had returned, but was now whispering rather foolishly and even crossly to his reinforcements and was clearly sending them off whence they'd come.

"And what," enquired Tenna, who had gathered up, John could see, into an invisible ball of gossamer thread the whole psychic aura of this improvement in the situation, "did Lord Nelson actually say to your ancestor, Mr. Lordy?"

The little man shut his eyes as if to shut out a world made up of imaginary horrors created by the activity of those accursed "thoughts" whose perilous frivolity the Commander wished to restrain. "What our relative told Lord Nelson," he announced, "was that they'd all be dead men by that time

THE INMATES

to-morrow; and what Lord Nelson replied was: 'Pump at the water—hammer at the nails! Leave till to-morrow who sinks or sails!'"

John stepped back a pace or two then, and so did Tenna, for it became clear that Mr. Lordy's tone in uttering this quotation, quite as much as the quotation itself, had saved the day. It was a commonplace tone and it was a conventional tone, but it was a tone that in its very conventionality conveyed so clearly the familiar picture painted by the Lord of Hosts himself all over our old island of brown beer in pewter-mugs, of leather-trodden sawdust on uneven floors, of mongrel dogs lifting grateful legs against whitewashed posts, of creaking sign-boards, and finally of "the wind and the rain and a little tiny wit making content with our fortunes fit", that it swept into Doctor Echetus's laboratory for lost dogs and demented men as if it brought a nepenthe that could redeem all sorrows and assuage all pain. At any rate, the strait-waistcoat expert and his colleagues had vanished, while the attendants who had been at the Commander's elbow had not even resumed their perambulation of the room but had seated themselves at a table near the door and were now sedately smiling at each other as they alternately shook a dice-box.

All this, John Hush soon realised, was no miracle. He had only to lend an ear to what the Commander, who had reseated himself in his armchair, was now saying to Mr. Lordy, to understand what the strait-waistcoat man, the second he came back, had realized in a flash, that—pro tem, anyway—the devil of insanity had been driven out and Commander Serius-Ocius was once more a quiet and competent ex-officer of the fleet.

Mr. Lordy himself, who had worked this temporary cure of the most distinguished of his fellow-inmates, solely and simply by becoming a medium for all the undistinguished persons who, from the furthest Hebrides to the Scilly Isles, had in the last hundred years uttered, and with no particular emphasis, the word "Nelson", was only anxious now that these well-meaning but abjectly heretical pair of friends should not altogether miss the significance of the coming among them, even for a brief hour or two, of a priestly successor to the apostolic revealers of the one Truth.

It can be believed that neither of our friends was lacking in interest in the fate of Attendant Gewlie nor at the same time very surprised to learn that since the particular kind of wickedness in which the wretch was such a master was not a "mortal" but only a "venial" sin, this weasel-like pursuer of human rabbits had not even been threatened with dismissal from Glint Hall. Well, he would only have gone to another asylum if he had been dismissed from this one; and, after all, there *was* his maniacal terror of Mr. Frogcastle to restrain him here, not to speak of Father Wun's awareness of his horrible vice.

"You were saying, sir—" John hesitatingly observed, for though the last thing he wanted to do was to arouse the officer's nervous eloquence again, he knew from his own feelings that while Tenna and he were, so to speak, in the psychic attitude, sitting at the man's feet, it would be embarrasing and difficult to attempt any sort of ordinary give-and-take conversation, "you were saying that the purpose of life is to enjoy ourselves. I didn't want to interrupt you then, but I'd be so grateful, sir, and I'm sure my friends Miss Sheer and Mr. Lordy would say the same, if you'd tell us a little more about your ideas as to the enjoyment of life and where we young ones are apt to get things mixed up.

"I don't want to bother you, sir, if you feel too tired to talk any more"—John added this after a pause, a pause too craftily short, however, for the officer to take advantage of it —"but I'd like to know, and so, I'm sure would my friends here, a little more about this 'plunging' you spoke of into all these various forms and colours of matter, and why it is that this brings us pleasure so deep that such pleasure can be regarded as the purpose of life."

The expression upon the officer's face as he listened to this crafty rigmarole touched John Hush to the heart. He longed to exchange glances with Tenna, who would he felt sure share this spasm of *tendresse*. Chance was as tender to him, however, as he felt towards the Commander, for had he met Tenna's

THE INMATES

look he would have found it unsympathetic. She was prepared to help the officer against the authorities, but when she perceived on his face the masculine unction of mental superiority and the philosophic pride of being in a position to "lay down" as we say, "the law", a fierce jet of rebelliousness shot through her veins, and the officer's face, that face which to John held a touching revelation of boyish simplicity in its glow of triumphant exposition, became an epitome of all she loathed most in the world; became, in fact, what the world loves to call "benign and fatherly".

John's chance-given luck certainly held out during the whole length of what followed, for if he had glanced but once into her face he would have been thunderstruck by its expression.

Mr. Lordy did glance at it; and what he saw compelled him to say to himself, "I wish the Father knew what a good Catholic this girl would be! I'm sure he'd try to convert her. She's the sort of girl who'd make a perfect mother to half a dozen obedient souls. She knows that all insanity comes from pride and can only be really exorcised, as the Father said upstairs just now, through that slit in the skin *we* call 'humility', that slit in the skin for which the angels have a heavenly word of their own!"

What had specially struck Mr. Lordy about Tenna was something that John, just because he was listening to her so intently, hadn't noticed—namely the startling difference between her profile and her full face. "She's a queer one," thought Mr. Lordy. "She's both a profile-girl and a full-face girl!"

And, indeed, Mr. Lordy's verdict approached the truth. Tenna *was* both these things. In profile, her soft dead-white skin was emphasised by the way her brown hair, hair that was so fine and filmy that it naturally clung together in smooth masses, fell so thickly, like a heavy shadow, over her ear and across the side of her face. Her delicate aquiline nose and small soft chin, together with the tender fluctuating lines at the corner of her mouth, indicative of the exquisitely childish curves with which her lips would part, composed a living portrait that simply and entirely vanished, like the vanishing of a lovely ghost at cockcrow, the moment she turned her head and you saw her full face. Then you realised how pitilessly her unbalanced sensibility, her subhuman shyness, her morbid shrinking from contact with events and people, hurt her and lacerated her; then you realised how all the complicated habits she had acquired of taking life so much harder than others took it left her suffering from a malady that might well have been called the malady of *being a skin short*.

The more he studied the girl's look, the more sorry for her Mr. Lordy became. It must be, he told himself, the absence from her life of the help of a good priest that caused her front-face to differ from her side-face and to be lined with an anxiety so far beyond the natural wont of her years. She had four deep perpendicular lines descending her forehead and no less than four horizontal ones—very faint, it is true, but the carefully concerned Mr. Lordy was able to count them in that electric-lit corner—crossing her forehead, while her eye-sockets were so deep, and the troubled brown orbs within them so swiftly moving and so glittering with a dangerously intent lustre, that Mr. Lordy experienced a sympathetic shock as she talked to him and even began vaguely wondering if there were anything that a simple person could do to ease her agitation.

One thing he could see clearly. The interest that her young friend Mr. Hush appeared to be taking in this voluble gentleman from the Royal Navy was extremely painful to her. All seven frowns, both the perpendicular ones and the horizontal ones, obviously deepened every time she looked in the Commander's direction, while her eyes in their hollow sockets almost ceased to be brown and took to themselves a peculiarly alarming golden tint as if she were some weird kind of metamorphosed bird—a sandpiper, perhaps, Mr. Lordy thought, considering her long thin limbs!—who might suddenly begin flying round the room and beating its wings against the walls!

But the officer's words, as fascinating to John Hush as they were infuriating to Tenna Sheer, were now beginning to arrest Mr. Lordy's own distracted attention.

THE INMATES

"We can't get away from it," Serius-Ocius was saying. "The 'I' in us—and that is of course the mind that uses our body and its senses—is the only soul we've got. The first great mistake a typical Member of Parliament makes is to assume that, because thought can't function without a thinker, there must be *within* the body, though quite capable of slipping out of it in sleep, or in a trance, or at death, a queerly functioning, formless entity called a 'soul'.

"According to this idea we are presented with the quaint situation of not only possessing two *thinkers* for one set of *thoughts* but with the danger that if one of these' thinkers ', for instance this fantastic butterfly called the 'soul', were to slip out of the body and take a holiday, whether in a sleep or a trance, it might take the mind's thoughts—that is to say *our* thoughts, the thoughts of our mind-self or the living thing that says 'I am I'—along with it, so that we should be left with nothing but a dumb, deaf, blind unconscious self, every one of whose thoughts have been stolen by the runaway soul.

"I well remember being told once by one of these political rogues—I think it was the Member for Wash Lane, the second son of the first Lord Antimacassar—that his soul always left his body when he was asleep.

"'You don't dream, then?' I said. 'Oh yes,' he cried, 'I'm a terrific dreamer!'

"'But how,' I protested, 'can an animal body deserted by the creature inside it which thinks, that is to say deserted by its own consciousness, have any dreams at all?'

"That *did* stump him, and he began at once, as they always do when defeated in argument, looking round for a policeman. You see now, don't you, my children, the mistake our preposterous rulers make? They are convinced that all thoughts must be the thoughts of thinkers—whereas, of course, there isn't a single traveller by sea who hasn't come upon derelict thoughts drifting on the waves like seaweed, and there isn't a traveller by road who hasn't come upon wind-piled ridges of desert-sand where thoughts are buried thick as the shards of beetles in the cracks of forgotten sepulchres.

HAMMER AND NAILS

"What these same Members of Parliament—good easy men! —are inclined to do, in their anxiety to fob off their thoughts upon their butterfly soul, is to forget that what we call our 'thoughts', speaking in the plural, are really only another name for the inexplicable phenomenon, speaking in the singular, that we call our consciousness. You can find lost 'thoughts' drifting about like fallen leaves or floating seaweed, but it is only from the consciousness in some sort of living creature that they are originally born."

Mr. Lordy had completely given up any further attempt to follow the peculiar reasoning of the man who thought he could teach philosophy to Members of Parliament; but it came rushing into his mind how quaint it would be if the souls of people really *could* leave their bodies and go roaming about! "Suppose," so he thought in his secret heart, "Father Wun were at this minute watching our proceedings and listening to our conversation; and suppose Father Toby came floating by, like a sea-urchin, mounted upon some great squid-like jelly-fish thing, would I be glad or sorry to see them fight?

"And what would they look like? Oh, how queer it all is! Why are people so odd-looking, anyway, quite apart from their souls? And why should there be people at all? Or a world at all? Or anything at all?"

At this point the Commander bent forward eagerly in his chair and the weird thought crossed the consciousness of John, who was watching the man's worn handsome excited face very earnestly, that his own ambassadorial politeness, learnt in the Balkans and which he knew had become a habit with him, was acting upon this honest sailor like a magic spell, and indeed was having an extremely curious effect on him drawing out from him, as if by an hypnotic process, thoughts and feelings such as in the natural course of events he would have hesitated to express even to those indignant Members of Parliament he was wont to waylay.

"A person's mind," the officer went on with impassioned vehemence, "is himself, his identity, his individuality, his conscious ego. We all of us feel this mind-self within us to be

THE INMATES

connected with our body, but yet at the same time we feel it to be independent of our body. But what we do *not* feel is that its self-consciousness, its power of realising its past as well as its present, its future as well as its past, is the self-consciousness of a living thing *within* our *body*, a living thing that could leave our body and go moving about quite freely through time and space. We do not feel this because it isn't there to feel.

"There is no soul to go rampaging about. What exists is our self-consciousness, our mind-self, and this, though we feel it to be independent of the body, we also feel it to be dependent upon the body. It is more than the body; but, while the body lives it can only escape from the body in imagination and in dreams. And thus I come, my dear boy——"

Mr. Lordy, who was growing more and more concerned by the expression of Tenna's face, by the gleam in her eyes and by the deepening lines on her forehead, told himself at this point that it was only just in time the officer *had* thrown in "my dear boy" and *had* lowered his voice and concentrated so definitely upon John Hush. "She'd have flown at him in a second," Mr. Lordy told himself, "just as she did at old Rumpibus that day."

"Thus I come," went on the Commander, "to my answer to your question about pleasure and happiness. These things indeed *are* the whole purpose of life. Faith, hope, and charity; truth, beauty, science and art; passion and compassion; all these are precious to us only in so far as they make us happy, only in so far as they enable us to enjoy life. And the point of it is that the nature of our ego, of our mind-self, the nature of this 'I am I' that is *not* lurking, like an ambiguous parasite, under our skin, but is the companion and mate of our old familiar doomed-to-perish dust-and-ashes body, the nature of our mind-self is such that when it plunges into the forms and colours, the sounds and scents, the atmospheres and wandering airs, of the elements that surround our body—when, I say, it resolves itself into these things, sinks into them, immerses itself in them, loses itself in them, and yet, by that

HAMMER AND NAILS

mysterious principle in life, which Jesus seems to have snatched from the air, draws out of them a magical nourishment, then and then only is it happy and content.

"It is this immersion of the mind-self in whatever it may be it chooses to feed upon, that constitutes its secret of enjoying itself; and we must never forget—— "

But here the Commander was compelled to drop his dominating flagship tone; not because anybody contradicted him, still less because anyone was jeering at him, but solely because there wasn't a single person at that moment listening to a word he said. Not that the Commander's voice ceased at that point. It went on. He was a determined gentleman and he had a message. And this message was to the broken intellects and drifting wits of the entire world. But he had ceased to lean eagerly forward, staring at John Hush. He had relaxed. He had stretched himself out in his armchair. He was twisting a large signet-ring with a Roman goddess engraved on it, along with the words "Sooner or Later", round and round the third finger of his left hand.

Nor would it be true to declare that, though the three persons he imagined himself converting had ceased to listen, and though Tenna was hating him, and Mr. Lordy was puzzled by him, and John's mind was wandering from him to Halfway House, the words he was uttering were wholly lost.

On the contrary, while Tenna held her hands over her face without being able to stop herself from glaring through her own fingers at those seafaring fingers twisting that classical ring, and while John thought, "*Will* she agree to marry him before Midsummer Day comes and changes everything?" Mr. Lordy, who had caught the phrase "constitutes the secret of enjoyment" discovered that the word "constitute" had a potent effect upon him. Mr. Lordy felt compelled to repeat the word. "Constitute, constitute," he muttered. "Constitute, constitute."

And it seemed to him as if the word "constitute" were a giant crane that had the power of seizing upon him and hoisting him up to heaven. Not unkindly nor clumsily was it ready to hoist him the moment he wished to be hoisted.

It hadn't intruded on him. It wasn't pushing itself forward. It had nothing in common with a bulldozer. *It was just there*, ready and able to hoist, anxious to hoist, but with no intention of hoisting until required by the hoisted.

Mr. Lordy began to feel faintly sleepy. "Not quite yet," he told the great being whose name was "constitute"—"I'm not quite ready to be hoisted; but I soon shall be—constitute—constitute—constitute."

10

THE ZEIT-GEIST

WHEN John Hush and Tenna Sheer had separated for the night, and John was once more alone in his bedroom, the first thing he did was to go straight up to the Rembrandt picture of the Supper at Emmaus and begin deliberately talking to the newly resurrected Christ as if he were Mr. Lordy; and, indeed, there was a remarkable resemblance between the unique painter's idea of how Jesus looked under that stone arch in the old inn and the way Mr. Lordy looked when seated at any meal in the Glint dining-room; and it struck John Hush with overwhelming force that the rays of divinity which were emanating from that timid, nervous, and unassuming person with such embarrassing persistence were a disturbing bewilderment to the man himself.

"Well, well!" John muttered. "So you can break bread in Doctor Echetus' research laboratory as well as anywhere else, can you? And that serving-boy can do his bit of day's work, can he, bringing you that fish's head to eat without bothering whether the fish-hook's still in its gill or not? Yes, by God! that boy can go on just the same, waiting at table and saving his wages and going to the bazaar to find a girl who can be kind, ard feeling no necessity to be more righteous than his parents or his playmates or to be so wise that he could say 'Rabbi' to

THE ZEIT-GEIST

the man under the arch when the others hailed him as master, and yet not be an absolute idiot in Israel!

"Yes, yes! Nor is there need—no need at all, is there, my little Lord Jesus—for this honest serving-boy to run round to the stable to see that the asses have water in case of their being wanted. He can bring the fish's head in, can't he, Lord Jesus, and carry it out, too, after the hungry travellers have scraped it clean, without worrying whether it was caught from the common beach or from the promontory preserved for Caesar's houschold?"

His mood changing again, John moved back to the door and turned off the light. This proceeding converted his bedroom into a twilit chamber in a city-wall, and he rushed across to the barred window and clutching the top of it with his hands where it was open and where the smell of trodden straw and lately dropped dung was blown in along with a vague waftage from the invisible sap of millions of misty grass-stalks and thousands of wet wind-stirred withy-buds drooping above the weirs and the dams and the muddy ditches where the unseen river made its sweeping curve to the north, he began pressing his forehead hard against that portion of his window that had been designed to be unmoveable.

And just here upon the steel frame of the windowpane he now proceeded to give several sharp taps with that portion of his skull out of which, if he had been the Devil, or even if he had been the humblest of the angels who followed the Devil, there might have sprouted, indeed there would naturally have sprouted, a fine pair of horns.

He could detect the light in the upper window of the north lodge where his friend the wife of the gate-keeper slept, that chamber which twenty-four hours ago had filled him with such frightening thoughts. Then, without turning on the electric light, he began rapidly pacing his room from wall to window.

The curious greenish light that washed back and forth in his chamber like an unpalpable estuary of air seemed, as he marched up and down, to pass through him as if his body were

THE INMATES

the plasm of a newly born spirit, or rather, if spirits can die, of a newly dead spirit. He was desperately wondering now about the four quarters of the dark sky; and the problem that particularly absorbed him was the question as to how far round this place the sweeping curve of the river went.

He had been strongly reminded just now of the river by the smell of damp mud, and he decided that Glint Hall must be surrounded by its flow in a vast curve of several miles, stretching from north to south across that western horizon where shone at night the lights of Halfway House.

If he were right in supposing the river's curve to be as extensive as this, there would be only one of all the four horizons free of this encirclement, only one with what you might call a dry approach. But which way, he kept asking himself, did the river flow? Did it flow from north to south across this western horizon? Or did it flow from south to north?

And there was another question that bothered his mind. What was the mysterious something that stood between those two Scotch firs that were growing side by side on the crest of the ridge, where that prehistoric camp was? He was sure there was something there in addition to those firs. What the devil was it?

It was something monumental, poetical, and very important; and it was something that separated those two trees! Ay, he remembered now. *It was the sun!* But he hadn't seen it himself. That's why he'd forgotten. Someone had told him that at a certain time in the year the sun rose exactly between those two Scotch firs as you saw them on the crest of that ancient camp from the windows of Glint looking east.

Yes, that was what it was—the sun! And he'd been told that it would soon be the time of the year when you could see the sun rise between those trees.

He suddenly stood dead-still in the middle of the room. Why the devil was it so extremely necessary to him to get the precise geography of Glint Hall and of the position of his room in regard to the points of the compass?

He concluded, but without much assurance of finality in the

idea, that it had something to do with a queer fear that had come over him ever since Tenna had been so upset by Mr. Rumpibus, namely the fear that his own mind was on the edge of playing him some outrageous trick! "Normal people," as he had grown accustomed to call the bulk of his fellow-creatures since he had become obsessed by the indescribable thrill of his peculiar use of nailscissors, "normal people" always seemed to take geography and the points of the compass for granted.

And yet they were assisted in their successful struggle to keep their mental balance far more than they realised by their dependence on the points of the compass. "I must get it clear! I *must* get it clear!" he told himself; and he began making a deliberate effort to put himself, naked and passive and free from every human purpose, into the power of the four winds.

He obstinately turned round as if he'd been a lighthouse on one of those mysteriously turning castle rocks, the idea of which and the planetary explanation of which, lost in an engulfing antiquity, keep reoccurring in the ancient Welsh books.

In this crazy process of behaving like a "turning castle" with four sides, he faced, first the north through his barred window, then the south through his closed door, then the west through the wall behind his bed, and lastly the east through the wall behind his chest-of-drawers. The Rembrandt picture was against this final barrier to the gulfs of space, so that it was from the direction of the old heathen camp that there had appeared, as if straight from the tomb of Joseph of Arimathea, and in as deep a daze of wonder at being resurrected as he was in a maze of wonder at being accounted a god, that Jesus of Nazareth had entered the research laboratory of Doctor Echetus.

And now as John Hush stared for half a minute at each of his four walls—at his window, at his door, at his bed, at his chest-of-drawers—he forced himself to call up before his mind's eye all that he could remember of each particular stretch of country between Glint Hall and its four horizons. Alder-swamps and

THE INMATES

willows and a flooded river lay beyond the gates to the north. Alder-swamps and willows and a flooded river lay beyond the gates to the south. Alder-swamps and willows and a flooded river lay beyond the walls to the west, where rose the roofs of Halfway House.

Meanwhile to the east there were only dry, heathery, sandy plantations of young firs and pines, spruce-firs, Douglas pines, and Siberian larches, all of these mounting up to that heathen camp on the top of which were the two gigantic Scotch firs, between whose trunks, so he now remembered being told, the sun rose at this time of the year. It was only when he had entirely satisfied his desire for revolving like an idolatrous weathercock to the four quarters of the sky that he approached his chest-of-drawers. This he did with a view to ascertaining if it contained a packet of cigarettes he had placed among his collars, not as a bait for a thief, but simply because it contained a particular brand that had been a favourite with his guardian and that out of a sort of piety he enjoyed as a special celebration on particular days.

Yes, the cigarettes entitled "The Smoke of Heaven" were in their place; and John felt, as he folded four of his collars in a consecrated half-circle about the box of pale-blue cardboard which contained them that as long as he had the job of keeping quite a lot of material objects clean and neat, while at the same moment he could "plunge", as the commander had recommended into the nonhuman elements of Nature, he would daily advance in wisdom.

It was at this moment that he found himself confronted by the fact that, not only was one of the round brass corner-knobs of his bed missing, but that one of the polished mahogany knobs of the drawer that held the cigarettes was badly chipped. He gazed at these mutilated things with an overpowering urge to do something to patch them up and heal them. After his fashion he had to analyse even this compulsion and to do so while he was deciding to yield to it. "It must be a reaction," he thought, "from that officer's talk about plunging into things! No, I really can't undress and get into bed with that unhappy screw craving for a knob and that knob so miserably chipped. It's things like this waiting to be properly fitted and united that cause so much misery in the world. The whole world of Glint Hall is simply full of inanimate inmates!

"Oh, I *can't* understand how living things can be so indifferent to inanimate things! Damn their souls! Till the bits that are broken off, and the pieces that are divided, and the parts that are lost, are joined together again, what's the use of talking about federations of the world?"

With a rush of more happiness than he had felt since he first saw Tenna under the tulip-tree, he now set himself to unscrew the chipped wooden knob. It yielded at first, then was recalcitrant, then yielded again; and while he worked at it he couldn't help deciding that there was a great deal in what Serius-Ocius had recently been asserting. "But," he told himself, "where the fellow went wrong was in not realising that any work you do, when done naturally, such as removing this chipped knob, means using the mind; and, though it doesn't mean thinking, it means being conscious, and, moreover, being conscious that you are being conscious!"

When he had removed the chipped knob from his collar-drawer, he found that it was a hard job to fasten it to the protruding screw at the corner of his bed. But his wrists were strong, and though the mahogany knob didn't completely conceal the base of the exposed screw, it hid the top of it quite successfully, so that his bed now possessed three brass knobs and one wooden knob.

This gave him extraordinary satisfaction, and he stared triumphantly for several minutes into a world of broken things that were no longer broken—spoons with restored handles, dolls with restored heads, horses with restored hooves, cups with restored saucers, teapots with restored spouts, chimneys with restored chimney-pots—while it seemed to him that all the *animae* of these inanimates, as they crowded round him, were crying aloud in a multitudinous chant :

THE INMATES

"Hail, mender of mendicants!
Hail, furbisher of fetishes!
Hail, tailor of totems!
Hail, mortiser of mascots!"

But soon, coming out of this godlike trance, he sat down on the edge of his bed beside the latest of his four knobs and gazed round his room. The strong electric bulb seemed to be saying all the while: "To the healthy all things are healthy!" and "Be strong and sane like me!" and "Let there be light, light, light, light!"

The divine Mr. Lordy watched him out of the great painter's chiaroscuro as if through a miraculous hole in the wall; and though he felt that the shadows were twisting and twining with shadows in that upper room of the north lodge, he could see nothing but the square panes and the imprisoning bars of his own uncurtained window. But it was at this moment that silence itself, eldest of all things, began to throb and beat and pump and pulse and bulge and rumble at him.

"Is it," he thought, "just my nerves that I hear sounds in the passage? Damn! That's the worst of these institutions. They're all right in the day. It's in the night that the thoughts and dreams of the sleepers come out of their rooms and shuffle about, and shiver, and squeak and gibber. Yes it's in the night they sob and go moaning up and down."

"No! No!" he told himself. "*That's* not nerves!" He had heard a door open; and now there were shuffling feet! Oh, there was no question about it. He listened intently. Yes, the person, whoever it was, must have seen the light under his door. "That's the worst of these electric bulbs," he thought, "you can't turn them *down*. You can only turn them *out*."

He rose from his bed and, with the intention of locking his door, turning the light out, and going to bed by the pallid greyness that came in through the window, he took two and a half of the three or four lazy steps he would have to take to reach the corner between door and wall where protruded the knob that worked the electricity. Then he suddenly became a

THE ZEIT-GEIST

waxwork image in the centre of which thudded a panic-stricken heart.

The door towards which he had moved opened a couple of inches, and about level with his face and near it, too, for he was only a yard away, a finger inserted itself as if it had been the snout of a peculiar animal. The finger had large knuckles and it had particularly long intersections between these knuckles. It could not have been called a deformed finger nor did it look like a finger dedicated to the service of actions that had, as the poet says, "no relish of salvation in them". But if it wasn't a devilish finger no one could call it a "good" finger, it was just a finger. It might have been a symbol in heraldry. It might have been a symbol in some occult pack of prophetic cards. John regarded it with fascinated horror.

But now the finger began to bend at its thick knuckle. It bent towards him. It waggled at him. It did more than waggle. It wriggled. John had seen terrifying objects in his time. He had seen ghastly objects. He had seen appalling objects. But this wriggling finger directed towards his face was different from anything he had ever seen.

And his consciousness as it contemplated this "moving finger" felt as if it were absolutely alone with it, in some cosmic vacuum beyond all worlds. But an atrocious idea now came gently sliding into his head. He was an agile performer with nail-scissors; and he had noticed just now, when he went to his collar-drawer to see if his package of "The Smoke of Heaven" was still there, that since they'd got him safely certified it hadn't occurred to them to search his toilet articles and remove those glittering snappers. Why, therefore, shouldn't he grab that wagging finger and cut its nails for it, cut them to the quick! But it was all very well to think of these terrestial performances. Here he was—and, in spite of Serius-Ocius, or any other king's officer, *for him the mind was everything* —floating like a vast mass of indivisible squid on an ocean without bottom, without horizon, without a ripple, while against his heart, his breast, his solar plexus, his mental nerve-centre, wriggled eternally, like the undying worm that Jesus

THE INMATES

beheld devouring those who wouldn't love him, the fumbling finger of the background material of the deepest abyss known.

The thing was more than obscene to John Hush. To his mind there was something about it like a monstrous ribaldry and as if an outrage were being perpetrated upon the inherent decency of matter itself. The spotted nakedness it embodied wasn't a phallic nakedness, and yet in some shocking manner it was super-sexual. It suggested the self-ravishing and self-impregnating sex-organism of some abysmal being in the process of whose eternal spawning the copulating opposites of mind and matter and male and female were as yet undifferentiated.

"Cut your damned nails for you—that's what I'll do!" he muttered aloud; and, swinging round, lurched heavily, for he felt weak in his legs, towards the collar-drawer from which he had just wrenched the chipped knob, leaving a lamentable hole behind.

Even in the midst of his perturbed state he experienced, and was surprised to observe himself doing so, a puzzled amazement at the unconcerned complacency of the thing's twin-handle. But before he could reach the outraged hole or its unsympathetic twin, the door of his room very slowly and very silently opened, and a middle-aged man in blue-and-white pyjamas waddled along the floor towards him, advancing on his haunches and his heels with his arms working like barge-poles, as if he were trying to imitate the motion of the circular man-woman of the Platonic symposium.

John's first feeling at the approach of this apparition, who was breathing hard and whose spasmodic movements were already losing their initial fling, was one of profound relief. And with this relief he got back his calmer wits to such a tune that he began to enjoy himself. "It shows," he thought, as he stared into the eyes of the creature on the floor, "that what I'm really afraid of is simply the vacuum; yes, simply the void, the inane, the empty, the vacant, that shocking gap or gulf concealed behind every motion of the consciousness that apprehends and every aspect of the thing apprehended."

Having in this manner stated his view of his own fear he

THE ZEIT-GEIST

suddenly began to continue his thoughts concerning it aloud just as if he were conversing with the intruder on the floor.

"I was thinking about fear," he murmured. "And I'm now convinced that what frightens us—well, frightens *me* anyhow!—is not what we actually see—*you*, for instance, playing the giddy goat in my room when you ought to be asleep—but *the empty space*, the vacuum, so to speak, *of the future moment*, the hollow place, so to put it, of the as yet unfilled gap in time, into which the whole caboodle, I mean the whole panorama of experience, is moving, to become, directly it occupies that gap, like yourself who are now interrupting my going to bed by acting the fool, to become something that may be annoying and may make us angry but which is not in the remotest degree what we call terrifying."

With a deep and extremely theatrical sigh and a shrug of his shoulders that had a somewhat foreign air, the man in the elegant pyjamas picked himself up and sat down on the edge of the bed.

"And now—" the fellow began, jerking up one of his feet under him, and tapping the floor with the heel of the other, both feet being tightly encased in embroidered slippers ornamented by green beads; "and now—" and he threw into his words the satisfied tone of a man just come to his club and with the best hours of the day stretching out like golden sands in front of him, "and now we can tell each other to our heart's content all about ourselves! And it might, don't you think, be a good thing if we shut the door and turned on the electric heater?"

John, who was now standing with his back to the door, closed it as silently as he could, and feeling very irritable and repeating to himself over and over, "I'll turn the chap out in a minute and go to bed," began vaguely looking round. Till this moment he had never realised that there *was* an electric-heater in his room. But there it was; and it was situated between his only chair, a chair which had its back to the wall, and his now somewhat reproachful chest-of-drawers. He turned it on; and seating himself upon the chair beside it, soon began

THE INMATES

to feel that he really did owe something to this preposterous person for indicating to him this fountain of agreeable heat.

He pulled the chair away from the wall, and keeping nothing but his profile directed towards his visitor and repeating to himself over and over, as a kind of incantation, "going to bed . . . going to bed . . . going to bed," he tried hard to put some authentic cameraderie into the tone with which he begged at least for the honour of learning his visitor's name.

"Name?" cried the invader of his bed. "Did I hear you utter that goose-girl word 'name'? Don't you remember the words of Faust concerned the Spirit? 'I have no name to give it—feeling is all in all—the name is sound and smoke'! But, since I *am* here, and we are alone, I may as well confess that I'm generally known in this absurd place by my title."

"And may I enquire what that is?" John murmured wearily, thinking, as he surveyed the coloured beads on the slipper with which the fellow was tapping the floor, that he would talk quite openly to Tenna to-morrow, when they met after the midday meal, and make her see that it was absolutely essential, however they might have to act or speak or dissemble with regard to the rest, to be completely frank with each other; and if they had—as no doubt they had—unusual peculiarities of their own, they must confess them freely to each other, and each obtain the aid of the other in getting them under control.

It indeed began to strike John very strongly that if, after only two nights in this place, a man like himself, who had served in all the embassies of the Balkans, could be so shocked and startled by the wagging of a finger through the crack of a door and in full electric light, and long before midnight, there was little to wonder at if Tenna's nerves had grown shaky after two years of this sort of thing? And he thought: "Can *anything* in our whole normal way of life be crazier than this throwing of extra-crazy people *together* with the idea of getting them back to normality? Of course, *really* it's just to get us out of the way!"

"Well, sir," he repeated, as the occupier of the bed remained silent, "and what *is* your title?"

THE ZEIT-GEIST

The man on the bed hesitated. His manner was that of a disguised monarch who is not absolutely sure whether his confession of identity will be made to a friend or an enemy. Then he said, "My title, good friend, is an unusual one; but not, I fancy an altogether unknown one, to a gentleman and a scholar like yourself."

Here the fellow leapt to his feet and gave John a dignified bow.

"I am the Marquis of the Fourth Dimension," he declared, "and I am, of course, much more than human. History doesn't contain me. I contain history. I am real and yet I am ideal. Some thinkers call me 'the Zeit-Geist'; but I prefer, as that German said, to be superficial out of profundity."

After this bold revelation of the riddle of personality, the Marquis of the Fourth Dimension drew back a step further, making, as he did so, a gesture that reminded John of a woman's curtsey. It must have been some kind of choreographic compulsion conveyed by telepathy from one mind to another, combined with the propitiatory training of an ambassador's secretary that brought it about that John, with an even lower obeisance than that of the Zeit-Geist, slipped into the precise position on the bed vacated by the other, imitating him even to the extent of drawing up one foot under him and tapping with the other upon the floor.

Moving, therefore, in this magnetised circle of reciprocity, the Marquis of the Fourth Dimension approached the bed and touched the knee which his host had just bent beneath him.

John surveyed this outstretched finger with a curious interest. It was the same finger, composed of bone, flesh, blood, and rather wrinkled skin, terminating in a horny but in this particular case a very clean fingernail, that had frozen his heart with terror ten minutes ago.

The very same finger! And yet he regarded it now with a quiet, humorous interest, but an interest that was not very lively or intense, and might, indeed, pretty soon change into complete indifference. What conclusion—such was his thought as this nobleman from a Dimensional House of Lords

THE INMATES

kept his finger upon him, and kept it in the position and, indeed, with something of the gesture of that pointing finger of the Father of Gods and Men in Michelangelo's picture where He is conveying the breath of life into Adam—what conclusion was he to come to in regard to pure fear?

For in this case that is what it was. It wasn't fear of death, or fear of a fall, or fear of a bullet, or fear of cancer, or fear of pain. Could it be fear of the supernatural? Not in any ordinary or traditional sense! He had never for a moment doubted that it was the real finger of a real person. "No; the truth is," John told himself: "this thing, fear, is as much a part of the original constitution of our souls as attraction and repulsion, advance and retreat, love and hate. If to be born is to enter battle, it is also to endure fear. The only creatures wholly free from fear are the dead."

"Well?" enquired the person who declared himself to be, as Homer would put it, the Time-spirit, "I came in dancing, and dancing I must go out!" Here he removed both his Michelangelical finger and the magnetic radiation that excited reciprocity. "But I can't go back to my pillow till I make you realise as a gentleman and a scholar exactly to what a pass human history has come in realising its final identity in me; for let me tell you this, my good sir, and see that you lay it to heart. They used to talk of the Peers of Christendom. Well, now they must deal *with us*, the Peers of the Fourth Dimension! And scholars like you and me"—here he lowered his voice— "know very well to what in reality all this fuss about evolution amounts!"

Here he approached so close to John that the latter felt a shivering in his stomach, like the under-the-skin shudder of an old maid compelled to contemplate a rape. The visitor put both his feet on the floor and struck the palms of his hands together with a smart shock as if he were killing a flea or summoning a waitress.

"It amounts," he whispered hoarsely, "to a bubble! And this dance you have had the privilege of witnessing is the dance of history, that is to say the dance of a bubble!"

THE ZEIT-GEIST

At this point John stood up, and, straightening his shoulders, discovered to his amazement that he was considerably taller than the Zeit-Geist, whose personal appearance, now that he had ceased to be afraid of him, he was free to take in. The man was nearly bald and had a plump round face with prominent ears. His chin was small and had a deep dimple in it. His eyes were pale grey, and they were so pale that as the electric bulb shone down on them they looked positively white. In fact, as John continued to inspect them, they seemed almost devoid of eyeballs, and the effect of this was to make them really ghastly.

John had never seen any eyes like them, and he made up his mind, then and there, to ask Tenna for every detail she could give him of this weird creature.

"When we meet again," he now presumed to enquire, "is there any *ordinary* name by which I can address you?"

To his surprise the plump round visage before him broke into a smile. "Well, well well! Think of that! And so you've never even heard of Professor Zoom of the College of Doom?"

John could only bow gravely; but when the fellow had danced himself to the door, and John had opened it for him, both the men began whispering. John whispered, "I hope you'll be able to sleep."

And Zoom whispered: "Oh, I'll sleep all right. I'll sleep like a—like a——"

"Like a top?"

"Like a burst bubble!" replied the Marquis of the Fourth Dimension.

HITHER AND THITHER

JOHN WOKE up before it was fully light. In fact he woke at the hour when human beings usually feel at their lowest level of courage, energy, and confidence.

The actual dawn could hardly be said to have begun, and yet the infinite restfulness and restorative anonymity of the

THE INMATES

all-obliterating night had vanished. It was that hour, or half-hour, or even that quarter of an hour, for the length of its lasting as well as the degree of its quality varies in proportion to what the clouds and the mists and the winds are doing in any particular locality, when a pallid diffusion of light enters our sleeping-place—"lumen intra limen", "light across the threshold"—and affects us in a manner quite different from any other phenomenon of nature.

As he awoke to consciousness this pallid light struck John Hush as if it had been a *fifth element*, as different from air and water as these are different from earth and fire.

John could see by means of this presence the objects in his room, and clearest of all he could see the windowpanes through which this presence was entering his room; but there was nothing that it revealed to him in his surroundings that was more startling, more strange, more solemnising than itself.

The queer thing about it was that it didn't make him think at all of the radiance of the sun's rays. Nor did it make him think of warmth in general or of the delicious sensation of being warm. It struck him as a thing in itself, as an absolute, as something which, though it may have been a normal apparition, was the essence of pure light, of very light of very light, and, as the creed says, "begotten not made". This fifth element that ere the coming of dawn was now establishing itself both outside and inside the weak barrier of his window seemed to him, as he watched it, to be the physical embodiment of some ultimate disillusionment that was older than the orbits of any of the stars yet known to us, older than the inhabitants of any planet revolving round any of those stars. He felt at that moment as if this strange, cold, prae-dawn light had nothing to do with the rays of any sun or with the rays of any star, and yet was totally different from any legendary *psychic* event, like the Fall of Man or the Revolt of the Angels. It struck him now, this prae-dawn light, as if its far-off origin had nothing to do with any war in Heaven, or with any prae-historic rallying of mankind to the cause of the devils or titans.

Something had happened, something had gone wrong, that

HITHER AND THITHER

was much further off and longer ago than any wars between Jehovah and Satan. And it had happened in the process of creation itself. Something like a ghastly *cosmogonic blunder* had been made by whatever demiurgic power it might be that had originally projected the "background material" of our dimension into overt existence.

The impression of immemorial antiquity made upon him by this cold white light that seemed so much older than sun, moon, or stars was indeed an impression of abysmal disillusionment; but it was the disillusionment not of the created but of the creator. This prae-dawn light was the diffused sigh with which the original world-builder had lamented some huge catastrophic mistake and with little hope of redeeming it had obstinately set to work to start all over again.

Thus did John Hush work it out to his grim satisfaction that this white light of disillusionment, which had recurred at irregular and intermittent dawns from the beginning of the world, could still communicate to us the oldest secret of all, the secret of the endurance of the burden of existence by inanimate things.

John, indeed, felt that the effect upon him of this faint prae-matutinal light was sobering rather than inspiring; and, though not saddening to his spirits, was a patient and stoical influence rather than an exultant one. He remembered a talk he'd once had with a Bulgarian scholar about their personal reactions to this particular prae-dawn light, and how the man had told him that each of the ancient classical races had special names for the influence of this hour, the Roman goddess of the light before sun-rise being named Matuta, whereas the Greeks had called her Leucothea.

This goddess, he explained to John, was, by reason of her own tragic experiences before her apotheosis, liable to have an unlucky effect upon any child of one's own, but a very lucky effect when a mother brought into her presence a neighbour's child.

"My feelings just now," thought John, "are certainly what you might call Leucothean. They are benevolent and yet totally irreligious!"

THE INMATES

He soon found that, as his present mood intensified itself and established itself, it excluded all human emotions except those of a mild expectation, a mild enjoyment, a mild pity, a mild amusement, and a strong desire to get Tenna and himself, together with as many of the other inmates and dogs as were still redeemable, out of the hands of Doctor Echetus.

In this cold, enduring, sobering, prae-dawn light the bubble-dance of last night's fourth-dimensional nobleman struck him as scarcely more real than two half-forgotten dreams whose scattered members he now vaguely began to reassemble; but save that one of them had to do with a dead sycamore-twig and the other with a little heap of rabbit's dung, the first associated with some terrible unknown fear, the second with the redemption of all matter, he could not summon them back.

"It's about time to go down to those sheds," he thought. "But one thing's clear! I mustn't think of girls' curls, even if such thoughts are, as I daresay they may be, a legitimate enticement of Nature. Tenna's my sweetheart, and I *won't* mix her up with my manias!"

He got out of bed quickly now, and stood for a second or two hesitating as to whether to put on his faded blue-and-black dressing-gown to go to the lavatory, or his overcoat. He decided on the latter, so as to feel less conspicuous in case he met anyone; but he couldn't resist drawing his fingers across the agreeable texture of the former.

"So the moment has come," he thought, addressing his dressing-gown as if it had consciousness, "when the deliciously safe tightness of your collar when its top button is buttoned, and all those things you make me remember when you flap round my legs, have to be hung up on a hook!"

And even as he touched it there came over him one memory after another of precious moments when the rainbow bridge of man's precarious *monochronos hedone*, that flickering perfection of the Ideal Now, spanned the abyss between the two horrors, the former of which our French drawing-rooms call *ennui* and the latter of which our German class-rooms call *angst*.

He met nobody on his way to the lavatory or on his way

back, and he only met men who were complete strangers to him as he went down to the yard. Once in the yard, nothing occurred to disturb his equanimity. He enjoyed his work out here at this hour. Oil-lamps and gas-burners, in addition to electricity, played their part in the illumination of the stables and sheds, where the less aged and frail among the male inmates helped the hired farm-hands from about half-past six to eight. Chance had so arranged it that John's particular job, into which he had been initiated yesterday, was singularly adapted to his complete lack of any sort of knowledge of cattle and horses. It was to clean out an airy shed and the couple of capacious stalls in which two white cows and two grey cows were milked every morning and evening.

The woman who milked these particular four cows was a sturdy creature of about thirty who "answered", as they put it in Glint kitchen, to the name of Nancy Yew, and to whom the gods had given an extremely passionate, though an indescribably ugly, physiognomy. It was her only child Seth by whose work with pitchfork and shovel this shed was kept clean and daily supplied with fresh straw from the neighbouring straw-stacks; and it was to help the frail and youthful Seth with the maturity of his own manly strength that Hush had been selected by the asylum authorities to work in the particular shed called Delta.

Why the sheds at Glint had been named from the letters of the Greek alphabet, nobody to whom John had so far put the question had been able to say. Some professor with a philological mania must have taken Greek mythology too lightly and the Greek alphabet too seriously.

Nor apparently had the learned man—for, as Doctor Echetus himself admitted, "the alphabet can lead anywhere"—confined his nomenclative mania to the inanimate. The most beautiful of these four beasts had in some way or other acquired the unusual soubriquet of Clytie, which at once suggested to John's mind the name Clytemnestra.

It was with electric light that the stalls of Clytie and of her sister-cow were lit these March mornings, and John had derived

THE INMATES

a good deal of pleasure from the various quite startling "chiaroscuro" effects that resulted from this modernistic illumination of prehistoric labours.

Nancy Yew's son was a bastard. He was also not entirely "there". But since to be not entirely "there" was likely to be less noticeable here than elsewhere, and since she herself was milking both Clytie and Clytie's sister, Whitey, in the shed, it was Seth's business to keep clean, Nancy Yew felt that though she couldn't always be there to keep an eye on him, there was bound to be a definite aura of maternal protection hovering over that Delta stall.

"And to you too, sir!" Mistress Yew now murmured in response to John's greeting. "And there'll be a nice drop"—"tling-tirroop! tling-tirroop!" went Clytie's milk into the pail—"a real nice drop of rain, I wouldn't wonder, by nick of noon this day, if I've not lost my what-do-you-know, if you catch my meaning, mister."

"Do you mean it's going to rain, Mrs. Yew?" enquired John, plunging his fork into several heaps of dirty straw, one after another, and trying to make a solid mass of them, thick enough to be transported out of the shed.

"Mummy's thinking," intervened young Seth in a gently explanatory tone, "of turn-ups."

John added yet another layer of dirty straw to his transfixed mass, and pressing it against the floor of the shed threw his whole weight upon the handle of his pitchfork. He perceived in a flash that, like other innocents, young Seth had the wit to see that what sane people always have at the back of their minds is their own concern, their own affair, their own purpose, their own interest.

"You'll be," he added with a sudden illumination of his long, sad, weary, resigned face, "wanting to see how this here place looks in sunshine."

John confessed that such was his desire.

"Me garding," murmured the idiot's mother, to the resounding noise of Clytie's milk, "be too dry for end of March."

John continued leaning on his fork while he watched the

HITHER AND THITHER

long thin wavering shape of Seth insinuate itself, like a patient slow-worm endowed with the power of perpendicular motion, between the stool on which his mother was sitting and the hindquarters of Whitey.

What passed through John's mind, as he watched the boy carry his shovelful of dung out into the yard, was the idea that on some far-off day when Tenna and himself had a house of their own, far from all their friends, they might have Seth as their retainer. Then he glanced at the rough, red, wind-tanned, rugged cheek of Nancy Yew, as it pressed itself against the incredibly soft side of the creature she was milking. "Maybe it would be all right," he thought, "if I asked Tenna straight out if she wouldn't mind my snipping off—now I've got the scissors in my drawer, and since I've got them it seems mad not to use them—just that one single little tiny curl? Yes, I must think, think, think, think, very carefully about this."

And while Mistress Nancy milked Whitey, and while he did quite a lot of Seth's share of the stall-cleaning in addition to his own, he went on wondering whether it wouldn't be quite a natural and sensible thing to do, since he *had* found at last a girl who suited him, if he used her as a lightning-conductor for this mania of his.

"His poor dear head," as Mrs. Toby Tickle would have said; but of course it wasn't his "head" at all, it was that desperate thing in him that was the bowsprit of his whole life's intention —"was ringing" with this idea when the asylum bell proclaimed that it was time for breakfast.

This bell began ringing at three minutes to eight, and went on until three minutes past eight, and it might be said that these six minutes were to some of the inmates of Glint the most precious of the whole twelve hours, if not of the whole twenty-four.

And they were this for a very powerful reason; namely that the clanging of the great bell of Glint produced such hurryings, scramblings, rushings, scurryings, jostlings, that those who weren't hungry, and those who wanted to avoid the notice of others, and those who were half-asleep, and those who were on the look-out for a minute or two's pretence that they were

THE INMATES

still free-agents and could come and go as they liked had the sort of interval not often offered to the inmates of an institution.

As John propped his pitchfork against the wall and with the help of a wisp of straw set himself to clean his boots, he noticed the devouring yearning in the one single round grey eye which, during all the while she was milking, Nancy kept fixed upon her offspring. Glancing from her to the lad himself, he became aware that Seth was now watching with an absorbed and fascinated interest one of the inmates who had strayed quite far from the sacred purlieus of the farmyard and was now skipping and dancing and nodding his head and taking fantastic leaps as he made towards one of the tall iron posts of the big gates guarded by the north lodge.

Seth's own long thin greyish face wore the intense expression, undisturbed by any need for action, which some spell-bound onlooker might have worn in a religious picture by El Greco.

"Who is that fellow, laddie, dancing up to that gate?" John enquired of the boy. The moment he'd uttered these words, though he hadn't spoken loudly and the noise of the squirted jets of milk came near to drowning them, he felt he oughtn't to have uttered them. Seth was so polite that it was pain to him not to answer at once, and yet he was so absorbed in the queer figure at which he was staring that it was worse pain to look away or to make any response.

But when the figure stood still between the dazzling sunshine and the dark velvety shadows on the green grass, he did at last turn to his questioner—"It's Twin Hither," he said. "It's the one as hunts shadows! If you hadn't got to go and eat sausages in hall, mister, you might have seen Twin Thither, too! She's the clever one, she is! *She* has got to have water or something like water for *her* hunt. And do you know what *her* hunt is, Master Hush?"

John looked at him gravely and shook his head.

"Reflections!" cried the boy. "Twin Hither's after shadows, and Twin Thither's after reflections! They're a funny pair, they twins! He be a boy and she be a girl, but they look awful-much the same!"

HITHER AND THITHER

Seth's long sad narrow face with its perpetually raised eyebrows and its life-weary detachment from everything that other human beings long for, was now to John's astonishment transformed by a radiance that seemed to reach it directly, instantaneously, and with an immediate physical contact, from the skipping and capering figure that was now approaching the northern gate of Glint. The towering gates themselves contained elaborate iron bars that had curious ornamental portcullises at intervals, answering each other in a sort of pattern of heraldic symbolism, as though they were perpetually chanting in metallic reiteration: "Stay where, you are! Stay where you are! Stay where you are! Don't try to escape! Don't try to escape! Here is your world! Here is your world!"

But this was not all. The gate-posts of these vast erections rose considerably above the complicated ironwork of the gates themselves and were terminated by dull specimens of that sort of totally meaningless ornamental foliation which at one epoch carried the very stamp and seal of successful builders of the type of Tenna's progenitor; and from both these tall gate-posts, if so they could be described, though they resembled gigantic metal lances that had been used to pierce titanic puffballs and had retained what they had transfixed of these cryptogamous growths like the spiked heads of condemned felons, there stretched across the sunlit grass two long narrow wavering shadows, and it was along one of these early morning shadows that Twin Hither was now skipping.

"What on earth will the boy do," thought John, "when he reaches the gate?"

John looked anxiously at Seth; and Seth looked anxiously at John. They knew by each other's eyes that they were both deeply concerned over what was going to happen; though the idiot was still exultant with his faith in the spirit that inspired that airy dancer.

Suddenly Twin Hither swung clean on his heel and went skipping back along his shadow-path towards the rear entrance of the building. When he came to the spot where the shadow ended, with a reproduction on the sunlit grass of that shapeless terminal, he took a run, and leaping over the gap which separated this object from the sun-illumined mat in front of the open door, he seemed literally to dive into the passage with his hands clasped in front of his face.

All that was left for the onlookers to do was to follow back with their heavy gaze the dancer's shadow-path as it returned to its monstrous origin, that "leave-all-hope symbol in shoddy cast-iron!"

"See you again in an hour," murmured John, "and good luck till then!"

But noticing the idiot's eyes and the desperate look in them, "Don't 'ee mind too much, Seth, my friend. He'll be out here again this afternoon."

"It isn't *that*, mister."

"*Not* that? What is it, Seth?"

But all the answer the boy gave him was a faint movement of his head towards the silken flanks of Whitey, which in that curious criss-crossing of artificial light with the long dazzling rays and deep shadows of the newly risen sun, made a perfect background for the profile of Nancy and the indrawing possessiveness of her insatiable maternal eye.

"I might have guessed it!" thought John. "Before we know where we are, it's on us again— *the Holy Family!*"

He swung round and bolted; yes, the private secretary to our country's special representative in four sovereign states bolted like a rabbit from the irresistible power of the loving eye. This particular projection of possessiveness was harmlessly pillowed against the silken side of Whitey; and it wasn't that he feared anything for himself, or that he had any thought that Nancy was a witch. He knew she was a good, kind, hardworking honest woman, who doted on her idiot son.

"And it isn't," he told himself, as he took his place beside Mr. Lordy at the dining-room table and commenced hungrily devouring his oatmeal and brown sugar, "it isn't as if there were anything unnatural or morbid in this mother's love for her offspring. It is a perfectly normal and natural feeling!"

Why then had a shiver of terrible sympathy shot through

him when we saw the boy's glance at that round shameless feminine eye staring at him out of the very belly, so it seemed, of that patient beast?

There was no escape. He had to face the truth. He might have to deceive a lot of other people, but it was silly and ridiculous solemnly to set to work deceiving himself. And what *was* the truth?

Ah, *there* was the rub! Well! He decided that since they had now both finished their porridge, he would consult Mr. Lordy. Mr. Lordy had quelled the storm in the breast of a naval commander; why should he not be able to settle the problem as to where "love" ought to yield to common sense?

"Will they bother us," he began, not exactly in a whisper but in quite a low tone, "if I ask you rather a crucial question; if I ask you, in fact, how far we ought to carry our obedience to love?"

Mr. Lordy must have taken stronger measures than usual to protect himself from the ghost of the old gentleman he had shaken to death, for John's first taste of the copious helping of scrambled eggs which was now on his plate, in spite of all the pepper with which he had freely sprinkled it, carried with it a perceptible smack of powerful disinfectant.

"In all well-managed institutions," replied Mr. Lordy in a firm voice, and John knew at once that the loyal little man was quoting from some printed sermon of Father Wun, "it is imperative to keep quite distinct what we say from what we think. Thoughts are one thing. Words are another thing. The space between thoughts and words must be kept like carefully preserved grass. This space must be cut. This space must be weeded. This space must be rolled."

Putting down his knife and using his fork like a spoon, in the American manner, and pushing to the side of his plate with the extreme tip of his longest finger, as if it were a piece of carpet upon which a corpse had been lying, the square of toast upon which the scrambled egg had been placed, Mr. Lordy drained his teacup to the bottom and continued his quotation. "When we talk of 'love' we talk of a thing so slippery, so fluid, so erratic,

THE INMATES

that there's nothing to which it can be compared except those moving bubbles under cat-ice which have, as everybody must remember, so striking a resemblance to wriggling tadpoles."

It was only with a slight shake of the head that Mr. Lordy refused an attendant's offer of more scrambled eggs. John, however, though fully aware that the satisfying of his hunger did to some extent diminish his attention, felt sure that as long as he imitated Mr. Lordy by keeping his profile at right angles to his interlocutor there was nothing in their conversation to draw "those men" a step nearer—John, I say, acquiesced quite shamelessly when he had the chance of a second helping.

"No one in this place," began Mr. Lordy, addressing his words to the distant row of female backs up and down which John was pathetically moving his lack-lustre gaze, not with any hope of seeing Tenna there, for she had told him that she was one of the lucky ones for whom Mam Tickle had coaxed from the authorities the privilege of going to the kitchen for a tray and carrying their tea and bread-and-butter up to their bedrooms, but with a foolish lover's fancy that, having been seen there once, she might be seen there again.

"No one in this place," quoted Mr. Lordy, becoming a little confused as he went on, "has the right to use the word *ought* in connection with that listing wind referred to in the Gospels or possibly in the Epistles, or even in the Acts, but referred to anyway as a precious something that comes and goes where it listeth, and none can increase it or restrain it by any effort of will, and none can bind it or loose it or create it or destroy it. The Church regulates marriage and overlooks the begetting and the conceiving of children. The Law regulates possessions and overlooks the acquiring and the inheriting of possessions.

"Conscience regulates our behaviour to all other living creatures. The State regulates our intercourse with other nations and takes upon itself the prevention of crime, and the certifying of—well, of people like us! But love is no more under our control than the clouds or the winds or the rain or the sun or the tides of the sea."

HITHER AND THITHER

"But don't people tell us, Mr. Lordy," John remarked in the particular diplomatic tone that conceals beneath a quiet emphasis the mischievous shaking up, like peas in a bag, of the whole subject, "that the opposite of love is *hate*; and that, if everything important to life is connected with love, everything dangerous and deadly to life must be connected with hate?"

But no ambassadorial niceties could side-track a man who had danced his stepfather to death like a badly-made puppet.

"Hate," said Mr. Lordy, with unruffled concentration on the row of feminine backs, "is *not* the opposite of love." He paused. One of the nearest attendants, and he could not be called *very* near, was at this moment removing the chief weight of his body from his left foot and transferring it to his right foot. Such relaxings, such rest-giving physical movements, such shiftings of bodily weight, such yawns and sighs, can in an unconcerned bystander have a momentous effect upon the manner and even upon the substance of a prophetic revelation. But when the bystander is an attendant employed to safeguard the nerves and moral sense of the public from untimely and improper revelations, the greatest of prophets has to be careful.

And Mr. Lordy had long ago learnt to take no chances in this danger-zone of official attention. "What I always say," he interpolated gravely in a firm, clear voice, "about Ayrshire cattle, is that you mustn't keep them too long in the same field." Then, when it became clear nobody was listening, "The point is," he went on, "that hate, which is just as much out of our control as love, has no connection with love at all. It resembles love in the sense that it is as completely beyond our power as the wind or the sea or the clouds or the rain. But it is no more the opposite of love than miserliness is the opposite of honesty or treachery is the opposite of extravagance."

"Well then," burst out John with some impatience, for he had become angrily conscious how many the hours were, and how slowly they were likely to pass, before he would have a chance of being with Tenna again, "what becomes of our behaviour to our parents, to our wives, to our children, to our neighbours and friends?"

THE INMATES

Mr. Lordy moved his head round apprehensively as if he were expecting a physical assault from all these directions.

"That," he murmured, "is as the Church decides. It is the Church that teaches us how to behave in this world so that we can inherit the world to come."

Here Mr. Lordy hurriedly crossed himself and carefully looked down at an elegantly bound volume of Milton which he had pulled out of his pocket and placed between the empty plate of brown bread-and-butter and the untouched plate of white bread-and-butter.

"You won't think I'm presuming on your kindness to me, Mr. Hush," he said, speaking shyly and in a low voice and pushing Milton against the untouched plate of white bread-and-butter, "if I confessed to you a fancy of mine? You really and truly won't? Well, it is this. I feel that the souls of original writers—for the more original a writer is, the more powerful is the pressure of his projected soul—are real presences that have their dwelling inside the printed pages of the author's books; not more than one, you understand, Mr. Hush—I mean not more than one soul to each separate book, though if the book has several volumes the author's soul will naturally have to flit from one to another of these separate volumes. You understand, Mr. Hush?—one, that is to say, for each volume."

John gravely inclined his head, indicating that he had no quarrel with the creative energy for thus confining the number of living souls in each book to one apiece. Encouraged by his friend's nod, Mr. Lordy now went on to explain that each book-spirit had its own natural appetite for appropriate nourishment, and that white bread-and-butter, thickly spread and thinly cut, was exactly what the fastidious soul dwelling between the covers of Milton's works would enjoy most.

"You see, Mr. Hush, though I am no good at Greek and Latin, I used to blow for the organist in our church; and I must take it for granted that when a spirit is very particular about the arrangement of poetical words it will be fastidious and even finical about what it imbibes of material sustenance."

HITHER AND THITHER

John Hush instantaneously forgot the attendants and incontinently turned his full attention upon Mr. Lordy. "If there is," he thought, "an exacting spirit between those covers ready to imbibe some ethereal essence from a plate of bread-and-butter, I'm damned if I've not got in me some still more fastidious and exacting spirit! Mine is not perhaps so austerely particular as Milton's; but by God it's more delicate in its taste! My spirit, in fact—I mean as opposed to Milton's, though they say at Cambridge he was called 'the Lady of —is the spirit of an old maid.

"I want to protect that heavenly wine-coloured leather-bound book as if it were a vestal virgin. In fact I can't stand the sight"—here he looked round almost ferociously—"of pages full of the subtlest verbal harmonies in Britain, being jostled by two great greasy plates, one of them greedily empty, and the other repulsively full." Thinking in this way and with an irrepressively urgent movement of hand and arm, Hush seized upon the poetical works of John Milton and inserted them in the nearest sanctuary he could see, which was one of Mr. Lordy's well-disinfected coat-pockets. This done he boldly leaned sideways towards the ear of the coat's wearer.

"Who the devil," he whispered, "is *that* fellow? And what bug has he got in his bonnet?"

In portentous gravity Mr. Lordy whispered back: "It's poor old Pantamount. He's perfectly harmless. Wouldn't hurt a fly. But they don't like him. They keep him in' the Wing' all they can. It's in 'the Wing' for anything, with poor old Pantamount. You see what he's like. Wouldn't flap at a fly. Wouldn't 'shush' at a midge. Wouldn't worry a wood-louse. Mam Tickle says he's the saint of Glint, but Father Toby don't like him and Father Wun can't abide him. He's been here as long as anybody, but lots of us have hardly seen him. They keep him in 'the Wing '. If he goes on as he's doing now, for instance, he won't last out the day. Back he'll go!"

John Hush sat up straight again, staring fixedly at the extraordinary figure thus presented to his attention.

THE INMATES

"What does the Commander think about him?" he enquired.

"He? He's probably never seen him or heard of him."

"Doesn't everybody talk about him?"

"I should say not!"

"What do they say about him?"

"Tottie Creambo says it's lucky to look at him, dangerous to meet his eye and fatal to speak to him. She says there are four of the rooms in the men's quarter—that where you and I sleep—empty because of him."

"You mean they died after speaking to him?"

"That's what Tottie says."

"What ridiculous nonsense!"

"Well, I'm not going to sit here any longer; and I'd advise you not to. In fact, Mr. Hush, only you mustn't think me impertinent, I beg you to come away with me." With these words Mr. Lordy rose to his feet. "If you're here at dinner I'll tell you more. I really am sorry, sir, but sometimes we just *have* to be rude."

And so now there was only Mr. Lordy's empty place by his side; and in front of him was the full plate of white bread-and-butter and the empty plate that had been full of brown bread-and-butter. There was also Mr. Lordy's empty cup and his own empty cup; and these two cups had the look of being absorbed in metaphysical speculation about nature of human fear.

"*Have* to be rude, have we," said John to himself. "And have to be frightened, too, eh? Here am I, a perfectly sane person save for a trifling sex-mania, so dominated by the deranged mind of this quaint individual whom I've been confusing with Jesus at Emmaus, that under the power of his crazy influence I am absolutely scared of even looking at this chap who's making now these extraordinary noises and who was just now on his knees! But I'm not going to yield to this crazy fear. Only I must fight it in my own way and nobody else's. Go on, you over there! Go on praying in hissings and scrabblings and rustlings and scrapings such as grass-snakes and slow-worms make when they pray! I'll look at you in a moment and, by God, I'll speak to you in a moment!

HITHER AND THITHER

"Whatever Mam Tickle may say, my room up there looking north, my room where the redeemer who's scared of being a redeemer comes out of a hole in the wall, won't be empty to-night, won't be empty for many a night, won't be empty till I've decided I've had enough of this place and am going to leave it; yes, and perhaps not only leave it, but leave it with *all* its rooms empty!"

And then while he could hear the slow steps of the two breakfast-attendants marching up and down, up and down, and while he wondered how soon they would start meddling with Pantamount, he set himself to find some mark, some sign, some crack, some blemish, some flaw, some stain, some defect, some deformity in one or other of the empty cups over which he was now bending so that he'd be able to distinguish them and know them again after they had been washed and dried.

And find it he now did! It was a small chip, a chip taken from the curve of the cup's handle just where the handle touched the side of the cup. The second he saw this chipped curve he knew that if there was a soul in that volume of Milton, a soul now safe from greasy plates in the left-hand pocket of its owner, there was also a soul in this chipped cup which was now from henceforth totally, inexorably, ineluctably, irremediably, separate from all other cups.

It might be broken, it might be thrown away, it might be flung to the bottom of a river, it might be thrown into the dog-pit among the spruce-firs; but its separate identity, its difference from all other cups ever made or ever destined to be made, was now, once for all, unalterably, fundamentally, absolutely established.

"It is a cup, take it for all in all the like of which—a cup is a cup: therefore it possesses a soul and from the depths of this soul I am draining enough courage, like the ichor from the veins of an immortal, to do what I want to do; enough courage, in fact, to face the man-god Pantamount, who at this moment is hiding his godhead by the simple device of kneeling upon a bench and pretending to pray."

THE INMATES

12

PANTAMOUNT

Laying the fingernail of his longest finger for the palpable passing of half a second on that chip in the cup, John now boldly rose to his feet, stepped backwards over the bench and walked casually towards one of their two attendants. While he did so, he noticed that the other attendant, with a casualness equal to his own, had languidly seated himself near the door. The attendant towards whom John now directed his negligent steps was the one who struck him as intending to approach the kneeling man, not directly but indirectly, in fact with that encircling movement that had already, even in the space of the forty-eight hours of his sojourn here, made John think of a dog-fish rounding up a shoal of mackerel and of a naked-necked vulture hovering round a corpse till the right moment to come down for its feast.

"Won't you try one of mine?" he now remarked, addressing this perambulating official. His silver case was in his hand and he was wishing for the first time since his guardian had given it to him on his twenty-first birthday that it was made of solid gold.

The man smiled agreeably but shook his head.

"Oh no, sir! Oh no!" he murmured. "Our regulations are very strict on this point. You see, sir, if once any of us permitted such a thing, the fat, as they say, would be in the fire."

"I understand perfectly," conceded John in his most ambassadorial tone. "'The fat and the fire.' Yes, I believe I *have* heard that before. It's a powerful saying. Yes, indeed, I can see what a lot of regulations there have to be to run a place like this with any kind of smoothness. But about that queer chap kneeling on the bench over there? Would he be angry if I said good morning to him? Would it be—all right —if I spoke to him? Of course, I know I mustn't ask you questions"; and as he said this he removed a couple of

PANTAMOUNT

cigarettes from the left side of his still open silver case and transferred them with exquisite nicety to the right side, bending his head a little towards the case as he did so and lightly blowing away a few feathery shreds of tobacco that in the airy fashion of wisps of cloud in a halcyon sky were flecking the polished silver. "Not personal questions, of course," he went on, "though I can't believe the poor fellow's name is really Pantamount. I expect that's a nickname, eh, like Tottie Creambo; one of those school nicknames—for, after all, Glint Hall *is* a kind of school, isn't it?—a school from which we poor inmates that you chaps are treating for our various manias are hoping—I'm sure I am"—and the crafty John straightened his shoulders and threw a wistful and nostalgic glance towards the window—"to soon return cured into the ordinary world! It would be more polite, I expect, don't you fancy so, Mister officer, if I were to address him by his real name? Some name, I expect, like Brown or Smith—though, of course, it might be, for we never know in these confused days, Romanoff or Hapsburg. In fact I might chance it, mightn't I, and call him Mr. Jones?"

The attendant had been regarding John as he talked in this style with an expression of suspended judgment. It was not an expression of serious suspicion and it certainly was not one of intimate trust. As he waited for him to reply, John hurriedly told himself that if there were not psychological training-schools for asylum servants there certainly ought to be; and then he told himself just as hurriedly that training in psychology was the last thing needed.

"All that is needed," he told himself as he watched the man's eyes and mouth, "is natural human sympathy, and reservoirs upon reservoirs of instinctive tact!"

But in a second the fellow *had* to answer! He couldn't go on looking at him with that peculiar expression whether he had *learnt* to look like that or whether it was an inspiration of his own. "Oh, chipped cup," John found himself silently praying, "if you inanimates have any soul at all, make him answer me!"

THE INMATES

But aloud he said: "I may be quite wrong, but my impression is that Pantamount was the name of a hobby-horse in the nursery of King Arthur."

Suddenly the attendant turned his profile to John and began talking to himself. "One thing's clear," he muttered audibly: "Brown-Smith must come off his bloody knees!"

After thinking aloud in this surprising manner, the attendant resumed his circumambient stalking-match.

But now on the strength, John told himself, of a single chipped teacup, whose soul, like that of all souls, whether Vegetable, animal, mineral, human or divine, was "totus sensus, totus visus, totus anditus, totus sui generis", he moved straight to the side of that kneeling figure. The neighbours of Mr. Brown-Smith alias Pantamount, who sat at their breakfast nearest to the man, were to John's surprise paying very little attention to him. Every now and then they whispered to each other; but though John couldn't be sure their whispers had nothing to do with the kneeling man, the fact that not one of them so much as glanced at the attendant seemed to suggest that their minds were far away from him, and very likely far away from the present moment.

Mr. Pantamount's own mind seemed far away, too, for his eyes were shut and his lips were moving in his concentrated prayer to some invisible hearer. The first thing John noticed about the man's face was that it was composed of very hard flesh. This flesh wasn't stretched out taut over prominent bones. It was just hard flesh where most people have soft flesh. The man had an aquiline nose, and the colour of his skin seemed yellow rather than white or brown, and though John looked at his head pretty closely, he found himself completely unable to decide whether his skull was bald or whether it was covered, like that of a baby, with very fine, very filmy, whitish-grey hair.

But the general effect of this hard-fleshed, strongly moulded skull, tilted upwards and a little backwards, was that it was not composed of human flesh at all, but was a very ancient image carved in some kind of hard-grained wood, the image,

PANTAMOUNT

so it struck John's mind at that first moment of encountering it, of some sage from the lost continent of Atlantis.

"No, no! I don't mean," so he decided he would interpret Mr. Pantamount to Tenna when they were together again, "the image of an Atlantean god; I mean an image, or, if you prefer, a statue, cut in hardwood and petrified, if that's a permissible word, by aeons upon aeons of aimless drifting, back and forth, to and fro, up and down, in the tides of the salt sea."

John's mind was in an odd state that morning, a more confused state than he had experienced since he first saw Tenna under the tulip-tree. He couldn't expel from his consciousness that possessive, in-drawing, in-sucking, maternal eye of the mother of Seth, issuing forth from the half of the face whose other half was hidden against the body of the milk-giving cow.

He could see all the time with horrible clarity the pitiful helplessness of the desperate little jerks which that unhappy idiot kept making, with the obscure hope of originating some independent life, some seminal sex-life, some self-chosen life, of his very own, that wouldn't at once, that *wouldn't ever*, be lapped up and swallowed up and drawn up into the veins and sinews and maternal juices of his doting parent.

How to deal with the terrible force of normal love was a problem John Hush felt he was himself spiritually too weak to undertake either for himself or on behalf of another; and when it came to abnormal or perverse love it would have been grotesque for anyone as degenerate as he knew himself to be to attempt a syllable of advice to another person!

But though he had spent the whole of the precious unreturning bloom of to-day's early-morning hours, hours that always had the effect of throwing him into a mood of almost painfully virginal receptivity, watching, watching, watching, with a dreadful absorption the vampirising suction of maternal love as its youthful victim squirmed beneath it, it still seemed to him that for him—though other men might risk such things—the only course was to dodge, with all the subtlety at his command, every conceivable kind of responsibility.

THE INMATES

But though he indulged to the limit a pitiful and almost wistful craving to escape responsibility, none of this mental spreading of wings seemed able to save him to-day from seeing before his inmost vision that insucking maternal eye, that eye wherein this much-praised "love" could be observed, in the serpentine coils of its devouring insatiability, swallowing its offspring's freedom to live a life of its own and exciting itself to swallow the more Voluptuously as its own pity for the helpless thing's struggles draws forth more maternal saliva to smooth the path of its re-enwombing.

And yet this question, John told himself now as he stared at the kneeling Pantamount, was a matter of cosmogonic psychology. Should the maternal eye, turning so quickly into the eye of a virtuous vampire, be violently *put out*, or could it be, so to say, philosophically diverted or even perhaps metaphysically hoodwinked by the evocation of some primordial illusion with the help of creative nature?

It was for help to meet the life-challenge of this demonic beautiful-horrible thing that he had come to Mr. Lordy this morning; but Mr. Lordy had failed him. Of course he ought to have known that Mr. Lordy, as a worshipper of the Mother of God, was bound to fail him.

"My irritation with Mr. Lordy," he told himself, "isn't quite fair! The Mother of the Redeemer has been worshipped for so long with the crucified on her knees that to rebel against mother-love as something deadly to natural life has become an unnatural gesture.

"But a carved wooden image of the last of the Atlanteans, an image capable of keeping itself upright on its knees on an ordinary schoolroom bench for something like twenty minutes, is an entity, call it Pantamount or Tom Thumb, or Tamburlaine the Great, that I can't afford to ignore when considering the crucial point whether in its essence love isn't a curse to the human race——"

What he felt at that moment was that if he could only explain to this Atlantean creature just exactly what that mother was doing when she kept her eye on her idiot boy, he might per-

PANTAMOUNT

suade the man to go out with him into the yard now at once and address a word of warning to the woman.

"Mr. Brown-Smith!" he accordingly began.

But he was so obsessed by the indurated woodenness of the man's appearance that it gave him a very curious feeling when the fellow lazily, easily, comfortably and quite casually opened his left eye and fixed it upon him. The eye was a heavy-lidded eye. It was an ichthyoid eye, and it gave John Hush a look that made him feel as if he had been dead twenty thousand years and in his ghostly peregrinations, while stumbling along the bottom of some prehistoric ocean-bed, had stumbled on a volcanic crack in that horrific floor of the universe and out of this crack had been arrested by the fixity of this eye. Then the other eye opened and then the mouth opened.

"Sit down and explain yourself!" said the mouth; and, as the creature who owned the mouth spoke, it itself slid down into a sitting posture and made room for John at its side.

Not one of the inmates who were finishing their breakfast at that end of the table gave John a glance; and as for the attendant who had encouraged him to speak to this "revenant" from before the Flood, he had calmly taken himself off and was now standing with his hands in his pockets quietly talking to his companion near the door.

"Mr. Brown-Smith!" began John again, as soon as he found himself comfortably seated beside this enigmatic fragment of antiquity. "What I've been wanting to ask you ever since I first saw you is this: Wouldn't it be a good thing to invent some other word in place of the word love?"

The piece of driftwood that had become immortal in its aeonian tossings on all the seas of all the world allowed its Atlantean head to wag slowly from side to side in an emphatic "no".

"Why not?" John persisted.

"Because," responded Pantamount, "words have magical power; and since the word 'love' has been used so long for all the meanings we give it in this part of the world, it would be silly to use another word unless we decided to break the spell.

THE INMATES

If we decided to undo all that this magic word has done, then we would have to use a word that was opposite in meaning; and not only so, we would have to try hard to feel whatever it was that the new word meant."

John looked at him uneasily.

"Would we have to say 'hate'?" he enquired.

But the driftwood man only smiled at him. Not a word did he answer.

"You mean," answered John, "that hate isn't the opposite of love?"

But still the driftwood man only smiled; and now his smile made John think of a queerly shaped piece of wood that he had found once in a rock-pool near Lulworth and that a fisherman had told him must have been carried backwards and forwards across the ocean for a million years.

"You mean," said John, "that hate is some kind of perverted love, and that the real opposite of love would be indifference; and that if we found some appropriate word either biblical or classical implying anyway the condition of complete imperviousness, we might if we used such a word for a few hundred years gradually turn off, before we knew what we were doing, the electric current that moves the entire world?"

Pantamount didn't even smile. The features carved in driftwood, from which John had never taken his eyes, remained as unmoved as a universe from which the dynamic polarity of positive and negative electricity had been totally withdrawn.

John felt frustrated and baffled. He felt like a boy who had at last found the way into the circus of his ideal desire only to be rejected as incapable of even collecting the dung of the elephant he longed to ride.

"I had hoped you could help me," he murmured rather pitifully. "It's this woman from the village who comes to the sheds to do the milking. She's got an idiot boy, you know, and this boy — " He fancied he detected a flicker of interest cross the man's face, and so he dropped the Brown-Smith and boldly called him Pantamount. "And she loves this kid, Mr. Pantamount," he said, "to such a tune that I saw a look of positively sick longing on the boy's face when he wanted to follow one of those twins—you know the pair, Mr. Pantamount?—as he danced over the shadows."

Once more a smile flickered over the piece of driftwood that had been crossing the Atlantic for a million years, and along with this smile there drifted into John's ears what sounded like a proposition of some elemental Euclid, a proposition that had come together out of the lines and curves of foam left by the ripples and eddies of half the tides of the Atlantic.

"What we tend to forget," murmured this elemental subhuman Euclid, "is that our choice is not between the chaoticism of 'love-hate' and the monotony of 'love-nothing'. It is between a less or a more of this lively and magnetic 'love-hate', that is to say a less or a more of the natural magic we've all been practising for a million years!"

John shuddered through his whole body and soul. He had never in his life felt so compelled to stiffen his whole being, and at the same time to bend it, metaphorically speaking, in that crouching movement, described by the Homeric word *aleis*, of a desperate creature at bay. He had never felt like this before, anywhere, or about anything. He sat straight up. He clenched his lean knuckles upon his hard, pressed-together knees. He felt as if in another second he might be compelled to butt with his head, as well as struggle with clenched hands and bony knees, against the impact of this cosmic 'love-hate' about which the man was talking.

"I don't think—" he gasped, in a voice that to his own internal hearing was like a rending and a splintering crack, cleaving its way through some vast, compact, adamantine rock, thick as the world, "I don't think I agree with you!"

He was astonished that the half a dozen men who were still lingering over their breakfast didn't rise and crowd round them. He was amazed that the attendant with whom he had been talking didn't come rushing up. But what was this? The arm that came round him was not the arm of any indignant attendant, nor was it the arm of any agitated neighbour. It was the arm of Mr. Pantamount himself; and no sooner was

THE INMATES

it about him than he was aware of the fact that he had totally and entirely misunderstood the man's meaning.

The arm thrown round him, the arm supporting him, the arm that was now leading him across the dining-hall towards the entrance to the passage and the stairs, wasn't at all the kind of "loving arm" the mere idea of which as approaching him and as touching him made him feel as if he could utter a scream that would crack "the thick rotundity of the earth".

"You misunderstood me completely, my dear boy," said Mr. Pantamount, allowing John to lean against the banister while he himself, relaxing his hold upon the young man, permitted his own arm to sink limply to his side and stood awkwardly and obviously Very uncomfortably on the second step of the staircase.

"You don't perhaps realise that what *you* call 'love' and I call 'love-hate' 'is an electric vibration, with an ebb and flow and a less and a more, as if it were an actual fluid, but a vibration whose activity, though not its essential nature, is affected by the amount of it you use.

"Thus while an ordinary amount of the 'love-hate' vibration or invisible fluid leaves things to all outward appearance very much the same as they were, the use of twice as much of this fluid has a totally different effect and a very sudden and sometimes a very surprising one. Can't I make you see, my dear boy, that in all these ultimate things in nature and life, it is not the difference of substance, but the difference of *quantity* that is the important thing? This nectar, this ichor, this miraculous semen of the gods, is simply the result of doubling, yes! and perhaps of more than doubling, the amount of love-hate you are using. This doesn't change the quality of the thing's creative magnetism; but it changes completely its effect. Can I make you understand? I tell you when you shudder, as you did just now, at the idea of the appalling power of ordinary human love mixed, as it always is, with ordinary human hate, you are entirely justified.

"And you are entirely justified in crying out that you don't agree with the abuse, examples of which we see on all sides, of

PANTAMOUNT

this divine force and power. Experiment with it yourself, my dear boy! Only the living experience of it will show you! And don't you see how easy it is? You don't have to say to yourself: 'Now I must mix my love for this person, for this stone, for this stump, for this grass, for this plant, for this mud, this rock, this empty air, this gulf between the stars, this horizon of moving ocean, this wall, this carpet, this bird, this cloud of gnats, or for these legs and arms that are yours, theirs, or my own, *with the proper amount of hate*! "I tell you you don't have to think what you're doing at all; or to understand what you're doing at all; or to stop for a moment to ask yourself' what am I doing?' All you've got to do is to do it.

"And if you say to me,' To do what?' I answer, 'To "love-hate" more than you've ever love-hated before!' That's all. To do it more. To do it more each time you do it!"

At this point Mr. Pantamount gave John a look; and this look John, in the quarter of a tick of the big clock just below them in the hall, decided that at all costs he must fix in his memory, exactly as it was so that he might recall every quiver and quirk of it, every up-lift and down-droop of it, to Tenna, when they met in the afternoon. It was, he decided he would tell Tenna, the most perfect example he had ever seen of the wisdom of the serpent and the harmlessness of the dove, fused in something else, something that John, whether Tenna understood him or not, could only describe as *magian*.

At the moment, however, John had no time to think out all that the man's look implied, since the words that followed it required instantaneous action.

"Better go down a couple of steps further," suggested Mr. Tantamount, "and let's both lean on this rail, so that you can keep watch past my shoulder on all who come up, and I can keep watch past your shoulder on all who are coming down. Our watchword, of course, is 'Inmates pass!' But if they're not inmates we'll both hurry down and be out of the front door before you can say 'Jack Robinson!'"

Hush obeyed him in every detail; and certainly if Doctor Echetus had appeared at the bottom of the stairs and Father

THE INMATES

Toby Tickle at the top of the stairs, they would never have given a second glance to these two active, practical, competent, energetic men exchanging a casual morning's greeting as they passed each other on the main staircase of Glint Hall.

"Forgive all this fuss, my dear sir!" murmured Mr. Pantamount. "And before I go on, let me assure you I don't give myself away to everybody like this; only I knew, even before you spoke to me, that you and I had a lot in common."

Meanwhile John's mind had been whirling round fifty times faster than the big entrance-hall clock, whose chief peculiarity compared with other institutional time-pieces was the bare, unbroken, unadorned whiteness of its face and the unvarnished blackness, an opaque dead blackness, more like soot than ink, of its broad flat hands, hands that resembled the gloved fingers of an implacable great-aunt raised to her face in mechanical prayer the moment her knees touched their familiar accomplice the straw-stuffed hassock.

"He's on the track of something," John thought, "but he's taken the wrong road to get there. This damned 'love-hate' business, however much he piles it up, can never get him there. He may be right that they're not opposites; or, if they are, that they depend on each other for their very existence; but I don't see how he can deny that they cancel each other out, and that no amount of 'more', 'more', 'more', 'more' can really fuse them together or produce the required magic. No amount of 'more 'can change the quality of a thing's essence."

John felt like a mediaeval theologian who has just nailed up a challenge on the gate of the university of the universe. But it was as if that far-carried fragment of Atlantean driftwood had read his thoughts.

"It is not," recommenced Mr. Pantamount, "that the hate-fluid neutralises or freezes the love-fluid, nor is it that the psychic-chemical atoms of love work upon the object to which we direct them in alternate activity with those of hate. To think in that way is to misunderstand the nature of both. The love-element or love-fluid or love-magnetism in us possesses as the larger portion of its nature psychic-chemical atoms that are identical with—and I have proved this from many curious experiments on these delicately mixed atoms in my own nature —identical with the psychic-chemical constitution of the hate-element or hate-magnetism in us. When we direct them towards any person or any thing, they create a link between ourselves and that person or thing. And this link, whether a love-link or a hate-link, or both together, as is usually the case, is not easy to break.

"And now consider this, my dear sir. The whole of our life is divided into two halves, the first action, the second contemplation; and the curious thing to note is that though they both tend to overlap each other, there is about twice as much over-lapping of action by contemplation as of contemplation by action.

"For instance, I am going out now to help trimming some young firs. My chopping and sawing is unquestionably action; but, as I do it, are my taste, my eyes, my ears, my nose, my touch, entirely absorbed in this action? Of course not!

"And what about women? A woman, let's say, is washing up at her sink. She is rinsing and drying; but while her fingers are at work she can see a stream of sunlight striking the woodwork at her side or striking a rack of clean plates over her head, and she can note a leaf blown across the bricks at her feet, while the sound of rooks is reaching her through the window from somewhere outside, or the long-drawn whistle of a train.

"We are thus compelled—as the academic logicians would put it, though, of course, really, we are *anything but compelled*, for all the world does the precise opposite!—compelled to recognise that contemplation occupies about three-quarters of our life, while action—though we may be supposed to be working twelve hours every day—really only occupies, that is to say entirely fills, our living consciousness for about a quarter of our life, or perhaps only a tenth. And now I come to my point——"

But at this moment a group of specially fortunate male inmates, favoured, as Tenna was, by being allowed to have their

THE INMATES

breakfast on trays in their bedroom, came leisurely downstairs, each one of them, without exception, John noticed, surveying Mr. Pantamount with fascinated interest as they passed.

"He must," thought John, "be some kind of a celebrity, perhaps a famous criminal of whom in those foreign places I never heard!" and he began conjuring up the most monstrous "Jack the Ripper" crimes, trying in vain to imagine his companion committing them. Then he told himself that perhaps Mr. Pantamount had a mad fancy that he was once a salamander who slept in a warming-pan under the stairs all day, but at night scurried about from room to room, all over the building, swallowing all the big black spiders it could catch by one leg and gobbling them up alive.

"But it must," he thought, "have been all a pure fancy! He may have crawled about in the dark all night for years with his head near the floor and his mouth open; but as for catching a single spider, I can't see him ever doing it. And whatever his crimes, whatever his manias, whatever his crazy delusions, whatever Jesuitical or Taoistical defence of 'love-hate' he may invent, calling it a 'magnetic vibration', I like this Pantamount. I feel a physical attraction to the fellow. But where the devil are my thoughts off to now?" He asked himself this when he realised that he was rubbing the slippery banister with the palm of his hand and imagining himself caressing the sea-polished, million-years-drifted woodwork of Mr. Pantamount's battered frame! That gentleman was now speaking once more, and speaking with a queer creaking sound in his voice that really did seem to John like the creaking in the skeleton ribs of some fantastic vessel from the ports of lost Atlantis, or even from the drowned harbours of Mu, the flood-city of the Pacific, a Vessel that had drifted for aeons of time across one, or both, of these two oceans, and in drifting had been scraped and scratched by huge extinct devil-fish and hammered by the frontal bones of marine mammals larger than any leviathans as yet recorded in the annals of the sea.

"Three quarters of our life," creaked Mr. Pantamount, "is contemplation; and so much does our happiness depend on

PANTAMOUNT

those three-quarters of our life that even if we are incredibly deft and adroit in our daily job we can be the reverse of happy in our lives!

"Now suppose, my dear sir, that that aggravating old clock ticking away down there were to recognise that you and I were both unhappy; and, further, were to decide like some shrewd old Nanny to tell us what to do to recover our spirits, what would it tell us? Well! I contend that it would tell us, as it saw us against this banister, that we must intensify our love-hate for everything in our consciousness at this moment. It would, in fact, tell us not to confine ourselves to the wood-work under our elbows or to the carpet-covered boards under our feet or to the sun's rays falling upon the marble squares upon the floor or to the heavenly scents of leaves and grass reaching us through some open window downstairs, that is to say, not to confine our intensification-scoop to what is round us at the moment but to include, in addition to the moment's plunder, all the most pressing images of pleasure, yes, and of pain too, that at this moment are disturbing, delighting, harassing, agitating, thrilling or lacerating us from our immediate past—that is to say, from the past that has power to hurt us still; the events, for instance, that brought us to Glint Hall and the personalities, both engaging and detestable, that were connected with our coming here."

At this point John Hush suddenly became aware of the countenance of that keeper of the north lodge whose sleeping-quarters and those of the woman who resembled his old nurse he could see from his bed. The man was staring at them with concentrated interest; but the moment he realised that John had recognised him he turned his head, shrugged his shoulders and went off.

"What makes up the larger part," continued Mr. Pantamount, though John Hush knew he had seen the man, "of everyone's life is our love-hate for the people of our life, for our wives and husbands and friends, for our parents and children and neighbours, for our employers and employees. Thus whenever we are oppressed by sadness or by annoyance

THE INMATES

the cause is our love-hate for other people, either a momentary and transient, or a permanent and abiding love-hate, with the stress on the hate, or on the love as circumstances dictate. Therefore, if the art of life consists in the supremely easy and yet supremely difficult art of being happy, it becomes clear that our deliberate intensification of the nervous magnetic flow from our soul into the clothes, the faces, the gestures, the bodies, the ways, the words, the expressions, of the people of our life will be associated with the material things immediately around us.

"For instance, at this moment I am myself grievously affected by two faces, faces that I love and hate, faces that swim about in my spleen and burrow in my bowels, faces that I know so intensely that I feel as if my own face, as I think about them, comes to resemble first one of them and then the other! Well, my friend, these faces mingle with these stairs and these banisters, with that pool of sunlight, with that old clock's ticking! Yes, and I've got to mix them with all the air around us and all the earth about us, and with the airy space beyond, and with the empty spaces beyond the airy-spaces, and with the great void itself."

Pantamount's words melted into so much before they died away that John's mind was left flying in circles over the things into which they'd sunk, like a seagull over miles and miles of wet sand.

But for John the oddest thing about that particular moment of his clinging to the banister of the main staircase of Glint was that suddenly, and without warning, his own life-consciousness which till now had felt completely dominated by this human eidolon of ghostwood that had drifted for a million years over the antediluvian cities of Atlantis and Mu and about whom heaven knows what sea-birds had floated and what flying-fish had flown, rose in revolt. Yes, the almost insanely humble life-consciousness in John's Shakespearean actor's frame, from feeling like the consciousness of a fly, of a gnat, of a midge, of a worm, of a newt, of a spider, of a flea, began to feel as if it were the life-consciousness of some great magician capable of making any enemy he might have wish to the devil he were his friend before it was too late.

And with this totally unexpected sense of power there came a clear memory of what, when he left the milking sheds and came into breakfast, he had wanted from Mr. Lordy and been unable to get from him because of his being a Catholic, namely some device, some trick, some incantation, some miraculous formula, by means of which he could liberate—spiritually, of course, not physically—that idiot village-boy from his possessively devoted mother.

"Oh, by the way, Mr. Brown-Smith"—he noticed that at the sound of those syllables Pantamount made a humorous grimace, screwing up his features in the most grotesque manner till he caused them to resemble the features of a sea-serpent to whom has been offered a dish of pond-eels; but John shamelessly went on—"what I want you to do now is to win the confidence of no less a person than the village idiot of this hamlet. Yes, this is serious, Pantamount. I want you to attract this boy to yourself, as I know you could if you only would, and draw off a little of this same 'love-hate' —intercept it I mean—as it flows between this possessive mother and this possessed youngster. Come on, my dear sir, and let me introduce you. You'll soon see just what I mean."

He laid his fingers on the man's sleeve.

"I don't know," he began again, as they descended into the hall, "whether you have a mother living, Mr. Pantamount? I am an orphan myself; but there are cases, I assure you, when—cases when ——" He broke off suddenly; and then, in quite a different voice, a voice that rose almost to a harsh scream: "There are cases, Mr. Pantamount ——" He stopped abruptly. "Cases when," he went on after a pause, during which he was clearly trying to control himself, "it makes anyone *murderous!*"

The sound of this dangerous word startled both of them; and it was with an access of caution, reticence and discretion that they crossed the threshold and walked out into the air. Oh, how clearly John could remember afterwards all that

THE INMATES

passed through his mind as he led the man from the front of Glint Hall clear round to the back and guided him into the particular portion of the big north yard where were the couple of sheds in and out of which Nancy and her son looked after their cows.

He imagined himself founding, with the money he would receive from a brilliantly savage book on the way Glint Hall was run, a completely new Glint Hall, in which all the attendants were men he himself had trained and among whom it would be impossible to imagine such a creature as Mr. Gewlie.

The wind had entirely gone down when they reached the cowshed, and the smell of dung and hay and grass and milk and oil and grease and sawdust and stagnant water and horse-piss and disinfectant and river-mist and new paint all mingled together in the windless warmth to create a morbidly agreeable earthly Hades quite as pleasant if not more pleasant to John's peculiar taste than any earthly Paradise of which he had read.

The brooding sunshine heaved and quivered and wavered and languidly floated between the buildings as if it were a diffused essence of *pot-pourri* drawn from the fecundity of the whole of the British Isles; and the singular notion now edged itself into John Hush's brain that the cockleshell creases of Pantamount's figure represented a cosmic reversion to some purely mineral world against which the friendly, animal-vegetable world had long ago revolted.

To John's fantastic speculation at this moment the ocean-drenched driftwood of this weird person's bodily form, to which just now on the staircase he had been so strangely attracted, had grown to be something not merely petrified, but transformed into some element older than uranium or helium or hydrogen or nitrogen, older than all the scoriac dust from all the extinct craters of the world.

But his crazy thoughts were now impinged upon by their arrival at the shed, and their vision of Nancy and her offspring, the sweat running down the ruddy, plump apple-hard cheeks of the one, and the sad, hollow, elongated, Quixotic cheeks of the other, while the former worked with bucket and mop at

PANTAMOUNT

the cribs, racks, receptacles for grain, and bins for mixing food and fodder, and the latter, with the biggest pitchfork Hush had ever seen, was shuffling back and forth, carrying the cow-dung and the trampled straw to a great heap in the corner of one of the small fields which were inside the walls of the institution.

So fast had John's imagination run ahead of what he was practically achieving that the process of introducing his friend to Nancy was well over, and the buxom middle-aged woman was already becoming infatuated with this refugee from before the Flood, by the time he himself had begun to talk to the idiot.

When his conversation with Seth, however, touched the performances of Hither and Thither, John had an agitating shock with regard to his own personal mental state. He suddenly experienced the extremely disturbing sensation that he was living in a dream that was inside another dream. There was terror for him in this. He had been dreaming and now was awake; but he found that he had awakened into a new dream, out of which he now had to escape again through any aperture, postern, skylight porthole, arrow-slit, airshaft, that in his desperation he could hit upon!

But what had happened to him? A minute or two ago, as he presented his new friend to the idiot's mother, and himself began talking in so mellow a tone to the boy, he not only felt that he was master of a very difficult situation but that he was master of it by the use of his own secret way of life that was totally outside the bounds of race or creed.

Yes, a minute or two ago he was on the crest of a great wave of life, in a *Flying Dutchman* of his own, and able to ride any storm and give any orders—like yesterday's crazy Commander —but now—Jesus Holy!—there was nothing to stand on, nothing under his feet, nothing to stop him going down, nothing to stop him going up, nothing to stop him going sideways, whether to left or right, and, with this, his senses had gone all askew, so that he saw sounds, heard smells, felt colours, tasted shadows!

THE INMATES

"What on earth has happened to me?" he asked himself. His actual body was swaying and lurching about; though it wasn't only in the outer world that things had become very queer. He kept asking himself, "Is this the proper way to breathe?" For the notion had crossed his mind that he ought to be breathing through his skin, but that he'd forgotten the trick of this! And then he thought: "Didn't I know how to fly when I was little? Weren't there once feathers on my wrists? Yes, yes—*feathers*! Didn't Plato talk of feathers? He's a good fellow. Where is he now?"

Everything in John's mind was rocking like bilge-water in the hold of a ship. He had begun talking to the idiot about love-hate. And now he was demanding of himself why it was that it had become impossible for the world ever to come to an end while there was so much love-hate to draw upon. What was the matter with him? Something must have gone wrong! "Is it possible that when I was getting sleepy and struggling and beating against sleep I broke through some barrier and slipped down some crack leading into a completely different world?"

And then in a flash of realisation he knew what it was! The whole atmosphere of psychic disturbance in Glint Hall—that is to say the magnetic cloud of *derangement under treatment*—was something totally different from the natural tradition of world-old rural aberration such as is rooted in the common earth along with rocks and stones and trees.

Yes, John Hush now saw clearly enough what had happened. Coming straight from insanity *within* Glint to insanity *outside* Glint, he had indeed quite literally slipped into a different world. The truth was that the insanity of the free outside world was capable of producing many startling effects upon Doctor Echetus's imprisoned patients. To them it seemed doubly real. It was real in its insanity, which the inmates naturally held to be a very especial form of truth; and it was also real in the manner in which it was taken for granted and given its particular and special place in the free, noninstitutional life of the ordinary world.

PANTAMOUNT

This idiot boy he was trying to assist in freeing himself from his possessive mother had managed in some subtle and indescribable way to hypnotise him into the poetically accepted and taken-for-granted aberration of a simple idiocy that was as old as the human race. This boy was, in fact, what in ancient races was called an "Innocent of God", and in line presence of this planetary human derangement that was older than Homer or Hesiod, this derangement with whose sacred innocence even Hippocrates dared not meddle, this derangement that affected every aspect of the human flesh, every member of the human body, every impulse of the human spirit, all these modern psychiatrists about whom his guardian and his guardian's friends were forever talking seemed frivolous and superficial and trivial and altogether unsound.

Yes, John realised now what had happened to him. By trying to help this rustic Innocent, this incarnation of all the traditional simplicities of all the Simple-Simons of the immemorial village-greens of England, he had given himself up to a lad whose whole soul longed to catch, to take hold of, to feel between his fingers, some wild free creature that he could make his own, and only in this way obliterate his secret knowledge that to his mother he himself was just such a wild creature, and that all this craving was born of his own flutterings and quiverings as he was pressed to his mother's heart.

And John saw that by giving himself up to this lad—for he told himself that what might be called "the insanity of nature" was a more powerful force than what might be called "the insanity of nerves"—he had himself taken the part, in this mad drama, of those airy-fairy twins for whom the heart and spirit of the lad were crying.

"Well, Nancy my dear," he could hear Pantamount murmuring in that peculiar tone of his that seemed to introduce into the actions of an hour the feelings of a thousand years, "I must get off now to my spruce-firs; but I'll see you again to-morrow and we'll talk more about that little matter!"

It was indeed with these words repeating themselves over and over again at the back of his brain—"that little matter, that little matter, that little matter!"—that John decided as he worked by the boy's side that what he was really doing for him was offering himself as the wild goose, as the wild lizard, as the wild shrew-mouse, or even as the wild hedgehog, for the idiot's imagination to overtake and hug to its heart, though its embrace killed the thing it loved!

But he knew he had contracted the last thing he wanted just then, namely a heavy human responsibility; and what if he had started towards this unknown Atlantean a foolish fancy in the breast of Nancy that might end by making the woman seriously unhappy?

"I must tell Tenna," he thought, "every word of this." And then there came over him a ghastly desolating sense that what he had particularly dreaded with regard to himself and Tenna was the very thing that had been brought to pass; namely that their individual manias should be swept into the current of their friendship—for he was actually beginning to wonder which of her locks he would most like to snip off; and there *she* was, scarce able to control her fury with that absurd old Rumpibus!

"I must have it out with her," he thought, "I must persuade her to enter into a sort of solemn league and covenant with me, so that I restrain myself about her curls and she restrains herself about that ridiculous old doddipole."

13

THE POLISHED TABLE

THE DAYS and weeks and months at Glint Hall went by with their scrapings of nerve-strings, their loosenings of nerve-knots, their meltings of nerve-glaciers, their combustions of nerve-dams, their scoopings out of nerve-cisterns, their crater-eruptions of nerve-volcanoes, their ice-fields of nerve-corpses, without any startling change in the average tempo of the affinity between John and Tenna, until the revolving

THE POLISHED TABLE

whirligig of fate, following its own rhythmical polarity of obsessions, brought time's pulsing locomotive to a pause on Saturday June the sixteenth, just a week before Midsummer Eve. The unequalled solstitial twilights of this particular summer, although entirely natural, were not without their temperamental effect upon the inmates of Glint.

This effect was primarily nervous, but it was emotional, too; and that open-minded scientist, the master of Glint, studied it just as carefully as he studied the recurrent effects of the waxing and waning moon.

It was as a consequence of these studies that he discovered that when subjected to a succession of twilights patients tended to become absent-minded and indulge in those vague daydreams in which all dangerous obsessions are lost. He was, indeed, famous all over Europe as the only authority who insisted on allowing protracted twilights their therapeutic effect.

This was on the principle of *like curing like*. For as Nature in her northern twilight falls into a mood suspended between a romantic worship of light and a romantic worship of darkness, so also does her paragon, man; and as Nature's temperate zones are healing and restoring to her poor creatures of earth, so nothing but good could come, the Doctor argued, from letting loose, so to speak, this solstitial suavity upon agitated human nerves.

And under what conditions, he must have asked himself, were his certified bedlamites most apt to be soothed by the innocuous daydreams of nature's twilights? Obviously when reading! And reading what books? Obviously old-fashioned books. From the pages of modern books the minds of readers seldom wander. It is from old-fashioned books that these touchingly abstracted heads are lifted up in their trances of absorbed daydreams.

Doctor Echetus never hesitated to rely upon the sound judgment of his chaplain, Father Toby, as to the difference between disturbing books and soothing books. Thus it was brought about that the chief inciters to insanity, to whose

THE INMATES

devilish influence, according to John and Tenna, these aberrations were due, namely religion, sex, and blazing sunshine, were all barred from this group of patients from whose carefully-shaded lamps, and from whose books chosen by Father Toby, not a few wholesomely dreaming heads were lifted up in the peaceful dusk.

The grand piano was an innovation. It had been steadily advocated for the reading-room by Ursie Mum; but for a long time Doctor Echetus had refused to consider it. It was only when Ursie Mum persuaded a specialist from Budapest to explain to the Doctor the value of adding good music to good books, and both to the influence of prolonged twilight—and then only when she herself offered to pay for the piano—that Echetus yielded.

In regard to the smoking-room, nobody interfered with the Doctor's method. Here he was startlingly original. Here he followed the purely empirical and experimental method. He insisted on the shutters being closed and the curtains being drawn and all the electricity being fully turned on. Thus when a patient moved from the reading-room into the smoking-room it was like leaving one hemisphere to enter another! There was no card-table in the room that wasn't brilliantly illuminated, and there could never be a doubt in the mind of the blindest player as to what cards he held in his hand.

It may be imagined it was found necessary in spite of the Doctor's experiments in normal nightclubism to open a couple of small windows near the door when the smoke-filled warmth of the room became too overpowering; but, that the Doctor's original idea shouldn't be interfered with, the particular windows letting in the air looked to the east and consequently opened on the darkest twilight that could be found round Glint Hall, and although in the twilight the old heathen camp could be seen, the lights in the room were so glaring that the view outside was considerably dimmed. The Doctor's idea in this whole scheme of the smoking-room was to evoke, as far as it could be done, an environment of metropolitan normality, thereby inducing the patients to forget that they *were* patients.

THE POLISHED TABLE

On this particular night of the sixteenth of June John Hush and Tenna Sheer were facing each other over the same familiar untouched draughts-board as had been their inanimate companion every night since Lady Day. "Nothing," John was earnestly whispering to her, "can stop my reading your feelings in your face. We know each other too well, my precious one, and we can't be put off by words. You can repeat that bravado till midnight and you won't make me believe you. I know you are as tense as a bowstring, and so are the rest of us, and every day now till we're off it'll get worse and worse. Tottie and Thither and Miss Bolster are just as strung-up as Mr. Lordy; nor are the Commander and the Zeit-Geist any better. Pantamount is the only one of the lot of us who seems unruffled, and, of course, it may be self-control even with him.

"I don't have to tell *you*, my treasure, what the worst danger is!" Her eyes, which had been growing larger and darker and rounder all the evening and had begun to surround themselves with cavernous circles that steadily grew hollower as the flickering orbs within them grew darker, now emitted a startling glitter that shot from their centre to their circumference as they reflected the rays from the nearest electric bulb in the ceiling.

"You mean *ourselves*?" she murmured. "Well!"

"Well! Not only you and I, my dear. I mean the whole lot of us who're in the secret. I mean all the Confederates."

Tenna bit her lips and was silent. Then, unable to restrain herself, she began speaking rapidly, though still in so low a voice that he found difficulty in following her.

"What's so unfair about you, John, is that you treat my instincts as if they were no more than your own manias which have merely to do with yourself! Do you know I sometimes feel I shan't be able to get into that plane at all with that abominable old man! I feel as though if he were there I'd throw myself out, or throw him out!"

John looked at her exactly as a devoted elder brother placed in charge of the "little ones" in the absence of their Nanny

THE INMATES

might have looked at the most excitable of these troublesome infants.

"Please, please, my treasure, listen to me for one second! Don't, for heaven's sake let it be like it was that awful time in May when neither of us could utter a word at the Confederates' table, and they all saw we'd had one of those lovers' quarrels at which—as I told you then—they say Jove laughs, and Miss Bolster said——"

Tenna gave him one of her most furious looks. "Who cares what Miss Bolster said? And you've no right to call it a quarrel in that stupid schoolboy way when naturally anyone's feelings would have been hurt by what you said."

"What *did* I say? No, no! I'm not trying to tease you! I really do want to know. It's very important I should know. Don't you see, when we're all so sensitive about certain teasing views of what we feel so strongly, it's maddening to be quite in the dark! We know that something we couldn't bear to be said is being said about us and yet we don't know what it is! Please, please tell me what it was I said that hurt you so! I *know* I could explain it."

But the only reply she gave was to turn her head away. She had come to know, by the experience of a quarter of a year, that nothing put him at her mercy so quickly as the simple gesture of turning her head away from him and keeping it turned away.

At this particular moment her head was turned in such a manner as to cause the electric light from the bulb in the ceiling to isolate, like shadowed ivory, from the rest of her face the white portion of her left eye, which, since the brown of Tenna's eyes was a very deep brown and a good deal deeper than the brown of her hair, gleamed, by reason of the contrast, with an almost phosphorescent whiteness, a whiteness so pure that it possessed a power of reflection.

This power of reflection possessed by the intense whiteness that encircled the brown of the girl's eye, and which at this moment, because of her half-averted head, was all John Hush could see of it, was now made use of by the nearest electric

THE POLISHED TABLE

bulb shining down from the ceiling to reflect mysterious gleams of an unusual lustre.

The truth is that, as in the case of certain historic women whose faces have come down to us in poetry and painting, Tenna's appearance, evasive and shadowy as it was, had the peculiarity of something transparent. Her inner soul, her astral identity, showed through.

It was through the sharp outlines of her profile, through the bony structure of her cheeks and eye-sockets that this was now emphasised. It was emphasised by the merest chance, by the most trifling and negligible accident.

John was hopelessly unobservant in these things. This mysterious golden lustre now reflected in the white penumbra of Tenna's eye as she kept her face half-averted was entirely due to something abnormal and unusual about the particular electric bulb above them from which the light fell. There was certainly something peculiar about this bulb, but John didn't glance up at it or give it a thought; though he yielded himself wholly to the effect it produced.

The bulb may have suffered some slight accident to its pure spotlessness and translucency that caused it to emit an uneven ray, or by some quirk in its glassy substance it may have flung down a more intense light than its original purpose warranted.

In any case it was a negligible accident in this hot illuminated chamber, where the intermittent airs from outside smelt of the thyme-scented grass of the high camp-ridge and not of the muddy reeds of the river that encircled Glint Hall in every other direction, that such a mystic gleam, or demonic gleam, or gleam from some temporary crack in the adamantine walls of our present dimension, shone from the delicate features of this old-fashioned girl that it never occurred to John Hush that the accidental concatination of a half-averted profile with an erratic electric bulb could be its sole cause. No revelation from the confounding workshop of Nature takes longer to establish itself in a clever diplomatic mind than that the greatest emotional events are often spontaneously generated by the flips and flurries of chance stirring into life the fecundity of chaos.

THE INMATES

As he gazed at her now John Hush made up his mind never to allow his reaction to any conceivable caprice of hers to divert the obstinate steering of the mental ship of his life towards the north-star of fidelity; and this in spite of any new mania of his own or any new madness of hers.

"We've only got a week more, dear heart. I implore you to remember that; only a week more before the moment comes for you to escape the visit of your father and for me to cut to pieces my jealousy of the American woman! Let's make a bargain, my one of all, that we can never break!

"But the important thing now needn't be as serious as that. It need only be a simple, honest, faithful bond between you and me for these few agitating days! Don't be angry with me any more, I beg you, my sweet, because of that wretched mania of mine. I frightened you unnecessarily about it.

"You see, Tenna my treasure, I have to confess all my manias to you; and that must give you the idea that I'm all manias, nothing but manias, whereas it isn't like that at all!

"I yield to them pretty often, I know. But I don't always yield to them! No, by no means always! You must remember that it's only *three times* in these three months—April, May, June—that I've done you-know-what! And I've got all three of you-know-what safely upstairs in my collar-drawer. I haven't done to them you-know-what. Well, as you know, I needn't talk like that—I mean I haven't put a match to any of the three, so as to lick up the smell of their burning, and so lick up my girl till she's part of me, though I've wanted to so much that my knees have knocked together and my stomach—you know those feelings!—has sunk inwards till it felt like a broken soap-bubble!

"Oh! I've come near it Tenna! I've lit a match and held it to one of those heavenly curls, closer—closer—closer —— But I didn't burn it! I tell you, Tenna, my precious, I really must have a much stronger will, now that I've met you, than I ever had before! Why, in the old days nothing on earth would have stopped me from burning those wisps of hair of yours! You don't mind my calling them curls, do you? I know your

THE POLISHED TABLE

hair's only wavy really and not properly curly, Tenna, but nothing has made my will stronger than this temptation! They're all three in my collar-drawer upstairs. One's in *Leaves of Grass*, one's in *Don Quixote*, one's in the *Odyssey* in Loeb's Classics. And though, of course, I've *thought* of burning them time and time again, I never have!

"It's extraordinary, really, when you come to think of it! Here am I in' the very lists of love ', as it says in *Venus and Adonis*, only it isn't exactly 'love', not love in the ordinary sense, anyway! But here I am, surrounded by people who have followed their personal manias *to the limit*—and there, in my collar-drawer are three of your darling curls"—he lowered his voice till she could barely catch the words—"yet I can't—"

He stopped. But had Mr. Lordy instead of being deep in chess in the reading-room with Mr. Candlemas, the mad lexicographer from Sheffield, been seated near them in the smoking-room listening to their talk he would have noticed the hurried, instinctive movement with which Tenna's hand went up to her head at the words "three of them".

But John was far too full of his own obsession and of his pride in controlling it to notice the fainter and more attenuated effects of his words. "I tell you my will has become what I never thought possible—really strong and powerful! It's queer, isn't it, my precious one?" His whispers were growing louder as well as more intense. "But, of course, it's all due to being really in love for the first time in my life. If I weren't in love it wouldn't have been long—in April probably!—that I'd have done the worst, and let myself go, as most of us here have done, to the limit. But you mustn't imagine, my one of all, that it's been easy to restrain myself. You'd scarcely believe what power of will my love for you has developed! Only last night I was on my feet three times in the night: once for the curl in *Leaves of Grass*, once for the one in the *Odyssey*, once for the one in *Don Quixote*! My will became a gigantic pair of tongs—I could feel it holding me. Yes, little owlet! I stopped being your gladiator-slave. I stopped being your emperor at Capri. I became your simple lover transported by a will as

THE INMATES

powerful as a pair of iron tongs; and I took myself up and put myself down as I decided I could best serve you and be your faithful bodyguard.

"I don't want you to think of this new will-power of mine as if it were using its power to pick up and put out of the window a vicious old rat who has already swallowed his granddaughter's tail and is nibbling at more of her. But don't you see, my treasure, how unfair it is—surely you *must* see!—for you to let yourself go about that old fool Rumpibus till you risk endangering our whole escape? I can't see how you *can* do it, Tenna! It seems unlike you. You become a different person when you do it.

"And don't you see the danger—danger to yourself in doing it? Don't you see what I mean, Tenna? Sir Warden Sheer will have made all his arrangements to come. We can't get off before Midsummer Day because my guardian won't be married before that day and the American plane won't be starting till he's married. And we must give them time to motor here from London.

"And don't you see that if you let yourself go as you're itching to do—and don't think I don't know it, my precious, and don't think they haven't noticed it, too!—let yourself go, I mean, to the limit, and do old Rumpibus in, as you easily *could*, don't you see they'll put you up there, in' the Wing', and when the moment comes we shan't be able to escape with the rest, and our miraculous chance will be over and have come to nothing and can never return. The American plane will be gone without us! You and I will be separated and kept apart till we die of old age, or manage to kill ourselves; and that, you mad nymph *in antro*, is no easy thing here where all the windows are barred and they've taken everything away!

"Shall I tell you something, Tenna, that you'll be surprised to hear? I've been lying awake half the night for the last couple of weeks—oh, more than that!—telling myself horrible stories about what'll happen, what can't help happening, in case your self-control breaks down and you attack old Rumpibus! It's gone so far with me, my treasure, that I've actually—but never mind that!

THE POLISHED TABLE

"The point is, it's simply cruel of you to be so unfair as to let yourself go, when for your sake, I mean for both our sakes, I've turned myself into a pair of tongs and have lifted myself up and put myself down and carried myself out into the yard as if I were a dead rat! Why should you let yourself go and I restrain myself?

"Answer me that, girl of my heart! Answer me that! For it's unfair, unfair, unfair!"

There had come to be something so like a sob in that "unfair, unfair, unfair" that one of the two attendants, after a glance at his mate, began stealthily threading his way through the card tables towards their corner.

In spite of his emotion it was John and not Tenna who noticed this movement; and in a voice completely different from the excited feverish whisper he'd been using, a voice so perfectly under his control that when Tenna heard it she couldn't—in spite of her agitation, and though she felt more inclined to cry than laugh—couldn't resist a flickering smile, "Come, little lady," he said, "it's time we stopped quarrelling over our sins!" and rising from his seat and stretching a hand across the draught-board to help her to do the same, he boldly and brazenly led her between the tables, clear past the nonplussed attendant, and out of the smoking-room into the long passage that ended, as John knew well, better indeed than any other inmate, with a view to the east where rose the ridge with the two Scotch firs and the ancient British camp. Thence, turning their backs upon the staircase to the bedrooms above, they moved slowly to the door of the reading-room.

"Sorry, kid," John murmured humbly, "I oughtn't to have got so worked up. I expect it's the terrible nearness to the time. But it's no good my warning you and then getting so excited myself! I wonder if we were idiots to go and call our little group the Confederates? I don't like what you tell me about Ursie Mum asking what Miss Bolster meant by saying to those women, 'No, I'm not a Catholic. I'm a Confederate'."

Tenna pressed hand. "I'll try," said gravely and simply; and it was clear to him that in her mind she had never

THE INMATES

felt the real danger, but now was seriously promising him to struggle against her fury with old Rumpibus.

No one interfered with them when they took their places at the round mahogany table in the centre of the reading-room, near which, as was his habit before locking up the room for the night, Bill Squeeze was taking his Heraclitus-doll, for that was one of the parts the bearded little image played in his life, on its good-night inspection of the bookshelves.

So accustomed had all the habitués of the reading-room grown to the murmuring sound of Bill's nightly dialogue, wherein silence represented philosophy and a series of "obstinate questionings" ordinary humanity, that only a few readers ever looked up from their books, and of those who did so to-day it was only Tottie Creambo and Arabella Bolster who smiled at the pair on the step-ladder.

There was only one attendant in the reading-room. It was clear that the opinion of Doctor Echetus that the most effective of all sedatives for the disorientated and distraught is an old-fashioned library had influenced the official arrangements in this case.

The attendant upon whom by some natural law of spiritual selection had fallen the duty of superintending the reading-room was the oldest of all the attendants at Glint Hall. His name was Davy Jones and he looked exactly as if he had reappeared from a locked sea-chest deep down in the ooze, where fabulous gems had glimmered from his skull with mysterious gleams, and pieces-of-eight had tinkled against his ribs with every movement of every fish's tail.

Davy Jones took no notice of any particular inmate except Pantamount, towards whom his attitude was extremely peculiar. It couldn't have been called hostile, nor could it have been called friendly. It might have been described as humorously and gravely self-protective.

Davy Jones would throw the same sort of glance on Pantamount as a dignified gentleman quietly following his accustomed path through his own wood but suddenly tripped by a stone, or a root, or a bramble, might turn to cast, in reproachful

THE POLISHED TABLE

but amused astonishment, at the object which upset his equilibrium. "If," thought John now, "Pantamount has flesh like a drifting log, and Davy Jones like a ship's keel, with a precious chest embedded in it, is it not natural that the latter should be apprehensive at the approach of the former?"

Since he had first met Pantamount John had been obscurely conscious that the man's fellow-inmates were uneasy in his presence. That the attendants were hostile to him was clear, and it gradually impressed itself on John that he himself was the only person among all the men and women in Glint who felt an unmistakable attraction towards this weird individual.

As to the solitary attendant in the reading-room, John felt nothing towards him except a lack of interest so extreme that it would have reached that dangerous limit of boredom that drives certain unbalanced natures to commit indecent crimes if it had not been for another element in the thing.

But just as the suggestion of immemorial driftwood in the flesh of Pantamount was a magnet of attraction to John, so the suggestion of sunken gems about the sleepy skeleton of Davy Jones produced in John a quite special kind of irritation.

One of the most startling conclusions he had reached as a result of his three months' incarceration was that the physical peculiarities of his fellow prisoners was a thing of much greater importance to him than their mental attitudes. These latter seemed arbitrary, fitful, fanciful, and unilluminating; whereas the former seemed to spring from terribly deep and tragic movements of human life.

Thus it was not Pantamount's theories about "love-hate" and the crucial importance of it's "less or more" that arrested John. It was his corporeal frame. And in the same way the kind of *ennui* that hovered in the air like a desolate sprinkling of grey sand whenever he contemplated Davy Jones was accompanied by a curious physical irritation with the old attendant's sleep-drenched flesh, flesh that concealed, fold upon drowsy fold, layer upon somnolent layer, unshared, unrecognised, unenjoyed, piled-up palimpsests of hoarded memory.

Davy Jones had the longest and whitest beard John had ever

THE INMATES

seen. It was a very thin beard, and when the old man twisted it, as he frequently did, round his wrist and even round his longest finger, where it shone like the silvery mane, caught in a tamarisk, of a lost and riderless Bucephalus, it gave some of the frequenters of that reading-room a curiously uncomfortable sensation.

It struck them, in fact, as possessing a sub-human life of its own, the life of a creature resembling a sea-anemone, whose tentacular filaments drew their lustre from the gradual dissolution of fathom-deep masses of gem-breeding scum, scum too heavy to stay on the surface, but since it was not heavy enough to sink to the bottom could only dissolve very slowly. Once in their places at the Confederates' table, and if not under the eye of Davy Jones, at least within the charmed circle of his imperishable beard, John and Tenna could hardly be deaf to the sound of the piano which as usual was being played softly and gently, but like most of the others who were gazing either at Bill Squeeze on his step-ladder with Heraclitus or at the tulip-tree framed in the open window, they were neither musical enough to be annoyed at the sound or placid enough to enjoy it.

The Confederates had now, for at least a month, entirely monopolised this round bare mahogany table. It was a table for whose particular polishing a servant called Mrs. Wohntscher, the only servant in Glint who wasn't an inmate, had a predilection that amounted to a passion.

Mrs. Wohntscher's wages were small enough, but if it hadn't been for Ursie Mum they would have been smaller still, for the simple reason that when once in her daily round of dusting she arrived at this big bare table in the reading-room she couldn't leave it. To polish it was to the soul of Mrs. Wohntscher such a heavenly delight that she could only be parted from it by the end of her day's work. But her rapt labour was certainly appreciated by John, if by nobody else. For when after the glare and heat of the smoking-room he saw Tenna's fingers sink to rest beside his own, and remain at peace folded upon that polished mahogany surface, which really in those June twilights

THE POLISHED TABLE

resembled a magic pool, a calm deep as a deep sea used to descend upon him.

As he led Tenna to their table of conspiracy this particular night and took his place by her side between the Zeit-Geist and the Commander, he deliberately tried to divide his receptivity to what was around him into two spheres of sensitiveness, so that with one he might enjoy the air that was coming in through the window, and with the other guard his girl from getting worked up over poor old Rumpibus and Tottie Creambo, for there they were, playing their usual game across the table, he on the further side of the Commander, and she on the further side of the Zeit-Geist, who certainly, as far as he was concerned, took no more notice of her than if she had been a belated specimen of the plump fluffy moth known as the "yellow-under-wing".

Apart from the danger to Tenna's nerves, both persons and things as John looked about him, were soothing to his spirit. Mr. Lordy, snugly ensconced between the twin dancers who were whispering across him, was smiling with an expression of unruffled benignity as the Commander expounded to him the absurdity of using the mind to think; and as John watched the youthful faces of the girl Thither and the boy Hither at such close quarters, for it was unusual for them to sit down with the other Confederates, he was struck by the complete absence of all ordinary human interests in their faces.

Their lovely little features—for lovely they remained in spite of this surprising lack—were absolutely devoid of expression. They looked neither sad nor happy. They looked as if they had no desire, no ambition, no fear, no hope, no regret, as if they were totally unaware that such feelings existed.

With most of the persons sitting round this table and with nearly all the rest in other parts of the room, our friend had struck up during his three months in Glint a friendly acquaintance; and, indeed, he would have found it hard to explain what it was about the twin dancers, of whom the rumour ran that it was the irresponsible indulgence of a titled father that had affected their wits, that had made him so cautious in their case and induced him to draw away from any close contact.

THE INMATES

The whole experiment of this music-and-twilight cure naturally implied that there should be as little exciting discussion of politics, crime, sex, or the cinema, as it was possible to avoid, and Davy Jones seemed endowed with the power of lifting his head and opening at least one of his eyes when any of these agitating topics emerged in the offing.

After glancing quickly at the peculiar ceremony proceeding on the step-ladder, where apparently Heraclitus had to utter an evening benediction to various heavy-weather sages of our feather-brained race, John allowed his attention to wander to the familiar window and the branches of the tulip-tree floating out there upon the flowing sea of twilight.

It seemed to him that what the air was bringing into the room that night was much more than the scent of flowering trees and fragrant shrubs. There was a scent upon it that was like an exhalation rising from a mass of cold grey water into which had been diffused long ago in aeons beyond all memory the souls of dead water-plants whose very shapes, not to speak of their names, were today totally extinct.

But from the tulip-tree under which he had first seen her John's spirit was now jerked back to Tenna. He shifted a little in his chair so as to be able to watch her face more closely. He had learnt by experience that such scrutiny was irritating to her even when it expressed nothing but the fascination of a lover; but he felt he had to risk it now, for he had already decided that at the first sign of her self-control breaking down he would get her out of the room even if he had to carry her in his arms.

He suddenly discovered that he had an ally in Pantamount who, with a sagacity and subtlety that bewildered him, had already sensed the danger and was leaning across Mrs. Wohntscher's circle of magic mahogany with his great bare arms outspread and his heavy king-log visage drooping as if across the rowlock of a ten-thousand-years-old Boat of Charon.

John soon realised that he'd been emptying "some dull opiate to the drains" and had "sunk lethe-wards" longer than he had intended while Tenna had been arguing with Pantamount.

THE POLISHED TABLE

When he became aware of their talk he found that though she had grown unusually excited she was keeping her head better than he had feared. Anyway, she was too absorbed to notice how he was watching her, so he could go on doing so without any fear of annoying her. She was gesticulating freely with her hands, as she always did when excited, but since when she was alone with him, and he took good care she should be alone with him most of their free time, he was absorbed in watching her face and listening to her words, these gestures were as a revelation to him.

And since she was now facing Pantamount and giving him her full attention, John was able to "take her in", as we say, in unbroken entirety, like a river-pool free from the ripple of a breath of wind, the rising of the smallest fish, the falling of a single leaf.

He noticed how relaxed her whole slender body was as she talked to Pantamount. It gave him the impression that it was the body of an exhausted dryad who had been on her feet so long as a captive odalisque in a tyrant's tent that she could only respond with her fingers to the call of her confederate-tree.

Her whole body suggested helpless weariness, and yet the life in her wrists and fingers was quiveringly electric. But not only had her body this look of helpless relaxation. Her brown hair was of so fine a texture and each strand of it so filmy and thin, that it sank across her high forehead with the massed effect of drifting seaweed, lifted and released, released and lifted, on the smooth surface of a recurrent wave.

The aquiline tilt of her nose and the old-miniature curves of her unreddened lips accentuated John Hush's feeling that she really did belong to those creatures of the elements known in the old books as Sylphs and Undines and that there was about her that sort of closeness to the more rarified aspects of planetary chemistry from which must have originated the weird fairytales about changelings.

John Hush had already discovered that there were aspects of Tenna Sheer that were as alarming as they were alluring.

THE INMATES

Indeed, the better they had come to know each other the more intimately had his obsession for her become associated with a boy's awareness of mysterious vistas of recondite adventures, while hers for him was more and more like a little girl's desperate craving to possess an inanimate companion that was absolutely and entirely her own.

It was the movements of her hands and fingers that carried him away now as he watched her for they were completely unlike any hands or fingers he had ever seen.

The extraordinary and even startling thing about them was the abnormally wide spaces between the fingers and the girl's power of moving them in a sort of rhythmic dance while her wrists and arms, whether recumbent or lifted, seemed to partake of the strange lassitude of the rest of her body.

Pantamount, as Hush could clearly detect, was finding his task of keeping her attention growing harder every moment. The man couldn't see as clearly as could her lover from his place at her side that in the midst of her gestures—which were merely being used to emphasise her discourse, a discourse that itself carried danger, for it had already begun to be directed without distinction against all old men—she allowed her mobile fingers to play round a heavy water-bottle which as a missile of retribution might have knocked a horn off the skull of Satan.

And she was getting dangerously worked up. She was now assuring Pantamount—and John didn't dare to put that water-bottle out of her reach—that devils are always waiting to enter the souls of men the moment they approach seventy and their natural strength abates.

She asserted that a new Act of Parliament ought to be passed decreeing that automatically, at the age of seventy, and without appeal to any Court or any official board, all old men without exception should be sent to prison; to pleasant, comfortable prisons, of course, and more agreeable than Glint Hall, but still to prison, where they, along with the vicious devils that take possession of their souls, could no longer do any harm.

There might even be, she explained to Pantamount, special

THE POLISHED TABLE

faraway islands in the Pacific reserved by the United Nations for the purpose of keeping these devil-possessed Strulbrugs in comfortable isolation for the rest of their days.

The unfortunate thing was that Pantamount took human emotion so casually and lightly that it was very difficult for him to imagine anyone getting agitated by the absurdly simple game that was going on between old Rumpibus and Tottie; a game that consisted as far as Hush could see in the former trying to steal a bit of bread from the girl's plate, while she, watching like a cat the approach of that long predatory finger and thumb across the polished table, would clap one of her plump little palms upon these extemporised tweezers and her other palm upon the bit of bread with a childish chuckle of triumph.

And then just what John most feared happened. The fingers of Tenna's right hand tightened upon the neck of the water-bottle and, leaping to her feet, she lifted it in the air.

John had never seen any human action performed with less time for human thought than Pantamount's action now. In the beat of a pulse he was on his long legs. In a second beat he'd caught the bottle before she had drawn it back for the fling. In a third beat he was leaning across the segment of polished mahogany that divided him from the girl, and then, while all the faces round that table turned towards them, he lifted her in the air and, heedless of her wild hysterical laughter, turned to carry her from the room.

Very rapidly now, however, but quite calmly and clearly and quietly, he spoke to John; and his words, below Tenna's laughter and all the hubbub in the room, sank into John's consciousness like a quick series of bullet-shots.

"Don't give me the lie. Don't contradict any of their nonsense! Let them take me upstairs. I can cope with anything they do. If *I'm* left behind when the time comes, it won't matter!"

All John could do was to follow them to the door through the crowd, clinging to Tenna's fingers, from which the bottle had already fallen on the floor, and fallen, oddly enough,

THE INMATES

without breaking, so that John was destined to remember more vividly even than Tenna's distorted mouth the particular look of the dark water as it flowed out over one of Ursie Mum's reddest rugs.

Of the white beard of Davy Jones, of Davy Jones himself, John could remember nothing. The old man must have hurried from the room for help at a pace that was like the subsiding of an ocean-wave when it has broken upon a ship's deck. It was from a position on his knees at Tenna's side as her hysterical convulsions subsided—for Pantamount had placed her on an old horse-hair sofa that stood at the foot of the staircase to the women's quarters—that John was able at last really to grasp the actual issue of what had happened; and it was an intense relief to him, one of the greatest reassurances of his life, when as he rose to his feet at Tenna's side and helped her, very pale and silent, but perfectly calm now, to get up from that horse-hair sofa and lean on his arm, to find, that as far as he could tell, nothing that threatened destruction to their plan of escape had so far occurred.

There was a great jostling and murmuring going on round them, broken by cries and outbursts of anger and exclamations of pity, but there was always this sort of hubbub when the inmates, dazed by cards or by exciting books, were crowding together discussing every detail of what had happened, and enjoying in lively gregariousness every sort of prediction as to what was going to happen.

John had caught a glimpse of the strait-waistcoat official among the attendants whom Davy Jones had summoned to the spot. Nor was he without his own secret and cruel wrestling with the dark angel. It seemed to him that as he emerged from the whirlpool of Tenna's convulsions on that horse-hair sofa—and he could even recall one moment when across his own wet mouth, full of a salty and yet dusty saliva that tasted as if he had been biting his lips face-down upon half a dozen such sofas, there seemed to be drawn some maddening wisp of Tenna's brown hair—he felt a throbbing guilt in some blackened gland of his memory, as if he and his love were

THE POLISHED TABLE

returning together from a crazed plunge into the blue-black interstices of some gigantic poison-fruit full of fatal though delicious juice.

What John Hush began murmuring to himself, as soon as Tenna and he were on their feet again and the attention of the other inmates had been drawn elsewhere, was anything but a clear-cut confession, nor was it a tragic appeal to divine or human mercy. He didn't form in his mind words that exactly expressed his feelings as these feelings presented themselves. The words he was muttering gathered themselves from his consciousness at random, like mists rising from the surface of a mountain lake, and formed themselves into palpable and visible shapes.

But the general burden of what his heart was now muttering to his head was that it was no good trying to dodge the not very nice fact that he had known perfectly well he was letting Pantamount sacrifice himself for them all and especially for himself and Tenna. He hadn't been private secretary to an ambassador for nothing. He knew there were plenty of subtle ways in which acceptance of a man's sacrifice could be justified by those for whom it is made.

Pantamount was one single person, for example, and *they* were many people, and among them were several women. Pantamount had acted so quickly and decisively that he had left him no time to decide the issue in any other way than by humble and grateful acceptance of the queer man's heroic gesture. But, in spite of all this, his conscience still felt guilty.

Tenna and he were now standing, both of them absorbed in their own thoughts, on the outside of a jostling group of inmates who had gathered in the corridor between the door of the smoking-room and the door of the reading-room. From what he heard of this group's excited chatter it seemed that Mr. Cogent Cuddle had brought a couple of new patients, each of them middle-aged men of an unusual appearance, to wait in the reading-room until either Doctor Echetus himself, or Father Toby, was free to conduct them to their quarters for the night, if not to give them some kind of official reception.

THE INMATES

By the time John had shaken off—and he felt as if he had done this for both of them—the distressing pressure on throat and lungs and nerves of that broken-springed, remorse-shiny, black-slug-slippery horse-hair sofa, he became aware not only that Father Toby was in sight but that Ursie Mum was at their side. This extraordinary lady, John had already decided, resembled Rabelais' Priestess Bac-Buc. He regarded her as the noblest creature with the breasts of a woman he had ever encountered; and to himself he always styled her Mother of the Hunted.

She took him aside for a moment now, which was easy enough. Tenna was so sad and weak and humiliated and reduced to the vanishing point that she could be safely left in the dazed trance into which she had fallen without the danger of any new harm coming from this isolation.

And once having got him to herself, Ursie Mum hurriedly explained that it would be a great mistake for Tenna to go now at once to the loneliness of her bedroom, for the vibrations in her nerves would in all probability lead her mind round and round and round, in circle after circle of confused memories, bringing her nothing but the shapes and faces of people, outlined with horrible distinctness, and all of them giving her pain.

"Take her back to that table," she whispered to John, "that Mrs. Wohntscher so loves to polish—and she really does it wonderfully, doesn't she?—and let her get a few other ideas and feelings into her mind before you let her go upstairs. I may put on my dressing-gown and look in on her later in the night—perhaps take her a cup of chocolate—that's the thing that always makes me sleep. But Father Toby's going to give a little talk in the reading-room presently and that may have the same effect as the chocolate. I've known it myself; and listening to the other Father, too."

And she pushed him back to Tenna with a smile that gave him the feeling that in her heart of hearts she regarded her husband's ministrations as so much hot chocolate and Father Allen Wun's as so much hot cocoa.

John obeyed her to the letter, however, and took Tenna

THE POLISHED TABLE

straight back to the polished table where they were warmly welcomed by the Marquis of the Fourth Dimension, alias the Zeit-Geist, alias Professor Zoom of the College of Doom.

"Well, you've sure come back at the right moment, children! What a lovely pair of ballad-babes you two are! The balloon's just going to burst. The drop at the tip of the Almighty's tongue's just going to fall! Lipperty-lopperty! It's gone! Wurra-lurra-buderpest! Laura's got it on the chest I The little birdies of fate have been beating their wings for sometime, but now they're really ready to fly! There comes a point you know, my pretties, there comes a point! Humbuggery's the word, of course, with all mankind. But things can happen, my dears. Not often, of course. But they can happen. And then there's no case for a cosmic crack and no need for the dung-cart to hurry back!

"Yes, things can happen, my pretties. Yes, after all, there do arrive moments when matters come to a head! It may be only a speck that does it. A speck of dust lodged in a wind-bag can blow a world sky-high! Explosions, you know, can be extremely unphilosophical. They can even be unscientific! Humbug, humbug, humbug—and then *crack, bang*—and where is the round world?"

As he beckoned them to sit beside him, John was staggered by the whiteness of the whites of Zeit-Geist's eyes. He shrank from even approaching the thought that there could be anything in common between this grotesque Eidolon of frivolity and the wild, tragic, staring eyes of Tenna, but where that unearthly gleam of God knows what sort of gold-dust had appeared on the whites of his girl's eyes under the electric light the appalling whiteness of the Zeit-Geist's eyes had horribly increased; and as John Hush watched it now it seemed as if it kept drawing to itself more and more of the man's eyeballs, till this pair of eye-centres, whose peering out from any living organism means to all of us poor creatures of earth our sole power of vision, was in danger of disappearing.

"With one illusion," the Zeit-Geist went on, "inside another illusion, and all these double and treble illusions inside

THE INMATES

bubbles that are themselves inside other bubbles, and all of them together, bubbles and illusions, floating on a dream-river in a dream-world, what, I ask you, could be more fitting for the last scenes of the last act of the sixteenth of June than to hear Daddy Toby tell us of a new discovery about God——"

He broke off suddenly and pointed excitedly with the very finger that had so terrified John. "You see," he cried, "what has happened? That idiot Cuddle instead of taking this pair of new inmates upstairs to their rooms has brought them in here, to hear a sermon on sanity, sobriety, and chastity from Father Toby, our great hooker of fish!"

And, sure enough, Toby Tickle's open-air voice, full of the harsh twitterings of reed-warblers, the splashings of water-rats, the cryings of plovers, the challenges of yaffles, the screamings of jays, the quackings of wild ducks, now rose and fell in its familiar plangency.

"All aberrations of the human mind, my dear people," declared Father Toby, while John, who knew too well how this sentence would end allowed his mind to wander, in company with his eyes, to the two new inmates, who, deserted by Mr. Cuddle and with nobody to welcome them except this impersonal open-air voice, were now standing side by side just across the threshold of the reading-room, surveying their surroundings with considerable curiosity and, as far as John could detect, with no apprehension at all.

There was, however, no question which of these two unusual events, occurring simultaneously twenty-five minutes before bedtime, namely the arrival in the reading-room of a couple of absolutely new patients and the delivery in the reading-room of a sermon by Father Toby, interested the present inmates the more. Toby, as Jesus would have put it, "*they had always with them*," and destiny might decide that they would find the newcomers more hopelessly devoid of amusement or entertainment for them than was usually the case even with patients who were incurably mad. But this was unlikely; and new guests at Glint were more exciting than new sermons.

THE POLISHED TABLE

As John gripped Tenna's left hand under the polished table, which at that moment seemed to gleam with a deep magic light as if its lustre were due to the anvil of Hephaestus rather than the duster of Mrs. Wohntscher, and looked anxiously about him, praying that their careful plot would not at this crucial moment, only a week from their escape, be broken up by Doctor Echetus. He couldn't help, any more than any other inmate could help, peering excitedly at the two newcomers, so unceremoniously landed here by Cogent Cuddle. This would have been a moment for Bill Squeeze, with Heraclitus in his pocket, to make it clear that the hour was unpropitious for new personalities.

But Bill must have departed for the night to Betsy and the south lodge. And then with a rush of shame and admiration he thought again of Pantamount, passive, patient, and unresisting, like an ancient camel with such a complicated experience of sand-storms and massacres and plagues and famines and the madness of strange gods that with a selflessness that was almost shocking in its natural ease he could let himself be carried off to that upper wing so that there should be no insuperable obstacle to the escape of the rest.

"And so, my friends," Father Toby was now saying, "I would like to appeal to you all, and especially to the two new patients, for I see we have two fresh faces here, whom I am delighted to welcome to our little intimate family of the good God, or, shall I say, to this 'great good place ', as some old writer calls it; to appeal to you all, I repeat, to remember the one Great Essence of our Holy Faith, which is its integrity. By its integrity I mean its perfect oneness with itself.

"Our religion can be summed up in two simple one-syllable words, the word *knot* and the word *tight*. We are all tied together in the tight knot of our holy faith. And outside this compact globe, or *ball*, if I may use such a word, of which God is the centre and circumference, there is nothing but nothing. You are all interested, are you not, in the noble game of football? And you know well, do you not, the difference between a soccer ball and a rugger ball?

THE INMATES

"Well, God's mysterious and eternal universe is like a soccer ball. It is rounder than a rugger ball and is more often kicked than carted. But the beautiful thing about our cosmic soccer ball is that it is *the all*. Outside of it there is absolutely and simply nothing.

"You have heard of Hell, dear people? Well, Hell is only our blasphemous and wholly impossible idea of something outside this tightly knotted soccer ball of a universe beyond whose circumference is nothing. You know, dear people, how the river flows round this' great good place' as that well-known ancient famous author—at the moment his name escapes me—called our happy home?

"Well, in the same way God's love radiating by the necessity of the Divine Nature from the Eternal Being flows round *all that is* and protects it from being dissolved into all that is not. That river of love guards from nothingness the memory of everything that has ever existed and every thought that has ever been thought. Yes, dear people, you know how the river flows round us at Glint? Round and round and round us the river flows!

"And so and in the same manner round this cosmic ball flows the river of salvation."

At this point there came a voice from the polished table and John couldn't be sure whether it came from the boy Hither or the girl Thither. "Who catches the little fishes from the shining river?" This interruption broke the spell.

The Commander himself leaned forward over the table and gravely uttered the words: "By the pricking of my thumbs something wicked this way comes!"

He spoke so solemnly and with so grave a face that both Hither and Thither burst into high-pitched shrieks of childish merriment. But it was at that moment that Tenna herself, who all this while had been staring, with eyes that kept opening wider and wider, at one of the two new patients whom the inconsequent Cuddle had thrust into the reading-room and left stranded there like a couple of sea-lions on a sheep-browsing promontory, waved her free hand—one of her elbows was on

THE POLISHED TABLE

the table and her chin was resting on that hand's inactive wrist —in the direction of the newcomer she'd been watching.

"He wants to answer him!" she burst out; and added quickly, when John turned an appealing look upon her, "Why don't you all let him speak?"

Just as if he had actually heard her, and he may have done so, though John didn't believe it, there now came, dancing forward into the space between Father Toby and the polished table, a man of about fifty in full evening dress and wearing patent-leather shoes. Had he been brought here in a car, John wondered, dressed like this? He was a striking-looking figure. His hair was grizzled and cropped close to his skull, while his high cheek-bones, sunken eyes, and hollow cheeks, gave his face a skull-like and a gargoyle-like appearance. His body was very short, but his arms and legs were long, and his hands and feet were abnormally large.

He advanced into the middle of the room in a series of skipping jerks; and it became in some queer way plain to everybody that if the caprice took him he could have used his big hands as feet and brandished his big feet like hands. But the moment he began speaking his absurdly short body and his startlingly long limbs froze into absolute immobility.

The sounds that issued from his mouth gave everybody the queerest shock, for his voice turned out to be more high-pitched than even Hither's and Thither's. It was indeed hardly human. It was as if some extremely bold insect were expressing its disapproval of the philosophical conclusions of the human race. Its protest was expressed in oddly constructed sentences, sentences so abrupt as to remind John of fifth of November squibs and crackers, yet what he said was simple enough and perfectly intelligible.

"Every word," he squeaked and gibbered, "of what has just been said is a lie! Nobody knows how many worlds there are—all totally different! *Our* realities, *our* worlds, our *truths*, *our* ideas, *our* impressions, are all different, and we may take it for granted that we are surrounded by millions of completely separate and completely different universes, some of them

THE INMATES

attainable from our dimension, most of them entirely beyond the scope, not only of our science, our reason, our logic, our intuition, our instinct but of our imagination, too!

"What the generations of mankind are like and what they've been like ever since they first appeared is the generations of the leaves of the forest! Leaves, leaves, leaves, leaves! Like leaves we come and like leaves we go! And if you want to know what we ought to aim at becoming with the whole of our intention I will tell you this first night I've set eyes on you! We ought to aim at becoming like a cloud of flies, a cloud of gnats, a cloud of midges! Thus and thus alone shall we escape places like this, preachers like this, and the silly solemn stupid humbug of taking for granted that a person is crazy because he doesn't accept the opinion of the hierarchy of ages, the academic poppycock of ages, the traditional abracadabra of a rabble of priests, professors, lawyers, doctors, scientists, politicians, divines, whose pontifical claptrap and up-se-daisy assumptions are simply the milk of those old moo-cows of habit, custom, tradition, and vain repetition, curdled by the holy horrors of hoodoos and taboos and put over on us, ever since man first appeared on the earth, by those who want to rule.

"How much better to do what I do and become a mob of midges, that is to say to blow up once for all this self-satisfied idea of wholeness and integrity and the beauty of a well-stuffed rounded-off person's person, and just say to all comers: I, *moi qui vous parle*, Johnny catch-as-catch-can, am not a pathetic tragical-comical *one creature* with a fatal power of choice between God and the Devil, but a host of creatures, a cloud of gnats, carried up and down on a welter of winds! Who and what can catch me, keep me, bind me, hold me, if I am true to myself? You say you can make me suffer and can force me to obey?

"Oh yes! And destiny, fate, necessity, chance, can beat me down to the ground. But what can they really do to me till they kill me *en masse* and finish me off *en masse*? They can do nothing! They can do nothing because I am *not one but a multitude.* And because every single thing and every single identical life is a multitude of things and lives!

"No, it's a lie that the universe is one. It's a multitude of personalities, of gods, of demons, of men, of animals, of midges and worms, of electrons and atoms! The reality of realities is not One but Many. And, of this many, nothing is eternal. Everything passes away! My thought, your thoughts, and the thoughts of every god, every demon, every insect, every worm, every minutest life that exists—*all* pass away, *all'* leave ', as the Great Magician says, 'not a rack behind '!"

Having thus expressed himself, this queer stranger balanced himself for a second on his head; and then rising on one of his enormous feet, whose size was emphasised rather than diminished by the elegance of the shoe that covered it, he uttered an audible sigh and murmured, loud enough for all to hear, but as if he were talking to himself, "The pleasure of life is expectation."

14

MIDSUMMER DAWN

THE DAYS before Midsummer Day were without question the most agitating of John's whole life. On the contrary, by some lucky chance, a chance that to John was quite inscrutable, Tenna was calmer during those six days than she had been for a long time, and of her own accord took the initiative in avoiding Tottie and old Rumpibus.

The fatal time came round at last, and on Sunday the twenty-fourth John was awake well before three in the morning, nearly a whole hour before the sun rose. He lay dead-still on his back in the cold greyness of the prae-dawn, deliberately keeping his eyes tightly closed but listening intently to the sound beyond sound that proclaims the approach, through dedicated abysses of infinite space, of the light of a new day. This sound is not the mathematical music to which the spheres dance their mystic dance. It is not the balanced rhythm of the

THE INMATES

advances and retreats of the galaxies and the nebulae. It is not the humming of the unfathomable dimensions that surround us. It is not the overheard inbreathing and outbreathing of the revolving mystery that is the nearest neighbour to the world to which we belong. It is simply the sound of the coming of light.

What John felt most aware of as he lay there listening on that twenty-fourth of June to that cold, wordless antiphony between being and nothingness, between the is and the is not, was a feeling of wonder that he wasn't more disturbed, more agitated, more tense and strung-up on this morning of all mornings than he felt himself to be. How could he be so calm when everything of value to him in this or any other conceivable world was swaying, reeling, shivering, rocking on such an intolerable pivot of suspense?

Well! It was no good asking himself how he could be like this. The point was that he *was* like this; and it was a damned good thing for him that he was. "But it's up to you," he told himself, "my good John, whatever may be the cause of this unnatural calm of yours, to consider every move you've got to make in the next hour or so; and consider it from more angles than one and along with every possible danger that such a move may bring with it.

It really is a wonder," he told himself," that things have got as far as they have. But I must get up and go out and have a look at those south-lodge spikes and make sure they're in working order. Everything depends on those damned spikes!"

Lifted up now as strongly by what he had to do as he had been by that weird fancy he had confessed to Tenna of his will being like a great pair of iron tongs with which he could pick himself up and plant himself wherever he might wish, or might decide he ought to wish, to be, he got out of bed in that queer pallid light that he kept telling himself was a sort of metaphysical light and began hurriedly dressing. While he put on his clothes he tried to arrange in his mind all he had to do if he was to have things really ready for their escape. This was no easy task, not only because, good diplomatist

MIDSUMMER DAWN

though he was, he was the extreme opposite of a competent conspirator, but because, owing to the special mental condition of most of the inmates, there were so many weak and ticklish spots in their conspiratorial phalanx that the most important and obvious duty of any leader fate might give them was to go up and down behind the front line, propping up the tottering knees and steadying the twitching lips of those whose shaky nerves, at a touch, at a straw, at a falling leaf on the air, at a ripple in the water, are plucked at by the madness of panic.

When he was dressed he stood hesitating for a moment, wondering whether to put on his boots or to carry them in his hand. The odd thing was that the idea of going to that stream flowing under the wall at the south lodge without his boots gave him the jitters.

"Why the holy Jesus should I feel like this from such a simple thing as carrying my boots and creeping downstairs in my stockings? Am I going dotty?" And then—but still standing in the same position with one of his boots dangling from a long leather bootlace in one hand and the other hand on the particular knob at the end of his bed that would always be associated with the wagging finger of the Zeit-Geist—he uttered that false artificial chuckle which is an essential attribute of a Nordic diplomatist in a Slavonic court.

On this occasion, however, the joke was against himself: "For what the hell," he groaned in his heart, "am I doing, talking of 'going dotty' when I've got in my collar-drawer those three wisps of Tenna's hair? God! How that does give this whole business away! Over girls' curls I'm as crazy as you like, but the horrors that come over me when I think of creeping downstairs carrying my boots are—and I don't deny it!—really and truly insane. Everything depends on the agreement of our minds about reality. That is sanity and everything is relative to that. There is no such thing as what the more simple-minded of our scientists call the 'objective world'.

"This room and that yard"—and John waved the hand from which his left boot hung by its bootlace towards the ghostly panes of his window—"only exist because all the

THE INMATES

various minds that keep them going see more or less the same room and the same yard.

"But the great difficulty about it is that some of these minds are superhuman and some of them subhuman. So the common vision of things that these silly sods call' reality' is a compromise between what souls of the elements see and feel and what the wood-ticks and the nuclear electrons see and feel. No wonder everything looks funny when we put our heads on one side and worse than funny when we stand on our heads.

"Nature isn't a static picture on a stretched-out canvas. It's a living face all puckered up with different feelings and with weeping and crying and putting out a galaxy of jeering tongues!"

He let the bootlace go and the boot fell with a thud on the floor. The sound of that thud and the thought of the many ears that might have heard it gave him a shock. He sat down on the edge of his bed and stared at his window. He counted six whitish-grey squares of window-glass above three rusty-black bars crossing a pallid gulf of dizziness that was scooped out of limitless space by the opposing wall of the north lodge.

"Of course, I ought to carry my boots when I creep down those stairs and unbar the hall door." He knew there were a couple of night-watchmen down there, great lusty prize-fighting fellows ready to stop any rush of inmates to escape. But he knew that in the summer dawn these guardians of the gate were always dead-asleep in the little entrance-office where they played their night-long games of chance; but, of course, the tramp of these thick-soled boots of his would almost certainly wake them—why the devil, then, had he got this queer horror of going down the stairs and crossing the hall with his boots in his hand? And why was it a still worse horror to think of following the gravel path between the tulip-tree and the flowerbeds, and along by the meadow-railings, with only his socks between his bare feet and the ground?

Damn! He had to face it. He had to admit it. It was the old supreme horror of his boyhood come back to torment him on this day of all days, this morning of all mornings!

MIDSUMMER DAWN

Yes, it was that old boyish mania about femininity, that blind sick horror of everything feminine that used to extend to everything that yielded to pressure, that horror which at one time associated itself with everything that was soft, with everything *that went in*, with everything that resembled children's india-rubber toys when they were squeezed!

It was all very well to boast to Tenna about his will being strong as a pair of iron tongs, and about his power to hold his manias in complete control, and about his inflexible refusal to let himself put a match to those three wisps of hair in his collar-drawer! Yet here he was at this moment of all moments, when it was absolutely essential he should get out of the house without being heard—here he was, suddenly confronted by the worst horror of his boyhood, the thing he had for years taken for granted would never trouble him again!

But why should touching the floor, or the steps, or the gravel, or the grass, bring all this back? Yes, it had been in him all the time, this peculiar association of ideas; but why on earth should touching things with his bare feet, or with only socks or stockings on, bring into his mind that appalling boyish dread?

Damn it all! Where was the connection? What on earth had the feeling of gravel and grass and flagstones and bare boards under his feet to do with his boyish terror of growing, when he grew up, *not into a man but into a woman*? Had any watchful observer crept into John Hush's room on *his* bare feet just then he would have noticed how John's head had sunk so far forward as he sat on his bed that by this time his forehead was only about eight inches from the boots on the floor.

His shoulders were hunched up as he sat there, and he had laid his hands on the pair of boots beneath him and was pulling their leather tops towards each other, making them *Just* touch, as if they were kissing each other, or whispering and conspiring with each other, and then he would pull them apart with a jerk, and then, after letting his long thin fingers hover languidly back and forth above them like sprays of seaweed

THE INMATES

over sea-anemones in a rock-pool, he would begin it all over again.

But suddenly he stopped, squared his shoulders, clasped his fingers tightly together and sat up straight. He had recalled a very curious conversation he had once had with his old nurse, the woman who resembled Mrs. Cogent Cuddle of the north lodge. This woman had been with his mother at his birth and had witnessed the performance of what was an ancient custom in that part of the country when by some chance the infant's feet appeared first.

On this occasion there had been a pause in the delivery while the doctor, a stiff-jointed old man, was still on the stairs, and to hasten the birth an ancient crone who was assisting rubbed the soles of the child's feet with a particular kind of pebble-stone, muttering as she did so some obscure ditty about boy-babes and girl-babes.

His mother, the nurse told him, had set her heart on the infant being a girl, "And if you, Master John," she had added, "be soft where women be soft, you may take it from me 'tis that pebble-stone fixed it—first in *her* mind, and then, half-born though ye were, in. *yours*."

The possibility that this insane dread in his boyhood of developing certain feminine attributes and necessities which was so oddly associated with a horror of going bare-foot might be explained by this incident impressed him very little in those early days, but it came back to him now with a revealing force. It was all very well to boast to Tenna about his will being strong as a pair of iron tongs, and about his power to hold his manias in complete check, and about his adamantine refusal to let himself put a match to those three wisps of hair in his collar-drawer.

Here he was at this moment of all moments, when it was absolutely essential he should get out of the house without being heard, here he was, suddenly terrified by that peculiar feeling of an intense neurotic outrage at contact with the floor or the gound without his shoes!

And now he realised why he must avoid this particular

MIDSUMMER DAWN

feeling. Oh, but he knew too well what the terror was! He felt it in every whitish-grey pane of that window and in all that he could detect across that scooped-out and barricaded-up gulf of space between his iron bars, bare to the faintly stirring breath of the dawn's pallid outriders, and exposed to those windows of the north lodge that were now staring back at him and taunting him and whispering at him: "Keep your boots on—and keep your hair on—and stay where you are! And bear this in mind—you double-dyed ass—the fields of dawn aren't the place for ugly cowards to creep about in!" Yes, it was when he touched anything cold or damp or wet or scratchy or sharp or rough with his bare skin that the feeling came over him *that he was turning into a woman.*

Yes, it was then that he felt his breasts beginning to grow and their nipples to distent and get longer and longer and longer and longer, get so long in fact that he could wave them about in the air! Yes, he felt them now, growing as long as elephant's trunks and groping about in the same sort of way! Why, he could take hold of those window-bars with his elongated trunk-like nipples, nipples made of that warm, intimate, flexible, baby-smelling, rubber-like stuff, that seemed to have been stripped off the very secretest organs of warm nature-hidden life, and pull himself from the bed towards the midsummer dawn!

Thinking thus—if it could be called thinking—John Hush made several feeble movements with his hands towards the places in the air on both sides of his thin chest, now well-covered by woollen vest, linen shirt, and cloth waistcoat, where these imaginary members were waving about like the flappers of a dying seal.

He got up from the bed and began walking up and down the short piece of carpeted floor between it and the window. Each time he approached his boots, one of which lay on its side with one single long bootlace trailing beside it, he touched the heel of this particular one, which was turned towards the window and from which a gleam of whiteness was thrown back from the head of a smooth well-hammered shining nail,

THE INMATES

and gave it a hesitant tentative poke with the tip of his big toe. And as he walked up and down this small strip of colourless carpet he was cruelly torn between alternative decisions. Should he force himself to disregard these imaginary appendages to his thin chest, leave his boots as they were at this moment, and his slippers, side by side under the bed, as they were at this moment, and, leaving his room, creep downstairs past the little office-room, and have a good try at opening the front door and slipping out on the gravel-path beside the tulip-tree?

Or should he obey his dread of this horror-mania, put on his boots and slip downstairs as quietly as he could, letting the inevitable creaking take its chance, and chance take its own risk, while he just simply hoped and prayed that the two men inside that little room would be too absorbed in their game or too fast asleep or too drunk to take any notice as he pushed the bolts and went out? Over each of these choices there hung a special and peculiar dread.

Over the first—going down in his socks—hung this horror of elongated nipples. Over the second—going down in his boots—hung the peculiar terror, which was always such a cruel compulsion with him, of feeling a coward, feeling, in fact, that he was dodging what he feared, and, worse than all, feeling that by taking this path of funk he was starting on a funk-slope that must inevitably lead him down, down and down, till he found himself hemmed in by every kind of fear and face to face with some unknown horror from which there could be no escape.

So—for this was what he kept telling himself—the end of the funk-slope must inevitably be that he would perish of pure unmitigated terror, while the end of the other decision remained unknown. He might by forcing himself to carry his boots in his hands while he let his monstrous nipples hang down in front, or buttoned them up tight inside his coat, get safely out of the building and be able without disturbing a soul to find out whether those sham wooden spikes were still safely in position only waiting to be removed *en masse*

MIDSUMMER DAWN

with the greatest ease when the final moment arrived, by which time he might easily have entirely forgotten the nipples-horror.

Or, on the other hand, he might reach such a point of horror with regard to them that he'd be able to think of nothing else; and in place of opening any front door or visiting the spikes of any under-road stream, he'd just rush deliberately into that little office-room and beg to be taken to "the Wing" and have "these things" cut off by Doctor Echetus!

It was, in fact, a choice between an action that risked ruining everything and everybody in a welter of madness, or an action that only risked the ruin of this one particular plan of escape. Well, he must choose the one or the other; on the one hand all or nothing, on the other hand much less than all or a good deal more than nothing.

After all, his boots might not creak, or not loudly enough to spoil everything, and if he were caught, well! it might not prove the end of everything! But could he face—in his own deepest self—knowing to the end of his life that he'd been a coward and had funked carrying his boots because of—of those things?

Well, he had faced already ere now a good many memories of contemptible cowardice and had, yes he actually had, either forgotten them entirely or could treat their memory with indulgence. Yes! He would try *it in his boots*!

But he never forgot to the end of his life what he felt as he put on his boots and laced up each of these objects with furious tightness over the instep of each foot, and then tied the laces in savage knots above his ankles. He remembered his concluding thought with special clarity as he rose to his feet and moved his body in odd jerks up and down as if performing some gymnastic exercise without lifting his feet from the floor.

He knew well that this conclusion was a final and very important one, as indeed it was; for it became a turning-point and a mile-stone in what might be called the wavering direction of his willed destiny.

"What am I doing?" he asked himself. "Well, I am choosing cowardice in this particular case quite deliberately so as to wrestle with life under the easiest and most unimpeded

THE INMATES

condition. By means of my cowardice I have won for myself now a completely free advance along a particular track of time, entirely irrespective of what may happen!

"I have chosen, in fact, the path *by which I can enjoy, and as I might say devour, every change in myself and every change in what is happening to me*, without bothering about my character or about my reputation! All I've got to do is to' press on regardless', as young Seth once told me he did."

All this being now settled, John went softly to the door, opened it, and closed it behind him. He congratulated himself that he'd dressed without turning on the electric light, since now he had no shock of contrast to face in the darkness of the corridor and the stairs. *Creak! Creak! Creak!* Of course it was quite impossible to go down these well-known stairs without this accursed sound. Well, he must just accept it as part of the carrying out of his great decision.

And what exactly was his great decision? "Oh, mother of the Muses, don't let me forget it—at least not till Tenna and I are safe! No, no, I can repeat it to a dot—though I'd be puzzled to remember how I reached it! Follow your worst cowardice and avoid the temptation to be brave, but press on regardless, doing the thing that in spite of your cowardice and all your stupidity it is your clear destiny, I mean the urge of your whole nature and the craving of your whole being, to do!" *Creak ! Creak ! Creak!* He tried to lessen this cursed noise by leaning all the weight he could possibly transfer from his feet as heavily as he could upon the wrist of the hand which was sliding down the banister.

There was no interruption, there was no sound except this devilish creaking, till he reached the bottom of the stairs; well, not precisely no sound, for from the very start, since from the moment he had closed his own door, he had been aware of a faint murmur of Voices from that little room on the ground floor where those two watchers were trying to keep each other awake.

But this he had expected, this was the recognised background, like the flow of the river, to the presence of night at

MIDSUMMER DAWN

Glint. But it was when he let his hand slip from the polished knob at the bottom of the banister, and giving each of his thighs little blows with his clenched fists so as to diminish—there could have been no other reason for such an odd gesture—the ridiculous noise these damned boots of his made at each step, and it was when he began to walk slowly and cautiously from the staircase to the front door, that he was aware of the figure of a man crouching against the wall.

In recalling this later he was struck by the fact that he wasn't by any means overpoweringly startled by this apparition. His impassivity, however, wasn't due to anything heroic in him. It was due to the indescribable relief he was feeling that those revolting figments of his imagination, those distorted elongated female nipples that he had actually felt—for obviously if he hadn't felt the loathsome things as well as conjured them up, it wouldn't have been so bad—were no longer with him.

So great was this relief that the sight of the egregious Gewlie huddled up there waiting for him troubled him hardly at all. "That's one advantage of having a mad imagination," he told himself, "*real* devilries are reduced." The "reduced" devilry in this case was the look in Gewlie's eyes of hollow, desolate, unhappy, in-drawing suction. It was this look the man turned on him now and he caught it by the light from the door-crack of the little room; for the fellow had turned the lantern he carried as a gesture of humble apology upon his own feet so that all that passed between them took place by the light of that door-crack through which along with the thin glare of electric illumination came the sound of the two watchmen's voices.

In his relief at having shaken off those imaginary feminine appendages John found his whole nature exceptionally alert. He recalled in a flash the galvanic effect on Gewlie's nerves of Tenna's mention of her friend the gardener, and moving as quietly as he could he advanced towards the man, stepping gingerly on his heels till he could actually have allowed the uplifted sole of his right boot to descend upon Gewlie's exposed left ankle, as the man crouched sideways under the wall.

THE INMATES

The ray from the lantern Gewlie carried flickered a little upon that prostrate ankle, which was covered, in spite of the season of the year, by a well-knitted woollen sock, for the unhappy creature, devil-ridden pervert though he was, had a grandmother in Canterbury, to whom his hideous physiognomy, whenever it was presented to her old eyes, was an angelic vision.

Gewlie's slippers above his Canterbury socks were not a reassuring spectacle, for there were ominous stains on them, and, indeed, he had been called to assist—for such perverts are as precious to scientists in research laboratories as they are to despots in political prisons—both in that upper wing, wherein recalcitrant inmates were taught the limits of institutional forbearance, and in the Doctor's vivisection annex, wherein, according to an hypocrisy deeper and more unpardonable than that of the worst religious humbug, human flesh was supposed to be healed by the torture of animal flesh.

Had the incorrigible Pantamount been present here, "whether", as St. Paul would say, "in the body or out of the body", he would doubtless in his Atlantean knowledge of the language of the inanimate inmates of our planetary bedlam, have been struck by that moment's vivid exchange of impressions between Hush's upraised boot-sole and Gewlie's prostrate ankle.

But John, even if he had known the way two such manifestations of matter exchange their impressions of a selfstricken planet, was now occupied in informing the wearer of the knitted socks that, early as it was, he had an appointment to meet the Glint Hall gardener at the south lodge.

Like a will-o'-the-wisp chased by a jack-o'-lantern Gewlie's light flickered now. It flickered so violently that John felt as if the man had been transformed into a swarm of fire-flies. But an event occurred at that moment that gave this strange creature an entirely unexpected command over himself. A fantastical dialogue between the two watchmen in the little room suddenly burst upon their ears. But apart from this dialogue, to which they both listened intently with their backs to the wall

MIDSUMMER DAWN

opposite the little room, John felt by a queer instinct that something in Gewlie, either a vein of deeper devilry or of deeper religion, had considerably diminished the gardener's power to scare him.

"Didn't you hear what I've been saying to you all this while, Gum? And if you heard what I said, didn't you understand?"

"I can't honestly say I did, Glue."

"Will ye listen, then, ye sodden gomorra, if I tells ye once again?"

"'Ere's me ear, Glue."

"It may be no more nor a bloody flea-bite to thee, Gum, old pard, but to me who've been a Third-Programmer ever since wireless were wireless, to me who've been president for ten months of the Take It or Leave It Club for Special Asylum Attendants, there's never been such news as I've just heard; news that if you had the brain of a badger, Gum, you'd jump out of your hairy skin when I uncovers it for you!"

"Has it to do with international football, Glue?"

"It has to do with international blowing to bits, Gum! But it said there's now arrived in this old British Isle a great mystery-man called Morsimmon Esty; and Parliament have sent him here, not, you understand, as an ordinary inmate, but to be given the once-over, on the q.t., by Doctor Echetus, to see whether he's a real miracle-man like Merlin or Moses, or just a lunatic like the ones we've got here. The fellow seems to have the run of the place, for 'ee only arrived after teatime last evening, and I'll be damned if he hasn't been prowling around like Sherlock Holmes all night long!

"They tell me he ain't slept for four and twenty years; seeing he's found some radio-stuff out there in Thibet or cooked it up 'isself most like, what'll keep a man 'ealthy, wealthy and wise without so much as a wink of sleep. They say he met this jibber-jabber crazy clown from Outer Cathay on his journey here; and a real tonic that bird is, and an honest-to-God inmate, too, and his proper name's Katch-as-Kan!

THE INMATES

"Yes, Katch-as-Kan, the dancing puss-moth, and, oh! but he does sleep! In fact, after that act he put on last night his head's been on pillow in number fifteen quiet as a baby, for the door can't lock and we've all 'ad a good look at 'im. *He* don't take no radio-urinny to drive dull sleep away! I wouldn't wonder if he don't ask for his tray on his counterpane and his cigarette in his soap-dish when he wakes up. One thing I do know. What he wants he'll ask for. And what he asks for he'll get!

"But this 'ere barmie-larmie, Gum, you old gambler, be none other than the greatest barmie-larmie that ever lived. They say he's the old boy who's back of all these flying saucers, and that he's now busy with flying coal-scuttles, and that the plane they've got at Halfway House is for him to fly to New York in.

"But the greatest thing they say about him, and you think of that, brother Gum, is that he can paralyse hundreds of thousands of people—millions if he wants to!—just simply by this funny business of teletitery or whatever its scientific name is; but it takes a brain like mine, as full of culties as a music-hall stage of tighties, to understand these things. And this is how it works, brother Gum. And put your wits to it, brother, and push hard, for it's backroom-boy stuff, Gummy old chrysalis, if ever there were! But as I explain it, knowing both *It*, as we might say, and *you*, as we might say, it grows clear as daylight; and so listen.

"'I'm in Thibet, you must understand, like this here barmie-larmie was, before he started to come here. Is that clear, Gummy? And I'm talking to you now, you being here, and me being there. And this is what I'm saying.' Don't you dare to move an inch, Gum! Lie down on your face, Gum! Kneel on the ground with your head between your knees, Gum! And stay like that, Gum, just as long as I tell you!' Don't you see, partner, how any man alive, not to mention a barmie-larmie of the top-grade who could make his voice ring and ting in your ears as if you was in a telephone booth, could stop these hoary Russians and these bleeding Chinks

MIDSUMMER DAWN

and march the lot of them, meek and mild as Mary's lambs into Holy Lizzie's compound."

At this point the voice of Head-watchman Glue died away, and it became clear that Under-watchman Gum had either been reduced to an awed silence or had successfully retreated into that blessed detachment from the most powerful logic and the most triumphant reason, open to mortals in the poppied oblivion of sleep.

Swift as the leap of a grasshopper, Gewlie now turned round to John, his lantern throwing a narrow, elfish ray, that, as it flickered here and there, seemed to want to dance alternately with the light that shone through the door-crack of the little room, and with the paler, wiser, less purely human light that came floating in through a small round window above the well-barred front door of the whole establishment.

"I was waiting for you," whispered Gewlie. "I thought you'd be glad of my help in getting away without their hearing you!"

But as if the accomplished Glue and the illiterate Gum had patched up, in fear of the "telepathy" they had been discussing, a sort of pact between knowledge and ignorance, they now turned without restraint to their private affairs. Here they were on equal ground, and they laughed and jested in so jovial a manner that John, when he began the process of drawing the bolts in dead silence, found he had no need of the feverish help proffered him by Gewlie. When once he had got the huge double doors open, both he and Gewlie, though what the latter's actual sensations at that moment were would have puzzled even such an expert in human obliquity and human redemption as Father Allen Wun to interpret, were instantaneously confronted by the naked presence of the midsummer dawn. To John's consciousness it was as if they'd been admitted through some "magic casement" into an enchanted Cimmeria of wandering airs that were at once exquisitely cool and exquisitely warm, and were full of faint yet quite distinguishable odours, odours that kept dodging

THE INMATES

one another, pursuing one another, overtaking one another, but never losing their identity.

Sharp grass-fragrancies came and went. Delicate rose-scents came and went. While in and out among them all, as if it were a weary serpent with dusky scales, such as might have been described in some heavily repeated burden to an old border ballad, floated the smell of river mud!

It was at this moment that turning round to confront Gewlie, with nothing in his mind but an obscure urge of animal instinct warning him of danger, he realized, just as if it had been a demon-headed worm in the central nerve of the man that could actually be touched, what it was that he was plotting. Was this sudden knowledge part of the new planetary telepathy by means of which this mysterious refugee from Thibet was minded to bridge the appalling gulf between the warring halves of the whole human race?

For it was a very curious experience that John went through at that moment. Herodotus himself, the master of wonders, would have hesitated at describing the millions of little clock-cells in Gewlie's skull that were ticking and tinkling and turning their tiny wheels on their electric pivots.

And yet all this was what John *did* actually behold! But it was much more than this that Master Glue's "barmie-larmie" had hypnotised our friend into embracing with his mental vision. It wasn't merely "as if" he could perceive millions of little clockcells in Gewlie's skull, ticking and tinkling and turning. There was no "as if" about it. This is what the intelligent inmate called John saw at the front door of the scientific establishment called Glint in the receptacle commonly known as Gewlie's head.

But he also saw what hasn't been permitted to many people —certainly to no other inmate of Glint—to see with mortal eyes, namely the insubstantial and yet not quite immaterial soul-covering or soul-skin which is the halfway house, "if one may", as Herodotus would put it, "speak in that manner", between the visible and the invisible! What he saw was in fact a cloudy shape in the form of a man, composed of semi-

MIDSUMMER DAWN

transparent mist, the colour of a puddle of dirty water upon which has just fallen some dark purplish shadow.

This misty shape might be called the chemical form of Gewlie's impalpable soul; but how well John could hear the clear, teasing, sceptical tone of Tenna's voice enquiring how in all this physical clockwork he managed to read the man's *thoughts*.

And then it was that in answer to this imaginary question he was compelled to admit that the man's thoughts came straight into his own head distinct from any clockwork and that he didn't "read" them in the wheels of Gewlie's skull.

No, it was into his own head they came, just as Homer makes Hector's brother confess that the truce between the two great opposed divinities, Athene and Apollo was *entheti thumo*, "slipped into his soul". But although Gewlie's thought was, as Homer says, "slipped" into John's soul, John was given, at that weird and never-to-return moment, the privilege of seeing the actual connecting link, duskier in colour than the cloudy image to which at the nape of the man's neck it was attached, between a human soul and a human body.

This link was apparently composed of an organic chemical substance which, in fact, conveyed the impression that a large living eel was the medium between Gewlie's soul and Gewlie's body! It was emphasised for John as something distinct from both Gewlie's spirit and Gewlie's flesh by the peculiar way it quivered and shivered, and still more by the extraordinary manner in which like a thin little inlet of seawater in wind-swept sand it kept being traversed from end to end by rippling vibrations just as if it were swallowing something not much smaller than itself!

All this accentuation and extension, to put it mildly, of John's normal powers of vision lasted for no more than thirty seconds, and as soon as it had ceased and he and Gewlie had returned to a simple staring into each other's faces, each face having grown both more ghostly and more ghastly in this pallid prae-dawn light than was possible under the electric glitter from the crack of that office door or the will-o'-the-wisp jerks of

THE INMATES

Gewlie's lantern, our friend John was once more aware of that look of indescribable suction in his enemy's eyes.

But it suddenly struck him that this indrawing "suction" of Gewlie's expression suggested a much deeper cause than a simple sadistic delight in creating intense fear or supervising calculated inflictions of pain. It seemed to belong to an older order of things than ours, and to a more confused dimension of life, where the differences between good and evil were much less clearly defined. In fact, Gewlie's expression actually suggested that the wretched man regarded himself as the Supreme Deity's avenger and inquisitor, in fact as a sort of little Minotaur of eternal justice, for whom to devour his master's enemies was a sacred duty.

John realised that the moment they separated and he himself went off to that stream where all those spikes had been changed into moveable wedges of harmless wood, the wretch would scamper off to the house of Echetus and claim from him God knew what reward for God knows what discovery!

But now as he looked into the man's face, himself with his back to the tulip-tree and Gewlie with his back to the dark hall and to the thin stream of light that, along with the two watchmen's noisy laughter, came from the door of the little room, he found himself startled by something he hadn't at all expected; in short, by something that he would have described, and indeed did subsequently describe to Tenna, as the very last thing he would have looked for from Gewlie. What he saw was nothing less than an urge to utter an oracle.

The countenance of the man, no Very attractive medium for any form of inspiration, least of all for a spiritual revelation, was actually convulsed and distorted under the pressure of what he was struggling to say or of what somebody or something was determined to make him say.

John was more than startled as he stared at the man's face in that unearthly morning light. He was shocked. Knowing, or at least *thinking* he knew, Gewlie's thoughts, and having just had, only a minute ago, not merely a super-sensual vision of the strange link between the man's soul and body but a direct

MIDSUMMER DAWN

intimation, by means of some new kind of telepathy of the man's intention to go at once and betray everything to Echetus, nothing could have surprised him more than that this weasel of hell should suddenly, instead of bolting off on his treacherous mission, be heaving and throbbing and contorting his horrible face in the spasm of a rending and tearing effort to utter an oracle!

And then suddenly the oracle burst forth from him in an appalling whisper. The spirit in Gewlie's soul, or the demon in Gewlie's soul, or simply the wretch's innermost self, had obviously not the faintest thought of addressing itself to John, as a sympathetic inmate of the asylum, or, supposing the pair could hear him, to the cultivated Glue or the illiterate Gum as fellow-attendants in the asylum.

No, this terrible whisper from the Coliseum of Gewlie's soul at bay was a bolt catapulted to the perimeter of his precious One-world-only in a desperate attempt to destroy for ever certain impious inmates who were trying to escape the cosmic glint of the living God. And the effect of this appalling whisper upon John was for the moment overwhelming. It struck him as the most poignant thing he had ever known. What thunderbolts of power lay in the miserablest human soul!

John felt like worshipping, not Gewlie or Gewlie's god, but the infinite divinity in the lowest human creature. He knelt on the mat in the doorway so that with his face close to Gewlie's face he could catch every syllable squeezed from that sponge of suction. And, as if the obsessed soul of the wretch did really have for its covering some kind of skin that could be torn in thin slits, there issued from its mouth, accompanying what he said, a queer sound that exactly resembled the tearing of some stiffly resistant fabric. "One God", whispered Gewlie; and the whisper as it lost itself in the morning air was accompanied by the hissing scream of torn silk.

"One God," repeated that wrung-out oval of porous human flesh, opposite to which John knelt; and it struck him, as he knelt there, in his thunderstruck worship of the intolerable, that not only were the eyes and mouth at work in this double process of sucking up and wringing out, but that the ears were

THE INMATES

doing their share, and the nostrils were doing theirs and that even the knuckles of the fingers clutching the lantern were doing theirs!

These fingers were in fact playing what might have been called "The March of the Cosmic Sponge", for they were beating a sort of indrawing and out-propelling tattoo on John's chest, in the process of which those fingers moment by moment seemed to be growing whiter and thinner and more bony, in their desperate attempt to combine the machinery of suction with the machinery of explosion.

"One God," hissed the eyes, mouth, nostrils, ears, and clenched fingers of Gewlie, "and therefore one Mother of God; one God, and therefore one Son of God; one God and therefore one Church of God; one God and therefore one Bride of God; one God and therefore one Spirit of God; and as in the Beginning God was All, so in the End God will be All. God, God, nothing but God! The One, the One, the One, nothing but the One!"

But a man's strength is a man's strength, whatever his will-power, and the legs of a man are that strength's measure and limit. Thus having flung his bolt back into the blue as a warning to the Titans to leave Pelion and Ossa alone and Olympus alone, the whole power and presence and personality of Gewlie cringed and cowered and crumpled and collapsed, as a creature drained of all life.

He made no further attempt to "kick against the pricks", in other words against all the thorny land-hedgehogs and spiky sea-urchins of multifarious Nature with her fathomless reserves of infinite backgrounds and undreamed-of dimensions. He sank down weakly and shamelessly on the litter and dust of the unswept floor of the entrance-hall to Glint. Mrs. Wohntscher wasn't due for nearly an hour yet, and between his exhausted body and the dust of that trodden threshold there seemed a natural reciprocity.

John's pity for the man under the tension of the oracle that convulsed him, combined with the fact that John himself was on his knees, made any assistance he gave him natural and automatic. What he did for "the sadistic little sod", as he called him later to Tenna, was simply to help him to collapse comfortably on his haunches, and, this done, to sink down by his side. After a little more shuffling, during which John treated his companion as if he were an exhausted infant, they were both seated on the capacious doormat, with their four heels on the doorstep.

The "sadistic little sod", however, though no longer with that painful accompaniment like the tearing of the Veil of the Temple, continued his dithyrambic oracle in praise of the One. "There will be," his voice wistfully wailed in John Hugh's left ear, "no more *you* and no more *me*, no more men and no more women, no more masters and no more slaves! There will be no more black, red, yellow and white among the nations. There will be no more French and English, no more Jews and Gentiles, no more Old World and New World.

"There will be no more individuals, no more persons, no more men, or animals, or birds, or reptiles, or insects, or vegetation. There will be no more heavens, or earths, or moons, or stars, or galaxies, or nebulae. There will be no more time and no more space. There will be no more of anything we know.

"Instead of life there will be only God! Instead of death, only God! Instead of me, wanting what I want and hating you, only God! Instead of you, wanting what you want and hating me, only God! Instead of the sane eating up the mad in places like this, only God, eating us all up according to His eternal and divine pleasure."

The high-pitched intoning of this diabolus-sanctus litany ceased at last, and John Hush, plucking his attention like an in-sucked cork from this exhausted conqueror-worm, considered what was, as Homer would say, the best counsel to be followed. He *had* to make sure that those sham wooden spikes were O.K., so that when the moment came it would be easy to pull them out and let the stream carry them off, and easy to climb out on the bank on the other side of the great wall when once they had followed the stream under that arch.

THE INMATES

But if he got up from the doormat and shut the door softly and cleared off wasn't there every chance that in spite of the fellow's belief in the final end of everything and his absolute conviction that he himself would vanish as utterly as a bubble of spittle from the mouth of one of the dogs in Echetus's torture-house, "the sadistic little sod" would scramble to his feet and for all the shakiness of his legs manage to shuffle off to the house of Echetus and find a hiding-place to wait there, as patiently as a cat watches at a mouse-hole, till the Doctor could see him.

And then John Hush thought of the appallingness for them all, for himself, for Tenna, for Mr. Lordy, for the mysterious Pantamount, for the heroic Commander, for poor old Miss Bolster and her besotted circus-freak, for those crazy twins, for the skipping Zeit-Geist, and even for Tenna's special human horror, that obsessed old masochist Rumpibus with his apple-cheeked Tottie, if their plot were discovered and the American plane went off without them!

"I'm responsible for the lot of them," he thought. "And if Tenna and I desert them, and *he* and that girl fly off with only Tenna and me, the fate of the inmates of Glint will be hopeless. Sometimes the worst of cowards simply *has* to be brave.

"Well, I rather fancy such a time has now come for me; and I've got to do something drastic." With a long fixed stare he contemplated the exhausted and wrung-out Gewlie.

Then, as we say, he gathered himself together, or, as Homer would say, he crouched to spring; and, having made up his mind, he acted with a rush.

15

"ON ALL FOURS"

IT MUST be confessed that when once his resolution was made John plunged head-foremost into a series of actions that would

"ON ALL FOURS"

certainly have struck his guardian as surprisingly rapid and competent. He clapped his hand over his companion's mouth, lifted him up in his arms, and, holding him pressed tightly to his chest, managed by squeezing him against the door-post to keep him dumb, while with his free hand, using exquisite care to shut them with scarcely a sound, he succeeded in closing the double doors of the main entrance to Glint Hall.

This accomplished, he staggered and stumbled eastward, away from the tulip-tree and the entrance-drive and the smooth lawn, following a narrow, neglected, overgrown path that led round the corner of the house where there were no windows on the ground-floor but above which, as he lurched and staggered on, he knew very well was that wide semi-Gothick window looking due east out of which on his first day in this place at the end of March he had seen the ancient fortress-ridge with its two Scotch firs, and seen it, in the rapidly darkening spring-twilight, as the background to Tenna's face when they first exchanged words.

He had to lean against the wall every half-minute, and he kept uttering loud panting gasps that seemed to himself to resemble the hoarse croakings of a mad raven who was carrying in its claws in some desperate insurrection of the fowls of the air one of the most vicious of game-keepers, in order to quell his expostulations in the pit Echetus had dug for his dead dogs.

During these moments of resting against the wall he kept assuring himself that he mustn't think about the threat to Tenna if Gewlie did get to Echetus and revealed their plot. "I mustn't squeeze the little sod to death," he thought, "or knock out his brains against this wall!"

But it wasn't only the roughness of the wall, making it an unpleasant object to rest against and a tempting smashing-block for the execution of a midget-minotaur of totalitarian omnipotence: it was the wall's endlessness that made every second of this struggle so appalling. And in addition to the rest there was this horrible half-dead, half-living, half-animate, half-inanimate jumble of things that clung to the wall for protection!

THE INMATES

To John's peculiar sensibility and half-crazy fastidiousness this over-growth of creature-life as it brushed against his face was incredibly repugnant.

Midges, spider-webs, small blue-bottle flies, snail-slime, trailing stalks without leaves, tickling insects without wings, tangles of leaves that completely hid their stalks, and finally thick red stalks that seemed to carry upon their smooth surface nothing but thorns, all these conspired with nameless grub-dust and pollendust to cause him that particular kind of discomfort, thick with a curious excretion of loathing and disgust from which he seemed to have spent his whole life in running away; and here he was with a jungle of it round his head!

The wall, indeed, seemed to stretch on in complete indifference to everything except some implacable necessity of the higher mathematics. But it was not ordained by the great goddess Chance, Nature's daughter and darling, and so much less of a wanton than many sages have surmised, that John should perish of a burst blood-vessel at that particular stage of his unnatural undertaking.

After a few steps more of stumbling and staggering he reached the end. The building turned away from them at right angles; and there in front of them, looking due east, was a clear open space ! So high did the up-sloping distance rise above their prison wall that the summit of the eastern ridge which he had seen from the window of that passage as a background to Tenna's head showed itself to him now through a wavering transparency of white mist, like a vision of magical escape, with its prehistoric camp and its two Scotch firs.

And above the ancient camp and between those two tremendous trees, red as the blood of a battle in heaven, rose the sun! It is true that neither the gasping and groaning John nor the moaning and whimpering Gewlie had the strength left to notice anything more than the most realistic aspect of what they saw or to observe that both the ridge and the trees upon the ridge had the air of having awaited this blood-red apparition, not for a mere twenty-four hours but for twenty-thousand years!

"ON ALL FOURS"

But there it was: and you might have thought at that moment from the expression on each face that the question as to which was the victor and which was the vanquished made small difference compared with the desperate welcome they gave to that red rim, knowing well in their strained and contorted bones that its presence brought at least a respite to their struggle.

There were several cows in the enclosed meadow whose iron railings had now given to this grotesque contest some sort of an end; and these somnolent creatures, who had themselves only just risen to greet the sun, leaving dim islands of enchanted greyness on the grass, like patterns on a map of undersea mountains, half-turned their heads on the obscure chance that it might prove possible to find a natural cause for the sudden manifestation at the boundary of their pasture of a man with well-laced leather boots and a scratched face pressing frantically against his breast another being of the same species with tattered slippers, a white face, and something in the expression of his eyes that even at that safe distance was disturbing.

But, having decided that neither the man carrying nor the man carried was aiming just then at any mischief to them, they turned back to the east, where the bloody rim of the lord of life challenged all profane men and all impious beasts to dare to utter a blasphemous sound.

John now behaved to Gewlie as if he were a child, and deliberately helped him to prop his slippered feet on the bottom rail of the fence and to clutch tightly with his trembling fingers, from which still dangled the palely jerking lantern-flame, the thin chilly rondure of the top rail. No piercing shriek burst from Gewlie's mouth to fly like an arrow across their prison-wall till it reached that crimson orb on the horizon.

All the sound that came out of him was just as if John had been squeezing a queer-shaped bagpipe, a bagpipe which, when balanced against the railings, could only repeat with a whistling long-drawn gasp: "Mother of Mercy! but I didn't know you were so strong!"

THE INMATES

Strong or not, our friend couldn't collect either his breath or his wits for a good half-minute, while with his arm round his prisoner's shoulder he stared at that crimson platter slowly projecting itself from between a pair of familiar black trees across a gulf in space.

And he now discovered that one of the cows they had disturbed had not returned to the grass but was still staring at that blood-red rondure on the high ridge. And while this black-and-white cow stared in awe at the sun, John Hush, recovering his breath, stared in awe at the cow. "She might be Io herself," he thought, "and that grand horned head with those liquid eyes and those quivering nostrils might be flinging its spirit across horizon after horizon, far over the Molossian plain, far beyond the oaks of Dodona, till it reaches the heaped-up mud of the Nile, where the gad-fly will cease from stinging and the great black king Epaphos will be born!"

And as he regained his breath, he asked himself what it was about the head of a horned cow confronting a sunrise that had such a peculiar effect on him? Was it, he vaguely pondered, mingling the remoteness of his thought with the aching of his muscles, that there exist within us certain life-germs inherited from primeval creatures of this planet who possessed an intimacy with the elements far closer than any known to us to-day; beings for whom what was happening now on that eastern ridge was the central ritual for all living things as they worshipped the cause of all life?

But everything was rapidly changing now about that crimson orb, and there had appeared above it what looked like an overhanging down-toppling mountain of woolly cloud edged with delicate silvery cornices and with coppery entablatures that were scooped into golden arches.

More slowly than he could have believed possible, that blood-red circle crossed the narrow chasm in space between the crest of the hill with its gigantic trees and these illuminated cloud-alps; and John had the feeling that it was crossing an irretrievable crack in our whole dimension! As he saw it now it was no circle, that orb of blood. It was the half-torso of a

"ON ALL FOURS"

cosmic creature, a creature born of a self-evolved, self-differentiated multiverse, not created by any god, and not a friend, or an enemy either, to any man!

John had never properly learnt Greek at school and it was due entirely to his guardian that he had made feeble efforts to keep up with it later; but the Heifer-Maid of the Aeschylean Prometheus had always had a special attraction for him, as a creature loved by one ultimate mystery and hated by another! "We are all haunted by mysteries," he thought, "and we have no more idea why we are what we are than why anything is anything!"

Whether it was that carrying Gewlie like a colossal insect, like the very gad-fly from which the Heifer-Girl couldn't be saved till she reached the mouths of the Nile and gave birth to the black Epaphos, John had over-strained himself, or whether it was that his drastic question addressed to life and flung in the face of the rising lord of life had blinded and dazed him, but for a minute or two his whole consciousness stopped dead and everything went dark.

He came to himself so quickly that his momentary loss of consciousness seemed to himself no more than the "blank misgivings of a creature moving about in worlds not realised", and when his mind came back it was an extremely disagreeable and totally unexpected shock to see his recent companion scuttling like a ferret escaped from a keeper's bag in the direction of that pit for vivisected dogs whence, as he knew well, there was a direct path leading to the House of Echetus.

"Oh, God!" he groaned aloud, "if I don't stop him now all is lost! He'll tell all he knows and he probably knows everything!" Had the wakeful Zeit-Geist possessed, as according to the cultivated Glue their visitor from Thibet did, "the run of the whole place", and at that silent hour been watching from the dew-soaked shadow of one of the young spruces John's desperate final rush to catch his enemy, he would doubtless have understood the subtle relief it was to our friend to utter his feelings aloud instead of keeping them to himself as his old nurse would have told him he ought to do, and understood

THE INMATES

also, no doubt, that the mere putting his feelings into words toughened them with that spiritual cement that might be called *the irony of expressed self-consciousness*. It may be doubted whether the wakeful Zeit-Geist could have produced from about his person by simply wriggling a finger an instrument for recording not only the substance of a thought but its precise verbal vesture, but he would have had a perfect opportunity for registering the effect of extreme emotional agitation upon the colours and forms of the visible world as these are imposed upon, and interpenetrated by, purely mental imagery, had he been watching this manhunt.

At last a perfectly simple and direct feeling broke through the blurred confusion of the chaos in John's brain, and, as he ran, this feeling tore its way out and tossed itself free of everything! In place of Gewlie it was Tenna herself he was now carrying in his desperation, and it seemed as if he were making the most frantic efforts to keep her soul as well as her body from escaping, and he felt as if it were these efforts to keep Tenna's soul in Tenna's body that kept forcing him to make certain convulsive jerks as he ran, and not only so, but to give vent to certain surprisingly animal noises, as he leapt over the small spruces and dodged the large ones.

To himself these sounds were the very talk of his heart to her heart. "Oh, my one true love!" was what these gruntings and groanings were really saying; but, in some obstinate knot of self-confusion, as if he'd been a spell-bound thick-skinned, inarticulate animal, he was troubled now by a blind doubt as to whether she understood what he was doing and feeling.

"*Tenna!*" he cried at last; and it seemed to him that this cry—wrenched like a gobbet of bleeding flesh from his body, and like a nugget of burning radium from his soul—had been flung forth upon the universe from within the mounting curve of the escaping sun as it burst into the mists! "Whether we die together," he cried, "or go on living side by side till my manias grow grey and your manias turn grey, I'll hold on to you while I am I; and if I lose you I'll hunt for you from one dimension after another! I'll ransack them, I tell you, these

"ON ALL FOURS"

dream-worlds! I'll break through them all till I get you again!"

It would have been a curious experience for old Mrs. Wohntscher, arriving, as she sometimes did, with all her paraphernalia for scrubbing and cleaning, long before even the most conscientious of the permanent staff had left their sleeping-quarters, if, as was her custom to do before settling down to work, she had taken her usual glance through the window at the end of the long corridor, and from thence had perceived the staggerings and the recoverings, the wild rushes towards the east, and the not less furious deviations to the north and the south, as these two figures, the one pursuing and the other pursued, the one bent upon reaching Echetus so as to reveal everything, the other still more bent upon preventing, if necessary by violence, the revelation of anything.

Whether the old lady, who never quite forgot, whatever else she was doing, that mahogany table at the end of her day, would have been able, simply from the outward appearance of the man pursuing, compared with the outward appearance of the man pursued, to decide whether it was the urge that was driving the first or whether it was the urge that was driving the second that was likely to prevail in the end, is a question difficult to answer.

Mrs. Wohntscher never gave a thought to outward appearances save in relation to inward urges. She had been brought up by the Salvation Army, having been left as a child almost literally on the Army's doorstep by one of those tender-hearted women who know by instinct, quite apart from logic or mathematics or even common sense, in what queer directions the vegetable substance of the second oldest mystery in the world is apt to make its unpredictable appearance; and although both Father Tickle and Father Allen Wun had more than once given her historical, archaeological, and even metaphysical instruction as to the true nature of the wood of the Holy Cross, there was something about the accelerated rhythm of the swing of her polishing-rag, as it swept dust and dirt from every grain of planetary wood, that led the old

THE INMATES

lady, in despite of geography, history, reason, and even of good taste, to reserve that honour for mahogany.

As a matter of fact, the philosophical charwoman did see the two figures behaving in that unusual manner by the first light of dawn, but when she turned back to the long corridor and set to work on its familiar floor she told herself that men *as* men, whether within or without the walls of Glint, were incurably demented.

For some while as she moved about on her hands and knees, Mrs. Wohntscher mingled the feel of each dust-crack she knew so well and of each queer mark in certain particular boards where great creative nature had indulged in some perverse caprice before the tree was cut down, with the peculiar aberrations of the male animal whether inside or outside this particular home of research.

"As I always say," she murmured to herself, "it's their trousers what does it. In them old scripture days"—thus her thoughts ran on—"when learned men painted proper Bible-pictures of the prophets and saints, they didn't paint the rest of the menfolk who were, of course, as men always are, playing at some silly game or drinking in pubs or sneaking into whore-shops.

"The saintly men they painted were always keeping their sheep or feeding their cattle or fishing from their boats, or with spears and shields taking captive great heathen cities from ungodly tribes of Midianites and Jebusites and Canaanites.

"Did we ever see in these Holy Sunday-book pictures even so much as one single pair of trousers? We never did! Where did I hear that timely saying:' When men first wore trousers in Cuckoldy Square their wives went a-whoring at Candlemas Fair'?"

But neither the philosophical cleaning-woman nor the wakeful Pantamount, who from his small window in the punishment wing had also caught a fleeting glimpse of this drama among the spruce-trees, remained long enough at their posts of observation to see what happened when John came

"ON ALL FOURS"

near to overtaking Gewlie at about a couple of hundred yards from the hole of the dead dogs.

Our friend was close behind the runaway; and Gewlie, aware of this, had already turned to face him, when from behind a spruce tree that was a trifle and a thicker trifle higher than the rest there suddenly appeared between them the most overwhelming personality that either of them had ever seen.

This person, if person he were and not a supernatural apparition, had his back to John and his face to Gewlie. Gewlie's own face, however, by one of those circus tricks so dear to that supreme virtuoso in historic pantomime the corybantic acrobat Chance, was clearly visible to John under the apparition's left armpit; for the man, if man he were, held his arms akimbo, and the expression upon Gewlie's face, thus exhibited within a living frame, completely bewildered his recent pursuer. It showed no fear. It showed no horror. It showed no surprise.

What it showed was ecstatic happiness! It had the look of those rather ugly supernumerary bystanders in some vast El Greco mystery-picture who nevertheless are quite as much transfigured and transported by what is occurring as the protagonists in that particular cosmic drama.

Very deliberately the imposing personage who had thus intervened proceeded to do what our friend had recently been doing for a different purpose and with another result. He lifted Gewlie in his arms. But instead of clasping him to his breast, as John had done, with a hug of desperate vengeance, this new performer in the Burlesque show of redemption held him high up in both his arms well above his head while he still kept his own face turned away.

John and Gewlie were therefore once again staring at each other; but this time only a couple of hundred yards from the dog-pit and with the prehistoric camp in full sight but with the risen sun concealed behind a mountain of mist.

And to John's amazement the ecstatic Gewlie, thus held aloft before the indrawn breath of all the creatures of the dawn, began to utter articulate speech.

THE INMATES

"So you see, master," announced the contorted image of this weird transfiguration, "you were wrong and I was right. Men and women are nothing. All is God; and all is death at the hands of God!"

Gewlie's face after he had uttered these words *broke in pieces*. Henceforth it was not as if Morsimmon Esty were carrying a dead man. It was as if he were carrying a figure of petrified clay that was in danger of crumbling to bits. A complete exhaustion that was like a collapse of living flesh, though it was parallel to Gewlie's almost chemical dissolution, now took possession of John Hush.

He caught sight of the stump of a large ash tree that had been left in the ground when the spruces were planted and upon this he sank down, clutching his shins with his fingers and pressing his forehead against his knees. Gewlie was done for. But John felt as if this Morsimmon Esty had found a crack in the heart of life, thrust an atom-bomb into it, and were now carrying towards it a fluttering and flapping flame that would blow up the world!

And John, with his skull pressed against his knees, knew that the flame the man was carrying towards this crack was the soul of Gewlie. The flame of that soul had curled itself up like a crouching tiger within the cauldron of the wretch's cruelty; but now it was released. It had leapt up. It had leapt out. The infernal cat was out of the holy bag. "What," thought John, "is this Morsimmon Esty going to do now? I wish I knew whether he's on our side or on the side of our enemies! Will he want to fly to America with us if we get out of this place?"

These questions adapted themselves in John's skull, as he kept that brittle structure pressed hard against his knees, to the rhythm of a peculiar jogging jig, a jig made, not with his heels against me stump he was sitting on, but with his fingernails on the edges of his shin-bones, scraping and rescraping these bony projections covered by corduroy trousers as if they were a pair of outstretched strings.

Suddenly he let his hands sink down and lifted his head. What he beheld in front of him was the figure of Morsimmon

"ON ALL FOURS"

Esty moving, in the manner of a priest approaching an altar, towards the dog-pit, with the rapidly disintegrating remains of the man he had caused to die of ecstasy held aloft in both hands. The remains of Gewlie were indeed dissolving fast, but as moment by moment they crumbled away they retained a simulacrum of human shape; and it was this shape that had a resemblance to a rain-soaked delapidated long-lost doll from some gargantuan Glint Hall for insane dolls into which one of the most scatter-brained of all Sons of Mischief had incontinently tossed it, either in pure caprice or out of curiosity just to see what would happen to it in such a Noah's Ark of crazy puppets, all fancying themselves creatures who could purr and growl and scrabble and wriggle and lick and bite and wag their tails, when once they were presented with a keeper *who enjoyed his job*!

"Inmates are we?" thought John. "But if crumbling images of corruption like this poor *eidolon* are to be allowed to go on driving us into worse insanity there's need indeed for rending and tearing, and a beginning again of the whole business! But of course"—and as he watched the inexplicable dissolution of the human-inhuman envelope of the entity upon whom the name Gewlie had been tagged he began to wonder if any atom of it, for the thing now seemed to be more than decomposing, it seemed to be trickling and dripping and melting away, would reach the dog-hole at all—"but of course," he thought, "if the whole of this weird puppet-show we call 'life' vanishes at the moment of death into a dream which in its turn dissolves into another dream without the sleeper waking up at all, and if neither the dream that has gone nor the dream that has taken its place touch, as we might say, bottom, in the sense of ever reaching any firm ground, what does it matter whether he gets to the dog-hole with anything of Gewlie left, or whether it's all gone before he gets there?

"I must call to him! But he knows I'm here, for he saw me. He came between us. No, I'd better not call to him. I'd better get up and go after him! But how solemnly he's walking now! It's as if he's carrying something that's very dangerous

THE INMATES

to spill, but he's spilling it all the time without knowing it! Yes, I must get up at once and go after him."

The man from Thibet was indeed advancing towards the dog-hole in a singular manner. He was walking not only slowly and cautiously but with a ritualistic gravity that was beginning to strike our friend as grotesque.

John Hush made an effort to rise. He *couldn't* rise. He made another effort. Again he couldn't! Had he been paralysed by this person whose face he hadn't yet seen? Had he a face at all? Like other victims of a disordered imagination John had often frightened himself by horrible fancies of featureless human heads. Was he destined, now, even now, when on the brink of escape, to be driven really and actually insane by what he might see if Morsimmon Esty turned round?

He tried desperately for the third time to rise from that ash-tree stump. In vain! And yet he didn't *feel* paralysed. Was the Thibetan a friend of the enemy and consequently hostile to any flight to New York? Was he himself destined to sit on this ash-tree stump till, like Gewlie, he crumbled and dribbled into nothing, his only advantage over that obsessed *voyeur* of cruelty being the questionable one that the bulk of his de-composition would take place while he was still conscious?

It may easily be imagined that John Hush had some very contradictory feelings, and as the result of these feelings some very contradictory ideas as he contemplated the prelatical back of Watchman Glue's "barmie-larmie" who was indeed making the utmost of what that well-informed attendant had called his "run of the place".

For one thing, some self-lacerating devil in John forced him to imagine the dead silence, for she was as secretive as he was himself over their feelings for each other, with which Tenna would hear that his room had been found empty that morning and that Mrs. Wohntscher had seen him chasing Gewlie across the spruce-plantation.

On the other hand, lie automatically began practising what he regarded as his most important discovery during his nine weeks in an institution devoted to research, nor was he so in-

"ON ALL FOURS"

fatuated with his own devices as to fail to give due weight tc the influence of the Commander in this, the royal trick, namely, of forcing himself to go through the motions of enjoying all the craziest and most abominable situations offered by life and death, as they arise, just as if instead of feeling them to be horrible he felt them to be delectable.

"Repeat these self-compelling motions of enjoyment often enough," he had of late explained to Tenna, who could only refute him by murmuring a preference for death, "and the most appalling things change their character and cease to be intolerable."

It was in accordance, therefore, with this august discovery, of which, so he had been driven to confess to Tenna, neither the Commander nor himself had hitherto made any striking use, that he now set himself to enjoy the sensation of imagining that the flesh below his ribs was falling away, and that, like the body of a dead sheep he had once seen in a ditch in Slovakia his decomposing torso was rapidly becoming a confused waterfall of living maggots.

If this was to be his fate, wasn't it only meet and right that it should come upon him when he was in a position like this, huddled, head to knees, and with his fingers clasping his shins? Wasn't this the very position in which in ancient days they buried people?

Wasn't it the position in which foetuses and embryos and abortions were wont to hug themselves before being bundled out of limbo into life and out of life into limbo? "Well," he thought, "if I can't get up I can at least find out how much of my body is paralysed!"

It was this vigorous and sensible decision of John's that resulted in his carrying out a series of muscular experiments which, even if they had struck Tenna as pathetically like the sort of experiments that a doll would have made if a doll's brain had been able to make the discovery that it possessed physical things called "muscles", a mental thing called "will", and an electric system of interior wires by which these two could be connected, would not have impressed her with that particular kind of special hero-worship that childless women who are not "in love", but who are deeply touched in their maternal hearts and at the same time mischievously tickled in their old-maidish sense of humour where their male heroes are concerned, are apt to feel.

To feel the true poignancy of our friend's situation would have taken not only the romantic sentiment of Miss Bolster but also the realistic and sweeping shrewdness of Mrs. Wohntscher, remembering the innocent timidity of Mr. Wohntscher, who perished in the Second World War leaving her still a virgin.

To have seen John so resolutely at work on his mysterious inability to get up from that ash-stump would indeed have deeply impressed both these admirers of his. What he did was simply to try out one by one every movement that it was physically possible for him to make, and every set of muscles that it was possible for him to use, and how far and exactly where these revolting members and muscles refused obedience to his will.

And to his perfect amazement he found he could move any separate portion of his body he liked! He was soon behaving in the manner of an electrified robot, nodding and wagging his head, knocking his knees together, tapping his heels against each other, shrugging his shoulders, snapping his fingers, slapping his arms across his breast, and even causing his haunches to rock to and fro, as though he were in the act of dodging or destroying a wasp's nest.

But no sooner did he suspend these activities and try to rise to his feet from his seat on the stump than once more complete immobility took possession of him and he became no better than a stone.

And all this time it was impossible for him not to gaze with infuriated desperation at the massive prelatical back of this "barmie-larmie" who could reduce one man to a pinch of dust and another to a prisoner on a tree-stump. Yes I this formidable back was still moving, with what might most literally have been called the remains of Gewlie, towards the dog-pit. "But I won't, I positively won't," he thought, "work myself into a fury over this. What difference does it make, in a

"ON ALL FOURS"

dimension of time and space like this, if a conscious entity called John should be compelled, yes, compelled to contemplate another entity, and one devoid, as far as the first can tell, of a single human feature in his terrestrial face, playing at a solemn entombment with the scraps of decomposition left from the crumbling body of an asylum-keeper called Gewlie? And, "after all," he thought, "it's all pure chance! The Aristotelian-scholastic God of Father Wun's metaphysic has no more real existence than the Evangelical-Anglican God of Father Tobie's river-bank intimations I And this unfair chance has chosen to make a hundred times luckier than the tortured dogs of Echetus's dog-hole. What's happened to me is simply that in coming near this ambassador from Thibet, who, I certainly hope, is on our side and not on our enemy's, I have been touched by some devolutionary cosmic ray that has the power of magnetising people back from human to animal, from animal to vegetable, from vegetable to mineral, and so on down the scale to bodiless gasses and even, perhaps, to atoms and mesons.

"I don't so much mind if it leaves me as a patch of moss or a clump of lichen or even as a scum of mould, but I don't want to finish as one of those weird mathematical suppositions or hypotheses belonging to some level of existence that exists only in the human mind."

And then John thought of Tenna. What would Tenna feel when she discovered he had vanished with Gewlie? Imagination of the nerves rather than of the heart was John's chief peculiarity, and at this moment the image of Tenna's particular look when she realised the fact of his disappearance hit him such a sharp blow that its first effect was to cause him to utter aloud the first syllable of her name and to repeat that syllable over and over again.

He must have uttered it four times. *"Ten! Ten! Ten! Ten!"* But to him it was as if he had desperately shrieked it a hundred times, and not upwards after the vapour-wrapped sun as he had done before, but downwards, "through the thick rotundity of the earth", downwards, cracking the innermost

THE INMATES

centre of "nature's moulds" till that *"Ten! Ten! Ten! Ten!"* broke out, erupting upwards once more, in New Zealand, and became audible as the voice of some ancient Maori ghost from the mountain-peak of Taranaki!

And then, just as he had begun to wonder whether the syllable "Ten" might have been some ancient prehistoric invocation understood at once by dehumanised presences hovering about the ridge of the two Scotch firs, he suddenly discovered that by letting his hands sink forward into the moss in front of his feet, and rolling sideways off the ash-stump, he was able, like the Titan who could only be strangled when lifted into the air, to draw renewed strength from the earth.

Aided by this contact, and exultantly grateful to find he could crawl, he began moving, as they say, "on all fours". It was in this way he tentatively followed Morsimmon Esty towards the dog-pit. It wasn't long, however, as may be supposed, before he was forced to stop to rest, for to move "on all fours" was a means of progression he hadn't practised since the age of one and a half.

The Thibetan stopped at the dog-pit and bent over it. Then he began to act as if he were removing from his hands something that might have been a little fluff, a little scurf, a flicker of scum, a speck of dandruff, a few scaly scabs, a wisp of hair, or a pinch of sticky dust.

Watching the tremendous back of Master Glue's "barmie-larmie" as he thus literally washed his hands of Gewlie, two rather unusual words came into John's head which he tried in vain to connect either with what he was watching of the person and of the proceedings of Morsimmon Esty, or with himself, as he peered out from under these sweet-scented spruce-branches. The first was the word *sorites*, and the second was the word *incunabula*.

Whether it was the prerogative of the feminine earth not only to allow a male human creature to draw "virtue" from his contact with her as the woman "with the issue of blood" drew virtue from Jesus of Nazareth, but also to supply him with a new metaphysical orientation by which he could avoid

"ON ALL FOURS"

the pitfalls of life, John was now made more vividly aware than he had ever been before, as with his left hand he touched the fringe of the small just-budding purple plant called self-heal, and with his right knee approached the trailing white-flowered wisps of the plant called bed-straw, of the monstrous fallacy, lying treachery, and infernal falsehood, of the idea of logical determinism and absolute fate in human affairs, of which the enemy made such compelling play.

It seemed to him, at that first moment of being "on all fours", that he became a medium for the secret wisdom of all those creatures of the earth, animal, vegetable, mineral, "up and down, down and up", who, unaffected by the attractions of logical scientific reasoning, lived by the true illusions of life; above all by the ultimate illusion of free will. "On all fours", as he was now, he was able to observe quietly and closely, and free from the fever of self-sadistic reasoning, not only all the unpredictable twists and turns of the living stalks and filigree-foliage of the fragile bed-straw, not only the globular curves and shell-like foliations of the shadowy self-heal, but all those fascinatingly casual shapes and positions of shapes, forming spears, swords, shields, gibbets, triangles, pikes, sceptres, squares, gates, hoops, spirals, jig-saws, crosses, rakes, horns, harps, trumpets, into which the indiscriminate litter and inland windrows and spindrift of the tiny microscopic wood-sticks and straws and grass-blades of dead vegetation had been led or driven. And like an animal he raised one knee and then one hand, thinking, "I will crawl there," or, "I will crawl *there*," and then thinking, "I will crawl a little in *that* direction, and then I will turn round, not urged by any motive at all, or by any urge at all, or by any desire at all, but simply and solely to prove to myself, for my own interest alone, and at a moment decided upon quite arbitrarily and capriciously by myself, that I possess, along with every other planetary identity, whether animal, vegetable, or mineral, together with all the atoms that compose us, the power to act or not to act, and the power to defy, unexpectedly, capriciously and wantonly, for the pure pleasure of proving to myself that I am free, every sort of cause

THE INMATES

and pressure exerted by every sort of material sequence as well as every sequence of thought or feeling or action!

"But oh, Tenna! Tenna! Tenna! The point now is, whether on our feet or' on all fours ', how many inmates we can save from Echetus!"

Slowly, cautiously, and forcing himself with a strange power in the depths of his spirit to taste a life-enjoyment beyond any he had ever known, he crawled towards the dog-pit.

Sorites? Incunabula? Did that first word mean an infinitely remote end to everything by a progression of mad logic leading to an impossibly absurd and therefore an absolutely nonexistent nothingness? And did that second word mean an infinitely remote rebeginning of everything out of the void?

Yes, out of the very vacuum of that absurdly logical nothingness? What magic there was in words I Mad it might be, but how miraculous it was that his absurd cry of *"Ten! Ten ! Ten! Ten !"* had summoned up those two mysterious words!

He moved his right knee and then his left hand. He moved his left knee and then his right hand. He was still crawling in the direction of the man from Thibet, who was still bending over the dog-pit. But then all in a moment he swung round! It seemed to him that a broken stick his right knee had encountered and a hollow bole full of black water into which he had thrust his left hand had spoken to him in a language totally beyond such words as *sorites* and *incunabula*! Faster than he had ever crawled in his infant life he now moved "on all fours" away from the Thibetan and away from the dog-pit; nor did he rise to his feet till he was in sight of the stream flowing under their prison wall, where the iron spikes had been changed into wooden ones.

16

THE ESCAPE

WHEN HE heard the news brought by his two chief retainers, Doctor Echetus was indignant. He was not upset—not, that is

THE ESCAPE

to say, out of due measure and suitable proportion—nor was he alarmed about the future. He was simply and quite naturally indignant.

It was an exceptionally beautiful midsummer morning; and the Doctor, after leaving his breakfast-room where he had enjoyed just the kind of breakfast he liked best, had proceeded to make his leisurely way to an earth-closet near the research laboratory with a view to relieving his bowels. On his return from this innocent objective, he had stopped to pick a white carnation.

It had been with this particular flower in his buttonhole that he had delivered the presidential address which had first announced to his colleagues the new line of research by which, alone among European empiricists, he had hoped, carrying science into a sphere where no one had ever dared to carry it before, to reach the electric contact between life and consciousness, that is to say between the magnetic vibration that acts and reacts, and whatever it may be that transforms these actions and reactions into consciousness.

The act of easing his bowels had increased the doctor's sense of well-being, so that when arriving at the door of his office and remembering that there were dogs still waiting to be crucified in his laboratory, he breathed a sigh of pure satisfaction. But he was faced by a surprise. Bill Squeeze and Cogent Cuddle awaited him with the startling news that there was not one single inmate left in Glint Hall; unless—but that was unlikely—the person called Pantamount was still tied up in the punishment wing.

Did Doctor Echetus, on hearing this information, burst into a fit of rage? Did he stand staring at the two men, white and ghastly and hit through the heart? He did neither of these things. He showed nothing but quiet vexation.

"*Ingratitude*, that's what I call it !" was the first remark. "But of course," he went on, "they can't have got far! What were all the staff doing, Squeeze? And where are they now, Cuddle?"

"Well, sir," began the latter, taking the initiative at once,

THE INMATES

"Bill here and I decided, before we came to you, to give the staff those some identickle orders that you yourself gave the day the bomb fell between the north lodge and the cattle sheds, blowing up the three best old sows and the three prettiest litters of little pigs we've ever had in this part of the county! So that's what we told them to do, and that's what they've done. Half of them have gone to search the village—every house of it. And I told that half clear and straight:' No beating about the bush, lads!' I said. And then I took the liberty, sir, of repeating your own strong language, the language referred to afterwards, if you remember, sir, in all our best papers, as the firm masterly hand at once scientific and Christian that our national institutions need."

Doctor Echetus withdrew the white carnation from his buttonhole and frowned at it for less than two seconds. Then, behaving as only Candidates for International Kudos can behave, he plucked a few caryophyllic petals from its corolla, converted his thumb and index-finger into an automatic catapult, and after replacing the flower in his buttonhole shot what he had removed from it straight at the philosophical head of Heraclitus. This head was now in full process of being furtively, but with a slow concentrated absorption, lured out of Bill's pocket into the light of day.

"Well, well, well!" murmured the self-controlled vivisector turning his attention to the retardative Squeeze. "And in what direction did the other half of our people pursue these silly fugitives?"

"Oh *that*, sir," cried the ingratiating Cuddle before Bill could speak, "was decided for us by one of those providential happenings, which, as I've so often heard you say, sir, in the annex laboratory of the dog-room, are the true scientist's reward for his pursuit of truth without fear or favour."

"Which way? Which way? I'm asking you, which way?" demanded Doctor Echetus.

"Straight down the North Road, sir! Some on bicycles, some on tricycles, some on motor-cycles, some in lorries and tractors!' The poor silly things,' as you, sir, so well call our

THE ESCAPE

runaways, were caught as they started in the middle of the night, for the whole thing must have been carefully planned; and the curious part of it is that our friend Gewlie—of all the staff, sir, as you know, the one most to be trusted—has completely disappeared, and it *has* crossed my mind that they may have murdered him; but, as I was saying, they were providentially seen as they were just starting by our distinguished visitor from the East—I believe you saw the gentleman last night, sir, and were seriously impressed by him? He was studying your methods, sir, by visits to the inmates at hours when they would least of all be expecting visitors, so he found out their ridiculous plot and he told us the whole thing. It was across the river they were to go and through the village—that's why we're having every house in the place searched—and then straight along the main road through Ghost-Privy and Pump-Handle to Integer Turnspit. Squeeze doesn't think—and I tend to agree with him—that there'll be any resistance to their recapture.

"The danger is—and Squeeze agrees with me in this as I agree with Squeeze that left to themselves they'll come back quietly—the danger is that when they go through the village some of the village-people will get into their silly heads that they are some sort of victims—you know, Doctor, what fancies village-people get—and try to hide them in their stick-houses and attics and pig-sties and straw-stacks and apple-lofts!

"That's why I sent the cleverer half of our staff to search the village from Stocks-Comer to Lovers Lane. And that's why I used the downright man-to-man language you used yourself, sir, on the occasion when ——"But Cogent Cuddle suddenly stopped, for it had become clear that the master of Glint was no longer giving him the slightest attention.

Doctor Echetus's head was indeed turned to the south as far as it would go and he was listening with absorbed intensity to a titanic helicopter, evidently a new American invention, that clearly could fly lower than airplanes usually do. And not only was this great air-vessel flying unnaturally low, flying so low that it looked as if it might very soon prove a serious menace to those who were watching it, but it was flying extremely slowly

THE INMATES

and with curious waverings to left and right as if searching for a suitable landing place.

It had such powerful engines that anyone would have supposed that the noise it made would have so disturbed the master of Glint that his brain would have become as confused as those of his runaway inmates. But not at all! This well-balanced guardian of public sanity retained his self-possession.

He again removed the white carnation from his coat, held it for a second to his left nostril, plucked out a few more of its musk-scented petals, and after returning its mutilated corolla and dangling stalk to his buttonhole, as if that innocuous slit had been a younger sister of the dog-hole among the spruces, "You're perfectly certain," he enquired, aiming, by aid of his firm square thumb and his sharp-pointed first finger, a new missile at the fox-hole of Heraclitus, "that this preposterous person from the East hasn't come on some special mission to make trouble in our English institutions? Foreign visitors to our research institutions have to be watched, you know; the——"

He was interrupted by the appearance on the scene of the oldest attendant, that same ancient-mariner-like individual who had been so cautious about making bad worse when Tenna Sheer suffered her seizure over Rumpibus and Tottie.

The old fellow was seriously out of breath and obviously very disturbed. "I have to tell you, Doctor——" he panted; but before he got any further he felt impelled to turn round and shout some extremely abusive words at somebody behind him who was at present invisible to the master of Glint. "Don't you dare to follow me, you fig-tree fornicator, you lousy grub-picker, you white-gilled worm-chaser I I won't be followed, I tell you, by a sneaking lemon-pip like you with a worm in his gullet and nothing but slug-slime in his stinking lubricating gizzard! Get away! Don't you hear? It's me that's seeing the Doctor about you, not you about me! Get away, you lubberly lobscouse!"

The classic physiognomy of Heraclitus, with that curiously complacent Greek-philosopher beard that must so often make

THE ESCAPE

an uncultured philistine long for an avenue of the busts of murderous Caesars, descended like a solemn Jack-in-the-box into the pocket of Bill Squeeze while he and Cogent Cuddle rushed forward and began waving their arms, just as in a crowded sale of cattle the auctioneer's assistants indicate by resounding thumps on the animals' backs the appropriate entrances and exits.

But as the ex-sailor drew back, his companion advanced, and it was not long before Doctor Echetus beheld the unruffled visage of Mr. Frogcastle, the gardener. With its multitudinous criss-cross wrinkles, the gardener's countenance had the peculiar quality, and it is likely enough that this was the very thing about him that Gewlie had found so disturbing, of compelling those who looked at it for more than a second or two to fall into a reverie. The face of the gardener resembled in fact all those segments and fragments of the surface of the earth—pieces of broken fence, patches of frozen mud, sections of the bark of certain growing trees, strips of cart-track in out-of-the-way lanes, shallow ponds crinkly with cat-ice, which, for no reason that can be named, lure us into a mood of abstraction just as if they were snatches from some familiar scene in a previous incarnation.

"Be quiet, you," cried the Doctor sternly, addressing his oldest attendant: "and now!" and he turned to the gardener, who was neither panting nor explaining his presence.

In fact Disraeli's great motto for practical life— "no complaining and no explaining" —seemed wholly fulfilled in the gardener of Glint.

"I thought I'd better warn everybody up here" —and the gardener gazed equably round him— "that the milking woman from the village is on the rampage. She would have been up here by now, only she met her gossip and neighbour, old Mrs. Wohntscher, the scrub-woman, at the north lodge, and went for her. I wouldn't have been the man to try and separate those two, but before I left them they had been separated; and it was done by the chaplain's wife. There's a real lady for you, Mr. Doctor I I sure do give her the prize. But how she

THE INMATES

does it God and the Devil alone know; the one because he wins by it the other because he loses by it."

Doctor Echetus looked at him gravely. "Why did the milking-woman fall upon the scrubbing-woman? Can you tell me that, Gardener?"

"Certainly I can tell you, Doctor. She attacked her because the boy Seth has taken to following the Heavenly Twins, as we call them, when they get their dancing fits, and Mr. Hush, who is always about with Miss Sheer, encourages the twins to take notice of Seth and be nice to Seth, whatever his mother says or does."

It was a calm, unruffled, and completely self-controlled master of Glint who now once again, out of his first finger and thumb, manufactured an effective catapult with which he ejected all the remaining petals of the carnation's corolla and, when this had been done, allowed its limp stalk to flutter unheeded to the ground.

But that queer habit of nature, known to ordinary folk as "it never rains but it pours" or "misfortunes never come singly," seemed unable to make an exception even of an official who could convert his very fingers into "disposal squads".

All the four men moved forward now in an amazed and indignant protest, for two struggling and panting women, one of them beside herself with furious anger, came reeling and staggering up the slope to this strip of level gravel between the entrance to the Doctor's house and the entrance to the research laboratory, which now seemed to have become the final rampart and ultimate barricade against rebellious inmates.

The women engaged in this murderous-looking tussle were none other than Mrs. Wohntscher and the plump red-cheeked mother of the idiot Seth.

"Cos you 'aven't got," the milking-woman was shouting, "any childer of your own, you needn't come barging and bustling into the affairs of them as 'as! Tell me who's got my boy Seth! Tell me who 'twas you seed'un with! And tell me quick, ye wurkus privy-cleaner, or I'll turn your yeller phyz into a turnip-field I Baalbub swallow my soul for mustard if I

THE ESCAPE

don't! Tell me who's got my Seth or you'll never have as much kissing space left in your yeller face as would tempt a horse-fly! One of your andy-dandy ones he was, I've no doubt, one of your well-behaved concertina-gents from abroad! Come on! Out with it! One of your fine loonies 'ave got 'im, sure as I'm born! Out with it, you devil's bitch! Who is it? You know you know and are only trying to keep my hands off 'im cos he's yours. Come on now, honest for once. Is it that Mr. Hush-a-baby of yours who sits, so they tell me, night after night with the worst loonies in the place and at a table you polishes hour by hour till it's as sleek as a suet-grub?

"No, not one of these gentlemen—don't you fancy it!—will stop me—no! not the Doctor himself—till I've got your ugly old-maid's mug down in the dust—and not then neither, till I've 'ammered with an honest country fist your filthy city-ways out of ye, ye slum-bitch what don't know a rake from a pitch-fork or a mattock from a hoe, and would be pulling up the best of the mangle-wurzels if you was told to do a bit of weeding before dark!"

Mr. Frogcastle had by this time withdrawn from the scene, while his recent antagonist, the old ex-sailor, had joined Cuddle and Squeeze in their attempt to separate the two women, or, to be more exact, to disengage the fingers, the knees, the few remaining teeth of the milking-woman from the clothes and person of the charwoman.

When they *were* separated, it became clear at once that Mrs. Wohntscher, though not wholly free from battle-stains, was a good deal the less ruffled and less upset of the two. The colossal helicopter now appeared to be following with concentrated care every curve of the serpentine river; that river that had struck so many among the inmates of Glint as being in league with their prison wall to draw closer the noose of their terrible isolation.

With all three pairs of absorbed masculine eyes watching this titanic air-omnibus from the outer world, it now became clear to the virgin mind of Mrs. Wohntscher that since nobody was detaining her by force, there was no reason against her

THE INMATES

immediate retirement from that over-crowded spot. Without any sign of her intention save the gentle extrication of her wrist from the heedless fingers of Bill Squeeze, she drew away from them all and hurried down the hill.

And the odd thing was that though at this very second Seth's mother lifted up her powerful Voice in a louder cry than ever, this particular howl of hers, which only caused Mr. Cuddle to redouble his grip, had nothing to do with Mrs. Wohntscher. The milking-woman had suddenly caught sight of her missing boy himself. She had seen before the rest of them what they all now, including Doctor Echetus, surveyed in astonished silence. A majestic car had driven up of a bright yellow colour and of unusual proportions and out of it had jumped not only the idiot boy Seth but, clasping the boy's hands, one on one side of him and one on the other, that excitable and restless pair of young inmates, the boy Hither and the girl Thither.

The three youngsters were immediately, though quite quietly, followed from the capacious body of this crocus-coloured conveyance by two extremely imposing and authoritative persons. One of these gentlemen was obviously, from the easy and familiar manner in which he permitted Hither and Thither to run off with Seth towards the river, the parent of these excitable twins, while his companion, the owner of this portentous vehicle, was none other than Tenna's father, Sir Warden Sheer. Each of Doctor Echetus's subordinates automatically turned towards their master to see how far this sight would disturb him. It didn't disturb him in the least.

He had now no longer any buttonhole to toy with. So, to make it quite evident, possibly to himself as well as to his retainers, that he had not forgotten how to "keep an equable mind *rebus in arduis*", he absent-mindedly moved his hand—for he was standing quite close to Squeeze—and scratched with a couple of fingernails the beard of Heraclitus, whose head was still just observable above the rim of Bill's pocket. The particular coat worn by Bill on that eventful day, though it is doubtful whether he had put it on for that reason, had neater and trimmer pockets than his usual one, so that the uncarved

THE ESCAPE

base, or "Herm" which terminated in the philosopher's shoulders—shoulders that looked as if they could, like those of Atlas, sustain the whole paradoxical world—must have rested, invisible to everybody, in a warm, tender, comfortable darkness through which could be felt, though without jolt or jar, every movement of the hip-bone of Bill the *Sophosopheros* or wisdom-carrier.

"I rather tend to think," announced Doctor Echetus, addressing nobody in particular, but watching with concentrated attention the butterfly antics of Master Hither and Miss Thither as the twins danced off with the enraptured Seth towards the watery archway where there were no longer any iron spikes, "I rather tend to think that Lord Tom Tiddler himself, those twins' father, is accompanying Sir Warden Sheer."

He paused for a moment, lifting first one foot and then the other, and stamping the turf with each leather sole, resolutely, firmly, and even defiantly, like an aged ram, perched on a rock, preparing for the approach of a couple of inquisitive dogs. "What I would like you fellows to do," he went on, "for my impression is that the two gentlemen have seen us and are coming straight up to us, is to remain here with me so as to be available for any action that may seem—" he paused for a second again, "that may seem *indicated*." The master of Glint put into the word *indicated* every nuance of moral weight mingled with every nuance of infernal caution of which the head of the most complicated of all conceivable Holy offices—that of pure knowledge through *licensed* torture—could possibly make use—"Yes, seem indicated!" he concluded with a faint fluttering of the fingers of the left hand.

"And my impression is—" he added, while one of his companions glanced from the approaching gentlemen to the panting stable-woman, whose wrist he was still clutching, and the other tried to turn the bearded visage of Heraclitus towards the escaping twins, "my impression is that Lord Tom is under the happy illusion that all is in order and that it is part of our curriculum in the cure of those children of his to entrust them with the care of a boy like that, and to encourage them to play

THE INMATES

with him at such innocent undertakings as damming up rivers and making tunnels under walls."

Both Cuddle and Squeeze nodded sagaciously; but the latter had to allow Heraclitus to turn his Athenian beard directly towards the woman he was holding, for the mother of Seth with her great round bulbous grey eyes "bursting", as Mrs. Wohntscher would have put it, "out of her turniptop head", had begun to heave and struggle and sob.

"Is it indicated," Doctor Echetus's look now said to his henchmen, "that we've got to separate this creature from her offspring? And, furthermore, have we the right to hold her back? She's a free villager. She's not an inmate. And mightn't she," so his look continued to hint, "be more of a trouble to our runaways, and to these damned agitators who are encouraging them, than she is to us?" Who can say whether Bill Squeeze was aware of all the implication of what he was doing in letting Seth's mother free to pursue her progeny?

But, aware or not, this eccentric "wisdom-carrier" must have heard these terrible sobs, must have felt these frantic and desperate efforts, even before Doctor Echetus had given him the glance that said: "Let the wretched woman go." It had long been the purpose of Betsy of the south lodge to make her husband follow, like a swift gnat "among the river-shallows, borne aloft, or sinking, as the light wind lives or dies", every curve and curlecue of a woman's conflicting emotions, so that as he released Seth's mother he used his free hand under his coat in the manner of a Punch-and-Judy showman, so as to permit his bearded doll to answer the woman's scream of maternal possessiveness with the philosophical retort of a free soul.

For that appalling scream as she rushed off came from her whole physical being. From her bulging eyes it came and from her twisted lips. From her belly it came, and from her protruding breasts. From her great thighs it came and from "the demesne that there adjacent lies".

The language of that cry was a language older than any English dialect from any English countryside, a language

THE ESCAPE

older than Sanscrit, older than Babylonian or Egyptian. "He has moved in my womb!" wailed that terrible cry. "He is my blood, my milk, my bones, my fibres, my flesh, my soul, *myself*! To let him leave me is to root out myself from myself! When his heart beats my heart beats! When his blood flows my blood flows! I can't eat save when he eats! I can't drink save when he drinks!

"For him to leave me and my warm love is a crime against God! He has no right to himself. He is mine and God's! He has no right to have any life save me, by me, and with me, who fed him with my food, swaddled him in my flesh, and grew him in the dark depths of my being like a ripe, sweet, lovely, round, obedient little bulb!" How low and faint was the voice from the bearded lips of a shocked and horrified philosopher that Bill Squeeze heard from the recesses of his pocket as he allowed his Heraclitus to sink down!

"Every living soul," sounded that faint voice from the pocket of Betsy's husband, "has one right that none can give or take away, one right in the infinite chaos of the innumerable warring worlds among which we are born, one right and one necessity, and that right is the right to be free and alone in our thoughts!"

But the mother of Seth was off now, bursting with the urge to whack and thwack and clack, with the law of the pack at her back, heading for the bed of the stream where the spikes were gone! Neither Squeeze nor Cuddle, however, could give any attention to the sequel of this maternal boy-hunt; for a second motorcar had appeared on the scene, driven by one person and driven at a most unusual speed. Out of it, the moment it stopped, leapt a tall, thin, lanky, aggressive individual, who began without delay shouting peremptorily and harshly at the figures of Lord Tom Tiddler and Sir Warden Sheer as they made their leisurely way towards the master of Glint and his two companions.

"Hie there, you two! Ho! Hie, you two I What's wrong with you? Can't you hear what a fellow's saying? Stop there! Stop! I want to talk to you! Stop, I say!"

THE INMATES

The two magnates, thus unceremoniously addressed, did turn round at this point, and after a word together awaited the newcomer in silence. Doctor Echetus and his two companions watched this encounter with considerable interest, but what would have struck our friend John, had he been sharing this contemplative suspense instead of being one of the trouble-makers, was the way in which both Bill Squeeze and Cogent Cuddle displayed no astonishment at Echetus's calm! They took this superlative self-control, so it would seem, completely for granted, just as a couple of boys in some great cathedral choir, absorbed in some affair of their own, would take it for granted, though the organ suddenly became silent and though one of the big lights hanging from the roof-rafters above their heads mysteriously went out, and there wavered a flicker of surprise across the Norman eyebrows of the Dean, that nothing would disturb the serenity of my Lord the Bishop—no! though every light in the place went out, and everybody lit a match, and they all danced down the aisle to the tune of *Widdicombe Fair*.

But where the unruffled Doctor and his two retainers, for a philosopher in a pocket can hardly be called a retainer, were in luck at that moment was in regard to the acoustics of that gentle eminence. There was scarce a sigh or a groan, far less a word, from those three men down below that was inaudible to the three men up above.

"To whom have we the ——" began the father of Hither and Thither.

"Do you know to whom you're ——" commenced the father of Tenna Sheer.

"My name is Cochineal, Colonel Cochineal," declared the newcomer, "and if you guys weren't mental patients, as I can see you are, of this peculiar bug-house of yours, where you seem to be treated with the easy therapy of doing what you damn-well like, I should have something to say to you, for where I live—Colonel Cochineal's my name—I should have something to say to you—no! I wouldn't call twice where I live after fellows like you—but if I did, there'd be some

THE ESCAPE

answering and some being answered!—you can take that from me, messieurs the uncured patients!

"And you can remember besides that it's Colonel Cochineal who is always at your service!"

Cuddle and Squeeze had hardly exchanged a look over this opening remark, when Sir Warden, who hadn't in his earlier days handled bricks and mortar for nothing, went straight to the point. "We are parents of patients, not patients, sir! This gentleman is Lord Tom Tiddler, whose two charming children are evidently being cured in the most sensible of all ways—at least that is my opinion—by being entrusted with the care of a village boy. I am the father, sir, myself, of a much sadder case, the case of a girl who has a passion for violence, sir—yes, sir, for physical violence, and I have no doubt you will understand me, sir, when I say that if I find her comfortable and quiet in this well-managed place, here I shall let her stay—yes, sir, stay till she has learnt to love her own father as the Book teaches."

The colonel from the Deep South suppressed his anger and looked at Sir Warden with real respect. It was clear that the brickmaster's straight man-to-man talk impressed him. At Lord Tom he cast a sharp appraising defiant look, as at a weird animal who might or might not bite.

"I may as well," he said, "inform you two patients—I mean parents—at once what I'm here for. Any little mistakes I may make in addressing you, you can balance up against your not answering me when I called. What I've come here about is a little private matter of investigation, entirely private and personal. I've heard it said where I come from — that is to say Cochinealville, Canister County—that you English allow social contact, drinking tea together, for instance, and even playing games like croquet and bowls, between buck niggers and white women. Now what I've come here to explain to you English about this nigger business is that in for a penny is in for a pound.

"What your English women haven't yet learnt, and what I've come here to teach them, is the excruciating temptation

THE INMATES

they are to buck niggers. A buck nigger playing croquet is a buck nigger playing with fire. I've got no quarrel with a nigger because he's black any more than I've got a quarrel with the rain because its wet or with a pot of honey because its sticky. I'm glad I've met you two men because I can speak plainly to you, seeing as you are connected with this important institution as parents and not patients. It's all in the understanding of the Unalterable. That's the grand key-word. That's the whole business; the *Unalterable*. The more I think of the word the more I like it. It is the grand secret of life as it should be. The mere sound of it makes you feel as if you were smoking a good cigar. Unalterable! It sounds like a rustle of the skirts of the woman you love. The great thing of course is to find out where the 'unalterable' begins and the 'alterable' ends. Can you make over a buck nigger so that when he sees a white woman playing croquet it don't make the blood rush to all parts of his black body?"

"I believe," broke in the father of Hither and Thither, "that the individuals who are staring down at us from the front of that building are the heads of this Institution. I am sure nobody will steal our cars if we leave them where they are. I can see my son and daughter are showing that little boy how to paddle in that pretty stream. Nothing could be more soothing to the over-excitable youngsters than paddling in cool running water. Gad! but this chap must be a good one at his job. My cousin Tit-Tat—the Dowager Lady Fly-by-Night, you know—wants me to send those children to America. She says America will knock the stage-struck nonsense out of them. It's all one great theatre, she tells me, over there, with everybody on the stage in ordinary life.

"Well, I suggest, gentlemen, since our cars are, so to speak, on holy ground, ha! ha! that we go and enquire of those fellows up there where this Doctor Echetus is to be found. Will you come, Sir Warden? Will you come, Colonel Cochineal?"

How Sir Warden reacted in his heart to this airy suggestion was not revealed in the words he uttered aloud. "God!

THE ESCAPE

how I wish," he "thought, I was safe back in the brickyard office with old man Bogger lighting his third pipe and young Jiggit making his best blueprint and pretty Miss Caryatid knocking at the door with a nice cup of tea! I only hope this Doctor what's-his-name will soon begin letting Antenna fish for minnows with little boys; for then, please God, she may settle down here for the rest of her days and I may be quit of her!"

But aloud he said: "Certainly, my lord; at your service, my lord; it's a pleasure to be a fellow-parent with you, my lord, not to mention visiting an institution like this in your company! I'm sure you feel as I do, Colonel?"

While the complacent peer smiled his approval of the downright yet respectful manners of the self-made magnate, he looked at the colonel, who had suddenly commenced gazing at him with positive awe.

"I'd split my bottom dollar," said Colonel Cochineal emphatically, "for my little woman down south to see me on the television talking to the owner of Tom Tiddler's ground I Yes, of course I'll come! This noble knight speaks for me. 'Colonel,' I say to myself, 'you're in luck today! Not only have you found exactly the right place to deliver your message to the ladies of Great Britain about buck niggers, but you are privileged to ascend a natural eminence in the company of a cousin of the Dowager Fly-by-Night.'"

The Colonel paused and looked up at the Doctor and his two retainers, while it became clear to Lord Tom, if not to Sir Warden, that, like so many orators, he saw a surging audience at a cross-road of life where others could only see a group of idlers smoking cigarettes by a closed museum door.

When the three newcomers, ascending the slope together, arrived at the door of the Doctor's research laboratory, Bill Squeeze and Cogent Cuddle drew back a little to enable their chief to greet his visitors.

But since the Doctor had already made it clear to his two retainers that, at this dramatic crisis in the history of Glint, it was essential that he should have their support, they did

THE INMATES

not retreat far. It was the lord of Tom Tiddler's Ground who "broke", as we say, "the ice", for after the three men had shaken hands with Echetus, both the colonel from the cotton-fields and the knight from the brick-kilns turned almost pathetically to that florid Etonian.

"I haven't failed to notice, Doctor," Lord Tom began, "how happy and normal my youngsters look playing with that little rustic—clearly an importation from the village, though I confess as we were climbing your hill just now I was disturbed to see a rather wild and frantic woman, no doubt one of your simpler and humbler patients, Doctor, who appeared to be trying to drag the boy away from my friendly progeny. I couldn't help noticing that the child was clinging in the most desperate manner to both Marmaduke and Eleanora, who were, I could see, resolutely refusing to hand him over." Lord Tom of Tiddler's Ground paused politely at that point.

"Sheer?" he murmured interrogatively, like an experienced butler encouraging a poor relation. "Cochineal?"

But Sir Warden shook his head, and the Colonel told himself that the longer he held his tongue the more pleased with him his wife would be when he recounted this scene.

"What I feel myself,—" continued Lord Tom, inclining his massive forehead a little forward as he turned to Echetus, and permitting his right hand to sail loosely and negligently through the air by his side as if he were touching with the tips of his fingers the shoulders of the persons and the backs of the chairs intervening between himself and the footlights, "what I feel myself is that all the moral and intellectual problems of this round world are much simpler than people realise. In fact they are"—here not only did Cuddle and Squeeze come nearer, but the hairy pate of Heraclitus emerged from the latter's pocket, though the philosopher's beard was still invisible—"in fact they are reducible to one simple—simple—simple—" It was clear that Lord Tom had forgotten the clue-word that was the whole point of this discourse.

But while the master of Tiddler's Ground hovered vaguely about the word he had forgotten, the Doctor had what really

THE ESCAPE

was a supreme opportunity to display that equanimity with which temperament or training or some queer vacuum in his sensibility had endowed him; for glancing through the gap between the left shoulder of Lord Tom and the right shoulder of Sir Warden he beheld what he knew must be the titanic helicopter from America, now safely and comfortably landed among the reeds close to the river, from which position, the moment it so desired, it could rise and float away into the upper sky!

Surrounding this amazing object in a tossing, surging, jostling, struggling, confused mass of men and women, was the whole heterogeneous company of the inmates! And they were not only swarming round, they were actually clambering into that monstrous apparition!

Along with this disorderly mob Echetus was aware of a large sprinkling of uniformed men, obviously the bulk of his official attendants, making feeble, helpless, hesitant, drifting, half-hearted, and evidently quite vain attempts to prevent their patients' escape. That both his quaint adherents, Cuddle and Squeeze, were watching what was happening was clear to him; but all they had dared to do was to move up close together. They were not speaking a word. They were hypnotised by the sight of what was going on.

From the monumental pose of their profiled heads as their condition forced itself upon the corner of Echetus's vision, they might have been stunned, petrified, dumb-founded, all but bereft of their wits; but Echetus was too shrewd to take any of this for granted, and in some extreme background of his consciousness the idea arose that both these men had known of all this from the start. Very slowly he slid his fingers into his right side-pocket and extracted a half-filled packet. Then he thrust a hand more rapidly into his left side-pocket, brought out a box of matches, and with his gaze on that airplane and that crowd, as if they had been figures on the stage of a theatre where he was entertaining his friends, he offered a cigarette to Lord Tom of Tiddler's Ground.

Lord Tom shook his head, and Sir Warden, imagining such a refusal just then to be the proper thing, followed suit and

THE INMATES

shook his head too. The Colonel, however, perceiving the crumpled condition of that unappealing half-package, with courteous American consideration for the Doctor's feelings, accepted with alacrity, and permitted their host to protect with his curved hand the flame of the match.

It was this well-meant gesture of the Colonel's that let the cat out of the bag, for Lord Tom, catching the excitement of Squeeze and Cuddle, followed the direction of their gaze and swung round. So did Sir Warden—and the fat was in the fire. It was, indeed, more than in the fire. It was burning and smoking. And it was leaping up the slope towards them. This it was doing in the familiar persons of Father Wun, the priest, and Father Tickle, the chaplain.

To meet these anxious men of God, our four gentlemen, followed by Cuddle and Squeeze, hurried down the declivity. Their encounter might well have been called memorable; but alas! in after days not one of these worthy men could properly remember it, so blurred with egotistical prejudices were their visions and so lacking in the faintest repercussion of the swift-darting mischievous malice of the old Attic touch that could clarify by a few wholesome explosions the nuclear core of an occasion of this kind.

"Ha, Doctor!" cried Toby Tickle, "I swore to the Father I'd spotted you, all right! And sure enough here you are, watching the battle of the kites and crows, shall we call it? or the whales and the flying-fish? A little 'Mutiny on the Bounty', eh, Doctor? Ho! Ho! The Father takes it too seriously. I told him you had only to appear on the scene and this confounded American invention would soon flap its wings and be off, hell for leather, and our little flock would return to its proper fold! You'll see it all, Father, for yourself in a minute if you come down with him and watch him handle it! You Romanists have so much truck with the beachcombing rabble of the Mediterranean that you've forgotten what a proper chieftain and a real living authority is."

Father Wun turned upon his Anglican companion a look that clearly said: "There isn't a thought in your float-bobbing

THE ESCAPE

brain, my good sir, that isn't as transparent to me as the thoughts of Cranmer or Ridley when they first smelt the smoke of their own burning. You think, you great silly ass, that this precious Doctor of yours has only to stroll down to that airplane and clap his hands and the plane will sail away to America and his patients will gather round him like the children round Our Lord, while the lion and unicorn of this Commonwealth of Commonsense, touched by the intimations of a tempered immortality, will pull the Ark of the Covenant of decent behaviour into the well-stocked home-farm of Glint Hall!"

Oddly enough, it wasn't the Reverend Toby, nor Lord Tom of Tiddler's Ground, nor Sir Warden Sheer, who returned this look of infinite contempt cast by Father Wun at the smiling weather-beaten face of the chaplain. It was the world-weary, life-tired, ungullible stare of one who had seen too many "beginnings" and too many "ends" to give way to human peevishness or human jocularity in these difficult matters.

It was, in fact, the grave detached stare of none other than Heraclitus himself, as Bill Squeeze edged that bearded head over the rim of his pocket.

What appeared to amuse Doctor Echetus, who evinced not the faintest tendency to move from where he stood even though the heavens fell, was the appeal flung forth upon the general air by Lord Tom of Tiddler's, who now beheld Marmaduke and Eleanora assisting the little Seth to clamber into the giant plane.

"Will anybody here," he called out, addressing the whole countryside: "Will everybody here who has the right to wear a public-school tie come with me to stop this nonsense?"

At this point Lord Tom paused for a moment. Then in a still shriller tone he began again—"I'm only asking for a few real gentlemen: that's not much to ask for, is it? A few real gentlemen? That's what our public schools are for, aren't they—at least the top half a dozen of them? Factories,

THE INMATES

aren't they, for turning successful men's sons into gentlemen! You agree, Sir Warden? You're with me, Sir Warden?

"Well! Come on then! Let's see what you and I can do to stop this nonsense! Come along, Colonel! Never mind about your niggers till we've got our palefaces under control! Come along! Come along! Come along!"

The voice of Lord Tom Tiddler died away as he approached the south-lodge gates. But through these gates he didn't go at once; still less through the low archway where the stream ran under the wall. At those great gates, though Betsy had already passed through them, leaving them unfastened, Lord Tom waited for Sir Warden. This hesitation of Lord Tom's failed not to interest quite a good deal the psychological eye of Doctor Echetus.

"It shows," the master of Glint told himself, "how the vibrations of biological change affect human character. The aristocratic lord of Tiddler's Ground daren't take his own twins out of an American plane till a brickyard magnate supports him!"

Echetus found less to interest him in the movements of his chaplain and Father Wun, who were quite clearly not at all anxious to get involved in the confusion that was going on outside the wall of the institution and within one of the snake-like curves of the river. Whether by mutual consent or by the compulsion and pressure of theological argument, they paused under an isolated group of spruce-firs, whence they could observe both the imperturbable Doctor above and the wild confusion below.

It was at this moment that a concatenation of small occurrences, at once fortuitous and unavoidable, at once ordained by destiny and grotesquely accidental, prepared the way for an event which was as startling as it was tragic.

Bill Squeeze became so anxious to enable his bearded pocket-totem to see what could happen in England when philosophical inmates revolt against unphilosophical scientists, that he left the Doctor alone with Cuddle and rushed off down the slope, following the same path as that which John Hush had traversed

THE ESCAPE

"on all fours" when he made his way to the now spikeless water-channel that ran under the great wall and out the other side.

It was in full view of his own house that this now unimpeded tunnel went under the wall; and it was no doubt his dread of his wife's wounding tongue, and some vague notion that if he crept through that orifice instead of through the great gates she was less likely to catch him, that set him at such a pace.

"Well! Well!" ejaculated Doctor Echetus, watching the half-hearted and spiritless attendants making their feeble efforts to prevent the reckless and desperate inmates from crowding into the giant helicopter. "Well! Well! And what's going to be the issue of all this?"

He had put back into his pocket those cigarettes and matches that had enabled the colonel from the South to show what man-to-man courtesy, save where buck niggers were concerned, a gentleman from Cochinealville could display; and now with a deliberate tranquillity that rivalled the natural calm of that particular spot upon the earth's surface with a latitude and a longitude so mathematically verifiable, Doctor Echetus calmly lit a cigarette for himself.

No animal second-sight, such as might have warned a less purely rational intelligence, rushed into the Doctor's consciousness to tell him if he didn't swing round, quick as hell, this would be the last puff of smoke that would ever pass his lips.

Any onlooker except Mesopotamia Cuddle would have been surprised to see Cogent Cuddle, that orderly and obedient fanatic, extract from *his* pocket, not tobacco nor any still wiser consolation in the form of a philosopher, but simply and solely a very large army pistol. A small puff of smoke from the front of the Doctor's skull now floated off towards the river in a perfect ring, while a large puff of smoke, accompanied by a distinct but not overpowering detonation obscured the back of that same skull.

Ever since he had been delegated to bring the Doctor's activities to an end the moment they ceased to be of use to the movement, Cuddle had repeated as soon as he was awake,

THE INMATES

like the most devoted of priests his office, every syllable of the unequivocal instructions he had received from headquarters.

What he hadn't been instructed in, however, were certain disturbing details of the transaction, when he came to carry the thing through. He had accepted too roundly perhaps the Shakespearean murderer's easy assurance that "when the brains were out the man would die". His instructions had been reticent as to how the victim after receiving his death-wound was liable to behave.

There was no allusion in this Spartan document to wounded bodies leaping into the air or diving into wet mud or offering to the murderer's unprepared eyes shattered bones, bloody hairs and oozing brains, in conjunction, as happened at this moment, with a horrible stare from a pair of eyes different from all other eyes in the world.

Still less did these laconic instructions give the faintest hint as to how an inexperienced killer was to calm his own nerves when his victim really was dead. On this particular occasion Cuddle had hardly replaced his pistol in his pocket before he caught sight of the well-known figures of Father Toby and Father Wun retracing their steps.

Apparently the professional concern for mortality natural to all priests had been as much excited by the sound of that shot from the hill above as their instinctive dislike of anarchy had been exasperated by the shouts of the crowd below. Cuddle's first instinct when he saw the two priests returning was the natural one of blind concealment. He couldn't see the reverend gentlemen when he lay flat, nor they him. So from this position he pushed Echetus's body away from him till he got it completely hidden amid the stalks, leaves and flowers of a bed of rhododendrons. Thus by the time he was on his feet again, with the pistol in his pocket and the body out of sight, he was ready to put on some sort of defensive mask.

"We heard a shot from up here, Cuddle," cried Father Toby, when they reached him. "The Doctor hasn't lost his head, I hope? We've nearly lost ours; haven't we, Father Wun?"

THE ESCAPE

"Perhaps you could tell us, my friend ——" began the priest.

But the chaplain had now heard a familiar voice behind them and he hurriedly swung round. Father Wun did the same. So, to the indescribable relief of the agitated assassin, he beheld their backs instead of their faces. But he, too, had heard the unmistakable voice of Ursie Mum, the only one of all the authorities of Glint who had no enemy among the inmates, for Mrs. Wohntscher, who resembled Ursie Mum in being a married virgin, was too confined, as you might say, to the floor, for the mahogany table only rounded off the events of the day, to be able to exercise her personal power.

"I'm surprised at you, Father Wun," Ursie Mum was now gasping indignantly, "encouraging Toby to leave his post like this! What have you got on your mind? And you too, Mr. Cogent Cuddle! I can't understand how you men can — Goodness-gracious! but what's this?"

Had she been the mother of all Britain, Ursie Mum couldn't have uttered that "Goodness-gracious!" with more astonishment. It was not natural to her to feel, still less to express, dismay, but she came as near to that emotion at that moment as she had ever done in the whole of her maternal and yet old-maidish life.

Well might Ursie Mum, whose married virginity gave her a protective instinct that was far less savage and far more subtle than the ordinary maternal one, an instinct that might have won for her as a saint, if she'd wanted to be a saint, some such nickname as "the aunt of God", well, indeed, might Ursie Mum come near to dismay, for between her and the two ecclesiastics there had suddenly manifested itself the figure of Morsimmon Esty, the refugee from Thibet. Without uttering a word, of giving any sign of warning, this mysterious stranger gripped the two Fathers with a double clutch of demonic power, Father Wun with his right hand and Father Tickle with his left hand, holding them in each Case by the nape of their necks and with the devil's own clutch of such supernatural force that to retain any dignity at all they were forced to submit as if he had been their executioner.

THE INMATES

The crouching and quaking Cuddle shuffled backward as best he could, feeling with his heels for the body of Echetus so as to thrust it further out of sight among the rhododendrons. There soon, however, arrived a point when this iron-handed executioner from Thibet, with his murderous hold upon those two men of God, compelled the agitated Cuddle to scramble backwards over the corpse of his master; and once there, far too exhausted by his antics to attempt further evasion, compelled him, drugged with the sharp taste of rhododendron-stalks, to await, crouching on his heels, the next bounce of the ball of fate, as Destiny and Chance played their game over his head.

Cuddle never forgot the extraordinary spectacle that these casual performers offered to his vision. Ursie Mum, that good and great "Aunt of God", was by no means petrified by fear. She moved forward a step, and seeing Father Toby's hand dangling in pathetic helplessness she clasped it in her own. Thus, if we had the curiosity to contrast the thoughts of these living centres of consciousnesses as they occupied together the same transitory bubble on the river of time, both Father Wun and Cuddle felt they were not alone but were portions of a larger entity upon which at this uncomfortable crisis they could lie back, whereas both Toby Tickle and Ursie Mum felt that they were, though a man and a woman holding hands, totally alone in infinite space and infinite time, although there was no doubt, floating vaguely around them somewhere, a sweet savour usually called "God" and a horrid stink usually called "the Devil".

It was at this point that Morsimmon Esty sank down on his own knees in front of the body of Echetus, where he faced across it the crouching figure of Cuddle. Then, having got his captives upon their knees, he intensified his iron clutch upon each separate skull and forced their faces downward till their eyes and noses and mouths and cheeks were buried in the Harris-tweed-smelling coat and laboratory-acid-smelling trousers of the dead scientist. Five separate times did the person from Thibet press down their faces in this manner into

THE ESCAPE

that dead body. And most vividly aware were both the ecclesiastics that, at each descent of their faces into the body beneath them, *there was less of the dead man* into which to sink.

Finally, when their skulls rose for the fifth time it was from earth mould and weeds and the stalks of rhododendrons that they rose. There was no longer any remnant left of Echetus, the maimer of dogs, nor was there any sign or shadow or semblance of the man from Thibet.

The two ecclesiastics were so physically exhausted by the weird experience they had been through that when at last released, and released in the attitude so natural to men of their profession, they were for a while unable to rise from their knees; and Cuddle, as he faced them with a piercingly sharp smell of stalk-sap in his nostrils, felt drawn to examine, with the desperate intensity of a hunted animal, the two faces that were now peering at him, towered over no longer by any supernatural stranger from Asia, but by the bent head, massive frame, and outstretched arm of Ursie Mum, that potential "aunt of God", who, however, was of less interest to Cuddle than a rhododendron-stalk.

"Only two of them now," he told himself, with an immense sigh of relief. Being a man of insight, in spiritual as well as other matters, it stuck him that his unquestioning use of the pistol, according to orders from above, need, as things had worked out, have no uncomfortable results for himself. The death of the master of Glint had in fact been lifted out of the sphere of the criminal and tragic into the sphere of the fantastic and miraculous. His personal apprehensions being so surprisingly eased he was now able to examine with something of his natural acuteness the faces of the two clerics kneeling before him and only divided from him by an oblong space about a foot and a half broad, where certain insignificant weeds, such as common veronica and groundsel, were now feebly rising from the prostrate position to which they had been reduced by the superincumbent weight of what was now thin air and a pinch of dust.

What struck Cuddle most about the face of Toby Tickle was

THE INMATES

its ruddiness and the thickness of the flesh that composed the nostrils and formed the bulbous knob of his healthy animal nose and the manner in which all the innumerable wrinkles from the corners of his eyes and the corners of his mouth seemed to be singing a little cheerful song of their own, a song that made Cuddle think of his wife when her special sort of female impulsiveness infuriated his logical mind.

And now, as he stared into the face of Toby Tickle, all the chaplain's good-natured little wrinkles seemed chirping like grasshoppers. And to the embittered integrity of Cuddle's fanaticism they really did compose themselves into a psychic ditty, though no doubt all Toby Tickle was feeling just then was that Ursie Mum had come to extricate him from the clutches of devils.

> *There's never a hook*
> *In a fish that you cook.*
> *What bell in the steeple*
> *Can bother a people*
> *Whose God's in the sky*
> *Where the great clouds sail by?*
> *The wind and the sun*
> *Wipe out all that's done.*
> *Let the sad wail dong-ding*
> *And the mud howl ding-dong.*
> *Forget everything,*
> *Whether right, whether wrong!*
> *'Twas to help us forget*
> *That the seas were made wet.*
> *'Twas to help us slip past*
> *That the rocks were made fast.*
> *If in one woman's looks*
> *Are a million books*
> *For one snow-flake of snow*
> *You can let them all go.*
> *When the sun goes down red*
> *The last word has been said.*

THE ESCAPE

But when he turned from reading these rhythms in Toby Tickle's face and gaped at the polished inscrutable countenance of Father Wun, he suddenly became convinced that this latter had actually winked at him.

And though this impression coincided with the uprising of both priests from their knees, and coincided, too, with an exchange of words between Toby and his wife that struck him as if the woman had been reassuring a little boy of ten who without quite knowing what had happened had received a stab in his self-respect by having been danced up and down with no power of retaliating by a person who had now completely disappeared, Cuddle made no bones about catching Father Wun by one of the buttons of his waistcoat and asking him bluntly and plainly whether he would be willing to take him on as a general servant at a low salary.

After his discerning scrutiny of the priest's impassive face, and after noting how the man was completely impervious to being turned upside down and bobbed five times against a corpse, he wasn't really very surprised at the reception his offer received.

"You are, of course," replied the Father quickly, "a lapsed member of the Greek Church?"

Cogent Cuddle admitted that such was the case; and in his heart he knew that the priest had accepted him. "Mesopotamia will have to go to mass!" he thought with vindictive and unholy joy. But life has a partner in her game of bagatelle with Destiny, and this partner is called Chance. According to what happens we call her pure Chance, blind Chance, wretched Chance, or sometimes lucky Chance. And on this occasion Chance had arranged it with this same Mesopotamia's natural impulse to escape that she should, by the hurried intercession of Mr. John Hush, find herself hugging herself with a healthy happiness she hadn't known for twenty years, in a comfortable hiding-place in the very heart of this huge newly-invented helicopter.

And though so quietly hidden herself in the heart of the confusion, it was permitted to Mesopotamia, as if she'd been a

THE INMATES

veritable pet of Chance, to behold episodes in this strange vessel's departure that not only would have absorbed the attention of her husband, that obstinate adherent of Oneness, but would have attracted a glance, though not, we may suspect, a turn of the head, from her husband's new master, the equally obstinate adherent of the Oneness of the faith revealed to St. Paul on his way to Damascus.

She saw, for example, though neither of them could possibly see her, the outburst of wifely fury, mounting up and up till it burst into a suicidal scream of hate, which Betsy Squeeze of the south lodge flung at Bill Squeeze; she standing amid the reeds of the river and he caught by her as he leaned over the central rail of the airplane in an obvious effort to give the bearded doll in his pocket a parting view of the hemisphere they were leaving.

Mesopotamia heard this appalling feline howl with a response altogether different from that with which Bill Squeeze himself received it, while the actual emotion experienced by Betsy and expressed in this manner was totally different from the emotion either of them attributed to her. Mesopotamia, the woman's gossip, and Bill, the woman's husband, did however agree that one of Betsy's dominant cravings was the craving to rise above the class into which she'd been born. For food and drink, for social jollification, for sexual ecstasy, for lively encounters, for pleasant parties, Betsy cared little or nothing. What she dreamed of, day in and day out, was for her neighbours to stare at each other in awed amazement and to murmur in their stunned and bewildered envy: "Think of our Betsy being a real lady born and nobody known it!"

But men are men, and women are women, and their association together through many years has the power of heaping up, day by day, and from thousands upon thousands of microscopic details, such smouldering stock-piles of explosive and even annihilating resentment that once released it seems to tap some Satanic crater that can draw upon the central lava of world-destruction!

What, however, brought Betsy's outburst of love-hate to an

THE ESCAPE

end was neither her own death by a broken blood-vessel nor the death of her husband by a stab of conscience: it was the actual death, by a ghastly fall from the helicopter, of the desperate and indignant mother of the idiot-boy Seth. She had followed the pair of reckless twins on to the very deck of this monstrous vessel and had tried to snatch the boy from them by sheer force; but others on the airplane had intervened, some taking her side, and some the side of the twins, with the result that in the confusion of the struggle the unlucky woman fell backwards from the deck of the plane, struck a twisted, sharp-edged six-foot iron stanchion fixed among the reeds close to where Betsy stood to deliver her imprecations, and broke her back.

The hurt to the cattle-woman's spine would alone have been fatal, even if her skull had not also been hit, and hit with the sort of crushing blow that kills at a stroke.

The disturbance that now arose, both on the deck of the vessel and on the ground beneath it, as a crowd composed of a motley mixture of inmates and attendants and villagers and onlookers surged round the idiot's mother confused every issue. Betsy Squeeze, although on her knees by the dead woman, hadn't by any means been shocked into silence, but, on the contrary, had found in this new tragedy a fresh cause for raving against "that cowardly idiot I only married out of pity for the brute, and he thinking of nothing but that bearded Beelzebub the crazy swine keeps in his filthy pocket!"

But it was rapidly becoming clear to John Hush, as he stood clutching Tenna's hand and staring at his guardian *with that girl*, that an indescribable jealousy was twisting like a snake round every nerve and every nerve-twitching fibre under the skin of his whole body! His guardian had seen him, and had seen Tenna with him, and so had *that girl*. What they were trying to do now was to talk to him above the uproar and through the same megaphone they had been using to give orders to their American crew.

It was queer how John managed to keep a small, cold, clear, uncynical, unsardonic observation-post in one corner of his

THE INMATES

consciousness that observed everything that was happening at that moment, together with its precise impact upon himself. "This is," he told himself, "the most hateful and horrible moment in my whole life! I've got to give him up whatever happens! Does he think he can hand himself over to that girl and keep me too? Not on your life, heart of my hell! Not on your life I"

What made things worse for John Hush at that devilish moment was the vicious and cruel struggle he was having, quite apart from his guardian and *that girl*, in what he called to himself his "Glint Hall conscience". What, in plain fact, he felt he ought to be doing now, before this air-dragon rose from its riverbed, was to rush into the main building of Glint Hall, climb the stairs to the punishment wing, and rescue Pantamount, that log-like waif from the Atlantic, who had sacrificed himself for Tenna and for him. Wasn't it his plain duty now to pay back this debt and return that sacrifice?

He couldn't help being troubled by the most horrible imaginations as to what might have been done to Pantamount. The most horrible rumours were always running through Glint Hall as to what punishment wing, or "Special Department of Corrective Treatment", as it was called, and as if his destiny wasn't being cruel enough to him at that moment by dangling him on a sort of gallows-bridge between his guardian and Tenna, it needs must now make him imagine the luckless Pantamount pinioned and trussed up in that bloodless crucifixion practised on the friend of the suitors in the Odyssey; one of the things, like the hanging of the suitor's girl-friends, that had always seemed to him an absolute proof of the Odyssey's infinite inferiority to the Iliad!

In addition to these private thumb-screws of the mind, John was now growing increasingly aware that the crowd about them had become dangerously hostile to this American air-vessel, to its foreign passengers, its foreign crew, and to its obvious intention of kidnapping as many crazy inmates as it could and carrying them across the Atlantic! All this excited shouting through the megaphone amounted, as far as he could

THE ESCAPE

follow it, to some sort of angry ultimatum. Either he and Tenna must climb on board at once, without further parley, or they would simply have to be left behind.

John felt as if there was an excruciatingly thin, sharp, high-pitched ice-edge in the centre of his heart, along which two distinct selves, each of them giving vent to a piercing soprano-shriek, were skating side by side and each endeavouring to thrust the other over the ice-edge!

It was at that moment that an extremely handsome, rather languid, exquisitely graceful individual of the male sex, with large brown eyes and an aquiline nose and an obscurely atmospheric but at the same time an unquestionable persuasive Jewish look in his air of approach, came lightly and gracefully up to them.

"Do you happen to know anybody," enquired he, addressing John, "who has any knowledge of the signs of the zodiac?"

From the remote position within the hinterland of his mind that contained an observation-post John couldn't help noticing how half-way across his frozen eel-bridge-edge of exquisite indecision, from the pain of which, if he'd been a woman, that woman would have had to fling herself with a rending shriek, he couldn't help noticing that mixed with his suffering there was a weird and diabolic spasm of enjoyment as he looked in his questioner's face and replied quickly: "Certainly I do, my friend, if I know anything of myself, for drawing up horoscopes has for some years been a habit of mine, and I can usually tell at the first glance under what sign of the zodiac a person is born."

The super-subtle and gravely ironical newcomer then turned to Tenna, whose attention had clearly been arrested by the beauty of his disillusioned eyes and Cardinal-Newman-like profile. "Do you, lady," he enquired, "happen to know anybody who knows anything of palmistry?"

John Hush couldn't help smiling, even from his ice-edge tragic indecision, as he caught Tenna's quick amused look.

"Certainly, mister, certainly," she murmured excitedly.

THE INMATES

"I'd like nothing better than to tell fortunes in a tent at a fair!"

Apparently very well satisfied with both these answers, their unknown interviewer went off, but John had a queer sense of something new in the wind when he saw the fellow hurry away to join none other than his old acquaintance, who had been the first inmate he had met when he arrived, namely that giant-dwarf from the circus who had been so attracted to Miss Bolster.

And then he was back again on the shrieking cutting ice-edge of his cruel indecision. As Homer is always saying: "his mind was" literally "divided into two".

Things were indeed growing more desperate every minute. His guardian's lady, the American to whom this gigantic invention belonged, kept whispering in his guardian's ear, and he could see clearly from her gestures that she was urging him to give the signal, whoever might be on board and whoever might be left behind, to rise from that river-side and be off at once!

The worst of the whole thing was that Tenna herself was beginning to get agitated with that old fatal agitation. He had known there *was* that danger. Too well for some time he had known it. Once or twice already he had caught sight of Tottie and old Rumpibus teasing each other in their accustomed manner as they leaned over the shining rail of the vessel's deck. And then as he was watching the preparations of a couple of the crew to haul up one of the few remaining gangways into the interior of the plane, he suddenly became aware of a much worse agitation in the frail form by his side and he noticed that she had twisted her head round and was straining her neck.

Yes! it had come—their worst danger! He knew it from the glimpse he got of her profile. He knew it from the frantic struggle she now began to get free of his hold; yes! to shake him off and rush wildly in the direction of the man she hated! Rumpibus and Tottie were nothing to this. This could only be one thing. This must mean the presence of her father.

THE ESCAPE

He had never seen the man before, but that it was her father was proved by the effect on her. Sir Warden was accompanied by some upper-class person who might have been any gentlemanly barbarian in the kingdom who didn't "give a damn" how he behaved; and it was evident as they approached the plane together that their appearance wasn't only throwing Tenna into one of her insane fits but was causing terrible consternation to Hither and Thither.

He had already noticed how the Heavenly Twins had been struggling to keep the fact of his mother's death away from the boy Seth. Would they be able now to defy their parent and refuse to leave the plane? God! But things were growing crucial. If the great flying creature didn't rise now—now at once—these two confounded men of rank and authority—and anyone could see they were that sort of thing—would send for the police—indeed he fancied he could see the helmet of a policeman already—and the police would search the plane—and the end of it would be that the Americans and their crew would have to set off alone!

It was at a curious little pattern of torn-off pieces of feathery reed-stalks, lying criss-cross together on the wet mud along with blackened wisps of moss, that John was now staring as he lifted the struggling Tenna from her feet and heard the gasping choking passion of the rending sobs that he seemed to himself to be squeezing from the core of her heart; and as he stared at that pattern in the mud, he plunged the very horn—for it felt like the horn of a crazed unicorn—of his whole soul into the very centre of this hieroglyphic writing in the mud!

He didn't pray. He didn't laugh. He didn't cry. Down, down, down, he seemed to be plunging the horn of his spirit; plunging it down into a secret of life that could only be known by a man who was squeezing sobs like black ambergris and golden myrrh out of the heart of his true-love!

His trance, or obsession, or whatever it was, was broken by the one voice that in all his days in Glint had never been associated with anything that wasn't comforting and healing—the voice of Mr. Lordy! And simultaneously with Mr. Lordy's

THE INMATES

voice he heard above him the resonant voice of his guardian giving the signal to start. The ground shook beneath John's feet with what seemed to him to be the same convulsive movements as Tenna was making in his arms; and the steel body of the air-monster above him shivered from head to tail, and then from flank to flank, and then with one grand heave and four great up-gathering wave-like cresting curves, the huge creature swayed upwards.

It was to John an astonishing sight, and in some ways a horrible as well as beautiful sight, to see it rise, for the people round it, as well as the people upon it, were so jammed together that it was like the human head and shoulders of a Centaur tearing themselves free from the four legs and flanks and tail of the same body!

John felt as if where he now stood the air ought to be wet with blood. But he noticed that from the thing's tail a long rope-ladder was still swinging in the air, a ladder that looked as if the hemp that composed it was made of some stuff much whiter than could be woven from any ordinary flax. Though the vessel which was carrying Mr. Lordy away was already heaving and swaying, and Mr. Lordy's voice was always rather faint, they were his words and nobody else's that remained in John's ears, and simple enough they were:

"Look behind you, mister!"

Yes, Mr. Lordy had now departed, and all that John could do was to obey him. So he swung round. And there at his back, as unmoved by the giant helicopter's leap aloft as he might have been unmoved by all the seas and oceans of the world, stood Pantamount.

"You thought of going to the punishment wing to look for me, didn't you?" he said quietly.

John gazed at him in complete bewilderment. The long rope-ladder gleaming so oddly white in the sun was swinging now between them.

"Catch it and go, for God's sake!" he gasped.

"I will, I will, I will!" cried the other. "See! I obey you! and I'll think of you all the way across!"

THE ESCAPE

It certainly offered no difficulty to this last of the Atlanteans to ascend this rope-ladder, though under his weight it serpentined over their heads like the tail of the chimæra. It was strange that it should have been just at this moment—though not out of keeping with a recurrent aspect of what happens to us in time and space where the negligible, the meaningless, the insignificant, the senseless, seems to take an impish delight in presenting itself to our attention—that the voice he heard upon the air was not the Voice of any of his friends but a Voice he hadn't heard since that day in March when he had had his first meal in the Glint dining-hall; the resounding voice, in fact, of the luckless young man who had been on that occasion removed by the attendants for making too much noise.

"My father," such were the last words that reached John's ears as his guardian left him for ever, "was the Flying Dutchman!" It was with the word "father" pounding and grinding and turning into powder within him something that seemed like the very marrow of his bones that John, with Tenna in his arms, stumbled blindly into the thick of the crowd. Though she had seen Sir Warden, he didn't think Sir Warden had seen her; and the chances were, he told himself, that the man took it for granted she was on board the plane.

Blindly he stumbled on, crying: "She's my wife, my wife, my wife!" when anyone tried to stop him. Then all in a moment everything had changed. They were out of the crowd. They were in a lane. They were just below that ancient camp with the two Scotch firs, where the river couldn't follow them. And now they were being helped into an old battered delapidated car by the circus-freak who had been so obsessed by Miss Bolster and the man whose profile resembled Cardinal Newman's.

It was explained to them now, and Tenna listened with relief as she sank into the ferret-smelling back-seat by John's side, that if they wanted to escape from the world and from their relatives in the world, the best of all disappearances was to be lost in a travelling circus. Miss Bolster's giant-dwarf, John noticed, spoke almost affectionately to the handsome

THE INMATES

gentleman who was now driving them and who had asked them a few minutes ago those pointed questions. And certainly after being rattled and jerked in that ferret-smelling car through a greater number of narrow lanes than John had imagined existed in that part of the country, they arrived at the biggest circus encampment either of them had ever seen.

The handsome gentleman, whom the giant-dwarf simply addressed as "Boss", but who, before they reached their destination, introduced himself in the most courtly manner as Mr. Livius, kept turning round to explain to Tenna, for he evidently considered John to be a convert already, that behind the disguise, in darkened tents, of fortune-tellers and zodiacal-diviners, no one could possibly discover them.

And there, indeed, a new life began for them. None knew them. None dreamed of their identity, none guessed their past. They had no past. They needed no future. Past and future, as they often told each other, were so perforated by the faces, voices, movements, gestures and all the wild and whirling words they had heard at Glint that their present was sometimes in the one and sometimes in the other, and sometimes had swallowed both!

Their saviour, the giant-dwarf, was so pleased with the favour they won in the eyes of his Jewish friend, the boss of the whole show, that it was only in the November of that year, and he had intended to wait till a year had gone by and the anniversary of their arrival had come round, that he presented them with a very special gift. This was nothing less than a black spaniel he had stolen from the Glint research laboratory before Echetus, the maimer of dogs, had got to work on it; and it was Tenna herself who chose its name. She decided to call it "Mr. Lordy".